THE MOROCCAN GIRL

ALSO BY CHARLES CUMMING

The Hidden Man

Typhoon

The Trinity Six

The Thomas Kell Novels

A Foreign Country

A Colder War

A Divided Spy

The Alec Milius Novels

A Spy by Nature

The Spanish Game

THE MOROCCAN GIRL

CHARLES CUMMING

St. Martin's Press
New York

THE MOROCCAN GIRL. Copyright © 2019 by Charles Cumming. All rights reserved. Printed in the United States of America. For information, address St. Martin's Press, 175 Fifth Avenue, New York, N.Y. 10010.

www.stmartins.com

The Library of Congress Cataloging-in-Publication Data
is available upon request.

ISBN 978-1-250-12995-6 (hardcover)
ISBN 978-1-250-12997-0 (ebook)

Our books may be purchased in bulk for promotional, educational, or business use. Please contact your local bookseller or the Macmillan Corporate and Premium Sales Department at 1-800-221-7945, extension 5442, or by email at MacmillanSpecialMarkets@macmillan.com.

First Edition: February 2019

10 9 8 7 6 5 4 3 2 1

For Luke Janklow and Will Francis

There is a point of no return, unremarked at the time, in most lives.

—GRAHAM GREENE, *THE COMEDIANS*

"Would you prefer to talk or to write everything down?"

"Talk," she said.

Somerville crossed the room and activated the voice recorder. The American had brought it from the Embassy. There was a small microphone attached to a stand, a glass of tap water and a plate of biscuits on the table.

"Ready?" he asked.

"Ready."

Somerville leaned over the microphone. His voice was clear, his language concise.

"Statement by LASZLO. Chapel Street, SW1. August nineteenth. Officer presiding: L4. Begins now." He checked his watch. "Seventeen hundred hours."

Lara Bartok adjusted the collar of her shirt. She caught Somerville's eye. He nodded at her, indicating that she should start. She brought the microphone slightly closer to her and took a sip of water. The American realized that he was standing in her eyeline. He moved to a chair on the far side of the room. Bartok did not continue until he was still and completely silent.

"In the beginning, there were seven," she said.

SECRET INTELLIGENCE SERVICE
EYES ONLY / STRAP 1

STATEMENT BY LARA BARTOK ("LASZLO")
CASE OFFICERS: J.W.S./S.T.H.—CHAPEL STREET
REF: RESURRECTION/SIMAKOV/CARRADINE
FILE: RE2768X

PART 1 OF 5

In the beginning there were seven. Ivan [Simakov], of course, who is still rightly regarded as the intellectual and moral architect of Resurrection; ██████████ and ██████████, both American citizens whom Simakov had met in Zuccotti Park at the height of Occupy Wall Street. ██████████, formerly of the Service; ██████████, the cyber expert who had been active in Anonymous for several years and was instrumental in planning and orchestrating many of Resurrection's most effective operations in the United States. Ivan had a way of contacting such people on the dark web, of gaining their trust over time, of drawing them out into the open. I used to say that he was like a child on a beach, pouring salt onto the sand so that the creatures of the deep would rise to the surface. He enjoyed this image very much. It is no secret that Ivan Simakov liked to think of himself as a man with extraordinary capabilities.

Also present that day were Thomas Frattura, former assistant to Republican Senator Catherine McKendrick, who had been a prominent figure in Disrupt J20; and me, Lara Bartok, originally from Gyula, in eastern Hungary, about whom you know almost everything.

These seven individuals met only once, in a suite at the Redbury Hotel on East 29th Street in Manhattan. Of course, no cellphones, laptops or Wi-Fi-enabled devices of any kind were permitted to be brought to the hotel. Each of the guests who entered the suite was searched by Ivan and myself and asked to remove watches and other items of jewelry, all of which we then took—along with personal belongings including bags and shoes—to a room on a separate floor of the hotel for the duration of the meeting. Ivan, who was meeting ███████ and ████████ for the first time, introduced himself as a Russian citizen, born in Moscow and educated in Paris, who was hoping to effect political change in his own country by inspiring "an international resistance movement directed against the advocates and enablers of autocratic and quasi-fascist regimes around the world."

Frattura asked him to explain in more detail what he meant by this. I remember that Ivan paused. He always had a good sense of theater. He crossed the suite and opened the curtains. It was a wet morning, there had been heavy rain all night. Through the glass it looked as though the thick fog of the New York skyline was going to seep into the room. What he said next was the best of him. In fact his response to Frattura would form the basis of all the early statements released on behalf of Resurrection outlining our movement's basic goals and rationale.

"Those who know that they have done wrong," he said. "Those who have lied in order to achieve their political goals. Those who consciously spread fear and hate. Those who knowingly benefit from greed and corruption. Any person who has helped to bring about the current political crisis in the United States by spreading propaganda and misinformation. Those who aid and abet the criminal regime in Moscow. Those who lied and manipulated in order to see England [sic] break from the European Union. Those who support and actively benefit from the collapse of secular Islamic states; who crush dissent and free speech and willingly erode basic human rights. Any person seeking to spread the virus of male white supremacy or deliberately to stoke anti-Semitism or to suppress women's rights in any form. All of these people—we will begin in the United States and countries such as Russia, the Netherlands, Turkey and the United Kingdom—are legitimate targets for acts of retribution. Bankers. Journalists. Businessmen. Bloggers. Lobbyists. Politicians. Broadcasters. They are to be chosen by us—by *you*—on a case-by-case basis and their crimes exposed to the widest possible audience."

The beauty of Ivan's idea was that it was *individually* targeted. This is what made it different to Antifa, to Black Lives Matter, to Occupy, to all those other groups who were only ever interested in public protest, in rioting, in civil disorder for its own sake. Those groups changed nothing in terms of people's behavior but instead gave various parties a chance merely to pose, to demonstrate their own virtue. There is a great difference between people of action and people of words, no? One thing you can say about Ivan Simakov, without a shadow of doubt, is that he was a man of action.

At no point did anybody suggest that the targets for Resurrection were too broadly defined. We were all what you would call in English "fellow travelers." We were all—with the exception of Mr. Frattura—in our twenties or early thirties. We were angry. Very angry. We wanted to *do* something. We wanted to fight back. We had grown up with the illegal wars in Iraq and Syria. We had lived through the financial crisis and seen not one man nor woman imprisoned for their crimes. All of us had been touched by the manifest corruption and greed of the first two decades of the new century. We felt powerless. We felt that the world as we knew it was being taken away from us. We lived and breathed this conviction and yearned to do something about it. Ivan was a brilliant man, possessed of fanatical zeal, as well as what I always recognized as considerable vanity. But nobody could ever accuse him of lacking passion and the yearning for change.

A policy of nonviolence was immediately and enthusiastically endorsed by the group. At that stage nobody thought of themselves as the sort of people who would be involved in assassinations, in bombings, in terrorist behavior of any kind. Everybody knew that deaths—accidental or otherwise—of innocent civilians would quickly strip the movement of popular support and allow the very people who were being targeted for retribution to accuse Resurrection of "fascism," of murder, of association with nihilistic, left-wing paramilitary groups. This, of course, is exactly what happened.

Ivan spoke about his ideas for evading capture, eluding law enforcement and intelligence services, men such as yourselves. "This is the only meeting of its kind between us that will ever take place," he said. There were silent nods of understanding. People already respected him. They had experienced firsthand the force of his personality. Once you had met Ivan Simakov, you never forgot him. "We will never again communicate or speak face-to-face. Nothing may come from what we discuss today. I have a plan for our first attacks, all of which may be prevented from taking place or fail to have the desired effect on international opinion. I cannot tell you about these plans, just as I would not expect you to divulge details of your own operations as you create them. The Resurrection movement could burn out. The Resurrection movement could have a seismic effect on public attitudes to the liars and enablers of the alt-right. Who knows? Personally, I am not interested in fame. I have no interest in notoriety or my place in the history books. I have no wish to spend the rest of my life under surveillance or in prison, to live as the guest of a foreign embassy in London, or to save my own skin by making a deal with the devils in Moscow. I wish to be invisible, as you should *all* wish to be invisible."

So much has happened since then. I have been through many lives and many cities because of my relationship with Ivan Simakov. At that moment I was proud to be at his side. He was in the prime of life. I was honored to be his girlfriend and to be associated with Resurrection. Now, of course, the movement has moved deeper and deeper into violence, further and further away from the goals and ideals expressed on that first day in New York.

They were so different, but when I think of Ivan, I cannot help thinking of Kit. On the boat he told me that I was like Ingrid Bergman in *Casablanca*, the faithless woman at the side of a revolutionary zealot. He called me his "Moroccan girl." Kit was romantic like that, always living at the edge of what was real, as if life was a book he had written, a movie he had seen, and all of us were characters in the story. He was kinder than Ivan, in many ways also braver. I confess to you that I miss him in a way that I did not expect to. I wish you would tell me what happened to him. In his company, I felt safe. It had been a very long time since any man had made me feel that way.

MOSCOW

The apartment was on a quiet street in the Tverskoy District of Moscow, about two kilometers from the Kremlin, a five-minute walk from Lubyanka Square. From the third floor, Curtis could hear the ripple of snow tires on the wet winter streets. He told Simakov that for the first few days in the city he had thought that all the cars had punctures.

"Sounds like they're driving on bubble wrap," he said. "I keep wanting to tell them to put air in their tires."

"But you don't speak Russian," Simakov replied.

"No," said Curtis. "I guess I don't."

He was twenty-nine years old, born and raised in San Diego, the only son of a software salesman who had died when Curtis was fourteen. His mother had been working as a nurse at Scripps Mercy for the past fifteen years. He had graduated from Cal Tech, taken a job at Google, quit at twenty-seven with more than four hundred thousand dollars in the bank thanks to a smart investment in a start-up. Simakov had used Curtis in the Euclidis kidnapping. Moscow was to be his second job.

If he was honest, the plan sounded vague. With Euclidis, every detail had been worked out in advance. Where the target was staying, what time his cab was booked to take him over to Berkeley, how to shut off the CCTV outside the hotel, where to switch the cars. The Moscow job was different. Maybe it was because Curtis didn't know the city; maybe it was because he didn't speak Russian. He felt out of the loop. Ivan was always leaving the apartment and going off to meet people; he said there were other Resurrection activists taking care of the details. All Curtis had been told was that Ambassador Jeffers always sat in the same spot at Café Pushkin, at the same time, on the same night of the week. Curtis was to position himself a few tables away, with the woman from St. Petersburg role-playing his girlfriend, keep an eye on Jeffers and make an assessment of the security around him. Simakov would be in the van outside, watching the phones, waiting for Curtis to give the signal that Jeffers was leaving. Two other Resurrection volunteers would be working the sidewalk in the event that anybody tried to step in and help. One of them would have the Glock, the other a Ruger.

"What if there's more security than we're expecting?" he asked. "What if they have plainclothes in the restaurant I don't know about?"

Curtis did not want to seem distrustful or unsure, but he knew Ivan well enough to speak up when he had doubts.

"What are you so worried about?" Simakov replied. He was slim and athletic with shoulder-length black hair tied back in a ponytail. "Things go wrong, you walk away. All you have to do is eat your borscht, talk to the girl, let me know what time Ambassador Fuck pays his check."

"I know. I just don't like all the uncertainty."

"What uncertainty?" Simakov took one of the Rugers off the table and packed it into the bag. Curtis couldn't tell if he was angry or just trying to concentrate on the thousand plans and ideas running through his mind. It was always hard to judge Simakov's mood. He was so controlled, so sharp, lacking in any kind of hesitation or self-doubt. "I told you, Zack. This is my city. These are my people. Besides, it's my ass on the line if things go wrong. Whatever happens, you two lovebirds can stay inside, drink some vodka, try the Stroganoff. The Pushkin is famous for it."

Curtis knew that there was nothing more to be said about Jeffers. He tried to change the subject by talking about the weather in Moscow, how as a Californian he couldn't get used to going from hot to cold to hot all the time when he was out in the city. He didn't want Ivan thinking he didn't have the stomach for the fight.

"What's that?"

"I said it's weird the way a lot of the old buildings have three sets of doors." Curtis kept talking as he followed Simakov into the kitchen. "What's that about? To keep out the cold?"

"Trap the heat," Simakov replied. He was carrying the Glock.

Curtis couldn't think of anything else to say. He was in awe of Simakov. He didn't know how to challenge him or to tell him how proud he was to be serving alongside him in the front ranks of Resurrection. Ivan gave off an aura of otherworldly calm and expertise that was almost impossible to penetrate. Curtis knew that he had styled himself as a mere foot soldier, one of tens of thousands of people around the world with the desire to confront bigotry and injustice. But to Curtis, Simakov was the Leader. There was nothing conventional or routine about him. He was extraordinary.

"I just want to say that I'm glad you got me out here," he said.

"That's OK, Zack. You were the right man for the job."

Simakov opened one of the cupboards in the kitchen. He was looking for something.

"I need some oil, clean this thing," he said, indicating the gun.

"I could go out and get you some," Curtis suggested.

"Don't you worry about it." He slapped him on the back, tugging him forward, like a bear hug from a big brother. "Anyway, haven't you forgotten? You don't speak Russian."

The bomb detonated six minutes later, at twenty-three minutes past four in the afternoon. The explosion, which also took the life of a young mother and her baby daughter in a corner apartment on the fourth floor of the building, was initially believed to have been caused by a faulty gas cylinder. When it was discovered that Zack Curtis and Ivan Simakov had been killed in the incident, a division of Alpha Group, Russia's counterterrorism task force, was dispatched to the scene. Russian television reported that Simakov had been killed by an improvised explosive device that detonated accidentally only hours before a planned Resurrection strike against the American ambassador to the Russian Federation, Walter P. Jeffers, former chairman of the Jeffers Company and a prominent donor to the Republican Party.

News of Simakov's death spread quickly. Some believed that the founder of Resurrection had died while in the process of building a homemade bomb; others were convinced that Russian intelligence had been watching Simakov and that he had been assassinated on the orders of the Kremlin. To deter Resurrection opponents and sympathizers alike, Simakov's remains were interred in an unmarked grave in Kuntsevo Cemetery on the outskirts of Moscow. Curtis was buried two weeks later in San Diego. More than three thousand Resurrection supporters lined the route taken by the funeral cortège.

London

EIGHTEEN MONTHS LATER

1

ike a lot of things that later become very complicated, the situation began very simply.

A few days short of his thirty-sixth birthday, Christopher "Kit" Carradine—known professionally as C. K. Carradine—was walking along Bayswater Road en route to a cinema in Notting Hill Gate, smoking a cigarette and thinking about nothing much in particular, when he was stopped by a tall, bearded man wearing a dark blue suit and carrying a worn leather briefcase.

"Excuse me?" he said. "Are you C. K. Carradine?"

Carradine had been writing thrillers professionally for almost five years. In that time he had published three novels and been recognized by members of the public precisely twice: the first time while buying a pot of Marmite in a branch of Tesco Metro in Marylebone; the second while queuing for a drink after a gig at the Brixton Academy.

"I am," he said.

"I'm sorry to stop you," said the man. He was at least fifteen years older than Carradine with thinning hair and slightly beady eyes that had the effect of making him seem strung out and flustered. "I'm a huge fan. I absolutely *love* your books."

"That's really great to hear." Carradine had become a writer almost by accident. Being recognized on the street was surely one of the perks of the job, but he was surprised by the compliment and wondered what more he could say.

"Your research, your characters, your descriptions. All first class."

"Thank you."

"The tradecraft. The technology. Rings absolutely true."

"I really appreciate you saying that."

"I should know. I work in that world." Carradine was suddenly in a different conversation altogether. His father had worked for British Intelligence in the 1960s. Though he had told Carradine very little about his life as a spy, his career had fired his son's interest in the secret world. "You must have, too, judging by your inside knowledge. You seem to understand espionage extraordinarily well."

The opportunist in Carradine, the writer hungry for contacts and inspiration, took a half step forward.

"No. I roamed around in my twenties. Met a few spies along the way, but never got the tap on the shoulder."

The bearded man stared with his beady eyes. "I see. Well, that surprises me." He had a polished English accent, unashamedly upperclass. "So you haven't always been a writer?"

"No."

Given that he was such a fan, Carradine was intrigued that the man hadn't known this. His biography was all over the books: *Born in Bristol, C. K. Carradine was educated at the University of Manchester. After working as a teacher in Istanbul, he joined the BBC as a graduate trainee. His first novel,* Equal and Opposite, *became an international bestseller. C. K. Carradine lives in London.* Perhaps people didn't bother reading the jacket blurbs.

"And do you live around here?"

"I do." Four years earlier, he had sold the film rights to his first novel to a Hollywood studio. The film had been made, the film had bombed, but the money he had earned had allowed him to buy a small flat in Lancaster Gate. Carradine didn't anticipate being able to pay off the mortgage until sometime around his eighty-fifth birthday, but at least it was home. "And you?" he said. "Are you private sector? HMG?"

The bearded man stepped to one side as a pedestrian walked past. A brief moment of eye contact suggested that he was not in a position to answer Carradine's question with any degree of candor. Instead he said: "I'm working in London at present" and allowed the noise from a passing bus to take the inquiry away down the street.

"Robert," he said, raising his voice slightly as a second bus applied air brakes on the opposite side of the road. "You go by 'Kit' in the real world, is that correct?"

"That's right," Carradine replied, shaking his hand.

"Tell you what. Take my card."

Somewhat unexpectedly, the man lifted up his briefcase, balanced it precariously on a raised knee, rolled his thumb over the three-digit combination locks and opened it. As he reached inside, lowering his head and searching for a card, Carradine caught sight of a pair of swimming goggles. By force of habit he took notes with his eyes: flecks of gray hair in the beard; bitten fingernails; the suit jacket slightly frayed at the neck. It was hard to get a sense of Robert's personality; he was like a foreigner's idea of an eccentric Englishman.

"Here you are," he said, withdrawing his hand with the flourish of an amateur magician. The card, like the man, was slightly creased and worn, but the authenticity of the die-stamped government logo was unmistakable:

FOREIGN AND COMMONWEALTH OFFICE
ROBERT MANTIS
OPERATIONAL CONTROL CENTER SPECIALIST

A mobile phone number and email address were printed in the bottom left-hand corner. Carradine knew better than to ask how an "Operational Control Center Specialist" passed his time; it was obviously a cover job. As, surely, was the surname: "Mantis" sounded like a pseudonym.

"Thank you," he said. "I'd offer you one of my own but I'm afraid writers don't carry business cards."

"They should," said Mantis quickly, slamming the briefcase shut. Carradine caught a sudden glimpse of impatience in his character.

"You're right," he said. He made a private vow to go to Ryman's and have five hundred cards printed up. "So how did you come across my books?"

The question appeared to catch Mantis off guard.

"Oh, those." He set the briefcase down on the pavement. "I can't remember. My wife, possibly? She may have recommended you. Are you married?"

"No." Carradine had lived with two women in his life—one a little older, one a little younger—but the relationships hadn't worked out. He wondered why Mantis was inquiring about his personal life but added "I haven't met the right person yet" because it seemed necessary to elaborate on his answer.

"Oh, you will," said Mantis wistfully. "You will."

They had reached a natural break in the conversation. Carradine looked along the street in the direction of Notting Hill Gate, trying to suggest with his body language that he was running late for an important meeting. Mantis, sensing this, picked up the briefcase.

"Well, it was very nice to meet the famous author," he gushed. "I really am a huge fan." Something in the way he said this caused Carradine suddenly to doubt that Mantis was telling the truth. "Do stay in touch," he added. "You have my details."

Carradine touched the pocket where he had placed the business card.

"Why don't I phone you?" he suggested. "That way you'll have my number."

Mantis snuffed the idea out as quickly and as efficiently as he had snapped shut his briefcase.

"Perhaps not," he said. "Do you use WhatsApp?"

"I do."

Of course. End-to-end encryption. No prying eyes at the Service establishing a link between an active intelligence officer and a spy novelist hungry for ideas.

"Then let's do it that way." A family of jabbering Spanish tourists bustled past pulling a huge number of wheeled suitcases. "I'd love to carry on our conversation. Perhaps we can have a pint one of these days?"

"I'd like that," Carradine replied.

Mantis was already several feet away when he turned around.

"You must tell me how you do it," he called out.

"Do what?"

"Make it all up. Out of thin air. You must tell me the secret."

Writers have a lot of time on their hands. Time to brood. Time to ponder. Time to waste. In the years since he had given up his job at the BBC, Carradine had become a master of procrastination. Faced with a blank page at nine o'clock in the morning, he could find half a dozen ways of deferring the moment at which he had to start work. A quick game of FIFA on the Xbox; a run in the park; a couple of sets of darts on Sky Sports 3. These were the standard—and, as far as Carradine was concerned, entirely legitimate—tactics he employed in order to avoid his desk. There wasn't an Emmy Award–winning box set or classic movie on Netflix that he hadn't watched when he should have been trying to reach his target of a thousand words per day.

"It's a miracle you get any work done," his father had said when Carradine unwisely confessed to the techniques he had mastered for circumventing deadlines. "Are you bored or something? Sounds as though you're going out of your tree."

He wasn't bored, exactly. He had tried to explain to his father that the feeling was more akin to restlessness, to curiosity, a sense that he had unfinished business with the world.

"I'm stalled," he said. "I've been very lucky with the books so far, but it turns out being a writer is a strange business. We're outliers. Solitude is forced on us. If I was a book, I'd be stuck at the halfway stage."

"It's perfectly normal," his father had replied. "You're still young. There are bits of you that have not yet been written. What you need is an adventure, something to get you out of the office."

He was right. Although Carradine managed to work quickly and effectively when he put his mind to it, he had come to realize that each day of his professional life was almost exactly the same as the last. He was often nostalgic for Istanbul and the slightly chaotic life of his twenties, for the possibility that something surprising could happen at any given moment. He missed his old colleagues at the BBC: the camaraderie, the feuds, the gossip. Although writing had been good to him, he had not expected it to become his full-time career at such a comparatively early stage in his life. In his twenties Carradine had worked in a vast, monolithic corporation with thousands of employees, frequently traveling overseas to make programs and documentaries. In his thirties, he had lived and worked mostly alone, existing for the most part within a five-hundred-meter radius of his flat in Lancaster Gate. He had yet fully to adjust to the change or to accept that the rest of his professional life would likely be spent in the company of a keyboard, a mouse and a Dell Inspiron 3000. To the outside world, the life of a writer was romantic and liberating; to Carradine it sometimes resembled a gilded cage.

All of which made the encounter with Mantis that much more intriguing. Their conversation had been a welcome distraction from the established rhythms and responsibilities of his day-to-day life. At frequent moments over the next twenty-four hours, Carradine found him-self thinking about their chat on Bayswater Road. Had it been prearranged? Did the "Foreign and Commonwealth Office"—surely a euphemism for the Service—know that C. K. Carradine lived and worked in the area? Had Mantis been sent to feel him out about some-thing? Had the plot of one of his books come too close to a real-world operation? Or was he acting in a private capacity, looking for a writer who might tell a sensitive story using the screen of fiction? An aficio-nado of conspiracy thrillers, Carradine didn't want to believe that their meeting had been merely a chance encounter. He wondered why Man-tis had declared himself an avid fan of his books without being able to say where or how he had come across them. And surely he was aware of his father's career in the Service?

He wanted to know the truth about the man from the FCO. To that end he took out Mantis's business card, tapped the number into his phone and sent a message on WhatsApp.

Very good to meet you. Glad you've enjoyed the books. This is my number. Let's have that pint.

Carradine saw that Mantis had come online. The message he had sent quickly acquired two blue ticks. Mantis was "typing."

Likewise, delighted to run into you. Lunch Wednesday?

Carradine replied immediately.

Sounds good. My neck of the woods or yours?

Two blue ticks.

Mine.

2

M ine" turned out to be a small, one-bedroom flat in Maryle-
bone. Carradine had expected to be invited to lunch at
Wheelers or White's; that was how he had written simi-
lar scenes in his books. Spook meeting spook at the
Travellers Club, talking sotto voce about "the threat from Russia" over
Chablis and fish cakes. Instead Mantis sent him an address on Lisson
Grove. He was very precise about the timing and character of the
meeting.

Please don't be late. It goes without saying that this is a private
matter, not for wider circulation.

Carradine was about halfway through writing his latest book, still
four months from deadline, so on the day of the meeting he took the
morning off. He went for a dawn run in Hyde Park, had a shower back
at his flat and ate breakfast at the Italian Gardens Cafe. He was excited
by the prospect of seeing Mantis for the second time and wondered what
the meeting would hold. The possibility of some sort of involvement
with the Service? A scoop that he could fictionalize in a book? Perhaps

the whole thing would turn out to be a waste of time. By ten o'clock Carradine was walking east along Sussex Gardens, planning to catch a train from Edgware Road to Angel. With a couple of hours to spare before he was due to meet Mantis, he wanted to rummage around in his favorite record store on Essex Road looking for a rare vinyl for a friend's birthday.

He was halfway to the station when it began to rain. Carradine had no umbrella and quickened his pace toward Edgware Road. What happened in the next few minutes was an anomaly, a moment that might, in different circumstances, have been designed by Mantis as a test of Carradine's temperament under pressure. Certainly, in the context of what followed over the next two weeks, it was a chance encounter so extraordinary that Carradine came to wonder whether it had been staged solely for his benefit. Had he written such a scene in one of his novels, it would have been dismissed as a freak coincidence.

He had reached the southwest corner of the busy intersection between Sussex Gardens and Edgware Road. He was waiting to cross at the lights. A teenage girl beside him was nattering away to a friend about boyfriend trouble. "So I says to him, I'm like, no way is that happening, yeah? I'm like, he needs to get his shit together because I'm, like, just not going through with that bullshit again." A stooped old man standing to Carradine's left was holding an umbrella in his right hand. Water was dripping from the umbrella onto the shoulders of Carradine's jacket; he could feel droplets of rain on the back of his neck. In the next instant he became aware of shouting on the opposite corner of the street, about twenty meters from where he was standing. A well-built man wearing a motorcycle helmet was raining punches through the passenger door of a black BMW. The driver—a blond woman in her forties—was being dragged from the vehicle by a second man wearing an identical helmet and torn blue jeans. The woman was screaming and swearing. Carradine thought that he recognized her as a public figure but could not put a name to the face. Her assailant, who was at least six feet tall, was dragging her by the hair shouting, "Move, you fucking bitch," and wielding what looked like a hammer.

Carradine had the sense of a moment suspended in time. There seemed to be at least twenty people standing within a few feet of the car. None of them moved. The rest of the traffic at the intersection had come to a standstill. A large white Transit van was parked in front of the BMW. The first man opened a side panel in the van and helped his accomplice to drag the woman inside. Carradine was aware of somebody shouting "Stop them! Somebody fucking stop them!" and of the teenage girl beside him muttering *"Fucking hell, what the fuck is this, this is bad"* as the door of the van slammed shut. The middle-aged man who had been seated on the driver's side of the BMW now stumbled out of the car, his hair matted with blood, his face bruised and bleeding, hands raised in the air, imploring his attackers to release the woman. Instead, the man in the torn jeans walked back toward him and swung a single, merciless punch that knocked him out cold. Somebody screamed as he slumped to the ground.

Carradine stepped off the pavement. He had been taking boxing lessons for the past eighteen months: he was tall and fit and wanted to help. He was not sure precisely what he intended to do but recognized that he had to act. Then, as he moved forward, he saw a pedestrian, standing much closer to the van, approach one of the two assailants. Carradine heard him cry: "Stop! Enough!"

"Hey!" Carradine added his own voice to the confrontation. "Let her go!"

Things then happened very quickly. Carradine felt a hand on his arm, holding him back. He turned to see the girl looking at him, shaking her head, imploring him not to get involved. Carradine would have ignored her had it not been for what came next. A third man suddenly emerged from the Transit van. He was wearing a black balaclava and carrying what looked like a short metal pole. He was much larger than the others, slower in his movements, but went toward the pedestrian and swung the pole first into his knees and then across his shoulders. The pedestrian screamed out in pain and fell onto the street.

At that moment Carradine's courage deserted him. The man in the balaclava entered the van via the side door and slammed it shut. His two helmeted accomplices also climbed inside and drove quickly away. By the time Carradine could hear a police siren in the distance, the van was already out of sight, accelerating north along Edgware Road.

There was a momentary silence. Several onlookers moved toward the middle-aged man who had been knocked out. He was soon surrounded by the very people who, moments earlier, might have defended him against attack and prevented the abduction of his companion. Through the mêlée, Carradine could see a woman kneeling on the damp street, raising the victim's head onto a balled-up jacket. For every bystander who was talking on their phone—presumably having called the police— there was another filming the scene, most of them as emotionally detached as a group of tourists photographing a sunset. With the traffic still not moving, Carradine walked across the intersection and tried to reach the BMW. His route was blocked. Car horns were sounding in the distance as a police vehicle appeared at the eastern end of Sussex Gardens. Two uniformed officers jogged toward the fallen men. Carradine realized that he could do nothing other than gawp and stare; it was pointless to hang around, just another passerby rubbernecking the incident. He was beginning to feel the first quiet thuds of shame that he had failed to act when he heard the word "Resurrection" muttered in the crowd. A woman standing next to him said: "Did you see who it was? That journalist from the *Express*, wasn't it? Whatserface?" and Carradine found that he could provide the answer.

"Lisa Redmond."

"That's right. Poor cow."

Carradine walked away. It was clear that activists associated with Resurrection had staged the kidnapping. Redmond was a hate figure for the Left, frequently identified as a potential target for the group. So many right-wing journalists and broadcasters had been attacked around the world that it was a miracle she had not been confronted before. Carradine felt wretched that he had not done more. He had witnessed street brawls in the past but never the nerveless brutality displayed by the men who had taken Redmond. He was not due to meet Mantis for another hour and a half. He thought about canceling the meeting and going home. Carradine told himself that it would have been rash to try to take on three armed men on his own, but wished that he had acted more decisively; his instinct for survival had been stronger than his desire to help.

He wandered down Edgware Road in a daze, eventually going into a café and checking the BBC for a report on what had happened. Sure enough it was confirmed that the "right-wing columnist" Lisa Redmond had been kidnapped by activists associated with Resurrection and her husband beaten up in the act of trying to protect her. Carradine opened Twitter. "Fucking bitch had it coming" was the first of several tweets he saw in defense of the attack, most of which carried the now-familiar hashtags #Resurrection #Alt-RightScum #Remember-Simakov #ZackCurtisLives and #FuckOtis. The latter was a reference to the first—and most notorious—Resurrection kidnapping, in San Francisco, of Otis Euclidis, a senior editor at Breitbart News who had been seized from outside his hotel shortly before he had been due to make a speech at Berkeley University. The kidnapping of Redmond was merely the latest in a spate of copycat attacks that had taken place in Atlanta, Sydney, Budapest and beyond. Many of the victims had been held for several weeks and then killed. Some of the recovered bodies had been mutilated. Others, including Euclidis, had never been found.

3

Carradine's apprehensiveness in the buildup to the meeting with Mantis had been completely erased by what had happened on Sussex Gardens. Arriving at the address on Lisson Grove, he felt numb and dazed. Mantis buzzed him inside without speaking on the intercom. Carradine walked up six flights of stairs to the third floor, slightly out of breath and sweating from the climb. The landing carpet was stained. There was a faux Dutch oil painting on the wall.

"Kit. Good to see you. Do come in." Mantis was standing back from the door, as though wary of being spotted by neighbors. "Thank you so much for coming."

Carradine was led into a sparsely furnished sitting room. He laid his jacket on the back of a brand-new cream leather sofa wrapped in clear plastic. Sunlight was streaming through the windows. The sight of the plastic made him feel constricted and hot.

"Are you moving in?" he asked. The flat smelled of old milk and toilet cleaner. There was no indication that Mantis had prepared any food.

"It's not my place," he replied, closing a connecting door into the hall.

"Ah."

So what was it? A safe house? If so, why had Mantis arranged to meet on Service territory? Carradine had assumed they were just going to have a friendly lunch. He looked around. Two mobile phones were charging on the floor by the window. There was a vase of plastic flowers on a table in the center of the room. Two self-assembly stools were positioned in front of a breakfast bar linking the sitting room to a small kitchen. Carradine could see a jar of instant coffee, a box of teabags and a kettle near the sink. The kitchen was otherwise spotlessly clean.

"Did you hear about Lisa Redmond?" Mantis asked.

Carradine hesitated.

"No," he said, feigning surprise. "What's happened?"

"Grabbed by Resurrection." Mantis opened a double-glazed window on to a small parking area at the rear of the building. Cool air poured into the room. "Thrown in the back of a Transit van and driven off—in broad bloody daylight."

"Christ," said Carradine.

He was not a natural liar. In fact, he could not remember the last time he had deliberately concealed the truth in such a way. It occurred to him that it was a bad idea to do so in front of a man who was professionally trained in the darker arts of obfuscation and deceit. Mantis gestured outside in the direction of Edgware Road.

"A mile away," he said. "Less! Three men kicked the living shit out of her poor husband, who's apparently some kind of hotshot TV producer. One of them had a pop at a have-a-go-hero who tried to save the day. It's all over the news."

"What do you think will happen to her?" Carradine asked, though he knew the answer to his own question.

"Curtains," said Mantis. "Another Aldo Moro job."

Moro, the Italian prime minister kidnapped by the Red Brigades in 1978, had been murdered in captivity, his body discovered in the back of a Renault two months later. Carradine wondered why Mantis had made such an obscure historical connection but conceded his point with a nod.

"I'm surprised she didn't have any security," he said. "People kept saying she was a target. In America, employees in the White House, staff at Fox News, prominent Republican officials, they've all been carrying guns for months."

"Quite right, too," said Mantis with an impatience that reminded Carradine of the way his temper had flared on Bayswater Road. "People have a right to defend themselves. You never know who's going to come out of the woodwork and take a pop at you."

Carradine looked at the sofa. Mantis understood that he wanted to sit down and invited him to do so "on the plastic cover." He asked Carradine to switch off his mobile phone. He was not particularly surprised by the request and did as he had been asked.

"Now if you wouldn't mind passing it to me."

Carradine handed over the phone. He was delighted to see Mantis place it inside a cocktail shaker that he had removed from one of the cupboards in the kitchen. He had used an identical piece of tradecraft in his most recent novel, stealing the idea from an article about Edward Snowden.

"A Faraday cage," he said, smiling.

"If you say so." Mantis opened the door of the fridge and put the cocktail shaker inside it. The fridge was completely empty. "And if you could just sign this." He crossed the room and passed Carradine a pen and a piece of paper. "We insist on the Official Secrets Act."

Carradine's heart skipped. Without pausing to read the document in any detail, he rested the piece of paper on the table and signed his name at the bottom. It occurred to him that his father must have done exactly the same thing some fifty years earlier.

"Thank you. You might want to take a look at this."

Mantis was holding what appeared to be a driver's license. Carradine took it and turned it over. Mantis's photograph and personal details, as well as a Foreign Office logo and a sample of his signature, were laminated against a pale gray background.

"This wouldn't be enough to get you into Vauxhall Cross," he said. It was necessary to demonstrate to Mantis that he did not fully trust him. "Do you have any other forms of ID?"

As though he had been anticipating Carradine's question, Mantis dipped into the pocket of his trousers and pulled out a molded plastic security pass.

"Access all areas," he said. Carradine had wanted to inspect the pass, if only to experience the buzz of holding a genuine piece of Service kit, but Mantis immediately put it back in his pocket.

"Always worried about losing it on the number nineteen bus," he said.

"I'm not surprised," Carradine replied.

He asked for a glass of water. Mantis produced a chipped William and Kate mug and turned on the cold tap in the kitchen. It spluttered and coughed, spraying water onto his hand. He swore quietly under his breath—"fucking thing"—filled the mug and passed it to Carradine.

"Who owns this place?"

"One of ours," he replied.

Carradine had met spies before but never in these circumstances and never in such a furtive atmosphere. He leaned back against the thick plastic cover and took a sip from the mug. The water was lukewarm and tasted of battery fluid. He did not want to swallow it but did so. Mantis sat in the only other available seat, a white wooden chair positioned in front of the window.

"Did you tell anybody that you were coming here today?" he asked. "A girlfriend?"

"I'm single," Carradine replied. He was surprised that Mantis had already forgotten this.

"Oh, that's right. You said." He crossed his legs. "What about your father?"

Carradine wondered how much Mantis knew about William Carradine. A rising star in the Service, forced out by Kim Philby, who had given his name—as well as the identities of dozens of other members of staff—to Moscow. Surely somebody at Vauxhall Cross had told him?

"He doesn't know."

"And your mother?" Mantis quickly checked himself. "Oh, I'm so sorry. Of course . . ."

Carradine's mother had died of breast cancer when he was a teenager. His father had never remarried. He had recently suffered a stroke that had left him paralyzed on one side of his body. Carradine made a point of visiting him regularly at his flat in Swiss Cottage. He was his only surviving blood family and they were very close.

"I haven't told anybody," he said.

"Good. So nobody has been made aware of our chat in the street?"

"Nobody."

Carradine looked more closely at his interlocutor. He was wearing pale blue chinos and a white Ralph Lauren polo shirt. Carradine was reminded of a line judge at Wimbledon. Mantis's hair had been cut and his beard trimmed; as a consequence, he no longer looked quite so tired and disheveled. Nevertheless, there was something second-rate about him. He could not help but give the impression of being very slightly out of his depth. Carradine suspected that he was not the sort of officer handed "hot" postings in Amman or Baghdad. No, Robert Mantis was surely lower down the food chain, tied to a desk in London, obliged to take orders from Service upstarts half his age.

"Let me get straight to the point." The man from the FCO made deliberate and sustained eye contact. "My colleagues and I have been talking about you. For some time."

"I had a feeling our meeting the other day wasn't an accident."

"It wasn't."

Carradine looked around the room. The flat was exactly the sort of place in which a man might be quietly bumped off. No record of the meeting ever happening. CCTV footage from the lobby conveniently erased. Hair samples hoovered up and fingerprints wiped away by a Service support team. The body then placed inside a thick plastic sheet—perhaps the one covering the sofa—and taken outside to the car park. Should he say this in an effort to break the ice? Probably not. Carradine sensed that Mantis wouldn't find it funny.

"Don't look so worried."

"What's that?"

"You look concerned."

"I'm fine." Carradine was surprised that Mantis had failed to read his mood. "In fact, it did seem a bit odd to me that a serving intelligence officer would talk so openly about working for the Service."

"Good."

"What do you mean 'good'?"

"I mean that you obviously have sound instincts." Carradine felt the plastic rippling beneath him. It was like sitting on a waterbed. "You obviously have an aptitude for this sort of thing. It's what we wanted to talk to you about."

"Go on."

"You have a Facebook page."

"I do."

"The other day you were asking for tips about Marrakech. Advertising a talk you're doing at a literary festival in Morocco."

Despite the fact that C. K. Carradine's Facebook page was publicly available, he experienced the numbing realization that the Service had most probably strip-mined every conversation, email and text message he had sent in the previous six months. He was grateful that he hadn't run the name "Robert Mantis" through Google.

"That's right," he said.

"Get much of a response?"

"Uh, some restaurant tips. A lot of people recommended the Majorelle Gardens. Why?"

"How long are you going for?"

"About three days. I'm doing a panel discussion with another author. We're being put up in a riad."

"Would you be prepared to spend slightly longer in Morocco if we asked?"

It took Carradine a moment to absorb what Mantis had said. Other writers—Somerset Maugham, Graham Greene, Frederick Forsyth—had worked as support agents for the Service at various points in their careers. Was he being offered the chance to do what his father had done?

"There's no reason why I can't stay there a bit longer," he said, trying to make his expression appear as relaxed as possible while his heart began to pound like a jungle drum. "Why?"

Mantis laid it out.

"You may have noticed that we're somewhat stretched at the moment. Cyberattacks. Islamist terror. Resurrection. The list goes on. . . ."

"Sure." Carradine felt his throat go dry. He wanted to take a sip of water but was worried that Mantis would see his hand shaking.

"Increasingly, things fall through the gaps. Agents don't have the support they need. Messages struggle to get through. Information can't travel in the way that we want it to travel."

Carradine was nodding. He knew that it was better at this stage to listen rather than to ask questions. At the same time he could feel his vanity jumping up and down with excitement; the flattery implicit in Mantis's offer, coupled with the chance to honor his father's career, perhaps even to surpass his achievements, was hitting a sweet spot inside him that he hadn't known existed.

"We had a station in Rabat. It was wound up. Folded in with the Americans. Manpower issues, budgetary restrictions. I'm sure I don't have to tell you that all of this is strictly between you and me."

"Of course."

"I have a desk responsibility for the region. I need to be able to put somebody in front of one or two of our agents out there, just to reassure them that they're a priority for London. Even though that may not be entirely the case."

Mantis flashed Carradine a knowing look. Carradine was obliged to return it in kind, nodding as though he was on intimate terms with the complexities of agent-running.

"I'm afraid it would require you to go to Casablanca as well as Marrakech. Ever been?"

Carradine had heard that modern Casablanca was far removed from the romantic image of the city conjured by Hollywood: a crowded, choking industrial conurbation entirely devoid of charm and interest.

"Never. But I've always wanted to check it out."

He set the mug of water to one side. In the distance Carradine could hear the sound of sirens, the familiar background soundtrack to life in twenty-first-century London. He wondered if Redmond had already been found and could scarcely believe that within hours of witnessing her kidnapping, he was being offered a chance to work as a support agent for the Service. It was as though Mantis was handing him an opportunity to prove the courage that had so recently been found wanting.

"Can you be more precise about what exactly you need me to do?"

Mantis seemed pleased that Carradine had asked the question.

"Writers on research trips provide perfect cover for clandestine work," he explained. "The inquisitive novelist always has a watertight excuse for poking his nose around. Any unusual or suspicious activity can be justified as part of the artistic process. You know the sort of thing. Atmosphere, authenticity, detail."

"I know the sort of thing."

"All you have to do is pack a couple of your paperbacks, make sure your website and Wikipedia page are up-to-date. In the highly unlikely event that you encounter somebody who doubts your bona fides, just point them to the internet and hand over a signed copy of *Equal and Opposite*. Easy."

"Sounds like you've got it all worked out."

"We do!" Mantis beamed with his beady eyes. Carradine must have looked concerned because he added: "Don't be alarmed. Your responsibilities will be comparatively minimal and require very little exertion on your part."

"I'm not alarmed."

"There's no need—indeed no time—for detailed preparation or training. You'll simply be required to make your way to Casablanca on Monday with various items which will be provided to you by the Service."

"What sort of items?"

"Oh, just some money. Three thousand euros to be paid to a locally based agent. Also a book, most likely a novel or biography of some sort, to be passed on as a cipher."

"Who to?"

"Yassine. A contact of mine from Rabat. Feeling slightly neglected, he needs to have his tummy tickled but I'm too busy to fly down. We usually meet up in a restaurant, Blaine's, which is popular with businessmen and—well—young women of low social responsibility." Mantis grinned at the euphemism. "Yassine will recognize you, greet you with the phrase, 'I remember you from the wedding in London.' You reply: 'The wedding was in Scotland.' And your meeting can proceed."

Carradine was surprised that Mantis was moving at such a pace.

"You really *do* have everything worked out," he said.

"I can assure you this is all very normal and straightforward, as long as you can remember what to do."

"I can remember . . ."

"As for the money, you are to leave that at the reception desk of a five-star hotel under the name 'Abdullah Aziz.' A very important contact. He is owed money."

"Abdullah Aziz." Carradine was trying to remember his answer to Yassine's question about the wedding. He wondered why Mantis was flooding him with so much information so quickly and wished that he was free to write things down.

"Sounds easy enough," he said. "Which five-star hotel?"

"I'll let you know in due course."

Carradine was seated with his palms facedown on the sofa's plastic cover. He became aware that they were soaked in sweat.

"And what about Marrakech? What am I doing there?"

Mantis was suddenly at a loss for words. Having rushed through Carradine's responsibilities in Casablanca, he became hesitant to the point of anxiety. Twice he appeared to be on the brink of replying to Carradine's question only to stop himself, biting the nail on the index finger of his left hand. Eventually he stood up and looked out onto the car park.

"Marrakech," he revealed at last. "Well, that's where things will become slightly more . . . *nuanced*." The man from the FCO turned and looked into the room, slowly rubbing his hands together as he moved toward the sofa. "It's why we've picked you, Kit. We're going to need you to use your initiative."

4

Mantis explained that there was a woman.

A "remarkable young woman, cunning and unpredictable." She didn't have a name—at least one that was still "operationally useful or relevant"—and hadn't been seen for "the best part of two years." She was on the books at the Service but they hadn't heard "hide nor hair of her for far too long." Mantis explained that he was worried. He knew that she was in trouble and that she needed help. The Service was "ninety percent certain" that the woman was living in northwest Africa under an assumed name and "one hundred percent certain" that she wanted to come back to the UK. She had been sighted in Marrakech in the winter and again in the Atlas Mountains only three weeks earlier. "Other officers and support agents" had been looking for her in a variety of locations—Mexico, Cuba, Argentina—but all the evidence pointed to Morocco. All Carradine had to do was keep an eye out for her. The woman knew the country well and it had been easy for her to "disappear" in a place with such a large number of Western tourists.

"That's it?" Carradine asked. The job sounded farcical.

"That's it," Mantis replied.

"You want me just to wander around Marrakech on the off chance I run into her?"

"No, no." An apologetic smile. "She's a big reader. Fan of books and literature. There's a strong possibility that she might show her face at your festival. We just want you to keep your eyes peeled."

Carradine struggled to think of something constructive to say.

"If she's in trouble, why doesn't she come in? What's to stop her making contact with you? Why doesn't she go to her nearest embassy?"

"I'm afraid it's a good deal more complicated than that."

Carradine sensed that he was being lied to. The Service was asking him to look for a woman who was doing everything she could to avoid being found.

"Is she Spanish?" he asked.

"What makes you say that?"

"Mexico. Argentina. Cuba. They're all Spanish-speaking countries. Tangier is a one-hour flight from Madrid, a short hop on the boat from Tarifa."

Mantis smiled. "I can see that you're going to be good at this."

Carradine ignored the compliment.

"What does she look like?" he asked.

"I have a number of photographs that I can show you, but I'm afraid you'll have to commit them to memory. I can give you a small passport-sized photograph to keep in your wallet as an aide-mémoire, but you won't be able to keep anything digital on your phone or laptop. We can't risk these images falling into the wrong hands. If your phone was lost or stolen, for example, or you were asked to account for how you knew the woman . . ."

The task was sounding increasingly strange.

"Who would be asking those kinds of questions?"

Mantis indicated with an airy wave of the hand that Carradine should not be concerned.

"If you carry on behaving exactly as you have always behaved whenever you've been on a research trip to a foreign city, it's very unlikely that you would ever be arrested, far less asked anything by anybody about the nature of your work for us. We take every precaution to ensure that our agents—by that I mean you, Kit—have no discernible relationship with British intelligence. Nevertheless, it goes without saying that you must never, under any circumstances, reveal anything under questioning about the arrangement we have made here today."

"Of course. Without saying."

"You and I will continue to communicate with one another *en clair* on WhatsApp using the number I provided to you. I will be your only point of contact with the Service. You will never come to Vauxhall, you will rarely meet any of my colleagues. As far as Morocco is concerned, you won't tell anybody about our arrangement or—heaven forbid—start showing off about it on the phone or by email. Did you put my name into a search engine at all?"

Carradine assumed that Mantis already knew the answer to his own question, but replied truthfully.

"No. I assumed it would be flagged up."

"You were right." He looked relieved. "By the same token, you mustn't Google the names of anybody you come into contact with as a result of your work for us, nor carry with you anything that might be at all incriminating. We don't do exploding pens and invisible ink. Does that sound like something you might be able to manage?"

Carradine felt that he had no choice other than to say: "Sure, no problem." He was perfectly capable of keeping a secret. He understood the mechanics of deceit. He was keen to do a patriotic job for his country, not least because his own professional life was so low on excitement. The only thing that concerned him was the possibility of being arrested and thrown into a Moroccan jail. But to say that to Mantis, to indicate that he was worried about saving his own skin, might have seemed spineless.

"Mind if I use the loo?" he asked.

"Be my guest."

Carradine crossed the hall and went into the bathroom. There were no towels on the rail or mats on the floor, no toothbrush or razor in the plastic mug on the basin. A stained shower curtain hung loose over the bath on white plastic hooks, many of which were bent out of shape. He locked the door and ran the tap, staring at his reflection in the mirror. It occurred to him that he was still recovering from the shock of the Redmond kidnapping and had not been thinking clearly about what Mantis was asking him to do. The job certainly promised intrigue and drama. It was a chance to perform a useful service for his country. Carradine would learn from the experience and obtain priceless first-hand research for his books. There was every possibility that he might be asked to work for the Service for a considerable period of time. In short, the situation was profoundly seductive to him.

"Everything OK?" Mantis asked as he came back into the living room.

"Everything's great."

"Come and have a look at these."

He was holding an iPad. Carradine sat next to him on the sofa and looked at the screen. Mantis began flicking through a series of photographs, presumably of the woman Carradine would be asked to look for in Marrakech.

It was strange. In the same way that he had recognized Lisa Redmond as she was dragged from the car, without at first being able to put a name to her face, Carradine was sure that he had seen pictures of the woman before. She wasn't a journalist or celebrity. She wasn't a likely target for Resurrection. But she was some kind of public figure. Perhaps an actress he had seen onstage in London or somebody associated with a news story or political scandal. He could not work it out. It might equally have been the case that Carradine had met her at a party or that the woman had some connection to the film or publishing worlds. She was certainly not a stranger to him.

"You look as though you recognize her."

Carradine decided against telling Mantis that he had seen the woman's face before. His explanation would have sounded confused.

"No. I'm just trying to take a photograph with my eyes. Commit her face to memory."

"It's a beautiful face."

Carradine was taken aback by the wistfulness of the remark. "It is," he said as they shuttled back through the album. The woman had long, dark hair, light brown eyes and slightly crooked teeth. He assumed that most of the photographs had been culled from social media; they had a casual, snapped quality and appeared to cover a period of several years. In two of the pictures the woman was seated at a table in a restaurant, surrounded by people of her own age; in another, she was wearing a powder blue bikini on a sunny beach, her arm encircling the waist of a handsome, bearded man holding a surfboard. Carradine assumed that he was a boyfriend, past or present.

"He looks Spanish," he said, pointing at the man. "Was this taken in Spain?"

"Portugal. Atlantic coast." Mantis reached across Carradine and quickly flicked the photo stream to the next image. "You were right. She has a Spanish mother. Speaks the language fluently."

"And her father? Where was he from?"

"I'm afraid I can't say."

There was a fixed, unapologetic look on Mantis's face.

"And you can't tell me her name either?"

"I'm afraid not. It's better that you know nothing about her, Kit. If you were to start asking the wrong questions, if you were tempted to Google her, for example, it's not easy to say what might happen to you."

"That sounds like a threat."

"It wasn't meant to."

Mantis directed Carradine's attention back to the screen. He had a good memory for faces and was confident that he would be able to recognize the woman if he came across her in Morocco.

"How tall is she?" he asked.

"Couple of inches shorter than you."

"Hairstyle?"

"She might have changed it. Might have dyed it. Might have shaved it all off. Anything is possible."

"Accent?"

"Think Ingrid Bergman speaking English."

Carradine smiled. He could hear the voice in his head.

"Any other, uh . . ." He reached for the euphemism. "Distinguishing characteristics?"

Mantis stood up, taking the iPad with him.

"Of course! I almost forgot." He extended his left arm so that it was almost touching Carradine's forehead. "The woman has a tattoo," he said, tapping the wrist. "Three tiny black swallows just about here."

Carradine stared at the frayed cuffs of Mantis's shirt. Veins bulged on his forearm beneath a scattering of black hairs.

"If it's a tattoo," he said, "and she's trying not to get recognized, don't you think she might have had it removed?"

Mantis moved his hand onto Carradine's shoulder. Carradine hoped that he wouldn't leave it there for long.

"You don't miss a trick, do you?" he said. "We've obviously picked the right man, Kit. You're a natural."

5

antis said nothing more about the tattoo. Carradine was told that if he spotted the woman, he was to approach her discreetly, ensure that their conversation was neither overheard nor overseen, and then to explain that he had been sent by British intelligence. He was also to pass her a sealed package. This would be delivered by the Service before he left for Morocco.

"I'm assuming I can't open this package when I receive it?"

"That is correct."

"Can I ask what will be inside it?"

"A passport, a credit card and a message to the agent. That is all."

"That's all? Nothing else?"

"Nothing else."

"So why seal it?"

"I'm not sure I understand your question."

Carradine was trying to tread the fine line between protecting himself against risk and not appearing to be apprehensive.

"It's just that if my bags are searched and they find the package, if they ask me to open it, how do I explain why I'm carrying somebody else's passport?"

"Simple," Mantis replied. "You say that it's for a friend who left it in London. The same friend whose photo you're carrying in your wallet."

"So how did she get to Morocco without a passport?"

Mantis took a deep breath, as if to suggest that Carradine was starting to ask too many questions. "She has two. One Spanish, the other British. OK?"

"What's my friend's name?"

"Excuse me?"

"I need to know her name. If it's on the passport, if I'm carrying her picture around, they'll expect me to know who she is."

"Ah." Mantis seemed pleased that Carradine had thought of this. "The surname on the passport is 'Rodriguez.' Christian name 'Maria.' Easy enough to remember."

"And mundane enough not to draw attention to itself."

"It does have that added dimension, yes."

They remained at the Lisson Grove flat for another half hour, going over further practical details of Carradine's trip, including protocols for contacting Vauxhall Cross in the event of an emergency. Mantis insisted that they meet at the flat when Carradine returned from Marrakech, at which point he would be debriefed and given payment, in cash, for any expenses he had run up in Morocco.

"Feel free to stay somewhere decent in Casablanca," he said. "We'll cover your costs, the extra flight as well. Just keep accurate receipts for the bean counters. They're notoriously stingy when it comes to shelling out for taxis and train tickets."

As Carradine was leaving, Mantis handed him two envelopes, each containing €1,500. There was no limit to the amount of foreign currency he was permitted to bring into Morocco and Mantis did not think that €3,000 would be considered suspicious. He told Carradine that the sealed package containing the passport and credit card would be delivered to his flat in Lancaster Gate the following day, as well as the novel which was to be used as a book cipher. Mantis reiterated the importance of leaving the sealed package intact, unless Carradine was instructed to open it by law enforcement officials in the UK or Morocco. He did not give an explanation for this request and Carradine did not ask for one. Carradine assumed that the package would contain sensitive documents.

"Good luck," Mantis said, shaking his hand as he left. "And thanks for helping out."

"No problem."

Carradine walked out onto Lisson Grove in a state of confusion. He was bewildered by the speed with which Mantis had acted and strung out by the painstaking assimilation of so much information. It seemed bizarre that he should have been asked to undertake work on behalf of the secret state—particularly after such a cursory meeting—and wondered if the entire episode was part of an elaborate setup. Clearly the content of his novels, the depictions of tradecraft, his observations about the burdens of secrecy and so forth, had convinced the Service that C. K. Carradine was possessed of the ideal temperament to work as a support agent. But how had they known that he would agree so readily to their offer? While working for the BBC in his twenties, Carradine had spoken to three veteran foreign correspondents—two British, one Canadian—each of whom had been tapped up by their respective intelligence services overseas. They had turned down the opportunity on the basis that it would interfere with the objectivity of their work, undermine the relationships they had built up with local sources and potentially bring them into conflict with their host governments. Carradine wished that he had shown a little more of their steadfastness when presented with the dangled carrot of clandestine work. Instead, perhaps because of what had happened to his father, he had demonstrated a rather old-fashioned desire to serve Queen and country, a facet of his character which suddenly seemed antiquated, even naïve. He was committed to doing what Mantis had asked him to do, but felt that he had not given himself adequate protection in the event that things went wrong.

Still in a state of apprehension, Carradine took a detour on the way home, purchased a roll of masking tape and found an internet café in Paddington. He wanted to be certain that Mantis was a bona fide Service employee, not a Walter Mitty figure taking advantage of him either for his own amusement or for some darker purpose which had not yet been made clear.

The café was half-full. Carradine stood over a vacant computer, tore off a small strip of the masking tape and placed it over the lens at the top of the screen. The computer was already loaded with a VPN. In his most recent novel, Carradine had written a chapter in which the principal character was required to comb the dark net in order to create a false identity. He had spoken to a hacker a few weeks before and still remembered most of what she had told him during their cloak-and-dagger meeting at a coffee shop in Balham. The trick—apart from disabling the camera—was to use the VPN both to create a false IP address and to encrypt his internet usage. That way, his activities would be concealed from any prying eyes in Cheltenham and Carradine could investigate the mysterious Mr. Mantis without fear of being identified.

As he expected, none of the "Robert Mantis" listings on Facebook could plausibly have been the man he had met in Lisson Grove. There was no Twitter account associated with the name, nor anything on Instagram. Carradine ran Mantis through LinkedIn and Whitepages but found only an out-of-work chef in Tampa and a "lifestyle" photographer in Little Rock. Remembering a tip he had been given by the hacker, he looked on Nominet to see if any variant of "robertmantis" was listed as a website domain. It was not. Whoever he had met that afternoon was using a pseudonym which had been cleaned up for the obvious purpose of protecting his true identity. Mantis was not listed as a director at Companies House nor as a shared freeholder on any UK properties. A credit check on Experian also drew a blank.

Satisfied that he was a genuine Service employee, Carradine put the computer to sleep, removed the strip of masking tape from the lens and walked home.

6

The following morning, Carradine was woken early by the sound of the doorbell ringing. He stumbled out of bed, pulled on a pair of boxer shorts and struck his foot on the skirting board as he picked up the intercom.

"Delivery for Mr. Carradine."

He knew immediately what it was. He reached down, grabbed his toe and told the deliveryman to leave it in his postbox.

"Needs to be signed for."

The accent was Jamaican. Carradine buzzed the man into the building. He waited by the door, rubbing his foot. A moth flew up toward the ceiling. Carradine clapped it dead between his hands. He could hear the lift outside grinding toward the landing as he wiped the smashed body on his shorts.

The deliveryman was a middle-aged, dreadlocked Rasta wearing a high-vis waistcoat. A Post Office satchel was slung over his shoulder. It was possible that he was a convincingly disguised errand boy for the Service, but Carradine assumed that Mantis had simply sent the items by Special Delivery. He signed an illegible version of his name on an electronic pad using a small plastic tool that slipped on the glass, thanked him and took the package inside.

On any other morning, Carradine might have gone back to bed for another hour's sleep. But the contents of the package were too intriguing. He walked into the kitchen, set a percolator of coffee on the stove and sliced the envelope open with a knife.

There was a paperback book inside. Mantis had sent a French translation of one of Carradine's novels, published four years earlier. He opened the book to the title page. It was unsigned. The rest of the text had not been marked up nor were any pages turned down or altered in any way. The book was in pristine condition.

He waited for the coffee to boil, staring out of the window at the treetops of Hyde Park. If the novel was to be used as a book cipher, then Mantis possessed an identical copy which would allow him to send coded messages to Yassine without risking detection. He was using a French, rather than an English version of the book because Yassine was most likely a French-speaking Arab. For Carradine to give him a copy of the novel at their meeting was an ingenious and entirely plausible piece of tradecraft. They would be hiding in plain sight.

He took out the second item, the sealed package for "Maria." The envelope was sturdy and bound with tape at both ends. Carradine weighed it in his hands. He could make out the outline of what he assumed was a passport. He bent the package slightly and thought that he could feel a document of some kind moving beneath the seal. Carradine had an obligation to open the envelope, because it was surely crazy to board an international flight carrying a package about which he knew so little. But he could not do so. It was against the spirit of the deal he had struck with the Service and would constitute a clear breach of trust. It was even possible that the package was a decoy and that the Service had sent it solely as a test of his integrity.

He set it to one side, drank the coffee and switched on the news. Overnight in New Delhi two vehicles had been hijacked by Islamist gunmen affiliated with Lashkar-e-Taiba and driven into crowds at a religious ceremony, killing an estimated seventy-five people. In Germany, an AFD politician had been gunned down on his doorstep by a Resurrection activist. Such headlines had become commonplace, as humdrum and predictable as tropical storms and mass shootings in the United States. Carradine waited for news of the Redmond kidnapping. It was the third item on the BBC. No trace had been found of the van in which Redmond had been driven away, no statement released by Resurrection claiming responsibility for the abduction.

Settling in front of his computer with a bowl of cereal, Carradine watched amateur footage of the crowds screaming in panic as they fled the carnage in New Delhi. He read an email written by the slain AFD politician, leaked to the press only days earlier, in which he had referred to Arabs as a "culturally alien people" welcomed into Germany by "elitist pigs." He learned that one in eight voters had given AFD their support in recent elections and that the group was now the second largest opposition party in the Bundestag. Small wonder Resurrection was so active in Germany. There had been similar assassinations of nationalist politicians in France, Poland and Hungary. It was only a matter of time before the violence crossed the Channel and a senior British politician was targeted.

Carradine took a shower and WhatsApped Mantis, acknowledging delivery of the package with a succinct "Thanks for the book." Within thirty seconds Mantis had replied: "No problem" adding—to Carradine's consternation—two smiling emojis and a thumbs-up for good measure. He put the package in a drawer and attempted to do some work. Every ten or fifteen minutes he would open the drawer and check that the package was still there, as if sprites or cat burglars might have carried it off while his back was turned. Later in the afternoon, when his once-a-fortnight cleaner, Mrs. Ritter, was in the flat, he removed the package altogether and set it on his desk until she had left the building.

Though he had yet to complete any specific tasks on behalf of the Service, Carradine already felt as though he had been cut off from his old life; that he was inhabiting a parallel existence separate from the world he had known before meeting Mantis and witnessing the abduction of Lisa Redmond. He wanted to talk to his father about what had happened, to tell him about Morocco and to gauge his advice, but he was forbidden by the Secrets Act. He could say nothing to anyone about what Mantis had asked him to do. He tried to work, but it now seemed ridiculous to be writing about fictional spies in fictional settings when he himself had been employed by the Service as a bona fide support agent. Instead he spent the next two days rereading Frederick Forsyth's memoirs and Somerset Maugham's *Ashenden*, trawling for insights into the life of a writer spy. He watched *The Bureau* and took a DVD of *The Man Who Knew Too Much* to his father's flat the night before he was due to fly to Casablanca. They ordered curry from Deliveroo and sat in semidarkness munching chicken dhansak and tarka daal, washed down with a 1989 Château Beychevelle he had been given by an old friend as a birthday present.

"Doris Day," his father muttered as she sang "Que Sera Sera" to her soon-to-be-kidnapped son. "Was she the one Hitchcock threw the birds at?"

"No," Carradine replied. "That was Tippi Hedren."

"Ah."

He tore off a strip of peshawari naan and passed it to his father saying: "Did you know she was Melanie Griffith's mother?"

"Who? Doris Day?"

"No. Tippi Hedren."

After a brief pause, his father said: "Who's Melanie Griffith?"

It was after midnight by the time the film finished. Carradine did the washing-up and ordered an Uber.

"So you're off to Casablanca?" His father was standing in the hall, leaning on the walking stick, which he had carried with him since his stroke. "Research on the new book?"

"Research, yes," Carradine replied. He detested the lie.

"Never been myself. They say it's not like the film."

"Yeah. I heard that."

His father jutted out his chin and pulled off a passable impression of Humphrey Bogart.

"You played it for her. You play it for me. Play it."

Carradine hugged him. He tried to imagine what life in the Service must have been like in the 1960s. He pictured smoke-filled rooms, tables piled high with dusty files, men in double-breasted suits plotting in secure speech rooms.

"I love you," he said.

"I love you, too. Take care of yourself out there. Call me when you land."

"I will."

Carradine opened the front door and stepped outside.

"Kit?"

He turned to face his father. "Yes?"

"I'm proud of you."

7

arradine had been on the Gatwick Express for only a few minutes when he saw the photograph. He was seated alone at a table in a near-deserted carriage finishing off a cappuccino and a fruit salad from M&S. A passenger had left a copy of *The Guardian* on a seat across the aisle. Carradine had picked up the paper and begun to read about developments in the Redmond kidnapping. The Transit van, which had been stolen from a North London car park, had been found abandoned and burned out at the edge of a wood not far from Henley-on-Thames. CCTV showed a bearded man wearing a woolen hat filling the van up with diesel in Cricklewood a few hours before Redmond was seized. Resurrection sympathizers had now claimed responsibility for the kidnapping but no images of Redmond in captivity had been released. "Experts" quoted in the article drew comparisons with the kidnapping of Otis Euclidis, pointing out that Resurrection had waited ten days before publishing footage of an apparently healthy and well-rested Euclidis sitting on a bed in an undisclosed location reading a book. The same experts claimed that the police were at a loss to know where Redmond was being held. At the bottom of the story there was a small box directing readers to a longer piece on the history of the Resurrection movement. Carradine had turned to the back of the paper, intending to read it.

Beneath the headline on the article was a layout of four pictures arranged in a square, each of them about the same size as the passport photograph of "Maria" that Mantis had given to Carradine in Lisson Grove. The photograph in the top left-hand corner showed Redmond taking part in a reality television show several years earlier. Beside it was a picture of Euclidis in characteristic Instagram pose, wearing a white, gold-encrusted baseball cap, a gold crucifix medallion and outsized designer sunglasses. The photograph in the bottom left-hand corner showed Nihat Demirel, a pro-government talk-show host in Turkey who had been kneecapped by Resurrection outside his summer house in Izmir in May. It was the fourth picture that rocked Carradine.

He had seen the photograph before. It showed Ivan Simakov, the deceased leader of Resurrection, standing beside the woman who was reported to have been his girlfriend when the movement was conceived: Lara Bartok. Carradine stared at her. She had long, dark hair and slightly crooked front teeth. It was "Maria."

He reached into his wallet. He placed the photograph of Maria alongside the picture of Bartok. There was no question that they were the same woman. He was about to pull up her Wikipedia page on his iPhone when he remembered that the search would flag. A young woman had taken a seat at the far end of the carriage. Carradine considered asking to borrow her phone to make the search but decided against it, instead reading the article for more detail on Bartok's background. A Hungarian-born lawyer, she had met Simakov in New York and become attached to Occupy Wall Street. Described as "a latter-day Ulrike Meinhof," Bartok was wanted in the United States on charges of armed assault, kidnapping and incitement to violence. She had reportedly become disillusioned with Resurrection and vanished from the couple's apartment in Brooklyn. Several months later, Simakov was killed in Moscow.

Carradine put the newspaper to one side. The train had come to a halt at a section of track littered with cans and bottles. He stared outside, trying to work out what Mantis was up to. He assumed that the Service had recruited Bartok as an agent, persuading her to inform against Resurrection. But how had they managed to lose track of her? And why was Mantis using an untried and untested support agent to try to find her? In the Lisson Grove flat he had refused even to reveal Bartok's name, telling Carradine that "several officers and support agents" were searching for her in places as far afield as Mexico, Cuba and Argentina. If that was the case, it was plausible that she was no longer a source for British Intelligence, but instead a fugitive from justice. Carradine had learned enough from his father about the workings of the Service to know that they were not a law enforcement agency. There had to be another reason behind Mantis's search. Carradine recalled the wistfulness with which he had spoken about her beauty, his irritation with the photograph of her surfer boyfriend. As the train began to move away, he wondered if Mantis was romantically involved with her. That might explain the furtiveness with which he had spoken about "Maria."

Gatwick Airport was rammed. Carradine checked the suitcase containing the book and the sealed package into the hold and cleared security without any complications. He was carrying €1,000 of Mantis's money in his wallet and the other €2,000 inside an envelope in his carry-on bag. The departure gate for the flight with Royal Air Maroc was a twenty-minute walk from security along increasingly deserted corridors leading farther and farther away from the heart of the terminal. A flight attendant wearing a headscarf and heavy mascara clicked a counter for every passenger that came on board. Carradine was one of the last to take his seat. He glanced at the counter as he passed her. There were fewer than fifty passengers on the plane.

As the flight took off, Carradine had the vivid sensation that he was leaving the old part of his life behind and entering a new phase which would in every way be more challenging and satisfying than the life he had known before. His thoughts again turned to Bartok. Was Mantis using him to try to get a personal message to her? If so, how could he guarantee that Carradine would find her at the festival? Was she a fan of his books? Did the Service think that she was going to show herself at his event? Perhaps she wanted to meet Katherine Paget, the novelist with whom he was due to appear onstage.

The sealed package was somewhere beneath Carradine's feet in the chill of the baggage hold; he knew that it would contain the answers to his many questions and felt his professional obligation to Mantis dissipating with every passing mile. He did not consider himself to be particularly cynical or suspicious, but neither would he enjoy the feeling of being duped. He needed to know what was inside the envelope. If that meant breaking his promise to the Service, so be it.

About an hour into the flight, Carradine was handed a small tray with a plastic knife and fork and told that alcohol was not served by the airline. Craving a beer, he ate a tiny, vacuum-packed trout fillet with a bread roll and something the flight attendant claimed was chicken casserole. Leaving most of it unfinished, he decided to go for a stroll. As he passed his fellow passengers bent over their in-flight meals, Carradine could hear a man with a deep, resonant voice speaking in Spanish near the toilets at the rear of the plane. He assumed that the man was talking to a friend, but when he reached the galley he saw that he was alone. His back was turned and he was looking out of the window. He was wearing shorts and a black T-shirt. Religious tattoos completely covered his arms and the backs of his hands. There were tufts of black body hair protruding from the neck of his T-shirt. He was holding a mobile phone perpendicular to his mouth and appeared to be dictating notes. Carradine spoke very little Spanish and could not understand what he was saying. The man sensed that Carradine was behind him and turned around.

"Sorry. You want the bathroom, man?"

The accent was Hispanic, the face about forty-five. He was well-built but not overtly muscular, with long, greasy hair gathered in a topknot.

Though not fully bearded, at least three days of dense stubble ran in a continuous black shadow from beneath his eyes to the hollow of his collarbone. He was one of the hairiest people Carradine had ever seen.

"No thanks. I'm just going for a walk."

The man lowered the phone. He was smiling with forced sincerity, like a technique he had been taught at a seminar on befriending strangers. Carradine had the bizarre and disorienting sensation that the man knew who he was and had been waiting for him.

"Out on the wing?"

"What?"

"You said you were going for a walk."

Carradine rolled with the joke. "Oh. That's right. Yes. So if you wouldn't mind stepping aside I'll just open the door and head out."

An eruption of laughter, a roar so loud it might have been audible in the cockpit. An elderly Arabic woman emerged from one of the bathrooms and flinched.

"Hey! I like you!" said the man. He leaned a hand against the doorframe and shook out a crick in his neck. "Where you from?"

Carradine explained that he was from London. "And you?"

"Me? I'm from everywhere, man." He looked like a mid-level drug dealer attached to a Colombian cartel: disheveled, poorly educated, very possibly violent. "Born in Andalucía. Raised in Madrid. Now I live in London. Heading out to Morocco for some R and R."

They shook hands. The Spaniard's grip suggested prodigious physical force.

"Ramón," he said. "Great to meet you, man."

"Kit. You, too."

"So what you doing in Casablanca?"

Carradine went with the story he had agreed with Mantis.

"I'm a novelist. Doing some research on my next book."

The Spaniard again exploded with enthusiasm. "A writer! Holy shit, man! You write books?" Carradine thought back to his first encounter

with Mantis. There was something similarly inauthentic about Ramón. "You get any of them published?"

"A few, yeah."

"Wow! So cool!"

A flight attendant came into the galley, obliging Carradine to step to one side. She was slim and attractive. Ramón stared at her as she bent down to retrieve a bottle of water from one of the catering boxes. He gazed openmouthed at the outline of her uniform, all of the liveliness and energy in his face momentarily extinguished. He looked up, pursed his lips and shot Carradine a locker-room leer.

"Nice, huh?"

Carradine changed the subject.

"What do you do for R and R in Casablanca?"

It turned out to be the wrong question.

"Oh man! The chicks in Morocco. You don't know?!" The flight attendant stood up, stared at Ramón with undisguised contempt and made her way back down the aisle. "Last time I was there, I meet this girl in a bar on the Corniche. She takes me to this apartment, we open a bottle of whiskey and then—bang! Oh Kit, man! One of the great nights of my life. This chick, she was . . ."

Ramón's recollection trailed off as a young child, accompanied by his father, was led to the bathroom. Carradine seized his chance to get away.

"Well, it was interesting to meet you," he said.

"You heading off?"

Ramón sounded distraught, almost as if he had been tasked with befriending Carradine and been judged to have failed.

"Yeah. I've got stuff to read. Work to do. Just wanted to stretch my legs."

"Oh. OK. Sure. Great to meet you. You're a cool cat, Kit. I like you. Good luck with those books!"

Carradine returned to his seat, oddly unsettled by the encounter. He

remained there for the rest of the flight. He thought that he had seen the last of the Spaniard but, having landed and cleared passport control in Casablanca, found himself standing next to him in the baggage hall. As they waited for their respective suitcases, some of the last remaining passengers to be doing so, Ramón continued to grill Carradine on his life and career, to the point at which he began to wonder if he was testing his cover.

"So, what? You're writing a kind of spy story set in Morocco? Like a Jason Bourne thing?"

Carradine had always thought that his novels occupied a literary space equidistant between the kiss-kiss-bang-bang of Ludlum and the slow-burn chess games of le Carré. For reasons of intellectual vanity, he would ordinarily have tried to distance himself from Ramón's description, but he was keen to stop talking about his work. As a consequence, he readily conceded that his "Moroccan thriller" was going to be "full of guns and explosions and beautiful women."

"Like *The Man Who Knew Too Much*?"

Carradine thought of his father the night before munching naan bread and drinking claret. He didn't think the comparison was accurate, but couldn't be bothered to enter into a debate about it.

"Exactly," he replied.

Ramón had spotted his bag moving along the carousel. He stepped forward, picked it up, slung the bag across his shoulder and turned around.

"You wanna share a cab into town, man?"

Had this been his plan all along? To get alongside Carradine and to accompany him into Casablanca? Or was he merely an overfamiliar tourist trying to do a fellow passenger a favor? Out of the corner of his eye Carradine saw his suitcase jerking along the carousel.

"My bag will probably be a while longer," he said. "I'm hungry. The food on the flight was terrible. I'm going to grab something to eat in the terminal. You go ahead. Have a great trip."

Ramón looked at the carousel. Three suitcases remained, two of which had passed them several times. Betraying an apparent suspicion, he shook Carradine's hand, reiterated how "truly fantastic" it had been to meet him and walked toward the customs area. Relieved to be shot of him, Carradine sent a WhatsApp to Mantis telling him that he had arrived, checked that the novel and the sealed package were still inside his case and walked out into the broiling Moroccan afternoon.

He had expected the chaos and clamor of a typical African airport, but all was relatively quiet as he emerged from the terminal. A hot desert wind was blowing in from the east, bending the tops of the palm trees and sending swirls of leaves and dust across the deserted concourse. Men in jeans and polo shirts were perched on concrete blocks smoking in the shade of the terminal building. When they saw Carradine, they popped up and moved forward, crowding him like paparazzi, repeating the phrase "Taxi mister, taxi" as he tried to move between them. Carradine could see Ramón less than fifty meters away at the top of the rank standing next to a pranged beige Mercedes. He was negotiating a price with the driver. The Spaniard looked up, waving Carradine forward shouting: "Get in, man! Join me!" Carradine was already uncomfortably hot. He was irritated by the drivers trying to force him toward their cars and intrigued enough by Ramón to want to know why he had taken such an interest in him. Was he working for the Service? Had Mantis sent him with instructions to keep an eye on the new kid on the block? Carradine raised a hand in acknowledgment as Ramón continued to gesture him forward. Should he stay or should he go? His curiosity began to tip the balance. Where was the harm in sharing a ride into town? He might even learn something. He duly rolled his suitcase toward the Mercedes and greeted Ramón for the third time.

"Chaos back there," he said. "Thanks for helping me out."

"No problem." The driver popped the boot. "Where you headed, man? I drop you off."

Carradine was staying at a Sofitel in the center of town. It transpired that Ramón was staying in a hotel less than five hundred meters away.

"No way! I'm at the Sheraton! Literally like no distance from where you are." A part of Carradine died inside. "We can meet up later, go for a drink. You know any good places?"

"Somebody recommended Blaine's to me."

The words were out of his mouth before Carradine had time to realize what he had said. He was due to meet Yassine at Blaine's the following evening. What if Ramón showed up during their dinner?

"Blaine's? I know it! Full of chicks, man. You're gonna love it."

He could feel his carefully arranged schedule being quickly and efficiently unpicked by the Spaniard's suffocating camaraderie. He didn't want to be put into a position where he had to work his cover, lying to Ramón about phantom meetings with phantom friends just to avoid seeing him. Why the hell hadn't he taken a separate taxi?

"Sofitel," Ramón told the driver, speaking in accentless French. *"Près du port. Et après le Sheraton, s'il vous plaît."*

Somewhere between the aircraft and the Mercedes the Spaniard had developed a case of volcanic body odor. The car was quickly filled with the smell of his stale sweat. It was hot in the backseat, with no air-conditioning, and Carradine sat with both windows down, listening to the driver muttering to himself in Arabic as they settled into a queue of traffic. Ramón offered Carradine a cigarette, which he gladly accepted, taking the smoke deep into his lungs as he gazed out onto lines of parked cars and half-finished breeze block apartments, wondering how long it would take to get into town.

"I never asked," he said. "What do you do for a living?"

Ramón appeared to hesitate before turning around to answer. His eyes were cold and pitiless. Carradine was reminded of the sudden change in his expression when the flight attendant had walked into the galley. It was like looking at an actor who had momentarily dropped out of character.

"Me?" he said. "I'm just a businessman. Came out here to do a friend a favor."

"I thought you said you were here for the rest and recreation?"

"That, too." Ramón touched his mouth in a way that made Carradine suspect him of lying. "R and R everywhere I go. That's how I like to roll."

"What's the favor?" he asked.

The Spaniard cut him a look, turned to face the oncoming traffic and said: "I don't like to talk too much about work."

Another five minutes passed before they spoke again. The taxi had finally emerged from the traffic jam and reached what appeared to be the main highway into Casablanca. Ramón had been talking to the driver in rapid, aggressive French, only some of which Carradine was able to understand. He began to think that the two men were already acquainted and wondered again if Ramón had deliberately waited for him to come out of the airport.

"You've met before?" he asked.

"What's that?"

"Your driver? You've used him before?"

The Spaniard flinched, as if to suggest that Carradine was asking too many questions.

"What makes you say that?"

"Oh, nothing. It just sounded like this wasn't the first time you'd met."

At that moment the driver—who had not yet looked at Carradine nor acknowledged him in any way—turned off the highway onto a dirt track leading into a forest.

"What's going on?" Carradine looked back at the main road. Paranoia had settled on him like the slowly clinging sweat under his shirt. "Where are we going?"

"No idea." Ramón sounded disconcertingly relaxed. "Probably has to visit his mother or something."

The Mercedes bumped along the track, heading farther and farther into the woods.

"Seriously," said Carradine. "Where are we going?"

The driver pulled the Mercedes to the side of the track, switched off the engine and stepped out. The heat of the afternoon sun was overwhelming. Carradine opened the door to give himself an option to run if the situation should turn against him. There was a small wooden hut about ten meters from the road, occupied by a woman whose face he could not see. The driver approached the hut, held out a piece of paper and passed it to her. Ramón put a tattooed arm across the seat.

"You look tense, man. Relax."

"I'm fine," Carradine told him.

He was anything but fine. He was convinced that he had walked into a trap. He looked in the opposite direction, deeper into the woods. He could see only trees and the forest floor. He used the wing mirror on the driver's side to check if there was anybody on the road behind them, but saw no sign of anyone. The stench of sweat was overwhelming. Through the woods beyond the hut he could make out a small clearing dotted with plastic toys and a children's slide. The driver was coming back to the car.

"*Que faisiez-vous?*" Ramón asked him.

"Parking," the driver replied. Carradine smiled and shook his head. His lack of experience had got the better of him. He looked back at the hut. The veiled woman was marking the piece of paper with an ink stamp. She slammed it onto a metal spike.

"Crazy!" Ramón produced a delighted grin. "In Casablanca they pay their parking tickets in the middle of the fucking woods. Never saw this before, man."

"Me neither," Carradine replied.

It was another forty-five minutes to the hotel. Carradine sat in the heat of the backseat, smoking another of Ramón's cigarettes. On the edge of the city the Mercedes became jammed in three-lane traffic that inched along wide colonial boulevards packed with cars and motorbikes. Ramón grew increasingly agitated, berating the driver for taking the wrong route in order to extract more money for the journey. The swings in his mood, from backslapping bonhomie to cold, aggressive impatience, were as unexpected as they were unsettling. Carradine followed the progress of the journey on his iPhone, trying to orientate himself in the new city, the street names—Boulevard de La Mecque, Avenue Tétouan, Rue des Racines—evoking all the antiquity and mystique of French colonial Africa. Mopeds buzzed past his door as the Mercedes edged from block to block. Men hawking drinks and newspapers approached the car and were shooed away by the driver, who switched on the windscreen wipers to deter them. Several times Carradine saw cars and scooters running red lights or deliberately going the wrong way around roundabouts in order to beat the jam. Stalled in the rivers of traffic he thought of home and cursed the heat, calling his father to tell him that he had arrived. He was busy playing backgammon with a friend and had no time to talk, their brief exchange leaving Carradine with a sense of isolation that he found perversely enjoyable. It was exhilarating to be alone in a strange city, a place about which he knew so little, at the start of a mission for which he had received no training and no detailed preparation. He knew that his father had been posted to Egypt by the Service in the early years of his marriage and thought of the life he must have led as a young spy, running agents in Cairo, taking his mother on romantic trips to Sinai, Luxor and Aswan. Ramón offered him yet another cigarette and he took it, observing that the smog outside was likely to do more damage to his lungs. Ramón went to the trouble of translating the joke for the benefit of the driver who turned in his seat and smiled, acknowledging Carradine for the first time.

"*Vrai!*" he said. "*C'est vrai!*"

That was when Ramón showed him his phone.

"Jesus Christ, man. You see this?"

Carradine pitched the cigarette out of the window and leaned forward. The headline on the screen was in Spanish. He could see the words REDMOND and MUERTA.

"What happened?"

"They killed the Redmond bitch," Ramón replied. "Resurrection fucking killed her."

8

They kept her in the van for the first thirty-six hours. She screamed when they took off the gag, so they put it on again and left her to rage. They offered her water and food, but she refused it. She soiled herself. When she had spent all of her energy, Redmond wept.

Toward the end of the second day they took her from the van, still blindfolded, and tied her to a chair in the basement of the farmhouse. They played the recording into the room. A loop of Redmond's words, repeated over and over again. A torture of her own making. The bearded man called it "The Two Minutes of Hate," after Orwell, but the recording lasted for more than twelve hours.

The immigrants attempting to cross the Mediterranean are the same insects already swarming over Europe. They choke our schools and hospitals. They dirty our towns and cities. They murder our daughters at rock concerts. They mow down our sons on the streets.

It went on and on into the night. Whenever Redmond looked as though she was falling asleep, they turned up the volume. She was prevented from sleeping by the words she had written. "Sentenced by your own sentences," said the man who had knocked down her husband.

The only answer is to lock up every young Muslim man or woman whose name appears on a terrorist watch list. How else to protect British citizens from slaughter? If we cannot take the sensible precaution, outlined by the government of the United States, of preventing potential terrorists from entering the United Kingdom from countries that are known sponsors of Islamist terror, then this is the only option remaining to us.

On the morning of the third day they removed Redmond's gag and again offered her food and water. This time she accepted. The bearded man asked her, on camera, if she wished to defend her words and actions. She said that she stood by everything she had written. She insisted that, given the chance, she would write and broadcast everything again. She had no regrets for exercising her right to free speech and for articulating views held by millions of people in the West who were too cowed by political correctness to speak their minds.

The bearded man was standing behind her as she spoke. He lifted her hair clear of her shoulders, held it in a fist above her head, and sliced her throat with a knife. Redmond's body was dumped at a stretch of waste ground on the outskirts of Coventry. A photograph of her corpse was sent to the editor of the British newspaper who had commissioned her column.

Somerville switched off the recorder.

"What are your feelings about what happened to Lisa Redmond?" he said.

Bartok shrugged.

"I do not know enough about it." She stood up and stretched her back, twisting one way, then the other. "I know that Kit was upset. He talked about it a lot. I think it haunted him."

"What about you?" the American asked. His tone was supercilious. "Were you upset by it? Were you haunted, Lara?"

Bartok picked up one of the biscuits. She turned it over in her fingers. She liked Somerville. She trusted him. She did not like or trust the American.

"As I have said. I did not know Redmond's writing. I did not have the opportunity to listen to her radio broadcasts wherever I was hiding in the world. She sounded like somebody who we might have pursued."

The American seized on this, closing the space between them.

"We?"

"Resurrection." Bartok looked at Somerville as if to suggest that the American was starting to annoy her. "In the old days. Before the violence

and the killing. She was the sort of figure Ivan would have looked at. Redmond, and those like her, men like Otis Euclidis, they gave encouragement to the bigots, to the ignorant. Ivan wanted to teach them a lesson.
We all did." She bit into the biscuit. It was dry. She could only swallow
by taking a sip of water to wash it down. "When I see what has happened
to Resurrection, I feel nothing but sadness. It began as something remarkable. It began as a phenomenon. Ivan had a conception of a new kind of
revolutionary movement, one which harnessed the power of the internet
and social media, one which was fueled by international outrage among
young and old alike. He wanted to take that revolutionary movement out
onto the streets, to fight back against those who had corrupted our societies. He knew that Resurrection would catch fire with people, inspire
groups and individuals, oblige the masses to mount operations of their
own—however small, however apparently insignificant—so that bit-by-bit
and step-by-step, democracy and fairness would be restored. But all of the
hope and the beauty of those ideas, the purity of the early attacks, has
been lost."

Somerville reached for the recorder. They needed to get the whole story
out of Bartok. There was no point letting her talk during the breaks if nobody was keeping a record.

"Would you like to go back to those early months?" he asked.

"Of course, whatever you want," she said.

"Please. Tell us how it all got started."

SECRET INTELLIGENCE SERVICE
EYES ONLY / STRAP 1

STATEMENT BY LARA BARTOK ("LASZLO")
CASE OFFICERS: J.W.S./S.T.H.—CHAPEL STREET
REF: RESURRECTION/SIMAKOV/CARRADINE
FILE: RE2768X

PART 2 OF 5

Euclidis was our first target. That was the first and most brilliant idea of Ivan's, to capture this snake, this poison in the bloodstream of public life, and to show the world that decent people were prepared to stand up to hate, to put an end to divisive words, to expose Euclidis for the narcissist that he was. For all his expensive clothes and his clever talk, we showed the world that he was just a self-interested clown. He blogged to make money. He spread lies to get rich. To get laid. He was not interested in changing the system, in making the world a better place. He and his friends—the alt-right, the white supremacists, the anti-Semites, the Holocaust deniers—they had no alternative ideology. They had no *ideas*. They just wanted to draw attention to themselves. They wanted to make decent citizens feel uncomfortable and frightened. That was their reason for living. They were bullies, high on hate.

How did Euclidis draw so many admirers? By making stupid people feel better about their stupidity. By allowing bigots to think they were justified in making anti-Semitic statements, saying that it was OK to hate women, to be aggrieved about people of color, about immigrants. The sad truth is that there were enough trolls buying his books, reading his articles, attending his talks to make him a rich man. They gave him the fame he craved.

Euclidis was a junkie for attention. And if they didn't give it to him in public, they gave it to him on Twitter, on Instagram, on Facebook. We had to take him down.

So Ivan, with my help, and with the assistance of Zack Curtis and ▮▮▮▮▮, seized him at Berkeley. Grabbed him as he stepped out of his hotel. It was so easy. We were in America so we were able to obtain guns. The hotel had no security, we possessed the element of surprise. We put a hood on him, we put him in cuffs, we threw his phone out of the window. He did not like that, he did not like being separated from his precious phone! We switched vehicles and drove into the mountains. Euclidis of course was a physical coward. He cried like a four-year-old boy. It was pitiful.

We filmed him in secret, as the world now knows. We were able to show on camera that Otis Euclidis was a charlatan, a fraud. He confessed that he had done it all to make money. He had never meant anything he had said or written to be taken seriously. His followers were "clowns" and "losers." When he had said in interviews that black lives "did not matter," he had been "joking." When he had written that feminism was "the worst invention since gunpowder," he had only been "fooling around." He showed himself to be a fraud who believed in nothing but fame. When we screened the film, when we put it out on the internet for the world to see, and we saw the reaction, well, it was a beautiful moment.

Almost immediately there were copycat attacks. Dozens of politicians and right-wing figures around the world came under threat. My favorite was done by the refugee in Amsterdam. The kitchen porter. A Muslim from Iraq who had been washing dishes in a restaurant so that he could feed his wife and baby daughter. He was no older than twenty-five or twenty-six. Samir. I've forgotten his surname. [JWS: Samir Rabou] He learned that

Piet Boutmy, the leader of the Dutch far-right party—again, I don't remember the name of this party [JWS: *Partij voor de Vrijheid*]—was eating in the restaurant. A waiter, a Syrian, I believe, came into the kitchen and told him Boutmy was there. Samir knew about the kidnapping of Euclidis, he told the police who later interviewed him that he had followed Resurrection from its very first statements and that he greatly admired Ivan Simakov. He took off his washing gloves, kept his apron, walked out of the kitchen and went directly into the restaurant. The security guard protecting Boutmy thought he was a waiter. The table was covered in many dishes, including—perfectly!—a soup prepared with beetroots which was still very hot. Also bottles of water, glasses of red wine, cutlery, a vase of flowers. Shouting "Resurrection!" Samir lifted the whole table on top of this racist animal, soaking him to the bone, also the colleague from the same party who was dining with him. I heard that he faced no charges and soon found another job at a rival restaurant. It was beautiful.

Everything that Ivan and myself had hoped for came to pass. Ivan was worried that the Resurrection movement would burn out. It did not. He wrote that he wanted Resurrection to have "a seismic effect on public attitudes to the liars and enablers of the alt-right." This is exactly what happened. The summer homes of criminal bankers were burned to the ground. Cars belonging to producers at Fox News were vandalized and damaged. Those who had attended white supremacist rallies were identified by their peers and targeted for retribution. They paid the price for their hate with the loss of their careers, their friends. All it took was one or two examples for everyone to follow suit.

But, of course, Resurrection changed. What started as a non-violent movement, symbolic acts targeted against deserving victims, quickly became violent. I was naïve to believe that this would not happen, but what distressed me was Ivan's willingness to change his position, not only toward nonviolence, but also concerning his own role as a figurehead. He wanted the limelight. He craved adulation. I had not identified these characteristics in him when we first met. His vanity, his stubbornness, his readiness to lose sight of what Resurrection was about and instead to place himself at the heart of what became a hijacked, paramilitary organization. It became impossible to live with him. I could no longer do useful work. I lost my respect for Ivan Simakov and I left him. That is when they began to hunt me down.

9

Carradine reached his room and switched on the television. Every major news network was carrying the story. The police believed the murder had been carried out by the same members of Resurrection who had kidnapped Redmond five days earlier. Tributes were being paid by friends and colleagues, inevitable expressions of outrage articulated by politicians, fellow journalists and friends.

Carradine muted the television. He sat on the bed and felt a hollowness inside him close to a feeling of personal responsibility in the death of an innocent woman. Had he done more to help, had he found the courage to cross the street and to confront Redmond's kidnappers, she might still be alive. He thought of the girl who had been standing beside him, chatting away to her friend. *So I says to him, I'm like, no way is that happening, yeah? I'm like, he needs to get his shit together because I'm, like, just not going through with that bullshit again.* Where was she now? How would she react to news of this kind? Would she share Carradine's remorse or experience nothing but a momentary, fleeting anxiety that Resurrection had again resorted to murder? Would she even be aware that Redmond had been killed?

He went to the window and looked down at the vast city. Low white-washed buildings stretched in a broad semicircle to the Atlantic coast. At the sea's edge the vast Hassan II Mosque dominated the skyline; to the northwest, the cranes and wharves of the port were blocks of shadow partly obscured by a high-rise hotel. Carradine had detested Redmond. He had abhorred her character and public style. She had weaved deliberate ignorance into casual prejudice with the sole purpose of inciting outrage, hysteria and fear. She had craved the spotlight of notoriety. In the wake of an Islamist suicide bombing on the streets of London, she had called for "internment" for male Muslims under the age of forty. Handed a column in a tabloid newspaper with which to disseminate her toxic views, she had advocated the use of naval warships to prevent refugees—many of them fleeing the horrors of Syria and Yemen—from crossing the Mediterranean. When her rhetoric became too vile even for the leather-skinned editors of the Fourth Estate, Redmond merely had to look across the Pond to find any number of right-wing media outlets in the United States eager to beam her prejudices into the homes of the ignorant and the dispossessed. Indeed, Redmond had been only days from moving to the United States to work for Fox News when she had been seized by Resurrection. Carradine knew that if he opened Twitter, or switched to Fox itself, he would be swamped in partisan bile and hate. For every person shocked by Redmond's murder there would be another openly celebrating; for every person applauding Resurrection for taking the fight to the goons and trolls of the alt-right, there would be another—like Carradine himself—who knew that violence only made the situation far worse.

He turned from the window and began to unpack. The sealed envelope was at the top of his suitcase. He took it out and placed it on the bed. To try to clear his head he did fifty press-ups, took a shower and changed into a fresh set of clothes. Whatever was in the package, he knew that he could now be incriminating himself by passing documents to a suspected member of a terrorist organization. The Redmond murder had changed the game. He had been transformed—without prior agreement—into a foot soldier in the global struggle against Resurrection. To hell with the Service; Carradine needed to do what he had to do. He picked up the package and felt it in his hands. He could make out the edges of the passport, the outline of the document.

He hesitated momentarily—then cut at the Sellotape using the knife on a bottle opener from the minibar. He reached inside the package.

It was a British passport, just as Mantis had said it would be. Carradine opened it to the back. A photograph of Bartok, identical to the one he was carrying in his wallet, looked out at him from the identity page. Bartok was identified as "Maria Consuela Rodriguez," a British citizen, born 8 June 1983. A Santander credit card fell out of the passport and dropped onto the floor. The name MS. M RODRIGUEZ was stamped across the bottom. The back of the card was unsigned.

Carradine reached into the package and pulled out a smaller rectangular envelope. The envelope was sealed. No name or address had been written on it, only the word LASZLO in block capitals. This time he did not bother using the knife. He tore the envelope open with his hands.

Inside was a single piece of white A4 paper, folded twice. The letter was typed.

IF THIS MESSAGE FINDS YOU IT IS A MIRACLE. TRUST THE PERSON WHO GIVES IT TO YOU.

YOU ARE NOT SAFE. THEY HAVE WORKED OUT WHERE YOU ARE. IT IS ONLY A MATTER OF TIME BEFORE THEY FIND YOU.

I CANNOT HELP YOU EXCEPT BY GIVING YOU THESE GIFTS. USE THEM WISELY. THE NUMBER IS 0812.

I AM THE MAN WHO TOOK YOU TO THE SEA.

10

Carradine read the message several times trying to decipher what was behind Mantis's language. He assumed that 0812 was the PIN number for the credit card though he doubted that Bartok, should he ever find her, would risk using it more than once; to do so would be to pinpoint her location to anyone tracking the account. "The man who took you to the sea" sounded romantic, but Carradine was wary of leaping to that conclusion without stronger evidence. Yet the tone of the letter was unquestionably personal. Mantis seemed to be distancing himself from the Service in order to send the warning. Who were "THEY"? The Service? The Agency? The Russians? Almost every law enforcement and intelligence service in the world was hunting Resurrection activists; all of them would have liked to get their hands on Lara Bartok. The only section that seemed unequivocal to him was the opening paragraph, which reinforced the idea that Mantis had employed Carradine in good faith and had been honest about the difficulty of finding "LASZLO."

There was a safe in his room. Carradine asked for some Sellotape to be sent up from reception. He sealed the letter, the credit card and the passport back inside the package and put it in the safe. Just as he was finishing he heard his phone ping. Mantis had finally replied.

Glad you've arrived safely. Meeting is at the Four Seasons later this evening. Let me know how it goes.

Carradine understood that he was to go to the Four Seasons and to leave the money for "Abdullah Aziz" at the reception desk. It was a simple enough task, yet he was apprehensive. He took the €2,000 from his satchel, adding a thousand more from his wallet, and wrote Aziz's name on the envelope.

He looked at the map of Casablanca. The Four Seasons was on the eastern side of the city, close to a cluster of bars and restaurants on the Corniche. It was too far to walk but Carradine set out on foot, intending to catch a taxi en route. He took nothing with him except his wallet, his phone and the envelope containing the money. He was wearing a dark blue linen jacket and walked with both the wallet and the envelope buttoned into the inside pockets. It was still very hot but he did not want to have to take the jacket off and run the risk of it being snatched by an opportunistic thief.

He quickly found himself in a maze of narrow, dilapidated streets in the old medina to the west of the port. This was Morocco as he had imagined it: low brick houses painted in blocks of pale greens, blues and yellows with shuttered windows and crumbling plasterwork. He took out his phone and began to take photographs in the fading evening light, the writer in him aware that the details of what he saw—the wooden carts laden with fresh fruits and spices; the old women fanning themselves in shaded doorways; the raggedy children kicking a football in the street—might one day be useful to him. At the same time he was working his cover. On the small chance that he was being followed, C. K. Carradine had carte blanche to snoop around, to be seen taking photographs and scribbling notes, to loiter in the lobbies of five-star hotels or to meet a contact in a fashionable restaurant. If asked to explain why he was carrying €3,000 in cash, he could say that he did not fully trust the safe in his hotel and preferred to carry his personal belongings with him. His legend was foolproof. This was, after all, why Mantis had hired him.

Carradine was lining up a photograph of a rusting truck laden with watermelons when he saw a WhatsApp message from Mantis drop down onto the screen.

Change of plan. Meeting at Sheraton, not 4 Seasons. Sorry for inconvenience.

He wondered if he was the victim of an elaborate practical joke. Ramón was staying at the Sheraton. Was the *Spaniard* Mantis's contact? Carradine hoped that the location was a bizarre coincidence, a consequence of the meager number of top-class hotels in Casablanca, but could not shake off a sixth sense that Ramón and Mantis were somehow involved with each other. Perhaps Mantis had arranged for them to catch the same flight so that Ramón could keep an eye on him? It was impossible to know.

Carradine looked along the street. He was standing at the edge of a busy market square, a smell of mint and burning charcoal on the air. The narrow switchback streets of the old city had spun him around; he had no idea if he was facing north, south, east or west. He used his phone to pinpoint his position and began to walk in the general direction of the Sheraton, eventually finding an exit from the souk through the old walls of the Medina. Twenty minutes later Carradine was standing on the steps of the hotel. It was just before eight o'clock. A bored, uniformed guard indicated that he should pass through a metal detector. Carradine did so. Despite the fact that an alarm sounded as he walked through, the guard—who was wearing gloves and holding a plastic security wand—waved him on.

The lobby of the hotel was a vast marble atrium dominated by palm trees and wide marble columns. A mezzanine balcony overlooked the ground floor. A cleaning woman was polishing a vase near a window on the street side of the hotel. Carradine was aware that Ramón might be nursing a preprandial mojito or cup of coffee in one of the nooks and crannies of the lobby. He did not want to be spotted by the Spaniard and engaged in conversation. He did not trust him and was sure that Ramón's ebullient good cheer was a front disguising a volatile, possibly even violent personality. It occurred to him that he was now involved in precisely the sort of scenario he had written about many times in his fiction. The spy—amateur or otherwise—was always at risk of running into a friend or acquaintance in the field. Carradine quickly prepared a cover story, on the off chance that he was identified, and walked toward the reception desk.

Had he dramatized the scene in one of his novels, he would have made more of the sense of trepidation his protagonist felt as he set about completing his first mission on behalf of the Service. In reality, Carradine found the task almost embarrassingly easy. He approached the youngest—and therefore potentially the least experienced—of three female members of staff, smiled at her warmly, explained that he wanted to leave a package for one of the hotel guests and handed her the envelope. The receptionist recognized "Abdullah Aziz" as the name of a guest, placed the envelope in a pigeonhole beneath the desk and did not ask Carradine for his name. At no point did he spot Ramón, nor any individual who might conceivably have been the waiting Aziz. It was all very straightforward.

Within ten minutes Carradine was back on the tenth floor of his hotel, basking in the cool of the air-conditioning, sending a message to Mantis informing him that "the meeting had been a success." A short time later Mantis responded, telling Carradine that "everybody was happy with the way things went." Despite completing the task successfully, Carradine experienced an unexpected stab of disappointment and irritation that he had not been tested more thoroughly. Perhaps it was the nagging sense that all was not quite as it seemed. He did not fully trust Mantis. He was profoundly suspicious of Ramón. Having read the note inside the package, he was concerned that there was a plot to kidnap Lara Bartok, perhaps even to kill her. If that was the case, was he being used as an unwitting pawn?

He took a second shower, went down to the bar, ordered a vodka martini and tried to convince himself that his doubts were just the flights of fancy of a novelist with an overactive imagination. A man sitting two stools away was wearing an aftershave so overpowering that it began to affect the taste of the martini. Carradine ordered a second, carrying it to a table a safe distance from the bar. As he walked across the lounge, a vodka martini in one hand, a packet of cigarettes in the other, he realized that he was casting himself as the central character in a spy story no different to the ones he had written in the pages of his books or seen a hundred times at the movies.

He sat down and tried to work out the link between Mantis, Ramón and Bartok. Carradine acknowledged that he was a need-to-know support agent, not a fully-fledged spy cognizant of all the intelligence about "LASZLO." In this respect, Mantis was not obliged to tell him everything he knew. By the same token, the Service was under no obligation to inform Carradine that Ramón had been sent to keep an eye on him. Besides, there was every reason to believe that Ramón was just an overly friendly passenger Carradine just happened to have bumped into on the plane. He had been shown no evidence to suggest that Ramón was "Abdullah Aziz," nor was it credible that Mantis would have wanted him to pay Ramón for his services. The only thing that Carradine knew for certain was that Bartok was on the run. Mantis wanted to protect her, for reasons that were not yet clear, but had not been in a position to leave London in order to do so. As a result, he had hired Carradine to assist in the search for her.

Carradine stared at the pitted olive at the bottom of the glass. None of it made sense. The vodka had blunted, not sharpened his wits. He had been active as a support agent for less than twenty-four hours and already felt lost in the wilderness of mirrors.

He settled the bill and walked outside. There was a taxi idling in front of the hotel. Carradine climbed in and asked to be taken to the Corniche. He offered a cigarette to the driver who placed it, unlit, in a recess behind the gearstick. Sated by alcohol, Carradine sat in the backseat texting his father, trying to forget about his responsibilities to the Service and to set aside his doubts about Mantis and Ramón. He enjoyed the sepia light of the Moroccan evening and the movement of the taxi as it weaved from street to street. He wanted to convince himself that there was no deeper meaning to the information he had gleaned from the letter, no dark conspiracy playing out on the streets of Casablanca. But it was impossible. He knew, in the way that you know that a friendship is doomed or a love affair coming to an end, that something was not quite right. He was sure that he was being manipulated. He was certain that he had been sent to Morocco for a purpose that had not yet been made clear to him. The chances of finding Bartok were so remote that the words of warning contained in Mantis's letter—"IT IS ONLY A MATTER OF TIME BEFORE THEY FIND YOU"—seemed to Carradine as vague and yet as terrifying as lines from a work of fiction. So why had he been handed such a task?

The taxi stopped at a set of lights. An elderly beggar came to the window, pressing his face against the glass. The driver swore in Arabic as the beggar knocked on the window, imploring Carradine to give him money. He dug around in his trouser pocket for some loose change and was about to roll down the window and pass the money to the beggar when the taxi accelerated down the street.

Carradine turned to see that the man had fallen over.

"Stop!" he shouted. *"Problème! Arrêtez!"*

The driver ignored him, made a right-hand turn and headed north toward the sea. Through the back window, Carradine could see the beggar being helped to his feet.

"He fell," he said in French, thinking of Redmond and his failure to act.

"They all fall," the driver replied. *Ils tombent tous.*

"Pull over!"

Again Carradine's request was ignored. "I want to go back," he said, lamenting the fact that his French was not good enough to make himself properly understood. "Take me back to the old man."

"*Non,*" the driver replied. He wanted his fare, he wanted to take the tourist to the Corniche. "You don't go back, mister," he said, now speaking in English. "You can never go back."

11

By the time Carradine had persuaded the driver to stop, it was too late. They had driven too far from the fallen man. As an expression of his annoyance, Carradine paid him off without a tip and covered the remaining mile on foot.

He found a restaurant on the Corniche where he continued to drink. On top of the two martinis, he bought a bottle of local white wine followed by successive vodka tonics at a bar across the street. Falling in with a group of businessmen from Dijon who knew a place nearby, Carradine found himself at a table in a packed nightclub on the oceanfront drinking Cuba libres until five in the morning. He eventually stumbled back to his hotel at dawn, his mind cleared of worry, his doubts put to rest.

He woke up at midday and ordered room service, necking two ibuprofen with a glass of freshly squeezed orange juice followed by three black coffees courtesy of the Nespresso machine in his room. There was a spa on the third floor of the hotel. Carradine booked a hammam, sweating out the night's toxins in a tiled steam room before falling asleep in an armchair to the sound of panpipes and birdsong. By four o'clock he was back in his room swallowing two more ibuprofen and repent-

ing at leisure the oversized tequila shot he had downed at the edge of
the dance floor, the entire packet of cigarettes he had somehow managed to smoke in less than seven hours of music and forgotten conversations. He was fairly sure that at a certain point in the small hours of
the morning he had consumed an enormous number of grilled prawns.

Mantis texted just as Carradine was preparing to head out to Blaine's.
Yassine was running late but would meet him on the first floor of the
restaurant as close to nine o'clock as he could manage. Annoyed to have
to wait another hour, Carradine tried to grab a quick siesta but found
it impossible to sleep. He was too tired to concentrate on the book he
was reading so instead ordered a hair-of-the-dog martini at the bar, listening to a local jazz quartet murdering standards from the American
songbook as he sat beneath an outsized reproduction poster of Humphrey Bogart and Ingrid Bergman. Just before half-past eight Carradine
returned to his room, retrieved the French translation of his novel and
took a cab to the restaurant.

It was after dark. Blaine's was not clearly marked. Carradine walked
for several minutes up and down Boulevard D'Anfa, eventually locat-
ing the entrance at the corner of a poorly lit street lined with shuttered
apartments and dusty parked cars. A shaven-headed Moroccan was
standing in the doorway wearing a black suit that fitted him like a cube.
He looked Carradine up and down, nodding him inside without a word.
Carradine climbed the staircase to the first floor. The martini had
begun to work through him but he felt no relief from the solemn
drudgery of his hangover, only a desire to eat a good dinner and to go
back to bed.

He emerged into a well-lit, low-ceilinged lounge upholstered in
whites and grays. There was an overpowering stench of fruit tobacco.
A woman was moving between the tables singing Arabic love songs with
the help of a cordless microphone and a preprogrammed synthesizer.
The music was very loud. One section of the room was occupied almost
exclusively by heavily made-up, well-dressed Moroccan women in their

twenties and early thirties. They were seated alone or in groups of two or three at tables toward the back of the lounge. They stared at Carradine as he walked in. He assumed they were prostitutes and ducked the eye contact. Men sitting nearby in gray armchairs were eating dinner and smoking cigars.

A waiter was cutting up a lemon at the bar. Carradine asked in French if he could have a table for two. The waiter appeared not to understand, indicating that he should speak to an older man standing in the center of the lounge. The man, who was wearing gray trousers and a white shirt badly in need of a washing machine, showed Carradine to a table on the street side of the lounge, close to a large television showing a football match between Real Madrid and a Spanish team Carradine did not recognize. The Arabic commentary on the game was inaudible above the noise of the music. A young Arab wearing a *thawb* was seated opposite, watching the match and smoking a hookah pipe. He did not acknowledge Carradine.

A waiter appeared carrying a long-handled frying pan lined with aluminum foil and filled with hot coals. He placed several of the coals on the foil cap of the pipe using a set of metal tongs. An attractive woman in a tight blouse and short black leather skirt was sitting at the table adjacent to Carradine's, engrossed in her mobile phone. She looked up and smiled provocatively as he sat down. When he placed the novel on the table she made a point of tilting her head and looking at it, trying to read the title from the spine. In different circumstances Carradine might have spoken to her, but he turned away.

A short time later he received a text from Mantis explaining that Yassine did not expect to reach Blaine's before ten o'clock. This time the delay suited him. He was famished and ordered a lamb tagine. It appeared within five minutes in a burned terra-cotta pot with a portion of chips piled over the meat. Carradine wondered if this was the traditional way in which tagine was served in Casablanca or if word had gotten through to the chef that he was British. In any case he ate it all, washed down with a beer, and was restored to something like his usual self. The manager cleared away the tagine and brought Carradine a plate of fruit—"on the house"—as well as a second beer. Carradine had line of sight to the top of the staircase and kept an eye out for Yassine while watching the game.

The match had just ended in a two-all draw when a slim, mustachioed man appeared at the top of the stairs, furtively looking around the lounge. Several of the women seated near the bar gestured toward him in the hope of encouraging him to join them. But the man, who was bald and wearing spectacles, did not appear to be interested. Instead he turned and looked in the direction of the television. Carradine was the only white Western male in the restaurant. The man picked him out immediately, raising a hand in silent acknowledgment as he approached the table.

"I recognize you from the wedding in London."

Carradine stood up and shook Yassine's hand. He had to speak loudly against the cacophony of the music.

"The wedding was in Scotland," he replied.

Mantis's contact smiled nervously and sat down with his back to the room.

"My name is Yassine," he said. "I am sorry to be late."

His voice had a low, rough quality and his cheeks were pinched and sallow. Carradine assumed he was a heavy smoker.

"It's quite all right," he said. "Kit."

Carradine poured Yassine a glass of water. The young Arab who had been smoking *sheeshah* had long since departed, but the woman wearing the black leather skirt was still at the next table. Carradine was aware that she was looking at Yassine out of the corner of her eye.

"Why did we meet here?" the Moroccan asked, opening a napkin on his lap.

Carradine was confused by the question. Perhaps Yassine was offended by the clamor of the music or the pervasive stench of tobacco.

"I was told it was what you wanted," he said.

"By who? London?"

"Yes."

The waiter who had earlier been carrying the pan of hot coals came to the table and spoke to Yassine in Arabic. Years earlier Carradine had been to Tanzania with the BBC and had sat in a safari hutch at sunset as impalas, zebras and giraffes gathered at a watering hole. The wild animals had seemed tense and jumpy, turning constantly to check for predators and bolting at the slightest noise or movement. He was reminded of this as he watched Yassine. He suspected that Mantis's contact wasn't merely a gopher for the Service, but a fully paid-up agent in a state of unremitting anxiety about being caught.

"Have a drink," he said, in an effort to calm Yassine's nerves. The Moroccan explained that he had already ordered tea from the waiter, but finished his glass of water in one continuous gulp. He then removed his jacket, placing it beside him on a gray armchair. He was wearing a striped green shirt with a heavily starched white collar. Carradine saw that his armpits were soaked in sweat.

"I brought you the book," he said.

"Good." Yassine withdrew a packet of cigarettes from his jacket. Carradine had borrowed a lighter from the manager and passed it across the table.

"Here," he said. They made eye contact as the flame jumped.

"Thank you."

Yassine blew a column of smoke at the ceiling and inhaled loudly through his nose, flaring the nostrils and releasing the breath as though applying a yoga exercise to control his anxiety. The music in the lounge was playing at a slightly lower volume, instruments Carradine could not identify over a fast electronic beat. Yassine briefly turned around to look back into the lounge. As he did so, the woman at the next table tried to catch Carradine's eye. He looked down and noticed that she had a second mobile phone poking out of the top of her clutch bag.

"How is our mutual friend?" Yassine asked, accepting a glass of mint tea. Carradine assumed that he was referring to Mantis.

"He's fine."

"And you live here now? In Casablanca? You are writing a book?"

"No, no." Carradine wondered how much, or how little, Mantis had told him. "I'm just passing through. On my way to Marrakech."

"And you have always done this sort of work? You write the books for C. K. Carradine or is this just a cover and somebody else writes them for you?"

Carradine was amazed that anybody could imagine that such a career was possible and laughed as he replied: "I write them. That's my normal day job. C.K. is just a pseudonym. My real name is Christopher Alfred Carradine. Everybody calls me 'Kit.'"

"I see."

Yassine continued to smoke the cigarette and to study Carradine's face with such intensity that he began to feel slightly uncomfortable.

"Why don't I give you the book?" he suggested.

"That would be a good idea."

Carradine passed the novel across the table. The Moroccan did not open it up or even look at the cover, but instead immediately lifted up his jacket and placed the book on the gray chair.

"Is this all that you brought for me?" he asked.

"I'm afraid so." Carradine wondered if he had failed to listen carefully enough to Mantis's instructions. Was some of the money he had been given intended for Yassine and not for the mysterious Abdullah Aziz?

"No, this is what I expected," Yassine replied.

The Moroccan ground out the cigarette and speared a slice of melon from the plate of fruit. Carradine saw the woman at the next table reach down for her second mobile phone, plucking it from the clutch bag.

"What does our friend think about the political situation?" Yassine asked.

"What political situation?"

"The death of this woman in England. The journalist. The one who hated Muslims?"

"Oh. Lisa Redmond." The name was like an echo chasing Carradine from city to city. "I only found out about it yesterday. I haven't had a chance to speak to London."

The ease with which Carradine had begun to use the term "London" spoke both to his desire to appear professional and to adapt to the language of the clandestine world. He felt self-conscious doing so, almost to the point of absurdity, but it was also oddly exhilarating to be speaking in real-life words that his characters had spoken merely in fiction.

"It is the first murder of this kind in London by Resurrection. I am right?"

"That's right. Up to now we've just had beatings, arson attacks, assaults in restaurants and at public meetings. That kind of thing."

"And what are you doing about it?"

"Excuse me?" Carradine could not prevent himself from laughing. "What am *I* doing about it? I'm just a writer, Yassine. Writers don't live in the real world."

"And yet you are here."

"And yet I am here."

They were silent. Carradine had begun to believe that he was sitting in front of a much sharper, more reflective man than he had first imagined. He tried to change the subject.

"What do you do for a living?" The woman at the next table was speaking quietly on her phone. Yassine skewered a chunk of banana and waved the fork in front of his face before answering.

"I do not want to talk about that," he said. "Let us not leave this conversation. I am interested to know about Resurrection. What you think will happen. Where you think all of this ends."

Carradine realized that he was being asked to speak on behalf of the

Service. Mantis's man wanted to know the party line in London, the thinking in Downing Street and Vauxhall Cross. Carradine was happy to run with the conceit.

"We're all biding our time," he said. "We're all living day-to-day not knowing what the future will bring." Yassine appeared to find this answer vague and insubstantial. Carradine endeavored to be more specific. "I'm about to turn thirty-six. My country has been in a permanent state of conflict for almost forty years. From the Falklands to Syria, Great Britain has always been at war. But it's never affected us."

"What do you mean?"

"I mean that we were able to go about our daily lives without thinking about the battles British soldiers were fighting on our behalf, without being concerned that our own lives might be at risk. We were oblivious to what was going on. In the last few years, all that has changed."

"In what way, please?"

"The war has come to the streets."

"This sounds very dramatic. I suppose that I am talking to a writer, so I should expect this."

Carradine was beginning to like Yassine. Two women, both in figure-hugging dresses and high heels, walked up the stairs, checked their reflections in a mirror beside the bar and made their way to a table on the far side of the lounge. One of them was very beautiful, with long, dark hair, causing Carradine momentarily to think that he had sighted Lara Bartok. But it was just his mind playing tricks. She was too dark, her features too angular.

"It's not meant to sound dramatic," he said, looking back at Yassine. "If you walk down the street in London or Manchester, at any moment you know that a bomb could go off, that some maniac in a van could come plowing through a crowd and mow down fifty innocent civilians." Carradine had seen huge concrete barriers, close to his hotel, protecting a wide pedestrianized boulevard in Casablanca for just that purpose.

"That was never the case before. We had the IRA, sure. The Spanish lived with ETA. But the existential threat was completely different."

Yassine removed his glasses and ran a hand across the pointed dome of his head.

"This word, please. I do not understand. . . ."

Carradine explained what he had meant by "existential" and realized that he was talking too fast and in too much detail. He felt a sudden headache flare at a point deep inside his brain and reached for the strip of ibuprofen he had been carrying around in his jacket.

"You are in discomfort?" Yassine asked as Carradine popped two of the pills.

"Nothing to worry about." It was as though one of the hot *sheeshah* coals had been placed behind his eyes and somebody was blowing on the embers. "What I was trying to explain is that Resurrection has added to this atmosphere of anxiety, of fear. People know that an incident could occur at any moment. People have been attacked outside bars and nightclubs. At concerts. They've been kidnapped in the street. If you happen to be in the wrong place at the wrong time, you can be caught up in an act of political violence. That was never the way things used to be."

Yassine was nodding. "Yes," he said. "This must be how Americans have felt for a long time. Living in a society where there are so many guns in the hands of so many people. A mass shooting can occur at any moment."

"Exactly. And Americans have learned to adjust to this, just as we are slowly learning to adjust to the threat from suicide bombers, from jihadists, from left-wing radicals."

The hookah waiter passed behind Carradine's chair carrying a pan of glowing coals. He could feel the heat of the coals on the back of his neck; it was like the blast of hot air that had greeted him as he walked off the plane the previous afternoon.

"And now this Lisa Redmond has been killed." Yassine skewered the last piece of fruit as he spoke. "Resurrection has changed every-thing, no?"

"In what way?"

"Murder has become normal for these people. Normal for them, nor-mal for their enemies. Violence is now the currency. People have taken courage from the aggression of others. They have seen how they have acted and they believe that they can behave in the same way."

"That's certainly what happened in America," Carradine replied. "Hate was unleashed. Now it's happening in my own country."

"Not in mine, thankfully." Yassine indicated to the waiter that he would like a second glass of tea. Carradine wondered why the Moroc-can was sticking around. The book had been handed over. Their busi-ness was concluded. Perhaps it was necessary for him to prolong the meeting so that it would seem less suspicious to anyone who might later become aware of it.

"Why do you think that is?" he asked.

"Control," Yassine replied. "Leadership." Carradine looked quickly to the woman at the next table. A man had joined her. His hand was lingering on the small of her back. "We have undertaken measures to ensure that jihadism is cut off at the roots before it has a chance to flower. Such groups are well infiltrated and—as you will know from your work in London—we share a great deal of sensitive material with our friends in Europe, and beyond." Carradine began to understand why Yassine had been of interest to Mantis. He seemed to be well connected in po-litical and intelligence circles. "Our ruling family has strategically placed individuals from the major towns and cities in positions of authority and influence so that each region feels fairly represented. Furthermore, we have ensured that our young men and women are educated in the correct way. . . ."

In other circumstances, Carradine would have continued to listen without distraction, but he had heard the sound of laughter emanating from the staircase. As he sat facing Yassine, Carradine looked over the

Moroccan's shoulder and saw two young women—one wearing a designer T-shirt and tight denim jeans, the other a long pink jilaba—climbing the staircase to the first floor. A few steps behind them came a man speaking noisily in a Hispanic accent, his long hair tied in a top-knot. The Spaniard's booming laughter was loud enough to be heard above the music playing in the lounge.

It was Ramón.

12

Carradine kept his head down. He knew that Ramón's presence in the restaurant was not a coincidence and cursed himself for recommending Blaine's in the taxi. The Spaniard sounded drunk and fired up, speaking in loud, slurred French as he stood by the bar with the women. Both were attractive and smartly dressed and looked as though they were accompanying him for reasons other than his charming personality. With any luck the manager would show them to a table on the opposite side of the lounge and Carradine would not have to speak to them. He did not want to have to go through the artifice of introducing Yassine.

"Do you recognize somebody?"

"No, no." Carradine had not realized that his reaction had been so noticeable. "I thought I saw someone I knew. False alarm."

"Holy shit! Kit, man! What the fuck are you doing here?"

The timing could not have been worse. Ramón was shouting across the lounge. Carradine looked apologetically at Yassine, half-stood up out of his seat and faced the bar.

"Great to see you, man!" Ramón was bellowing over the music and waving his hand. Carradine excused himself from the table. Weaving past a waiter ferrying a hookah pipe across the lounge, he reached Ramón and shook his hand. He was immediately clutched in a bear hug so tight that it transferred the sweat on the Spaniard's clothes onto Carradine's shoulders and neck.

"I thought I'd find you here, man! How are you doin'?"

"I'm just having a quiet dinner with a friend."

"Right!" Ramón put his hands around the waists of the two women. He looked like a Formula One impresario posing for a picture in the paddock. "You wanna join us?"

Carradine could smell the fumes of several hours of drinking. He was aware of the women staring at him, sizing him up as a potential catch.

"No. No thanks. You're kind to ask." He played the caricature of a staid, disapproving Englishman. "We're just doing a business thing. I had a big night last night and . . ."

"A business thing?" Ramón pronounced "business" like "beezness." "I thought you were a novelist, man?" The Spaniard glanced down at the chunky wristwatch nestled in the forest of hair on his forearms. "How come you doing business in Casablanca eleven o'clock at night?"

Carradine was not given the opportunity to formulate an answer.

"Hey girls," Ramón continued. "This guy, he's famous writer. In England. Kit Carradine. C.K. right? Not J. K. Rowling. C. K. Carradine. You know him?"

Both women smiled in a polite but obvious demonstration of their ignorance of the Carradine oeuvre. Carradine smiled back. One of them—the girl in the pink jilaba—was extraordinarily beautiful.

"So look," he said. "I've got to get back to my friend. Maybe I'll come and join you once he's gone?"

The offer seemed to satisfy all parties.

"OK good, fine." Ramón slapped Carradine on the back, as if attempting to dislodge any stray chunk of food that might have become lodged in his windpipe. "We'll be right over here." He pointed at a table close to the bar. The woman in the pink jilaba jolted Carradine with a bedroom gaze and walked toward her seat. "Come say hello."

Carradine turned around and indicated to Yassine that he was going to use the bathroom. As he did so, the woman with long black hair whom he had earlier mistaken for Lara Bartok walked straight past him. She sat in the seat behind Yassine that had previously been occupied by the young Arab smoking *sheeshah*. Carradine went into the gents, tipped the maid twenty dirhams on the way out and took a stick of Juicy Fruit from a metal plate by the door. When he came back into the lounge, a man in a checked shirt was moving between the tables crooning an Arabic version of "Careless Whisper." Carradine could hear the boom of Ramón's laughter above the amplified sound of the music. He walked toward the table and saw that Yassine was checking his mobile phone.

To his consternation, there was a photograph of Bartok on the screen. Carradine was certain that it was one of the pictures Mantis had shown him in London, but Yassine swiped it away before he was able to take a closer look. The sighting troubled Carradine to such an extent that he did not speak for the first few moments after sitting down. Yassine placed the phone on the table.

"I think I will also go to the bathroom," he said.

As the Moroccan stood up, Carradine noticed him staring at the woman with the long, black hair. His interest in her was so obvious that she returned his gaze. Had Yassine also mistaken her for "Maria Rodriguez"? The likelihood of such a coincidence seemed remote—unless several Service operatives in the region had all been tasked with finding her? Carradine recalled Mantis's remark at Lisson Grove: there were "other officers and support agents" looking for Bartok. Yassine could be one of them.

The Moroccan walked toward the bar. He did not take his phone. Had he deliberately left it on the table as a trap? There was no way of knowing.

Carradine realized that he must act quickly. Touching the screen to keep it alive, he leaned forward. In the same movement he picked up the bottle on the table and poured himself a glass of water. He was aware that Yassine was moving in his peripheral vision, passing in front of the bar. He did not want him to see what he was about to do.

As soon as the Moroccan was out of sight, Carradine picked up the phone. He clicked the button at the base of the handset, taking the display to a home screen populated by icons bearing Arabic script. Carradine's hand was shaking very slightly as he studied the screen. He was frustrated by his inability to control his nerves. He tried to remember the logo for "Photos," mistakenly opening Facebook Messenger, Instagram and Safari before tapping the technicolor flower that at last took him to the Camera Roll.

He looked up in the direction of the bathroom. No sign of Yassine. He prayed that there was a queue for the gents, that the Moroccan would bump into a friend or be delayed by a woman trying to pick him up. He looked down at the phone.

The screen displayed a patchwork of photos of Lara Bartok, identical to the ones Mantis had shown him in Lisson Grove. Carradine could see the same picture that he was carrying in his wallet, the one used in the Rodriguez passport. He clicked on the photo of Bartok standing next to the bearded man with a surfboard—then closed the Camera Roll, tapped back to the home screen and locked the phone.

His body was flushed with sweat. He looked up to see Yassine coming back from the bathroom. As the Moroccan passed behind a pillar, Carradine placed the phone back in its earlier position on the table and took a sip of water. His hands were shaking uncontrollably. He decided to sit on them, taking a series of deep breaths, elated that he had successfully managed to access the phone without being caught, but surprised by his inability to conceal his anxiety.

"Your friend is having himself a good time," said Yassine as he sat down. He had applied cologne in the bathroom. The smell reminded

Carradine of the arrivals hall in Casablanca airport. "Where is he from?"

"Spain," he replied, rocking forward on his hands. "Or America. I couldn't really work it out."

"And the girls?"

"Maybe they're his sisters?"

Carradine had intended the remark as a joke but Yassine took it at face value, indicating with a patronizing frown that he thought Carradine was being naïve.

"How do you know him, please?"

Carradine explained that he had met Ramón on the plane and had shared a taxi with him from the airport.

"Do you also know the man who is sitting with him?"

Carradine was caught off guard. He had not noticed that a fourth person had joined their table.

"I didn't see anybody else," he said. "Who's there?"

"Somebody I have recognized. Somebody I do not like."

Carradine peered across the lounge, trying to locate Ramón's table. He could see only the beautiful woman in the pink jilaba and the side of Ramón's head.

"You recognized him?"

Yassine lit a cigarette.

"He is known to me, yes. To the government. He claims to be an American diplomat."

Carradine understood the euphemism and felt the strange sensation of slipping and losing his balance.

"He's Agency?"

Yassine nodded. All of Carradine's doubts about Ramón crystalized in that moment. He lit a cigarette of his own to hide his disquiet.

"And my Spanish friend? The hairy one. Have you seen him before?"

"Never," Yassine replied. "Believe me. I would remember a man like this."

So who was he? And why was he meeting an Agency officer in Casablanca? Carradine was now certain that he was being followed.

"You look worried."

He tried to set his concerns aside with a gulp of beer.

"I'm fine," he said. "Totally fine." Needing an excuse for the change in his mood, Carradine plucked a lie out of thin air. "To be honest, that headache just came back. I should take another pill."

"I am sorry to hear this." Yassine immediately gestured for the bill. It was as though he had been waiting for an excuse to end their meeting. "Why don't we call it a night? Perhaps you should go back to your hotel and rest?"

Carradine heard the bulldog roar of Ramón's laughter burst across the lounge. He thought of all the fictional Agency officers he had written about in his books—the patriots, the traitors, the murderers, the saints—and realized that, for the first time, he was a handshake away from being introduced to the real thing.

The manager brought the bill. Carradine understood that it was the responsibility of the Service to pay for dinner. Yassine did not disagree. He paid in cash, left a generous tip, and kept the receipt for Mantis.

"Before we leave," said Yassine. "I have something for you."

The Moroccan had put on his jacket. He reached into a side pocket and retrieved a small, rectangular object that he passed to Carradine as he shook his hand. Carradine took whatever it was that Yassine was giving him without breaking eye contact, placing it in his back pocket.

"This is for our mutual friend?" he asked. The heat and sweat of his earlier disquiet had suddenly returned like a fever. Mantis had said nothing about Yassine giving him something to bring back to London.

"For our friend, yes."

Carradine probed the object between his fingers. He was certain that it was a memory stick of some kind. At the same time Yassine picked up the novel. Only then did he look at it more carefully and see the name C. K. Carradine printed on the cover.

"Wait," he said. "This is *your* book?"

"One of mine," Carradine replied.

Yassine walked toward the bar, shaking his head.

"You must forgive me," he said. "I did not realize."

"That's quite all right."

"Have you signed it?"

Carradine wondered why Yassine was concerned to have a signed copy of a novel intended only as a book cipher. As he returned the lighter to the manager, he asked if he could borrow a pen. Within earshot of the conversation at Ramón's table, Carradine rested the book on the bar, opening it to the title page.

"Who should I make it out to?" he asked.

"Just your signature, please."

Carradine signed his name and handed the book to Yassine. Anybody within a few meters of the bar would have been able to see the exchange take place.

"Well, it was very good to meet you, Kit," he said. They shook hands, Yassine making it plain as they did so that he did not want them to leave the restaurant at the same time.

"You, too," Carradine replied.

Yassine suddenly moved a step closer.

"This individual," he whispered, nodding in the direction of Ramón's table.

"Which one?"

"The one I spoke of," he said. "The American."

"Go on."

"Be careful with him." There was a foreboding in his eyes. "Be very, very careful."

13

Carradine was acutely aware of his isolation. An overweight woman seated at a nearby table looked up and curled a smile. He took out a cigarette, turning toward the bar. He felt like a man standing on his own at a party with nobody to talk to. The singer was crooning the end of another love song, drawing out the final notes. All around him middle-aged men were striking deals with women half their age over glasses of cheap champagne and untouched plates of fruit. *Sheeshah* and cigarettes were being smoked in every corner of the lounge; Carradine watched as one of the waiters picked up the foil crown of a hookah pipe, turned it over and blew a small cloud of ash toward the ground. The private, disciplined side of his nature was in conflict with his hunger for intrigue. The sensible course of action would have been to slip quietly out of the restaurant and to take a taxi back to his hotel. But he wanted to know the truth about Ramón. Who was he and why was he following him? Carradine also wanted to get eyes on his American contact, to try to discern the nature of the relationship between the two men. He knew that he was potentially putting himself at risk by meeting someone suspected of working for the Agency, yet he was constitutionally incapable of walking away without at least finding out if Yassine's warning had been justified.

He walked toward Ramón's table. The woman in the pink jilaba was speaking rapidly in French. Her friend laughed at something she had said and carefully attended to her mascara. Ramón was subdued, the ebullience and bonhomie sucked out of him. He looked up. Carradine saw the same cold, pitiless look in his eyes that he had witnessed in the cab. There would be no bear hug this time, no slap on the back.

"I just wanted to say goodbye before I head off," he said.

The American turned. The two women were looking at Carradine with interest. They had their catches for the night, but the solitary English tourist might be worth keeping in reserve for future evenings.

"How are you?" Ramón asked with indifference. He gestured across the table. "This is my new friend, Sebastian. Sebastian, meet Kit Carradine."

The American stood up. "Hey there. Sebastian Hulse. Good to meet you."

Hulse was a square-jawed forty-five with recently barbered brown hair and blue eyes. Boxing classes had given Carradine a habit of sizing people up in terms of their potential strength and physical fitness. Hulse's bespoke linen suit looked East Coast Ivy League and there was something easeful and well rested about him. Nevertheless, he looked as though he could handle himself in a fight. Carradine wouldn't have been surprised if he had once been in the military.

"You, too," he said. "New friend?"

"Yeah." Was it Carradine's imagination or did Ramón sound uncertain? "We just met tonight in my hotel. Had a couple of drinks, I told him you'd recommended this place. . . ."

"Great bar," Hulse added.

The meeting sounded plausible enough, but Carradine was wary of what Yassine had said about the American. If Hulse was Agency, could he have engineered the meeting with Ramón in order to find out more about him? Given that they had met at the Sheraton, was it possible that he was "Abdullah Aziz"?

"Look, I don't want to interrupt," he said. The remark was an expression both of Carradine's innate politeness but also of his desire not to be drawn into whatever web Hulse might be weaving for him. "I can leave you in peace."

Ramón's face suggested that he was hopeful that Carradine would indeed slip away. Hulse had other ideas.

"No, please join us for a drink," he said. "You don't have a girl with you?" He glanced in the direction of the overweight woman who had earlier smiled at Carradine. "There's one over there. I can't tell if she's built that way or six months pregnant."

Ramón grunted a halfhearted laugh. The two women seated at the table did not appear to have understood what Hulse had said. He introduced them.

"This is Maryam. This is Salma. Girls, this is Mr. Carradine."

"Kit," said Carradine, shaking Salma's cool, manicured hand as she adjusted her jilaba. "And how do you know each other?"

It was a naïve question for which he received a suitably blunt look from Hulse. Obviously the women had been plying their trade in the bar at the Sheraton.

"We met earlier this evening," he replied pointedly.

"Yeah, that's right," added Ramón.

There was a half-finished bottle of champagne in front of Salma and an empty chair positioned a couple of feet from where Carradine was standing. He did not feel that he could walk away without losing face.

"As long as you don't mind," he said. "I'll just have a quick drink."

In the time it took Carradine to consume half a glass of cheap champagne, he worked out the dynamic between the two men. Slick and self-confident, Sebastian Hulse exuded all of the class and education that Ramón doubtless aspired to but would never conceivably attain. The American was charm personified, asking all the right questions through a mist of aftershave and expensive education. *Have you been published in the United States? Did you enjoy visiting California? Does the current political situation in America look as bad on the outside as it looks from the inside?* At the same time, the two women were vying for his attention. If Ramón was a wallet, Hulse was an ATM. He was solicitous toward them, generous with the flow of champagne, even suggesting to Maryam and Salma that they visit him at his home in New York. Carradine knew that it would be impossible for them to do so: even if they could afford the flights, obtaining visas for the United States would take months. In short, Hulse had ended up cramping Ramón's style. Carradine noticed that he was wearing a wedding ring on his left hand and suspected that the American surfed from bed to bed on a bow wave of charisma and candlelit dinners. An evangelist for the easy, nodding smile, for the steely eye contact that lasted a beat too long, he was at once utterly charming and completely repulsive.

"So how are you finding Casablanca?" he asked.

"He loves it," Ramón replied on Carradine's behalf, recovering some of his characteristic bombast. "Our driver take him into the woods. Poor guy thought he was going to get fucked up."

"That's not exactly true," said Carradine, wondering if "our driver" had been a slip of the tongue. "I wasn't worried."

"And?" said Hulse.

"And what?" said Carradine.

"What do you think of the place?"

It was the second time Hulse had asked the same question. Either he was possessed of a talent for feigning interest in subjects that were of no importance to him, or he was suspicious of Carradine and testing his cover.

"I like it," he replied. "More than I expected to. I'm planning to write a book partly set in Morocco. Thought I'd end up writing about Marrakech, Fez and Tangier. Didn't think I'd be interested in Casablanca."

"So why d'you come here?"

It may have been his hangover, it may have been a consequence of seeing the photographs of Bartok on Yassine's phone, but Carradine was beginning to feel unsettled. For an almost fatal moment, he could not think of a suitable reply.

"For the waters," he said, sure that Hulse would recognize Bogart's famous line. "I was misinformed."

"What's that? I don't follow."

There was an awkward silence. Carradine explained himself.

"It's *Casablanca!*" he said. "I was quoting the movie. I write spy novels, political thrillers. The city is so famous. It has such an ineluctable quality. . . ."

"Ineluctable," Hulse repeated, slowly shaking his head as if to suggest that Carradine was being pretentious. "What a word. Haven't heard that since they made me read *Ulysses* in college . . ."

Carradine wondered if he had used it in the correct context.

"I'm just here for two nights," he said. "Been strolling around, taking photographs, making notes . . ."

"And then I walk in here and find you having dinner with Mohammed Oubakir," said Hulse, staring at him. "Of all the gin joints in all the towns in all the world . . ."

"So you *have* seen *Casablanca!*" Carradine replied, feeling his insides dissolve with anxiety.

"Yeah. I've seen *Casablanca*. Who hasn't?"

Ramón weighed in.

"What does he do, this friend of yours?"

"Who?" Carradine replied, trying to buy time.

"Oubakir," Hulse answered pointedly.

Carradine scrambled for a cover story.

"Mohammed? He's in the public sector. Friend of a friend. Put me in touch so I could ask him some questions about life in Morocco."

"Is that right?" Hulse left a pause long enough to suggest that he knew Carradine was lying. "So what exactly does he *do* in the public sector?"

"What does he *do*?" The American was staring at him. "I'm not one hundred percent sure. Something in politics? Something in finance? Those guys speak a different language. I never know the difference between a hedge fund manager, a mutual trust and a leveraged buyout. Do you?" Hulse appeared to be enjoying the sight of Carradine digging himself deeper and deeper into a hole. "We didn't really get into his job. We mostly talked about books. About Islamist terror. Resurrection."

Ramón flicked his eyes across the table. It was as if Carradine had used a code word for which he was primed to respond. "Resurrection?" he said. "What about it?"

"Nothing," Hulse replied. He didn't want Ramón interrupting.

"Nothing," Carradine repeated, and smiled at Hulse in an effort to take some of the sting out of their exchange.

"So you know people out here? You have contacts?" the American asked.

"A few." Carradine seized on the opportunity to talk about the literary festival, sketching out what he knew of the event's history and trying to draw Hulse into a conversation about literature. It transpired that he had read a book by Katherine Paget, with whom Carradine was due to share a panel two days later. Carradine offered to arrange some free tickets if Hulse felt like making the trip to Marrakech.

"I might just do that," he said. "I might just do that."

There was a sudden flutter of activity on the other side of the table. Salma was taking a selfie with Maryam. They were adding Snapchat butterflies to their faces and giggling at the results. Carradine hit on an idea. If he could somehow get a picture of Ramón and Hulse, he could send it to Mantis and have London run a check on them. But how to do so without raising suspicion?

"We should join them," he said, taking out his own phone, activating the camera and looking at Hulse. Seeing that no objection was raised, Carradine reversed the lens, held the phone at arm's length and grinned. "Say cheese."

To his surprise, Hulse allowed Carradine to fire off several shots while beaming a matinee idol smile at the camera. Encouraged by this, Carradine turned it on the girls and took several photographs of Ramón sitting between them.

"Do I look nice?" Maryam asked in French.

"You look beautiful," Carradine replied and received a wink for his troubles. "Why does nobody want a picture of *me*?"

"*I* want a picture of you," Salma exclaimed, adjusting the pink jilaba as she raised her phone. A septuagenarian Moroccan businessman at the next table lit up a Cuban cigar the size of a cruise missile. The smell of the tobacco drifted across the room as Salma took a photograph of Carradine and Hulse, their glasses raised, their smiles fixed.

"Man, isn't it great to smell that cigar?" Ramón exclaimed. "Beautiful! What is it? A Romeo y Julieta? Montecristo? Makes me wanna smoke one. I'd risk getting cancer for that shit."

Nobody laughed. Carradine was busy watching Salma take the photographs. He placed an arm around Hulse's back. There were years of gym weights in his shoulders.

"Are we done?" the American asked, a sudden edge in his voice. "That's enough now."

It was difficult to discern if the source of Hulse's irritation was Salma's flirtatiousness or the fact that Carradine had taken his photograph.

"Don't put those on social media, OK?" he said to the girls in terse, fluent French.

"*Bien sûr,*" Salma replied.

Ramón also seemed concerned by the sudden shift in Hulse's mood. As though wary of upsetting him further, he offered the American a cigarette—which he declined—and ordered another bottle of champagne. Carradine sensed an opportunity to leave. He was strung out and wanted to get back to his hotel. Taking the photographs constituted a good night's work.

"Don't get any for me," he said. "I'm going to take off."

This time there were no objections. As Carradine stood up, Hulse placed a territorial hand on Salma's thigh. Light bounced off his wedding ring. Taking his jacket from the back of the chair, Carradine offered to leave some money for the drinks but was waved away by Ramón.

"Next time, man," he said. "Get us next time. And thanks for recommending this place."

The memory stick was pressing into Carradine's leg as he stepped away from the table. Thanking Ramón for his generosity, he kissed both women on the cheek and shook Hulse's hand.

"You got a card?" the American asked.

It was the same question Mantis had put to him a week earlier. Carradine had been to Ryman's and had five hundred printed up. He passed one to Hulse.

"What about you?" he asked.

"Me?" The man from the Agency smiled at Carradine as though he was being too trusting. "Don't have one with me tonight. Must have left them back at my hotel."

There was nothing for it but to leave. Carradine went downstairs, tipped the doorman fifty dirhams and made his way out onto the street.

Boulevard d'Anfa was deserted. There was a strong smell of urine as he walked along the road. Carradine knew what would now happen. Hulse would have his phone soaked, his emails analyzed, every call and message Carradine had made and sent in the past six months crosschecked for evidence of a relationship with the Service. The basic invasion of his personal life was irritating, but whatever privacy he had once enjoyed was now a thing of the past. Carradine had nothing to fear in terms of Hulse learning about his relationship with Mantis; their communications on WhatsApp had been en clair and encrypted. Furthermore, there was nothing in his online behavior to suggest an interest in Bartok. What worried him was Oubakir. If "Yassine" was a source not only for Mantis but also for the Americans, Carradine would inevitably fall under suspicion. He felt for the memory stick, moving it into the side pocket of his jacket, wondering why the hell Mantis hadn't warned him that he was going to have to act as a courier.

Carradine lit a cigarette, trying to gather his thoughts. He stopped beside a branch of Starbucks about twenty meters from Blaine's. The doorman was staring at him. A cab drove past but it was occupied. Carradine opened Uber and booked a ride in a Mercedes six minutes away on Avenue de Nice. Seconds later a taxi turned into Boulevard d'Anfa with its light on. Carradine swore and let it go past, walking farther down the street so that he was out of sight of the doorman. He checked Uber to discover that his own car was still six minutes away, the icon turning in 360-degree circles on Rue Ahfir. He was about to cancel the ride when the car straightened out and began to move. He used the time to check the photos he had taken of Ramón and Sebastian, cropping out Salma and Maryam. He sent three of them to Mantis on WhatsApp with the message: "Fun tonight at Blaine's. Do you recognize any of these people?" but only a single gray tick appeared beside the message, indicating that it had not yet reached Mantis's phone. Moments later the Mercedes pulled up alongside him and he rode back to his hotel.

Carradine had been lying in the darkness of his room for more than half an hour, wired and unable to sleep, when the screen on his phone lit up, filling the room with a pale blue light. He sat up in bed.

Mantis's message was as straightforward as it was ominous.

You've taken on too much. Thanks for tonight but don't worry about Maria. Other people can handle that side of things. Just enjoy the festival, have a break, come home refreshed and finish your book! Interesting to meet you. All the best for the future, R.

14

Carradine did not know whether he should respond to Mantis's message or even if there would be much point in doing so. It was clear that he had been fired. Sending the photographs had been a grave mistake. Either the Service now wanted to protect him because they knew he was out of his depth or, more likely, were concerned that he was about to jeopardize an operation in which Ramón and Hulse were somehow involved.

Carradine felt an anger and humiliation as intense as any he had known in his working life. The Service had put their faith in him and he had shown himself to be a reckless amateur. He began to compose a reply asking what he should do with the memory stick and the package for Maria but knew that such a message would be pointless. As soon as he returned to London, he would most likely be picked up, taken to Mantis and asked to explain himself. The Service would want the items returned. The fact that he had already opened the package only made the situation worse.

He was exhausted. The long night of drinking, the confusion of finding photographs of Bartok on Oubakir's phone, as well as his subsequent encounter with Hulse and Ramón, had compounded this. Carradine opened his laptop and tried to access the contents of the memory stick, but it was encrypted and would not open. He took a sleeping pill and waited to pass out. There was nothing to be done except to leave for Marrakech, to take part in the festival and to head home. His career as a support agent, a counterpart to Maugham and Greene, and his attempt to live up to the example set by his father, had ended in ignominy.

15

Otis Euclidis was moved three times.

He spent the first two months of captivity in a cabin in the Flathead National Forest, about two hundred miles north of Missoula. He was driven there by Ivan Simakov, Lara Bartok and Zack Curtis and watched by a rotating team of two Resurrection volunteers who were given responsibility for feeding him, making sure that he did not try to escape and filming him for the purposes of propaganda.

When the Montana winter became too severe, Euclidis was driven south to an isolated house outside Round Rock, Texas, where he was kept in a soundproofed attic room for four weeks. Footage of Euclidis denouncing his political views and disparaging his followers as "clowns" and "losers" had been widely broadcast. By then, Simakov and Bartok had left him in the hands of Thomas Frattura and two married Resurrection activists who had provided the house. They quickly came to realize that Euclidis had been lying in his filmed statements and still adhered closely to the prejudices that had so enraged Resurrection. Euclidis developed a reputation among his captors for being charming and intelligent. It was obvious that he was quicker on his feet than Frattura and enjoyed puncturing what he described as his "high-minded left-liberal self-congratulation." On several occasions, Resurrection volunteers videotaped conversations between Euclidis and Frattura which were later destroyed when Simakov concluded that Frattura had been made to look a fool.

"How can you call yourself a feminist when you defend the right of Muslim men to wrap their wives up in black bedsheets when they walk down the street?" Frattura had been unable to frame a response. "What's 'modern' about that? I'm a gay man with a black boyfriend but your precious gender and racial signifiers are so fucked up you think it's OK to kidnap me on the street with an assault weapon and keep me in captivity for six months just because we disagree on abortion and climate change. Who's really the dangerous person here, Thomas? You or me?"

Frattura eventually left Euclidis in the hands of Raymond Powers, a former British civil servant with links to Momentum who had contacted Simakov on the dark net and traveled to the United States as a volunteer. Powers transported Euclidis to his Brazilian girlfriend's rented house in suburban Indianapolis where the basement had been converted into a small, soundproofed prison with minimum ventilation. The room was too low for Euclidis to stand up in and he was chained to a radiator twenty-four hours a day.

Approximately three weeks after Euclidis's arrival at the house, he developed a kidney infection. Rather than risk taking him to a hospital or leaving him out on the street to be cared for by a passerby, Powers and his girlfriend, Barbara Salgado, took the decision to leave him in the basement with a supply of food and water and some antibiotics. His health deteriorating, they packed their few belongings into a GMC Yukon and drove to Indianapolis International Airport where they caught a flight to London via Newark.

A fortnight later, in the same week that Ivan Simakov was killed in Moscow, Raymond Powers was arrested by British police on charges of premeditated grievous bodily harm. He was sentenced to three years'

custody in HMP Pentonville. Salgado, who had been subjected to physical abuse throughout their relationship, recovered from her injuries
and moved back to Brazil. She did not tell the British authorities about
the whereabouts of Otis Euclidis. The house in Indianapolis remained
empty for more than a year.

16

Carradine woke up at nine with a heavy head, went down to the pool, swam thirty laps and sat in the sauna thinking about Lara Bartok. He still had her photograph. He still had the Rodriguez passport and credit card. Mantis did not know that Carradine had identified her as Ivan Simakov's estranged girlfriend. Nor did he know that he had seen photographs of Bartok on Oubakir's phone.

During breakfast he resolved to keep looking for her. Screw Mantis and screw his WhatsApp message. The idea became a fixation. Should Carradine find her and be able to pass her the documents given to him by the Service, Bartok would be saved and his reputation restored. He did not want to return to the mundanity of his working life, the same groundhog routine day after day, without at least putting up the semblance of a fight.

He went back to his room and packed his bags. He took the items out of the safe, wondering why Mantis had not sent any further messages. Surely he knew about the memory stick and was expecting Carradine to deliver it? Perhaps he was taking on trust the fact that

Carradine would fly home from Marrakech and hand it over. After all, what other course of action was available to him?

He took a cab the short distance to Gare des Voyageurs. The first-class carriages were full so Carradine bought a second-class ticket, sitting on his suitcase in the shade of the platform as the passengers for Marrakech began to crowd around him. He was one of only half a dozen foreigners in the station. Two French girls in their twenties were taking giggling selfies a few feet from where he was seated. A Spanish couple, closer to his own age, were waiting on the southern side of the platform, both engrossed in books. At the opposite end, where Carradine expected the first-class carriages to pull in, an elderly man in a Panama hat was engaged in conversation with a member of the station staff. Carradine picked at the idea that he was a British or American official sent to watch him, but knew from his understanding of overseas surveillance operations that locals would have been hired for such a job. On that basis, he had no chance of knowing whether or not he was being tailed. With another fifteen minutes before the train was due to arrive, there were already at least seventy Moroccans on the platform, any one of whom could be keeping an eye on him.

The train was half an hour late. In the scramble to board, Carradine found himself at the front of a crush of passengers, each of them rushing forward to grab a seat. It was fiercely hot in the carriage and no quarter was given as people shoved and barged their way through. Carradine was still dogged by a black mood of annoyance and pushed through forcefully until he had managed to sit by the window at a table occupied by a husband and wife and their two small children. The father nodded at Carradine politely as he stowed his luggage overhead. Those passengers who had been unable to find a seat were packed tightly in the aisles, reaching out to steady themselves as the train pulled away.

The carriage was mostly filled with young Moroccans chatting to one another in Arabic and communing with their mobile phones. Across the aisle, a man with a neat mustache had opened a briefcase and was busy flicking through the pages of a file. Carradine succumbed to the paranoid notion that he was under surveillance, yet he could not tell who was watching him nor exactly how many people had been tasked with the job. An attractive woman of about thirty was standing nearby and kept smiling at him, but he could not know if she was a honeytrap set by Moroccan intelligence or just a pretty girl passing the time by flirting with a foreigner. In a fleeting moment of dread, he thought that he saw the face of Hulse at the back of the carriage, but a second look confirmed that it was just his mind playing tricks. Drifting off to sleep in the clogging afternoon heat, Carradine thought it more likely that the Americans would have organized for a team to be waiting for him at the station in Marrakech. After all, he was hardly going to jump off the train en route. The Agency had him exactly where they wanted him.

A sudden movement of the train woke him more than an hour later. He had been dreaming of Lisa Redmond. Carradine looked across the table and saw that the family of Moroccans had left. In the seat opposite his own was the elderly man who had been standing on the platform at Casablanca wearing a Panama hat. Carradine was surprised to see him; he had assumed that he would have traveled on a first-class ticket. A young, veiled woman had taken the seat beside the window and was listening to music through headphones. The man was reading a paperback book and chewing on the end of a pen. He acknowledged Carradine with a brisk nod. The book was a Lawrence Durrell novel whose title—*Nunquam*—Carradine did not recognize. He was about sixty-five with sparse white hair that in the heat had become matted to his head. There was a bottle of water in front of him, two overripe bananas and an unopened packet of Bonne Maman biscuits. There had been no food for sale at Gare des Voyageurs save for a snack bar selling nuts and crisps. Carradine had bought a tube of Pringles and a bottle of water, both of which were in his suitcase. He was hungry after his siesta. He was about to stand up and fetch them when the man lowered his book and touched the packet of biscuits.

"Would you like one?"

He looked, for all the world, like a well-educated, retired Englishman of a certain class and background, but the accent was Central European, possibly Czech or Hungarian.

"If you've got one spare, thank you."

The man smiled in a slightly self-satisfied way and prized open the packet of biscuits. He had large, thick hands with incongruously manicured nails. He was wearing an antique wristwatch with a signet ring on the little finger of his left hand. Carradine assumed that he was comfortably off: his pale blue cotton shirt and beige linen jacket were of high quality and his shoes—at least the one that Carradine had glimpsed beneath the table—expensive Italian loafers.

"Are you going all the way to Marrakech?" the man asked, holding up the packet. It was noticeable that he did not offer a biscuit to the bearded Moroccan nor to the veiled woman sitting beside Carradine. This minor detail was enough to make the already paranoid Carradine think that he had been singled out for attention and that their encounter was not a coincidence.

"I am," he replied, taking two. "You?"

"Indeed. We are still two hours away, I think."

"That far?"

Carradine did not feel like talking yet was pinned beside the window with no chance of escape. It transpired that the price of two biscuits was a conversation of blistering tediousness covering the man's views on everything from Brexit to the difficulty of obtaining a reasonably priced bottle of French wine in Morocco. Carradine suffered in polite silence, occasionally tuning out to look at a cactus crop at the side of the railway or to follow the progress of a donkey and cart bumping along in a small rural settlement. Only as the train was passing through the foothills of the Atlas Mountains, still forty or fifty miles from

Marrakech, did the man—whose name was Karel—begin to ask Carradine about his reasons for traveling to Marrakech.

"I'm a novelist," he said, expecting at least a modicum of enthusiasm on the subject, given that Karel was reading Lawrence Durrell. Instead he replied: "Really?" in a flat monotone. Carradine might as well have said that he was an Operational Control Center Specialist at a suburban accountancy firm.

"What sort of things do you write about then?"

Carradine was in an indifferent mood, resentful that the elderly man was taking up so much of his time. He was sick of spies and wanted to forget why Mantis had hired him but knew that he could not lie about his cover.

"Espionage."

"Ah. No better place for that than Casablanca, I suppose."

"No better place," Carradine replied.

The discussion was abruptly interrupted by an announcement, in French and Arabic, on the public address system. The train would be arriving in Marrakech in half an hour. Carradine took the opportunity to get up from the table and to walk to the back of the train where he smoked a cigarette with some students from Tangier. When he came back, the veiled woman had left and the seat next to his own was empty. Karel was reading a newspaper. As Carradine sat down he saw that it was a copy of *Le Monde*. There was a photograph of Lisa Redmond on the front page and a headline suggesting that Resurrection had "crossed the line in the United Kingdom." Karel folded the paper over and looked at Carradine.

"Ah. You're back."

"Just went for a cigarette."

"Terrible outcome with this journalist."

Carradine had the sudden, lurching intuition that their entire conversation up to this point had been manufactured. Karel's sole purpose in sitting with him had been to draw Carradine out about the Redmond

kidnapping. He had no evidence for this theory save for his own burgeoning paranoia and the deliberation with which Karel had set about
talking to him. But under whose orders was he working? Hulse? Mantis?
Or someone else entirely?

"Yes," he managed to reply. "Awful."

"There will be repercussions."

"What do you mean?"

"They will find whoever did it and they will go after their families."

Carradine was astounded. He looked around the carriage to ascertain if anybody had picked up the remark.

"Excuse me? You're saying the British government is going to start
killing people?"

"I said no such thing."

"I must have misunderstood."

"Not the British government. The Russians. It is well understood
among people who know such things."

"Know what things?"

"That Moscow is systematically murdering the families and loved
ones of known members of Resurrection."

It was not the first time that Carradine had heard such an accusa-
tion. The Russian government had a reputation for threatening—even
for killing—the parents and siblings of slain Islamist terrorists. He had
not considered the possibility that the policy extended to Resurrection.

"Why would Moscow care about Redmond?" he asked.

"That's hardly the point." Karel placed the newspaper on the table.
"I assume you know what happened to Ivan Simakov?"

It was as if a ghost had passed through the carriage. Carradine was
conscious of Karel studying his face with great intensity. The mention
of Simakov's name was surely intentional; whoever had sent Karel knew
that Carradine was searching for Lara Bartok.

"What about him?"

"Blown up by the Russians. The explosion in Moscow was made to look like human error, but they knew exactly what they were doing. . . ."

"Agreed," said Carradine. He had always believed that Simakov had been murdered by Russian intelligence.

"Well, the same applies to his parents."

"What do you mean?"

A warm breeze was blowing through the carriage. Karel had eaten one of the disintegrating bananas. He used the discarded skin to weigh down the pages of his newspaper.

"I am retired," he said. "I speak Hungarian, German, English, French and Russian. I use my time to educate myself. I have met intriguing people in the course of my life—politicians, journalists, civil servants, academics—and these people tell me intriguing things." The old man had a bland, smug manner that almost short-circuited Carradine's desire to delve deeper. "They also send articles to me. Books, links to websites, this kind of thing."

"But what if—"

Carradine began to ask a question but Karel raised his hand, silencing him with an extended index finger. He looked like a cricket umpire giving a batsman out caught behind.

"You merely have to look at the evidence. The parents of Ivan Simakov were killed in a car crash on the outskirts of Moscow. No other vehicles were involved. Mechanical failure was blamed, despite the fact that their Renault was less than two years out of the factory."

Carradine had known that Simakov's parents had died in a car crash. He did not think that this constituted evidence of a criminal conspiracy.

"You are aware of the name Godfrey Milne?"

Carradine said that he was not.

"I am surprised by this." Karel employed his customary tone of condescension. "Milne was a British intelligence officer who lost the faith. Joined Resurrection. Found a new faith in degrading those on the Right with whom he disagreed politically. It is said that he threatened to shoot dead the infant grandson of a senior figure in the NRA. That he waterboarded a member of the Ku Klux Klan. Alleged member, I should probably say. Charming fellow. Some people believe the Americans went after Milne's family as a result."

The train jolted suddenly to one side at a set of points. Carradine was briefly thrown toward the window. He grabbed the armrest to steady himself.

"The *Americans* are involved in this, too?"

Karel shrugged. "Milne was responsible for orchestrating an attack in Washington, D.C., in which acid was thrown into the face of a lawyer working on behalf of a Republican Congressman accused of taking kickbacks from big pharma. Four weeks later Milne's brother was taken from his apartment—in Salcombe or Padstow, I think, one of those English seaside towns—and murdered."

Carradine looked out of the window. He did not believe what Karel was telling him. The man was likely a fantasist, a spinner of tall tales and conspiracy theories. The American intelligence community would no more embrace a policy of state-sponsored assassinations against the families of suspected Resurrection activists than they would relocate Langley to the Gobi Desert. It would be political and moral suicide.

"If this is a policy to deter people from joining Resurrection, how come more hasn't been heard about it?" he asked.

The train was passing through the suburbs of Marrakech. In his romantic imagination Carradine had expected mud huts and camels, mosques and souks, but the outskirts of the city were wastelands of concrete housing and roads cluttered with litter. Karel shrugged a second time. He had the self-important man's habit of suggesting that society was beset by depths of ignorance and sloth which caused him great anguish; that his own personal philosophy was the One True Way; and that it was only a matter of time before mankind realized this and came to share Karel's worldview.

"There has been plenty said about it," he replied. "Plenty written. But perhaps it is not in the British media's best interests to accuse their governments of targeted killings against their own civilians."

"Hang on," said Carradine, with a tone that he hoped would convey his contempt for Karel's theory. "Are you suggesting the British are involved as well?"

"I never said there was British involvement." Karel fixed him with a sharp gaze. "But how would I know? Certainly there have been Agency plans to torture or kill the family members of anybody who carries out a Resurrection attack on American soil. It will be very interesting to see what happens to young Otis Euclidis, if he suffered the same fate as . . ." Karel unfolded the newspaper, turning to the photograph on the front page so that he could remind himself of the name. ". . . the same fate as this poor woman, Lisa Redmond, whose only offense, as far as I can tell, was to write a few immature, reactionary articles about Islam and Brexit and occasionally to be critical of the regime in Moscow. If Euclidis is found dead, you can guarantee they will go after the kidnappers. They probably already know who took him. After all, these people are not amateurs."

As was always the case when listening to fantasists and provocateurs, Carradine experienced a creeping self-doubt. There was something about Karel's demeanor that convinced him that he should probe more deeply into the accusations he was making.

"Is everything all right?" Karel asked.

"Absolutely," Carradine replied.

He wished that he had the means to contact Oubakir, to ask him outright what he knew about Sebastian Hulse. Why had the Moroccan warned him as he left Blaine's? What did he know about the American? The other passengers had begun to gather up their belongings and to stand in the aisle. Carradine found himself muttering, "No, they're not stupid," as Karel stood up, leaving his newspaper and banana skin on the table.

"What did you say?"

"Nothing," Carradine replied.

Karel looked nonplussed. "Well, enjoy your visit to Marrakech."

"I will. You, too." Carradine wondered if they should swap numbers. "Do you have a card?" he asked. He took one of his own from his wallet and handed it to Karel. He wanted to take the old man's photograph but could not think of a natural way of doing so.

"I do," Karel replied. He reached into the breast pocket of his jacket and pulled out a die-stamped business card. The name KAREL M. TRAPP was printed on the front. Carradine thought of Mantis and assumed that "Trapp" was a pseudonym in the same style. He turned the card over. There was a black-and-white photograph of what looked like a lotus leaf on the reverse side.

"Thank you," he said. "It would be good to keep in touch."

"Indeed."

Karel retrieved his Panama hat from the luggage rack and placed it on his head. He smiled courteously and made his way toward the door on the platform side. Carradine reached up for his bags, lowered them onto the table and sat down. The train moved slowly along the platform, eventually coming to a juddering halt. A woman close to Carradine was knocked off balance. He caught her by the arm. She thanked him in French and smiled gratefully.

Stepping out into the heat of the afternoon, Carradine could not shake off the possibility that Karel was onto something. Simakov. Milne. Redmond. The names were like a roll call of the dead. Bartok could be next on the list. If that was the case, was Carradine being used as a patsy? What if Mantis was not who he had pretended to be? What if the Service had sent C. K. Carradine to Morocco not to save Lara Bartok, but to assist in her assassination?

"I don't like your American friend. I don't trust him. What is his name?"

"Hulse," said Somerville. "Sebastian Hulse. He's with the Agency."

"Tell me something I didn't already know."

"He was the one trailing Carradine in Morocco."

"I knew that, too."

They were walking near the safe house. Bartok was wearing sunglasses with a hat pulled down low over her head. Somerville hadn't eaten in over six hours and was cranky for a cigarette.

"What happened to Kit after he left the boat?" Bartok asked.

"I'm afraid I'm not at liberty to say."

"Why not?"

"Because we don't yet know all the facts."

Bartok took off the sunglasses. She wanted him to be able to see the despair she was feeling.

"I don't believe you. You know exactly what happened to him. You have all the facts, all the information, but you refuse to tell me."

"Lara . . ."

"Where is he? What happened to him?"

"Let's go back to the flat."

She tucked the sunglasses into the pocket of her coat and turned away. Somerville's willpower broke and he finally succumbed to the desire for a cigarette, only to reach into his jacket and realize that he had left the packet at home.

"Let's finish the interview, get it done," he said. "Afterward I can tell you everything you need to know about Carradine."

"Everything I want to know, not just need to know," she said. "You don't control that."

He was astonished to see a tear in her eye. Bartok wiped it away and turned in the direction of the safe house.

"Fine," he replied. "I'll answer all your questions."

"All of them," she said. "Let's get it done."

SECRET INTELLIGENCE SERVICE
EYES ONLY / STRAP 1

STATEMENT BY LARA BARTOK ("LASZLO")
CASE OFFICERS: J.W.S./S.T.H.—CHAPEL STREET
REF: RESURRECTION/SIMAKOV/CARRADINE
FILE: RE2768X

PART 3 OF 5

I left Ivan [Simakov] in New York. One day I was there. The next I was not. I didn't explain myself. I didn't write him a letter or give any reason. I knew that if I told him I was going he would try to prevent me leaving. Surprise was my only chance of escaping and making a new life. Sometimes I regret the choices I have made. I never regretted that choice. His behavior had become intolerable. He was drinking a lot. He cheated on me with other women. On one occasion, during an argument, he had hit me.

I did not feel that I could go to ███████████████ or contact ██████████████. I didn't trust anybody—even ████████████— to protect me. I had money, I had passports, some of which were known to you, some of which were not. I had enough knowledge of what the Service and the Agency were capable of in terms of trying to find me that initially it was not particularly difficult to vanish and to try to start again.

I went to Mexico, as you know. I always worked on the same set of principles: that it was better to be in cities, where a kind of anonymity was guaranteed, than to present myself in, say, a smaller community where I could be noticed as I tried to blend in. I found men. Not serious men, but lovers who would want me only for their own short-term pleasure. If a man began to expect more of me, I shut him off. I was ruthless. These men had apartments, houses, places I could go if suddenly I needed to leave wherever it was that I was staying. I lived in hotels, hostels, apartments—at one point in a cabin on a beach in Cancún. I never stayed in the same place for more than a few weeks. At first I relished this freedom. I did not miss Ivan or Resurrection. I felt that I had escaped from a prison of my own creation. I was a free woman—or, at any rate, as free as a person in my situation could ever be.

Then I learned of the deaths of the relatives of Resurrection activists in Russia. I read about Ivan's family. I wanted to contact him, to reach out and to console him. I knew that it was the Russian method and—of course—it is noticeable that while Resurrection actions around the world have continued to increase in the last two years, in Moscow, St. Petersburg and elsewhere in the Russian Federation they have come to a stop. Moscow got what Moscow wanted. If you do not care what the other side thinks, if you have no moral compass or sense of shared human responsibility, anything is possible. That is one of the lessons we have learned from the past few years, no? The liars and bullies of the alt-right, the apologists for the NRA, the gluttons of the corporate world, they found a new voice, a new encouragement from the mass population. They became energized. They thought: "We can do what we want. We can spread lies, we can spread hate, we can spread fear. We do not care about the consequences." Moscow merely added a sadistic dimension to this: "We take pleasure in the destruction of our enemies and in the accumulation of power."

When I heard the news that Ivan himself had been killed, I did not believe it. I screamed. I remember nothing other than falling to my knees and crying for hours. My grief was inconsolable. I knew that Ivan had become paramilitary, that he was planning attacks, bombings and so forth. I didn't think that he would be stupid enough to try to create his own device. He had people to do that. People he knew who could facilitate such things. To be killed while in the act of preparing a homemade bomb, it was tragic and stupid and humiliating. So of course I blamed the Russians. I thought at one point that both the Agency and Moscow was behind it. The Agency or Moscow or even the Service. Who knew? Anybody in the secret world is capable of anything.

I wept also for Zack Curtis. We had worked together. I knew him well. He was a decent man with only good intentions. He was the best of us. There are things that I did, choices I made, actions I took in those early months of the movement which I regret. I was no angel. One of the newspapers compared me to Ulrike Meinhof, which was ridiculous and lazy journalism. I was never paramilitary. I never fired a gun or planted a bomb. But I was vicious, at times cruel. Zack was better than that. Purer. He had joined Resurrection because he believed in the power of individual action. He believed that one man can change the world by his deeds, however small.

Zack had a favorite analogy. He would say: "Resurrection will be like the effect of closed-circuit cameras on criminals. If a thief knows that his robbery of a convenience store or the mugging of a defenseless old lady is going to be recorded by CCTV and submitted to the police for prosecution, he stops robbing the convenience store. He does not mug the old lady. Suddenly he is *accountable*. He begins to think about his behavior and to *reform*." That was all Zack wanted. Reformed behavior. A greater accountability. You'll say that I was naïve, perhaps even deluded, but I really thought that in time Resurrection would bring about some kind of return to basic human decency.

We were talking about Kit. This I can tell you with absolute certainty. Before Marrakech, I had never heard of C. K. Carradine.

I had never read his books, I had not seen the movie they had made of his novel. He used to joke that the film was "apocalyptically bad." His work and career had passed me by. I knew nothing about him personally. That is the truth. I had had no contact with Robert Mantis for more than a year. You suggested that Mantis may have told me about him. How could he? How could this be possible? None of you had any idea where I was.

17

The festival organizers had sent Carradine the address of a riad in the heart of the old city. He was scheduled to stay for two nights. Though his taxi driver claimed to have been born and bred in Marrakech, it quickly became clear that he had no sense of direction and even less idea of the location of the hotel. Crisscrossing the Medina three times, Carradine eventually used his iPhone to pinpoint the riad to a building in the Kasbah. There was no air-conditioning in the car and he was soaked in sweat by the time he arrived at the address. A well-known American author was knocking on a nondescript wooden door half-hidden between a bakery shop and a makeshift stall selling cleaning products. Carradine settled the fare with the driver. He had barely removed his bags from the boot when the taxi screeched off, leaving him standing at the side of a noisy, dusty street in the full glare of the afternoon sun. Carradine crossed the road and followed the American into the building, closing the door behind him.

It was an oasis. Within an instant the clamor and heat of the Kasbah had subsided. Carradine walked along a narrow passageway toward a reception desk where a young male Moroccan was attending to a guest.

Both were speaking in Arabic. On closer inspection Carradine recognized the guest as an Irish novelist, Michael McKenna, who had won a prestigious award for his most recent book. A genial middle-aged Frenchman with a trimmed goatee appeared from a side door and introduced himself as the owner of the hotel.

After five minutes Carradine had been checked in and shown to his room at the edge of a pretty, tiled courtyard with a fountain at its center. The only sounds were of birdsong and cascading water. He left his bags in the room and explored the rest of the building, passing beneath a series of exquisitely carved Moorish arcades offering glimpses into dark, secluded rooms furnished in leather and mahogany. A woman in a dark green bikini was sipping a glass of mint tea beneath a parasol at the side of a long rectangular swimming pool. The pool was lined on both sides by orange trees in full fruit. Beneath them, dining tables covered in white linen cloths had been set out in neat rows. Carradine felt as though he had been deposited in a travel brochure for the superrich.

"Enjoying yourself?"

He turned around. The question had been directed at another guest, a celebrity historian with a nest of peroxide blond hair whom Carradine recognized from the television. Behind him, standing in a small group at the edge of a tiled colonnade, were several other writers and academics clutching cameras and bottles of water. Carradine assumed that they had returned from a sightseeing trip. Under normal circumstances he would have approached them and introduced himself, but in the aftermath of all that had happened in Casablanca, he felt strangely alienated from his fellow writers. Writer or spy? He was neither one thing nor the other.

He walked back to his room and began to unpack.

He woke up half an hour later, fully clothed, having fallen asleep on his bed. He looked at his watch. It was almost six o'clock. He searched for a safe in the room in which to keep the memory stick and the package for Bartok but did not trust the small metal box in the wardrobe with only a simple key to secure it. If he was under suspicion, his room would be searched and the envelope discovered in a matter of minutes. Having taken a shower and changed into a fresh set of clothes, Carradine instead took the package and the stick to the reception desk and left them, along with his own passport, in the hotel safe. A member of the staff gave him a receipt for the items which he placed in his wallet. He drank an espresso in the dining area before leaving the riad to explore Marrakech. He wanted to search for Bartok, even if his hopes of finding her were infinitesimally small. Mantis was banking on the fact that she might show her face at the festival, but there was also a slim chance that Bartok would go for a walk in the evening, when the intense heat of the Moroccan day had passed, and risk being seen as she searched for a place to eat.

As Carradine walked outside into the chaos of the Kasbah, he recognized the scale of the task facing him. There were hundreds of pedestrians in every direction; it was like looking out over a crowded railway station at rush hour. The pavements were so packed, the streets so jammed with cars and buses and bikes, that surely it would be impossible to make out Bartok's face even if she happened to be in the Medina. Almost all the women Carradine saw—locals and foreigners alike—had their heads covered with shawls or hats. Bartok knew that she was being hunted and had perhaps chosen a Muslim country precisely for this reason; she could conceal her features from the lenses of distant drones and satellites, as well as from the prying eyes of those, like Carradine, who had been sent to look for her.

He walked around the Kasbah for more than an hour. He saw a veiled mother, her children in rags, begging at the side of the road, a sign propped up beside them on which had been scrawled in both French and English: SYRIAN FAMILY IN NEED OF HELP. He saw an ornate green-and-white painted cart being pulled through the clogged streets by a starving horse, a young couple kissing on the backseat. He spotted hand-painted teapots and wooden chess sets for sale, groups of women sitting on plastic chairs offering henna tattoos to tourists. What he did not see, however, was LASZLO.

Twice Carradine took out Bartok's tiny, crumpled photograph to remind himself of her face; he had begun to doubt that he would recognize her even if she passed him at the festival the following day. At around half-past seven he gave up on his fruitless search and settled in a restaurant at the edge of Place des Ferblantiers, an open square to the south of the Kasbah filled with children playing in the last of the sunlight. He ordered spaghetti bolognese from the Italian page of a pictorial menu and did *The Times* quick crossword on his iPhone.

Just as Carradine's food was arriving, an older couple settled at the next table, placing hats and guidebooks and a Leica camera on the seat closest to him. The woman, who was strikingly beautiful, smiled as she opened the menu. Her husband had gone to the bathroom and she ordered a beer for him. She took out a brochure for the literary festival and began to flick through it.

"Are you going?" Carradine asked, leaning across the gap between their tables.

"Excuse me?"

He put his fork down and raised his voice above the wail of the call to prayer. The woman had an English accent and was wearing a silk headscarf.

"Are you going to the literary festival?"

"We are!" she replied. "Are you?"

It transpired that the woman, who introduced herself as Eleanor Lang, was a retired lawyer from Canterbury who had been sailing around the western Mediterranean with her husband, Patrick. They kept a yacht in Ramsgate that was currently moored in the marina at Rabat and were coming to the end of a three-week visit to Morocco that had taken them to Chefchaouen, Fez and the Atlas Mountains. Patrick, who shook Carradine's hand vigorously when he returned to the table, was at least ten years Eleanor's senior and had the easygoing charm and worn good looks of a man who had probably made a great deal of money in his life and spent it on at least two wives. In appearance he reminded Carradine strongly of the elderly Cary Grant.

"Kit here is a novelist appearing at the festival tomorrow," Eleanor told him. Carradine was tangling with his bolognese.

"Really? What sort of novels do you write?"

They chatted for more than half an hour, gradually pulling their chairs closer together and sharing recommendations on places to visit in the Medina. Carradine explained that he would be appearing on a panel at two o'clock the following afternoon. Eleanor declared that she would download everything he had ever written—"It's so easy with my Kindle"—and promised that they would come to his event.

"You really don't have to do that," Carradine told her. "Thousands of better things to be doing in Marrakech."

"Nonsense! We find it's so hot during the days, don't we, darling? It'll be nice to be in the air-conditioning listening to some intelligent conversation."

"She doesn't get much of that at home," said Patrick, reaching for Eleanor's hand.

Carradine was reminded of his parents' marriage. Every now and again he would meet a couple who seemed so content in each other's company that it made him yearn for a relationship of his own.

"Where are you staying?" he asked.

"The Royal Mansour."

He wasn't surprised. The Leica was state-of-the-art; Eleanor and Patrick were wearing his'n'hers Omega wristwatches; their yacht, an Oyster 575, had been built on spec three years earlier. They could afford five hundred dollars a night at the Mansour.

"I hear it's nice," he said and listened as Patrick talked about his career in advertising and his "second incarnation" as a property developer. The conversation felt like the first authentic, relaxed interaction

Carradine had experienced since leaving London. Initially it had occurred to him that they might have been Service personnel sent to watch over him and that the meeting in the restaurant had not been a chance encounter. Yet Eleanor and Patrick had seemed so relaxed and happy, and their legend so watertight, that Carradine had quickly set aside any doubts. It was almost eight-thirty by the time he had settled his bill and said good night. They swapped numbers and promised to meet after the panel the following afternoon.

"You can sign one of your books for my daughter," said Patrick.

"Happy to," Carradine replied.

"She's single," said Eleanor with a stepmother's knowing wink. "Doctor, lives in Highbury."

Carradine went out into the square. Darkness had fallen and swifts were swooping over the rooftops in the moonlight. He walked back in the direction of the riad, quickly becoming lost in the switchback side streets of the souk. Mopeds came at him from both directions, buzzing and weaving along the narrow alleyways. He learned to hug one side of the street and to trust that the drivers would steer around him, just as they steered around the other pedestrians wandering past the jewelry stores and carpet sellers and barbershops lining the souk. Men pushing metal trolleys piled high with boxes would appear suddenly from side alleys, clattering and bouncing along the uneven lanes. There was a constant noise of engines and conversation, smells of exhaust fumes and burning charcoal cut by mint and cumin and manure. Carradine studied the faces of passing women but saw nobody who resembled Bartok. Most of the Moroccan women were accompanied by men or part of larger groups; in an hour he saw only two or three female tourists walking on their own.

Eventually he came into a large open area lined on one side with brightly lit stalls selling orange juice and fresh fruits. Carradine assumed that he had reached Jemaa el-Fna, the great square at the western edge of the souk which he had spotted earlier from the cab. A drumbeat was sounding beneath a black sky lit by the shard of a crescent moon; it was as though the thousands of people crowding the square were being lured to a feast or ancient festival. The central section of the square was crammed with outdoor restaurants serving food to customers at trestle tables under white lights. If Bartok was in Marrakech, this might be a place that she would come to eat, assured of relative anonymity. Each of the trestle tables was crowded with customers, some of them backpackers on a budget, others Moroccan families and groups of friends feasting on fried fish and *merguez* sandwiches. Carradine passed tables piled high with sheep's heads and raw livers, booths selling snails drenched in garlic butter. To a soundtrack of ceaseless drums and wailing flutes he moved through the thick crowds, dizzied by the nighttime circus of Jemaa el-Fna, the glow from mobile phones and open fires throwing eerie light onto faces, the atmosphere acting on him like a narcotic dream. Ever since he had met Mantis, Carradine had felt transported into a parallel world, another way of thinking about himself and his surroundings; a world that was as alien to him as a chapter in the *Arabian Nights* or the Berber poem passed down through the centuries and now repeated by an old, bearded man, seated on a tattered rug in front of him, taking coins from passersby as he intoned his ancient words.

Carradine sat on a bench beside a wall at the edge of the Medina. He had bought a half-liter bottle of water from a stall in the square and drank it while smoking a cigarette. He looked at his watch. It was already ten o'clock, but the city showed no sign of slowing down. The pavements were still packed with pedestrians flowing in and out of the Medina; the traffic on the road leading north into Gueliz was almost bumper-to-bumper. He stood up from the bench, offering his seat to a frail, elderly man whose face was scarred and as dry as sand. As he walked along Avenue Mohammed V, boys as young as five or six, sitting alone on the pavement with no adults in sight, plaintively offered him cigarettes and plastic packets of Kleenex, begging for coins as he

passed. Carradine gave them whatever change he could find in his pockets, their gratitude as wretched to him as their solitude.

An hour later, having walked in a wide circle which had brought him
to a shuttered concrete shopping mall in Gueliz, Carradine stubbed out
a final cigarette and began to look around for a taxi. He was due to appear at the festival in less than twelve hours' time and had done nothing to prepare for his event. At no point had he seen anyone resembling
Bartok, nor felt much confidence that he would do so the following day.
This, after all, was a woman who had proved so adept at eluding capture that the Service had been forced to resort to the luck of amateurs
such as himself and Mohammed Oubakir to try to find her.

Speaking of the devil. Standing directly opposite him on the other
side of the road was Oubakir. The man he had known as "Yassine" was
looking at his phone while speaking to a middle-aged woman wearing
a yellow veil and a pale blue kaftan. To judge by their body language,
she was a close friend or relative; perhaps she was Oubakir's wife. Carradine concealed himself behind an orange tree at the side of the street.
A taxi pulled up alongside Oubakir's companion. She opened the passenger door and stepped inside, leaving Oubakir alone. Carradine
shouted across the road.

"Yassine!"

Oubakir looked up and squinted, as though he was having trouble
bringing Carradine into focus. For a moment it looked as if Mantis's
agent was going to ignore him, but he eventually raised his hand in slow,
bewildered acknowledgment and watched as Carradine crossed the
road.

"Mister Kit," he said. "What are you doing here?"

"I was going to ask you the same question. Let's get a drink."

18

They went to a café on the next corner. It was empty save for two old men playing dominoes at a table on the far side of the terrace. Carradine ordered a Coke, Oubakir a black coffee. He was wearing clothes almost identical to those he had sported in Blaine's: dark cotton trousers and a striped shirt with a plain white collar. The lenses of his glasses were blurred with grease and dust. Oubakir wiped them on a paper napkin. He looked very tired.

"You are here in Marrakech for the festival," he said.

Carradine took it as a statement rather than a question.

"That's right. And you? London didn't say anything about you coming here."

Carradine had decided to play the role that Oubakir had assigned to him in Casablanca: that of the experienced writer spy sent by the Service to run "Yassine."

"They did not?" The Moroccan looked surprised. "Perhaps I should have mentioned it."

"That's all right."

"You are also looking for the woman?"

Carradine lit a cigarette. He had not expected Oubakir to be so explicit about the search for Bartok. Nevertheless he ran with the conceit, wondering if the Moroccan knew about Bartok's links to Simakov and Resurrection.

"We have people looking for her all over the place," he said. "There's a strong chance she may show her face at the literary festival. Have you had any luck?"

Oubakir took a sip of the black coffee, losing his gaze in the cup. "None."

"Don't worry about it. Me neither."

The Moroccan looked up and smiled gratefully, running a hand over the bald dome of his head.

"You know about tomorrow?" he asked.

Carradine played for time. "What part of it?"

"The envelope. The package for the woman. You are to give it to me at the festival, yes?"

It was confirmation that Carradine had been sacked. He felt a collapsing sense of annoyance and irritation. Why hadn't Mantis told him personally that he wanted the passport and credit card handed over? He checked his phone. Sure enough there was a message waiting for him on WhatsApp.

Yassine is going to come to your talk tomorrow. Can you give him the package I sent to you? Very important that you do so. Hope all is going well out there at the festival. Thanks again for all your help.

Carradine lowered the phone. If he did as Mantis asked, and then happened to find Bartok, he would no longer have any way of assisting her. He had to continue to defy Service orders in order to do what he thought was right.

"You look concerned," said Oubakir.

Carradine forced a smile. "I'm just tired," he said.

"*You* are tired!"

Oubakir's temper suddenly flared. He drained his coffee, setting the cup down angrily.

"I am risking my life for you. My family. My job. I did not expect to do this sort of work when I agreed to help your country."

Carradine found himself in the unusual position of pretending to be a bona fide British intelligence officer trying to mollify a Service agent on behalf of a man who had just fired him for incompetence.

"Yassine," he said, wondering if he should have referred to Oubakir as "Mohammed." "Please. We understand the risks you are taking. The Service is very grateful for the sacrifices you are making. Believe me, I know the strain you are under."

"Yet you are the one who complains of being tired. . . ."

Carradine squeezed the Moroccan's forearm in an effort to reassure him.

"I'm sorry. It was ridiculous of me to talk about my own tiredness when you are the one under stress." He was as bemused by his ability to act out the part of an agent runner as he was bewildered by Oubakir's willingness to lap it up. "What can we do to help you? Do you want to go back to Rabat?"

The Moroccan's pride prevented him from yielding to Carradine's suggestion. With a stiff shake of the head he folded his arms and looked out at the street.

"I am fine," he said. "I am just concerned about the American, that is all."

"You mean the man in Blaine's?"

"Yes, of course I mean the man in Blaine's. I have seen him in Marrakech."

Carradine was again obliged to conceal his consternation.

"You saw him today?"

"Yes. Tonight, in the Medina. He was sitting in a café alone. What do you make of this?"

Carradine did not know what to make of it. Sebastian Hulse could have a dozen different reasons for being in the city. Had he come to Marrakech specifically to follow him or did he have other plans? Carradine also wondered what had become of Ramón. Were they working together or had Hulse left him behind in Casablanca? He wished that he knew why Mantis had fired him. It would have been so much easier to confess to Oubakir that he was playing a role for which he was neither trained nor sanctioned, but his pride would not allow it.

"Did he see you?"

Oubakir leaned back in his seat, folded his arms and said: "Of course not. I was careful. I used my training."

"Good. I'm sure you did." Carradine stubbed out the cigarette, wondering what to say next. He came up with: "Why did you warn me about him?"

"That was in my report," Oubakir looked affronted. "Two months ago."

"I don't see all your reports." The lie came to him as easily as switching on a light. "The product you send us is considered to be very sensitive. The circulation on the intelligence is limited to my superiors."

Carradine had rarely seen a man trying so hard to conceal his delight. Oubakir swayed to one side, fighting to suppress a smile, and turned to order a second cup of coffee.

"Will you have something?" he beamed.

"Not for me, thank you."

The owner of the café acknowledged the order and went into the kitchen. There was a moment of silence. Carradine could see that he was going to have to prompt him.

"You were going to tell me about Sebastian Hulse."

"Oh yes." Oubakir lowered his voice and leaned forward. There was no chance that they could be overheard—the two old men playing dominoes had left the now deserted café—but the Moroccan was plainly keen to sustain an atmosphere of the clandestine. "Hulse is under suspicion. We think he has made links with the Russian program."

Carradine immediately thought of Karel's claim that the Russian government was actively killing the friends and relatives of known Resurrection activists. Did Hulse's presence in Morocco verify Agency collaboration with Moscow's plan?

"I see," he said. He was trying to think of a way of putting questions to Oubakir that would not reveal his ignorance. "The Russian program is something the Service is keeping under wraps. What does your side know about it?"

"Only what the British have told us at a government level. That Moscow is carrying out state-sponsored assassinations. And that Miss Bartok is a target because of her relationship with the late Ivan Simakov."

So Karel wasn't just a jumped-up fantasist peddling conspiracy theories to strangers on a train. The threat against Bartok was real.

"And you think Ramón and Hulse are involved with them?"

For the first time Oubakir looked at Carradine with a degree of suspicion.

"That is not for me to say," he replied. Carradine could sense his reluctance to continue with the conversation. Partly out of irritation, partly out of a desire to push Oubakir into further indiscretions, he took a risk.

"It's something that London is worried about." He lit another cigarette, trying to look nonchalant. "We've known about the Russian policy for some time. We've been trying to find out what's going on from the American side."

Oubakir shrugged. He would not be persuaded to talk in more detail about what he knew: perhaps he had concluded that Carradine was too far down the pecking order to be trusted with such sensitive information.

"Well, no doubt we shall see," he said.

Carradine indicated that the owner was coming back with the second cup of coffee. With the obvious purpose of changing the subject, Oubakir embarked on a discussion about tourism in Marrakech. Less than five minutes later he had finished the coffee and proposed that they go their separate ways.

"Why don't you meet me at my riad tomorrow afternoon?" Carradine suggested. "Is five o'clock OK? I can give you the package."

"That would be great."

They swapped numbers. Carradine gave Oubakir the address of the riad, realizing that he would have only a few hours the following day in which to try to find Bartok. That idea now seemed increasingly pointless: he would need to spend the morning preparing for his panel. They hailed separate cabs, Carradine reaching the riad a short time later and banging repeatedly on the wooden door before it was opened by a sleepy night manager in a stained shirt. He was asked to show some identification before being allowed inside.

"I am sorry, sir," the night manager explained, once it had been established that Carradine was a guest. "We have many people trying to come into the hotel. It is my job to keep you safe. To preserve your privacy."

It was only when Carradine was back in his room, swallowing a sleeping pill and setting his alarm to wake him in less than five hours' time, that he began to question whether he should blow the whistle on what he had discovered. A secret Russian plan to kill the innocent friends and family members of known Resurrection activists, a plan with possible American involvement, was a scandal. He had signed the Official Secrets Act—yes—but what was to prevent him contacting one of his old colleagues from the BBC and leaking the story? Something had to be done, not only to protect Bartok but also to expose whoever was behind the alleged plot. Yet Carradine had no evidence to support Karel's theory, nor any way of finding out if Oubakir had been telling him the truth.

What he needed was proof.

19

The chambermaid's name was Fatima. She had been working at the Sheraton for four years, starting in the laundry, graduating to rooms when one of the girls got married and moved to Fez. Fatima was thirty-one. She had two children—a boy of six and a girl of four—with her husband, Nourdin, who was a builder.

Every now and again she would come into conflict with a guest. Usually it was with men, very occasionally with the foreign women who stayed in the hotel. They would shout at her, they would curse, barking orders to change the towels or find softer sheets or make sure they were not overcharged for the minibar. Often Fatima would walk in and find guests asleep or wandering naked around the room. On a few occasions, she had opened the door and heard couples having intercourse in bed. All of this was a normal part of her job. She liked the Americans best because they made sure to leave her money when they left. One man, from San Francisco, told her that tipping was like the time zones on a map: the farther east you went—"chasing sunsets" he called it—the less generous people became.

Only on two occasions had she experienced serious trouble with a guest. Very soon after she first started cleaning the rooms on the upper floors of the hotel, she had encountered a man who was drunk and became very aggressive toward her, closing the door of the room and pushing her up against the wall. Fatima had managed to escape and the guest had subsequently been questioned by the police. She later discovered that he had been mixing prescribed medications with alcohol and that a French diplomat had been summoned from Rabat to represent the guest's interests with the police and with the hotel management.

Never before had any kind of financial offer been made to her. The Spanish man who propositioned her on Tuesday evening was disgusting—his clothes dirty, his skin covered in tattoos and thick black hairs. He offered her two hundred euros to stay in the room with him, waving the money in his hand back and forth with a revolting smile on his face, as though he believed that everything could be bought in Morocco, that he could own any woman. Fatima had never been told that she was beautiful; she did not think of herself as attractive, as the sort of person in whom a guest would be interested for sex. The Spanish guest—she discovered that his name was Ramón Basora—had not seemed drunk or high on drugs. He was instead most probably one of those men who needed a woman all the time, in the same way that some people could not help themselves eating too much or drinking excessive quantities of alcohol. The Spaniard was greedy and vain and arrogant. She had told him no and had left the room immediately.

All the girls knew the story about the French politician and the chambermaid in New York. They had received advice and training from the management in how to deal with sexual aggression from guests of this kind. Even so, Fatima had been so shocked by the offer, so appalled and upset by what the man had proposed, that she had not reported it. She had said nothing to the other girls, nothing to her mother, not a word to Nourdin. She was worried that the Spaniard might be an important man and that she could lose her job. She had felt ashamed and wanted to forget all about what had happened.

She had not seen Mr. Basora since he had waved her out of the room on Tuesday saying: "Fine, no problem, I'll just find somebody prettier." She had not worked the next day and had hoped that he would have checked out by the time she returned to the Sheraton at dawn on Thursday. This was not the case. She checked the list and saw that he was still registered at the hotel, in the same room on the sixth floor. Passing the room at eight o'clock she saw a DO NOT DISTURB sign hanging on the handle. It was still there three hours later and had not been moved by midday, when she was due to go off shift. She assumed that he had left the hotel to attend whatever meetings had brought him to Casablanca and knocked gently on the door.

There was no answer. Fatima used her passcard and slowly opened the door, whispering "Hello, sir, hello" as she walked inside.

The stench of vomit was so overpowering that she gagged and went out into the corridor to take a towel from the trolley with which to cover her face. Fatima then returned to the room.

A man was lying naked on his back, close to the bed, his eyes open, his mouth hanging slack to one side and filled with what seemed to be a dried white paste, like milk which had been left out too long in the sun. She could see a torn condom wrapper on the carpet beside him. Fatima retched, running out of the room into the corridor. She knew that she was not supposed to alarm the guests—she had been trained to be modest in her appearance and behavior—but she screamed as she ran toward a family at the far end of the corridor. There was a man with them. She grabbed him by the arm, imploring him to find a doctor.

"There is a man," she said, pointing in the direction of Basora's room. "A guest. Please help him. He is Spanish. Something has happened to him. Something terrible."

20

arradine took breakfast beneath the orange trees, eating scrambled eggs on toast while watching a celebrity chef doing freestyle laps and tumble turns in the swimming pool. The famous American author and the equally celebrated Irish novelist were seated opposite each other at separate tables, the former eating muesli and yogurt, the latter attempting what appeared to be a Sudoku puzzle on his iPad. Neither man acknowledged Carradine.

He went back to his room to prepare for the festival. He learned what he could about Katherine Paget—speed-reading her Amazon reviews, memorizing salient points from her Wikipedia page, watching an interview she had given on *Newsnight*—but felt suspended between two worlds. The first—that of his profession, of his peers—now seemed to him a place of fantasy and escapism which he found faintly preposterous; the second was a real world consisting of tangible threats far removed from the stories C. K. Carradine had woven in the pages of his thrillers. Yet he could no more afford to cancel his appearance at the festival than he could pretend to be a significant actor in the hunt for Lara Bartok. Carradine made his living from writing fiction; men like

Sebastian Hulse and Mohammed Oubakir were men of action. He was a writer, not a spy. To think that he could intercede in the Russian plan to assassinate Bartok was foolish, perhaps even delusional.

The festival was taking place at a five-star hotel in Gueliz. The lobby smelled of cedar wood and oil money. Arab teenagers in Yankees baseball caps were slumped on sofas decorating selfies to send on Snapchat. Carradine followed signs to the conference area. A green room had been set up for the guest speakers. Carradine registered with the organizers and introduced himself to a group of sponsors from London, one of whom had read all of his novels and enthusiastically fetched him a plate of biscuits and a cup of coffee before asking him to sign a first edition of *Equal and Opposite*. At around midday Katherine Paget swept into the green room with an entourage consisting of her husband, her publicist, her literary agent and her American editor, all of whom looked exhausted by the heat of Marrakech and the strain of attending to the Great Author's every caprice. It was like witnessing the arrival of a head of state. Her eyes peering over coral-colored half-moon spectacles, Paget introduced herself to Carradine as "Kathy" and asked immediately if he had read her latest book.

"Cover to cover," he told her. "It's magisterial."

Paget produced a self-deprecating smile. She did not return the compliment. Instead she said: "I don't usually appear with thriller writers. Have you written many books?"

"A few," Carradine replied.

Every ticket for their event had been sold. They were introduced by one of the sponsors from London and invited to the stage by a Moroccan radio broadcaster who had been tasked with chairing the discussion. It quickly became apparent that Paget was interested only in the sound of her own voice, regularly interrupting both Carradine and the chairman in order to promote her latest book and to voice opinions on everything from the BBC license fee to the Tudor monarchy. In his rattled state, Carradine was happy to take a backseat, managing coherent answers to only a handful of questions, including—inevitably—his views on Islamist terror and government surveillance.

Paget was halfway through an interminable monologue about her daily writing routine when Carradine tuned out and glanced around the room. There were perhaps another five minutes before the chairman was due to take questions from the floor. The vast majority of the audience was comprised of young Moroccan students and elderly European tourists. Carradine spotted Patrick and Eleanor Lang halfway down the aisle on the left-hand side. He gave Eleanor a discreet nod. Patrick caught his eye, looked in Paget's direction and drew a finger across his throat. Carradine suppressed a smile. He looked back at Paget and tried to concentrate on what she was saying.

"Whenever I feel a little bit defeated, a little bit low and flat, I make myself a nice cup of tea and think of my readers." A bashful smile, a modest tilt of the head. "I can remember my last publisher but one telling me that the book I dearly wanted to write simply wouldn't sell in today's marketplace. I was dismayed, of course, but I went ahead and wrote it anyway and—thanks to the marvelous people who bought the book all over the world—it became an international bestseller." Carradine looked at the chairman, wondering how long he would allow her to continue. "I suppose it's a question of bravery. A writer has to keep up her morale, her desire, her *courage* to tell the stories she wants to tell. For me it's never been about prizes—although I've been lucky enough to have been nominated, sometimes even to win, many more times than I ever expected to—but rather it's about keeping one's spirits up, not getting too dejected, not feeling cross when yet another television adaptation of a period one knows inside out keeps making basic errors of historical fact, time and again." Paget appeared briefly to have lost the thread of her argument. Sensing that the chairman was about to interrupt, she quickly picked it up. "Ultimately it's about the *readers*," she said. "It's about *you*. I never forget that."

Carradine looked out at the audience, half-hoping that Lara Bartok had slipped in at the last minute and was sitting in one of the rows toward the back. But of course she was nowhere to be seen. The chairman was directing a question at him. Carradine turned to listen. As he did so, he was distracted by a face in the crowd. Only three rows from the front, staring at him intently, was Sebastian Hulse.

"Mr Carradine? Kit?"

Carradine was momentarily rendered incapable of speech.

"I'm sorry," he said. "Could you repeat that?"

To a gasp from an irritated member of the audience, Paget repeated the question herself and began to answer it, only to be silenced by Carradine.

"Oh yes, the movie business." He had been asked about the process by which *Equal and Opposite* had been turned into a film. "Everything you hear about Hollywood is true. It's beguiling, it's ruthless, it's exciting. There's a lot of money flying around, some big egos, some very clever people. What people don't tend to say about Hollywood is how hard they work and how good they are at their jobs. We tend to give the Americans a hard time, depict them as shallow and sentimental. That's not the case—at least, no more than anywhere else. They don't get credit where credit is due."

Carradine again looked over at Hulse. He had not intended to shape his answer in order to curry favor with the Agency, but the man in the bespoke linen suit looked suitably gratified. He had a smile on his face that might have been interpreted as encouraging and friendly, but which seemed to Carradine slightly forbidding. He recalled the way Hulse had laid on the charm in Blaine's before more or less ignoring him as he was leaving.

"Could I speak briefly about my experiences with the various adaptations of my novels?" Paget asked. It was a rhetorical question. She had soon embarked on a lengthy critique of *Sherlock* and *Doctor Who*, before attacking the "deleterious effects" of Simon Cowell on popular culture. Carradine scanned the room again. There was no sign of Bartok.

The event ended shortly afterwards with a series of questions from the audience, most of which—to Paget's palpable fury—were directed at Carradine. Both authors promised to sign copies of their novels in the pop-up bookstore adjacent to the conference room. More than thirty people queued for Carradine, the last of whom were Patrick and Eleanor Lang, who told him that they were leaving Marrakech the following morning to return to *Atalanta,* their yacht in Rabat.

"It was absurd the way that ghastly woman monopolized the conversation," said Eleanor as they walked outside into the furnace of the afternoon.

"Unadulterated egomaniac," Patrick concurred. "I've known North Korean dictators who were less self-absorbed."

Carradine thanked them for buying the books and wished them a safe trip to Gibraltar, their next port-of-call. There were perhaps twenty or thirty people milling about outside the hotel in the searing afternoon heat. He wanted only to get back to the riad, to have something to eat and to swim in the pool. A line of taxis had queued on the road, the drivers arguing with one another for prominence in picking up passengers as they emerged from the hotel. A young Moroccan student approached Carradine and thanked him for the event. Carradine signed a French copy of *Equal and Opposite* which the student had thrust into his hands. He was about to hail a taxi when he spotted the Irish novelist, Michael McKenna, standing beneath a palm tree about twenty meters away. Perhaps they could share the ride home. McKenna was talking to a young European woman wearing Audrey Hepburn sunglasses and a cream-colored headscarf. The scarf completely surrounded her face but not enough to disguise the fact that the woman was very beautiful. Carradine began to watch her. In order to make eye contact with the great Irish novelist, the woman removed her sunglasses and smiled at something McKenna had said.

Carradine froze. McKenna was talking to Lara Bartok. Her face was unmistakable, right down to the slightly crooked front teeth. This was surely the woman in the powder blue bikini with her arm around the waist of the bearded surfer. This was surely the woman from the photograph in *The Guardian,* the estranged ex-girlfriend of the late Ivan Simakov. Carradine fought the urge to go immediately toward her, to interrupt her conversation and to introduce himself, not as Kit or C. K. Carradine, but as "a friend of Robert Mantis." Another student approached him, asking him to sign a book. Carradine did so, unable to take his eyes from Bartok. As he passed the book back to the student, McKenna gestured at one of the drivers and took a step toward the queue of taxis. Was this his opportunity?

Carradine turned around, looking for Hulse in the crowds. The American was nowhere to be seen. Why had he come to the event only to disappear afterwards? Was his intention simply to unsettle Carradine or was he watching him? In the short time that it took Carradine to scan the crowds, both McKenna and Bartok had made their way to a taxi. McKenna held the back door open as Bartok eased inside.

Without pausing to worry that he might be under Agency surveillance, Carradine whistled for a driver and walked toward the nearest of the taxis on the rank. A young Moroccan man in denim jeans and a Paris Saint-Germain shirt greeted him with a cheery, "Hello there, sir, where you go today?" as Bartok's cab pulled off the rank.

"You see that taxi?" he replied in French.

"Yes, sir."

"Follow it."

21

Carradine tracked McKenna's taxi to the riad. Instructing his driver to hold back at a distance of about fifty meters, he watched as McKenna emerged from the front seat and opened the door for LASZLO. Like a celebrity ducking through a channel of fans and paparazzi, she hurried into the riad and quickly disappeared.

Carradine paid the driver and jogged the short distance to the front door. He was embalmed in sweat, assaulted by the chaos and noise of late afternoon Marrakech. He walked past the reception desk and entered the main courtyard leading out toward the pool. It occurred to Carradine that Bartok might have gone to McKenna's room; that they were already acquainted and that McKenna was passing her a message of some kind. Perhaps he was also working for Mantis? Perhaps they were lovers? The latter possibility seemed highly unlikely—McKenna was a bald, psoriatic Catholic homunculus in his early sixties who had been married to the same woman for forty years—but anything was possible when it came to the private lives of novelists.

Carradine stopped in a short passage leading out to a patio in front of the pool. He could hear McKenna's voice. Peering out at the gardens, he saw the Irishman sitting in a low wicker armchair at the edge of the swimming area, already deep in conversation with Bartok. Bartok herself was still wearing the cream-colored veil and Hepburn sunglasses. A waiter had brought them a bottle of mineral water and two glasses. Hoping to catch Bartok's eye, Carradine walked past their table, eavesdropping on the conversation as he stuck his hand in the shallow end of the pool, ostensibly testing the temperature of the water.

"This is what is so interesting about your books." Her voice was exactly as Mantis had described: Ingrid Bergman speaking fluent, heavily accented English. "The ability to sustain a kind of political commitment in literature without losing sight of the essential part of storytelling which is the characters and the relationships and the way we live our lives, yes?"

Bartok must have intuited that Carradine was staring at her because she looked up. He smiled back, trying to appear nonchalant. Bartok gave him a short nod of acknowledgment. He did not want her to be suspicious of him; he knew that she would be on guard against anyone who might have recognized her. Nor did he want to lose what would surely be his only opportunity to talk to her. Walking back past the table he looked down at McKenna and muttered: "Forgot my goggles," a remark to which neither McKenna nor Bartok responded. On the other side of the tiled colonnade, Carradine then turned sharp left and walked toward the reception desk.

There was a young Moroccan man on duty.

"What can I do for you?" he asked.

Carradine's heart was hammering. "I gave a package to one of your colleagues yesterday to put in the hotel safe," he said. "A large envelope. Can I get it out, please?"

"Of course, sir. Do you have the receipt?"

It was like the feeling of being prevented from boarding a train that was about to leave a station. Carradine explained that the receipt was in his room and that he would have to fetch it. He was desperately worried that in the time it took him to retrieve the piece of paper, Bartok would leave the riad.

"In the meantime," he urged the receptionist, "if you could get the envelope. As quickly as possible. It's very important."

Carradine rushed to his room, scampering through the riad. He unlocked the door, found his wallet and grabbed the receipt. Leaving the room, he looked out toward the pool to check that McKenna and Bartok were still talking. They were. He rushed back to reception.

"Do you have it?" he asked.

"I do, sir," the receptionist replied.

To Carradine's relief, the package was on the desk. He was asked to sign for it. He did so and took the package back to his room.

What to do next? He heard the sound of movement outside and pulled back the curtains. A maid was sweeping around the fountain on the far side of the courtyard. He picked up the package and wrote LASZLO in large capital letters on the front. He then opened the door and gestured to the maid. She set her broom to one side and came toward him.

"Oui, monsieur?"

She was shy, almost wary of him. In his clearest French, Carradine asked if she would take the package to the woman sitting with Monsieur McKenna. She was to tell her that the guest in room five, the man who had forgotten his swimming goggles, had sent it.

"Oui, monsieur. Quel est votre nom, monsieur?"

"Je m'appelle Monsieur Carradine. Je suis l'un des écrivains au festival."

He was sure that if the maid did as he asked, Bartok would take the bait. Carradine tipped her fifty dirhams and sent her on her way.

"Remember my name," he whispered in French as she walked off. "Carradine. Room five."

He had line of sight to the table from a narrow doorway linking the courtyard to the colonnade around the pool. He watched from the shadows as the maid headed for McKenna. After a moment's hesitation, she interrupted their conversation, gestured in the direction of Carradine's room and handed the package to "LASZLO."

Bartok immediately turned around. McKenna also looked in Carradine's direction, placing a hand over his eyes to block out a shaft of sunlight. Carradine was sure that he could not be seen. He took a step farther back in the shaded doorway as Bartok thanked the maid. She was about to put the package on the table when she saw what had been written on the front. Carradine could sense her shock from fifty feet. Yet he noticed that she controlled her reaction, placing the package facedown on the table before continuing the conversation as if nothing had happened.

Carradine waited. The maid came back and asked anxiously if she had given the envelope to the right person. He said that she had and gave her another fifty dirhams. Other guests came into the courtyard. Carradine wondered if he should go back to the pool and try to signal to Bartok when McKenna wasn't looking. Far from being elated that he had found "Maria Rodriguez," he was annoyed by the fact that he possessed neither the wherewithal to get her to do what he wanted her to do, nor the training to ensure that their meeting, should it ever take place, would go unobserved.

Another fifteen minutes passed. Carradine hovered around in one of the lounges off the courtyard. He sat in a leather armchair with a view through a partly opened window toward Bartok's table. At no point did she pick up the package nor show any interest in doing so. A third man joined the table. He was African but did not appear to be local: he was too well-dressed and carried himself with the easy confidence and swagger of a European or American. Bartok smiled at him warmly when the man sat down. Carradine hoped that he was not her boyfriend. Then the male receptionist who had fetched his package from the safe came into the lounge. Carradine pretended to be reading a magazine.

"Monsieur?"

Carradine looked up.

"*Oui?*"

"I have been searching everywhere for you, monsieur. There is a gentleman at the entrance who wishes to speak to you. Should I let him in?"

Carradine glanced at an ormolu clock above the fireplace. It was not yet four o'clock. Oubakir was due at five. Why the hell had he come so early?

"Did he give you his name?"

"No, sir."

Carradine had no choice other than to abandon his surveillance and to find out who was waiting for him. He stood up, walked out of the lounge and followed the man to reception.

There, sitting alone in the narrow passageway, was Sebastian Hulse.

22

K it! How are you? Great event."

The American stood up and shook Carradine's hand, pulling him forward in a power grab that served only to amplify Carradine's sense of confinement.

"I'm well, thank you," he said. He was trying to work out what the hell Hulse was doing doorstepping him at the riad.

"Thought I'd pay you a visit."

"I see that. How did you know where I was staying?"

Hulse ignored the question.

"Enjoyed your talk," he said.

"Thank you. Slightly took it out of me."

"What do you mean?"

"I don't know. I don't feel a hundred percent. . . ."

"Oh. I'm sorry to hear that."

Carradine knew that he had to get rid of him. If Hulse came into the hotel, he would see Bartok. Acting as though he was unwell seemed the most plausible strategy.

"It was a surprise to see you in the audience," he said.

Hulse grinned. "Gee, I hope I didn't make you feel sick."

"No, no!" Carradine tried to laugh. "I think it's a combination of the heat, the food. I'm just exhausted. I was resting actually when you asked for me."

Carradine glanced in the direction of his room, hoping that Hulse would get the point. He looked down and saw that he was holding a copy of one of his books.

"You bought one!" he exclaimed with more enthusiasm than he had intended.

"That's right."

"And you came all this way just to ask me to sign it?"

He was certain that Hulse had come for a different purpose. Perhaps Bartok was already under surveillance and had been observed entering the riad. He wondered if Hulse would try to book a room in order to gain access to the building. He had heard that the riad was full for the festival and prayed that this was still the case.

"Would you mind?" The American held up the book, producing a pen from the hip pocket of his trousers.

"Delighted. Who should I make it out to?"

"How about my wife?" Carradine thought of Salma and Maryam, of Hulse's hand on Salma's thigh.

"Sure. I hope she likes it. What's her name?"

"Lara."

Carradine had already written "To" at the top of the page. The pen stopped in his hand, a tiny circle of ink forming on the paper as he registered what Hulse had said.

"Lara? That's your wife's name?"

"Last time I checked. You look surprised, Kit."

"No, no. It's funny. I have a friend called Lara. Dating a pal of mine. In London. I was just thinking about them actually."

It struck Carradine how easily and seamlessly he was able to conjure the lie. Years of thinking about deception and subterfuge for his fiction had given him a kind of ghastly expertise. He completed the inscription, handing the book back to Hulse. The American looked at him with the same seemingly benign, yet sinister half smile he had adopted during the festival. It was a look that told Carradine he was not trusted; a look that promised payback should Hulse discover that he was being deceived.

"Well, thank you for coming," Carradine told him. He tried to appear slightly unsteady on his feet and winced in apparent discomfort. "I'm sorry not to invite you inside for a cup of tea but I really need to rest."

"Sure."

Hulse shook his hand again, moving back toward the door. Carradine was almost in the clear, but at the last moment the American hesitated and turned around.

"You seen Mohammed Oubakir at all?"

He knew it was a test. The Agency probably had Oubakir under surveillance. The two of them had been seen talking in the café the night before. It would be pointless to lie.

"Yeah, as a matter of fact I ran into him last night. We had a coffee up in Gueliz."

Hulse seemed surprised that Carradine had admitted the truth.

"Really?"

"Yeah. Why?"

"No reason. I thought I saw him at the festival, at your talk. I wasn't entirely sure." Hulse looked down at the floor, as though lost in thought. He was about to pull open the street door when he said: "Remind me how you know him again?"

Carradine decided that enough was enough. He had to push back.

"You ask a lot of questions, Sebastian." A car blasted its horn outside. "Did you come here to get me to sign a book for your wife or is there something else on your mind?"

"Forget it," Hulse replied quickly. He stared hard into Carradine's eyes, holding the gaze.

"It's just that you've behaved pretty strangely around me. . . ."

"Is that so?"

"Yeah, that's so. I didn't particularly enjoy our meeting in Blaine's." Hulse looked genuinely offended. The ruse was working. "Then you show up at my event and kind of stare at me like you're trying to put me off. . . ."

"Kit, I can assure you—"

Carradine plowed on.

"Let me finish. I didn't invite you here. I don't know how you found out where I was staying. The thing is, it's awkward for me. I don't feel comfortable around you. You keep asking about Mohammed Oubakir. I don't know why. I don't really know very much about him. There's somebody who helps me with my books in London. An intelligence officer. A spy. She was the one who gave me Mohammed's number. That's why I was meeting him in Casablanca. I'm not really supposed to talk about it but you keep pressing me. I don't know who you are or who you work for."

To Carradine's delight, Hulse took a step forward and touched him on the shoulder.

"Look," he said. "I'm really sorry, man. I didn't mean to make you feel bad. Oubakir is just somebody I know from Rabat. I was trying to work out your connection."

"It's fine." A female guest walked between them. Hulse stepped back to allow her to pass. "But now I really need to go and lie down. I need to rest. I'll see you around, Sebastian. Take good care of yourself."

23

As soon as Hulse had closed the door, Carradine hurried back to the lounge. Of all people and of all things, he found himself thinking of Simon MacCorkindale in *Death on the Nile,* scurrying along the side of a ship having committed murder in the dead of night. He returned to the same armchair in which he had been sitting ten minutes earlier and strained to see what was going on at the swimming pool.

Bartok had gone.

The table where she had been sitting was now empty. There were no guests seated on the patio, nobody swimming in the pool. Panic stretched out inside Carradine. He hurried to the reception desk, looked in the dining room, searched each of the lounges on the ground floor. There was a tradesman's gate at the back of the riad leading to a maintenance area where a van and two cars were parked at the edge of a quiet street. Carradine peered over the gate but could see no sign of LASZLO. He went to the spa and asked if a woman fitting Bartok's description was receiving treatment. The receptionist shook her head. Carradine went out into the gardens, looked up and saw Michael McKenna coming out of his room on the first floor of the riad.

"Mr. McKenna!"

McKenna squinted, again raising a hand to block out the sun.

"Hello?"

Carradine walked up a short flight of steps.

"I'm sorry to bother you," he said. "I'm Kit Carradine, one of the writers . . ."

"I know who you are."

"I was just wondering. The young woman you were talking to by the pool. Is she staying here?"

McKenna gave him an appraising smile, making the immediate—and not entirely incorrect assumption—that Carradine was attracted to Bartok and trying to track her down.

"I'm afraid not," he said. "I met her at the festival. She wanted to talk about books. I invited her in. Lovely girl. Clever. Hungarian originally."

"I know," Carradine replied.

"You were the fella that sent the package. What was that all about?"

"Long story. Did she say where she was going? Did she leave a number, a card?"

McKenna shook his head. He was carrying a swimming towel and a bottle of Factor 50 suntan lotion. His skin was the color of chalk.

"So you have no idea where she went?"

"Afraid not. You might have to go looking for her. . . ."

"Tell me about it," Kit replied. "Who was the other man there? The black guy? I thought I recognized him."

"Oh, just some big-shot editor from New York. Think he was trying his luck as well." McKenna chuckled to himself. "Sorry not to be more helpful, young man. To be honest she did look a bit taken aback when she read your billet-doux."

"She opened it?"

Carradine was impressed that Bartok would have taken such a risk in the open.

"Absolutely she did. Caused quite the intake of breath."

They walked down the steps. McKenna suggested that Carradine join him for a drink at seven o'clock, an invitation he accepted on the basis that he expected never again to set eyes on Lara Bartok and would need several consolation martinis. McKenna headed for the pool, waving the bottle of suntan lotion over his head as he went.

"Good luck!" he cried out. "May Cupid strike!"

Carradine continued to look in every corner of the riad. He headed to the reception desk with the intention of finding out the name of the editor from New York. It was possible that he was staying in the riad and that Bartok was in his room. He was about to speak to the same member of the staff who had earlier removed the package from the safe when he saw Mohammed Oubakir sitting in the same chair that Hulse had occupied less than an hour earlier. In the dismay of losing Bartok, he had completely forgotten about their meeting.

"Mohammed."

"I apologize, Kit. I am early. I was going to . . ."

"It's OK."

They shook hands. Carradine was wondering what he was going to say about the package: Mantis would expect it to be handed over intact. If Oubakir was still under Agency surveillance, Hulse would now know that he had visited the riad. Carradine could feel the outside world pressing in on him, the slow, irrevocable squeeze of American power.

"You look well."

"Thank you," he replied. "Listen, I need to talk."

"Of course."

He led Oubakir to the table where Bartok had been sitting with McKenna. The Irishman was lying on a sun lounger on the far side of the pool wearing sunglasses and a pair of bright red Speedos. His short, hairless body was entirely caked in sun cream. He looked like a patient in a burns unit.

"What is the problem, please?" Oubakir asked.

"I should have texted you." Was it his imagination or could Carradine smell a trace of Bartok's perfume on the chair? "I saw the girl. I've given her the package."

The Moroccan was stunned.

"Really? This is good news. Have you told London?"

Carradine nodded. It had been an afternoon of lies. One more wouldn't do any harm. "So you can go back to Rabat," he suggested. "No need to stay in Marrakech."

"I see."

They ordered mint tea, drinking it in the shade of the colonnade. They talked about politics and Morocco under French rule while the award-winning Irish novelist in red Speedos turned pink by the side of the pool. As the conversation progressed, a distracted Carradine began to feel that he had reached the end of the road. He had defied the Service and found LASZLO. Bartok had been given the package; her future now lay in her own hands. Doubtless she was already on her way to the airport or to the train station armed with the Rodriguez passport and several thousand dirhams extracted from the nearest ATM. There was, however, a silver lining. Mantis had doubted Carradine's ability to find Bartok and had fired him. Yet he had proven his worth, not least by putting Hulse off the scent. If Bartok survived and made it to London, Carradine could surely expect further work from the Service.

As their conversation drew to a close, he shook Oubakir's hand and wished him well. Oubakir congratulated him a second time on making contact with Rodriguez and headed back out into the Medina. Settling the bill for their tea, Carradine glanced toward the pool. McKenna had long gone. The water looked calm and inviting. He decided to go for a swim and made his way back to his room.

The maid was still sweeping up in the courtyard. When she saw him, she smiled, moving quickly into another section of the riad. Carradine took out his key, turned it in the lock and went into the room.

Bartok came at him as soon as he had closed the door.

"Who are you?" she said, pushing her hands into his chest. "And how the fuck do you know Robert Mantis?"

24

Carradine fell backwards toward the bed.

"Jesus!" he said, regaining his balance and looking quickly around to see if anybody else was in the room. "How did you get in here?"

"Answer me," she hissed.

Bartok was taller and physically stronger than he had expected. She had removed her veil to reveal hair dyed peroxide blond and cut short above the neck. Her eyes were fierce and unforgiving. Plainly she wasn't interested in explaining the whys and wherefores of how she had managed to break into the room. Carradine suspected that she had found it extremely easy.

"Answer you about *what*?" he said.

"Keep your voice down."

"Answer. You. About. What?" he replied in a comic stage whisper. Bartok looked baffled.

"I want to know why you are here," she said.

She picked up the remote control and turned on the television, the news headlines on BBC World smothering the sound of their conversation.

"My name is Kit Carradine," he replied. "I'm a writer. . . ."

"I know who you are."

"I met Robert a couple of weeks ago. Less. Or rather he met me. He asked me to work for him. For the Service. To do them a favor while I was out here in Morocco. He asked me to look for you. He wanted me to try to find you."

Bartok was watching Carradine very carefully, sizing him up, trying to assess if she was being lied to. He heard the sound of laughter in the courtyard and suggested that they move down into the bathroom, which was excavated below ground level and sealed with a heavy wooden door.

"Thick walls," he explained. "We won't be heard."

"Fine," Bartok replied.

They stepped down into the bathroom. Bartok sat in a narrow rattan chair beside the sink. Carradine perched on the edge of the bath. He looked for the tattoo on her left wrist but could see nothing.

"Mantis gave me a copy of your photograph," he said. "The same one that's in the passport. I saw some others in London and Casablanca. That's how I recognized you."

"What photographs in Casablanca?" she said, plainly concerned. "Where? How?"

"It's a long story."

Her watchfulness made him think of the animals at the watering hole, wary of predators, alert to every threat. Yet Bartok seemed at the same time fearless and capable. He had the sense of an intuitive, highly intelligent woman who had made an assessment of his character and intentions within seconds of meeting him.

"I've got all night," she said.

"I'd better start at the beginning then," he replied.

He did just that, describing his first encounters with Mantis in London, his subsequent discovery that "Maria Rodriguez" was the estranged girlfriend of Ivan Simakov. He told Bartok about the €3,000 payment he had left at the Sheraton for a man named "Abdullah Aziz" who may, or may not, have been Ramón, the Spaniard he had met on the flight to Casablanca. He told her about the photographs he had seen on Oubakir's phone and their subsequent meetings in Marrakech, the most recent of which had wrapped up less than an hour earlier. He described Ramón's appearance in Blaine's in the company of a man identified by Oubakir as an American spy. That same American, Sebastian Hulse, had paid Carradine an unsolicited visit at the riad earlier that afternoon and had asked him to sign a book to "Lara," a tactic probably designed to unsettle him. Bartok listened intently, interrupting frequently to check a detail and to ensure that she had understood Carradine correctly. She was particularly interested in Mantis's assertion that she had been spotted in northwest Africa and that the Service was "100 percent certain" she had settled in Morocco.

"Why did he think that I wanted to return to the UK?" she asked.

Carradine told her that he did not know the answer to her question. Rarely had he experienced somebody attending to his words so closely and assiduously. At no point did Bartok give any outward indication that she was frightened, yet her tireless, detailed questions left him in no doubt that she was deeply concerned. The picture he was painting— of a possible Russian-American plot to kill her—was as malign as it was morally indefensible. By the time Carradine had finished, they had moved back into the bedroom. Bartok sat on a leather armchair beside the television, Carradine on the side of the double bed farthest from the door. The television remained switched on to disguise their conversation. The same set of headlines on BBC World had been broadcast three times, at hourly intervals. A man had been arrested for the murder of Andreas Röhl, the AFD politician assassinated in Germany. Bartok made no comment on the story other than to point out that Röhl had been accused of taking money from sources inside Russia in order to further his political career.

"What more do you know about Robert?" she asked. Carradine could not tell if the question was an attempt to find out how deeply Carradine himself was embedded within the Service or a more personal inquiry into the well-being of a man for whom she possibly harbored romantic feelings.

"I think he's in love with you," he replied.

To Carradine's relief, Bartok looked irritated.

"Still?" she said, as though she expected a man's desire for her eventually to pass a sell-by date.

"I read the note he wrote to you. 'I am the man who took you to the sea.' It sounded like you were in a relationship of some kind."

Bartok seemed surprised. "Really? You concluded this? You must have a very romantic imagination, Mr. Carradine."

"Please, I keep asking you to call me Kit."

"And you had permission to read this note?"

"I did what I had to do."

Bartok liked that reply. She smiled for the first time. Light came into her face and, for a fleeting moment, Carradine saw the woman she must once have been, before Simakov, before Resurrection, before a life on the run had turned her into a fugitive, watchful and suspicious.

"Robert took a great risk by sending me the passport. I suppose I should be grateful to him for that."

Carradine was not in the mood to give credit to Mantis for anything. He indicated that he had nothing to say in response. Bartok stood up, stretching her back.

"Why did you send the maid with the envelope?" she asked. "Why not come up to me in person?"

There was a sudden noise from the riad, a door slamming in the distance.

"I thought it was better that we weren't seen together," he explained. "In case there was somebody watching me or watching you."

"So you decided just to stare at me beside the swimming pool?"

She grinned, moving to the opposite side of the bed. He realized that she was beginning to relax.

"I hadn't expected to see you," Carradine explained, enjoying the shift in her mood. "I wanted to be certain it was you. You took me by surprise."

"Evidently."

She sat on the mattress and began to look at the books stacked on the bedside table. They were both fully dressed, on opposite sides of the double bed, each with one foot secured on the ground. It occurred to Carradine that they must have looked like a married couple in an old Doris Day movie, keeping their distance for the benefit of the censor.

"Did you think it was unlikely I would survive Marrakech?" she asked, flicking through a copy of *Eastern Approaches*. Carradine was reading it for the sixth or seventh time. He found the question interesting. Did she think that Mantis had overestimated the threat against her? Did she think that Carradine himself was being paranoid about Ramón and Hulse?

"I was worried, yes," he said. "There were too many moving parts. One minute I was being told the Russians and Americans were bumping people off, the next I was being fired by the Service. I wasn't in a position to know what was really going on. I'm not trained. I write about this stuff. I've never *lived* it."

"You mean you have no proof that these men mean to kill me?"

"None. No proof at all."

"But the theory of this man on the train—Karel, was it?—this was confirmed by Mr. Oubakir, no? Robert believes that there is a Russian plan to kill me, not simply to arrest me and to bring me in for questioning. That is why he sent this warning."

"I guess." Carradine certainly could not think of any other reason why Mantis had acted as he did. "Isn't that what you think?" He was beginning to feel out of his depth. "Is there something else going on that I don't know about?"

Bartok placed one of the pillows behind her back and sat up against the headboard. She kicked off her shoes, stretched out her legs and bounced up and down, like a customer testing the mattress in a showroom. Her legs were tanned, her toes slightly bent and calloused. Carradine noticed that the sides of her feet were marked with cuts and patches of dry skin. She saw this and said: "I have ugly feet."

"You don't."

She looked across the bed and flashed him a smile. It was almost as if they had met before and were old friends. Of course, Carradine was aware that this was a misconception: creating an atmosphere of trust and intimacy with a man was doubtless a trick that Bartok could pull off as easily as she had kicked off her shoes. Yet he was convinced that she wanted to remain in the room, not only to extract information from him, but also because she felt safe there. She had stumbled on some sort of sanctuary.

"I was foolish," she said suddenly.

"What do you mean?"

"I became lazy. I have known that they have been looking for me ever since it was announced that Ivan had been murdered. Before that, even. Robert is correct. Your friend on the train and Mr. Oubakir last night. They are all correct. The Russians want me dead. Until this moment, I did not know that the Americans had joined their death cult as well."

"I don't have any proof that the Americans are involved," said Carradine. "Only this guy Hulse creeping around and the theories of Karel and Oubakir." Some kind of machine had been started up in the courtyard outside. "What do you mean, you got lazy?" he asked.

Bartok gestured into the room. Her gaze was both amused and cynical, betraying the intense strain she had been under for months and months.

"I went to Havana for a long time. Then to Mexico. Eventually down

to Buenos Aires. Isn't that what all fugitives do? Run to South America?"
Her uneasy smile encouraged Carradine to agree. "Butch Cassidy. The
Sundance Kid. Where did they go?"

"Bolivia."

"That's right! Bolivia!"

He saw that she had an ability to take pleasure in small, amusing details, even as the world outside continued to press in on her.

"I got scared," she said. "In Argentina. Too many repeating faces. Too
many strangers coming up to me in bars. I developed a paranoia."

"So you came here?"

"Not at first, no." Bartok's answer seemed to conceal a secret that she
was not yet prepared to divulge. "I went to Italy, then to Egypt. Eventually, yes, to Morocco . . ."

"Which is where you got lazy?"

"Eventually a person gets tired of running, you know?"

"I can understand."

"It becomes almost as if you *want* to get caught, just to bring an end
to it. That's how I felt. That's how I *feel*. I don't know how much longer
I can go on hiding."

Carradine was often at his most candid with perfect strangers. He
wondered if Bartok had shown more of herself to him in the preceding
two hours than she had revealed to any person in a long time.

"Do you have family back in Hungary?" he asked.

She shook her head quickly and decisively, as if to fend off any further questions of that kind. The telephone rang beside the bed and they
both flinched. As Carradine reached to pick it up he caught her eye.
They looked at each other and he felt his heart kick with desire.

"Hello?"

It was Michael McKenna.

"Michael, I'm so sorry." He had forgotten about their drink. "I fell
asleep."

"That's OK. Assumed that was the case. Did you find your beloved?"

Carradine had a sudden, paranoid vision of Sebastian Hulse standing over McKenna in his room, directing the conversation, listening in.

"Sadly not," he replied. "Vanished into thin air."

"Pity," said the Irishman. "What a shame."

"A real shame, yes."

Bartok looked at him quizzically. Carradine mouthed the words: "Don't worry."

"We're all away in the morning," McKenna continued. "What flight are you on, Kit?"

Carradine had not looked at his schedule. He had a vague memory that he had been booked on an easyJet flight out of Marrakech that evening.

"I think I'm leaving after lunch," he said.

"OK. So perhaps we'll see you at the airport."

They hung up. Carradine explained to Bartok that he had forgotten to meet McKenna for a drink. She did not seem suspicious that Mc-Kenna had rung and laughed when Carradine told her about their conversation earlier in the afternoon.

"*Billet-doux*?" she said, a phrase she had never heard before and had difficulty pronouncing. "I like this expression. He is a brilliant man. We had a wonderful conversation."

"Didn't you think it was a risk coming to the festival?" Carradine asked. "That somebody might recognize you?"

She bowed her head. "That is what I meant about getting lazy. The people who know me, they know that I love literature of all kinds, that I read everything. I devour books. These men who are looking for me, they would also know this. So perhaps they put two and two together and took a chance that I would come to a literary festival, out of curiosity, out of boredom."

"They were right."

There was a moment of silence. Carradine was vain enough to wonder if she had read any of his books, but too proud to ask. He picked up two bottles of water from the bedside table and handed one of them to Bartok. In ordinary circumstances, they might have left the room and gone to the bar of the hotel for a cocktail. He would have invited her to dinner, taken her to Le Comptoir or al-Fassia for a tagine and a bottle of red. Simple pleasures that were denied to them. It was becoming increasingly clear that they were going to be stuck in his room. If Bartok showed her face outside the riad she would be scooped up by Hulse and his henchmen within minutes.

"Why didn't you leave straightaway?" he asked.

Bartok frowned. "What do you mean, please?"

"Take the passport. Take the card. Get some money. Why didn't you take a taxi to Fez or Casablanca?"

"I needed to know who you were," she said. "Besides, the passport is useless."

"Why?"

"It has no entry stamp."

Of course. Any official at a Moroccan passport desk would want to know why there was no record of "Maria Rodriguez" coming into the country.

"Can't you just say you lost it in the souk and this is a replacement?"

Bartok honored Carradine with a patient smile.

"Possibly," she said. "That was certainly Robert's idea. Or it is a trap and there is a flag on the passport. The Moroccan authorities get suspicious, they make a telephone call, it is all over for me."

"Why would Mantis be trying to trap you?"

Bartok appeared to have no answer to Carradine's question. He wished that he knew more about the nature of their relationship, but she had closed off his questions whenever he had raised the subject.

"Maybe he is not," she conceded. "I don't know. It is even possible the passport is a fake."

"But it came to me from the Foreign Office!"

Bartok walked around the bed and came to sit next to him. Her perfume was the same scent that had been on the chair by the pool. Their knees briefly touched. She put a hand on Carradine's back, but it was not a new moment of intimacy. Rather it was the sort of gesture that a nurse or social worker might make on the brink of delivering bad news.

"There are things perhaps I should tell you about Robert," she said.

"Go on."

"I am afraid you are not going to like them."

25

Carradine knew what Bartok was going to say before she said it. He let her deliver the coup de grâce.

"Robert Mantis is not a British spy."

"I see."

"Robert Mantis does not work for the Service."

An awful, hollow feeling of shame opened up inside him. It was the secret doubt that had always nagged at him, but he had never allowed himself to face it head-on. He had wanted Mantis to be genuine. He had wanted to be a latter-day Maugham or Greene, to live as his father had lived and to experience the things he had known. Carradine had taken a business card, a copy of the Official Secrets Act and a photo ID as irrefutable proof that Robert Mantis was a British intelligence officer. He had been comprehensively duped.

"Who does he work for, then? Or is he just a conman? A fantasist?"

Bartok asked if he kept any alcohol in the room. Carradine had bought some Johnnie Walker at duty-free in Gatwick; the bottle was in his suitcase. He took it out, handed it to her and fetched two glasses from the bathroom, briefly staring at his own reflection in the mirror as though to remind himself what a fool he had been. She poured him two inches neat and encouraged him to join her in a toast.

"To honest men and women," she said, clinking his glass.

"To honest men and women."

Carradine was touched that she was trying to raise his spirits, but he was in shock. He tracked back to the long conversation in Lisson Grove. He wanted to work out why Mantis had made the last-minute switch to the Sheraton. He did not understand why he had set up the meeting with Oubakir in Casablanca. What was it all for? He could not make sense of any of it.

"I can explain." Bartok sipped the whiskey and held it in her mouth, lips pursed, as though reading his mind. She swallowed it, letting out a sigh of pleasure. "Robert's real name is Stephen Graham. He was born in London, educated at private schools in England. He went to Cambridge, married a French schoolteacher who left him for someone else."

"He told me he was still married."

"He told you a lot of things that were not true." Carradine acknowledged the remark with a defeated shake of the head. "His father was an academic. From Scotland. You call this a Scotsman?"

"A Scotsman, yes."

"Gordon Graham. His wife was Russian. This is the key. Yulia. I do not remember the patronymic. She came to England in the 1960s after Stephen's father met her in Moscow on an academic visit behind the Iron Curtain."

"So she defected?"

Bartok held more of the whiskey in her mouth, savoring it, indicating with quick eyes that Carradine was being impatient.

"Wait," she said. "Whether she defected or not is not important. I believe they fell in love and she was allowed to emigrate. Stephen Graham has worked for Moscow for his entire professional career."

Carradine slumped forward, shaking his head. The breath went out of him.

"It's OK," whispered Bartok and touched his back. "Mantis tried to recruit me, too. Shortly after I left Ivan and moved from New York. Ivan had become violent, both toward me and in the context of Resurrection. . . ."

"Simakov *hit* you?"

She waved away his concern.

"Never mind about that. All anyone needs to know is that I had had enough of him. Mantis wanted me to inform on the people I knew inside the movement. His typical modus operandi, the technique he has used in London and, I suppose, all over the world, with great success, is to pose as the traditional British spy. You said he had a briefcase, that he seemed slightly untidy and disorganized. . . ."

"But also sharp, determined, thorough." Carradine realized that countless others in his position had been comparably gullible. It was scant consolation.

"Of course, of course." Bartok placed the glass of whiskey by the side of the bed, allowing her to gesticulate more freely. "All of these things. He presents himself as a Service officer, he recruits agents, he runs them, they think they are working on Her Majesty's Secret Service, but all of the information they give to Stephen is channeled back to Moscow."

"It's very clever."

"Very simple and very effective. Yes."

Carradine looked at her. The whiskey had brought color to her cheeks. The nape of her neck was flushed pink.

"So you fell for this as well?" he asked.

Bartok hesitated. "That is another story, for another time." It was the second occasion on which Carradine had sensed that she was holding something back from him, something of significance. "The short answer is that I did work for him, but in the knowledge that he was a liar and a fraud, a false flag. A conman as you describe him."

Carradine asked the obvious question.

"How did you know he wasn't a British spy?"

Did Bartok possess powers of insight and analysis far beyond his own? Had she rumbled Mantis within minutes of seeing his crumpled FCO business card?

"I just knew," she replied. "He slipped up. His story didn't make sense. I allowed Robert to believe that he was running me."

"Does he still think you're on the books?"

Bartok looked at him as if he had lost his mind.

"Gosh, no!" Someone clipped past in the courtyard. Bartok waited until they had passed before continuing. "A lot has happened to me since then."

Question after question formed in Carradine's mind. He still did not know the truth about Bartok's relationship with Mantis, just as he did not understand why Mantis had recruited him under false pretenses. Was it simply to use him as an extra pair of hands in the search for LASZLO—or did Moscow have a darker purpose?

"Why me?" he asked.

Bartok picked up the bottle of whiskey, refilled her own glass and offered more to Carradine. He nodded and she poured him another two inches.

"It sounds as though he is going behind the backs of his employers in Russia. He knows about Moscow's plan to have me killed. He has no means of contacting me, he does not know where I am, he has no way of warning me in person. So he hires anyone he can think of who is coming to Morocco. He uses agents in place in Rabat, such as Mohammed Oubakir, to look for me. From what you have told me, Ramón is almost certainly working for him. Graham knows from Facebook that you are coming here to speak at the festival, so he takes a chance and uses you as another set of eyes."

"But that's crazy. You were a needle in a haystack."

"Maybe it is crazy, maybe it isn't. You *found* me, didn't you?" John Simpson was plugging his latest program on BBC World. The headlines were about to come around again. "Who is to say there are not five or six other people, all agents of Robert Mantis, walking around Marrakech tonight looking for 'Maria Rodriguez'?"

"All armed with passports and credit cards?"

Bartok shrugged. She did not have the answers to all the questions Carradine might ask. She did not pretend to.

"But why send me to the Sheraton?" he said. "Who was Abdullah Aziz? And why the fuck did Mantis have me deliver a book cipher to 'Yassine'?"

She smiled patiently, easing Carradine through his embarrassment.

"Agents need to be looked after," she explained. "They need to be serviced. Mantis asks you to meet 'Yassine,' to carry out a simple task, he is killing two birds with the one stone. Maybe he needed to get the book to Oubakir for other reasons. You said yourself that this man thinks you are a British spy." She paused, seeming to weigh up the good sense of teasing Carradine. "You are no different to Stephen Graham!" she exclaimed. "You have pretended to be somebody you are not."

Bartok was apparently delighted by this insight and giggled as she drank the whiskey. The sight of her enjoying herself had the effect of making Carradine feel slightly less angry and self-conscious. She was the best sort of company: intelligent and forthright, honest and kind.

"So who was the money for?" he asked.

"I have no idea."

"Ramón?"

"You meet this Spaniard on your plane. We can say this is a coincidence. There is—what?—one direct flight to Casablanca from London each day? Two, maximum. Therefore it is not unusual that you are on the same journey. He is also probably working for Robert Mantis, looking for me just as you were, just as Mr. Oubakir was doing. As for the money, perhaps it was to test you. Perhaps it was for this Ramón. Who knows?"

Carradine stood up. One of his legs had cramped. He walked around the room, shaking it out. Bartok looked as if she found the sight of this endearing.

"Are you all right, Kits?" she asked.

"Yes, thank you."

He liked the way she mispronounced his name, making it sound like "Keats."

"So perhaps now I should leave you in peace."

Carradine stopped moving. He looked at her. It had not occurred to him that she might leave.

"What do you mean?"

"I mean that I should go. You have done a lot for me. You have an airplane back to London in the morning. I have taken up too much of your time."

"What will you do?"

Bartok hesitated. "I do not know."

As strong and resourceful as she was, in that moment she looked vulnerable. Carradine felt a duty of care toward her, a responsibility to protect her from the danger outside.

"Lara, if you walk out of this hotel, you'll be assassinated. The Russians know you're in Marrakech. Now the Agency will suspect I'm involved with you in some way. . . ."

"You *are* involved with me in some way!" she said, trying to make light of it.

"You know what I mean."

The BBC headlines were counting down on the hour. Carradine turned to the television, expecting the same anchorman, the same news, the same guests. He was about to switch channels when he saw that a story was breaking.

"*Gunmen associated with Resurrection have seized control of Poland's parliament building in central Warsaw. . . .*"

"Jesus Christ," he said.

Bartok stepped toward the television in a state of consternation. The anchorman continued:

"As many as three hundred men, women and children are being held hostage inside the Sejm building. Gunshots have been fired and Polish police are reporting a number of fatalities. We join Peter Hackford, who is live at the scene. . . ."

They watched in silence as the reporter explained that as many as sixteen Resurrection gunmen had managed to shoot their way past security guards and take control of the Parliament building. Carradine was as fascinated by Bartok's response to the unfolding story as he was by the scale of the attack. She knew, as he did, that nothing like this had ever been attempted by Resurrection before. To go after a nationalist government in the heart of Europe, shooting to kill with little chance of personal survival when the siege ended, marked a sea change in the evolution of Resurrection, perhaps even the death throes of what had metastasized into a violent cult. This was no longer a group of idealistic center-left activists kidnapping journalists or tipping tables of food and wine into the laps of extremist politicians. This was terrorism, pure and simple.

"The movement is dead," said Bartok. "They have stolen it."

"Who has?" Carradine asked, but saw that she was in no mood to answer. LASZLO was sitting on the edge of the bed, shaking her head in disbelief.

"Why do they continue to come for me when this is happening?" she said. "Why do they still *care*?"

"I don't know," Carradine replied.

He had no means of helping her. She was trapped and surrounded, just as the gunmen inside the Sejm were enclosed by those who were determined to bring them to justice. Carradine was merely an ordinary citizen with ordinary powers. When it came to helping Bartok, he knew that he was in over his head.

"I need to leave," she said, picking up on this moment of self-doubt.

"Leave to go where?"

"Don't worry," she said. "I have ways of escape."

"What sort of ways?"

"A driver. Someone I trust. He can get me to Tangier. I can catch a boat."

"How are you going to do that? The Moroccans have eyes everywhere. They'll be watching the ports, the train stations, the airports. The Agency asks them to find you and bring you in, they will find you and bring you in."

"Why would they involve the Moroccans?" It was as though Bartok thought that Carradine was now exaggerating the threat against her. "I have been here three months, never had any trouble."

"It's a risk," he said.

"This is the nature of my life," she replied matter-of-factly. "I could be arrested at any time."

Carradine thought more carefully about the driver.

"Let's say you get to Tangier. How will you get out on the ferry? You said the new passport was useless."

"I have another passport."

"With you now?"

"No," she replied. Bartok was carrying a small shoulder bag. "Not with me now. At my apartment."

"You have a place here in Marrakech?"

"In Gueliz, yes."

He was amazed by this. How had she managed to rent an apartment without detection?

"What's the name on the passport?"

"Why?"

Bartok seemed impatient with Carradine for asking so many questions, but a plan had coalesced in his mind. The feeling was not dissimilar to those moments in his life as a writer when an ingenious plot device, born of creative necessity, materializes out of thin air. Carradine suddenly knew how to help her.

"Just tell me."

"The name in the passport is Lilia Hudak."

"Is it Hungarian?"

"Yes. Why? What is it, Kits?"

"Kit. No 's,'" he said.

"Kit, then!"

All Carradine needed was the driver and a slice of luck.

"I think I can get you out of Morocco another way," he said. "A safer way. What's the address of this apartment?"

26

Carradine ordered some food for Bartok on room service and waited for it to be delivered before going out alone into the Kasbah. It was just after nine o'clock. He walked the short distance to the Royal Mansour Hotel, asking for Patrick and Eleanor at the reception desk. They had already finished dinner and sent a message that Carradine should join them in the bar.

The Langs were taken aback by his suggestion at first but it did not take him long to persuade them. The key was his Hungarian girlfriend's love of the sea and the once-in-a-lifetime opportunity to surprise her and sail up the coast of Morocco. He would have been crazy not at least to ask if it would be possible to join them on their yacht for a couple of nights; maybe the extra pairs of hands might also make the journey up to Gibraltar a little bit easier?

Eleanor was the first to warm to the idea, telling Patrick it would be fun to spend a couple of nights at sea with a "famous novelist" and to get to know his "lovely young lady" in the bargain. Patrick couldn't remember Carradine mentioning her in the restaurant, but when he saw the passport-sized photograph Carradine kept of "Lilia" in his wallet, the old man's eyes lit up and he said he couldn't see any reason in the world why the trip wouldn't work. Carradine bought a second round of drinks to celebrate and they spent the rest of the conversation talking about the siege in Warsaw.

"What times we live in," said Patrick. "Used to be that you knew who the enemy was. The maniacs who hijacked airplanes, drove trucks through crowds, blew themselves up on the Tube. They were identifiable. Nowadays the terrorists look just like you and me—or your nice girlfriend, Kit. Ordinary people bearing a grudge."

"You mean white people," said Eleanor archly.

Patrick didn't bother denying it.

"I suppose I do," he said. "I can't pretend I haven't worried about Resurrection myself. I've got money offshore. I voted Conservative. I think Brexit, by and large, will be a good thing for Europe in the long term. Apparently that makes me an enemy of the people. I could be kneecapped. Our house in Ramsgate could be burned down. These people are callous." Patrick took a sip of his Chablis. "Resurrection isn't about change. It's about hate. Hatred of the rich. Hatred of those in power. They're just thugs. We might get to Rabat and find they've put a hole in *Atalanta* and she's at the bottom of the marina."

"Let's hope not!" said Carradine, trying to sound cheerful.

"At least we're insured," Eleanor muttered.

By the time his hosts were ready to call it a night, they had given Carradine instructions on where and when to meet them and asked only that he and Lilia both buy a pair of suitable shoes for the boat.

"No high heels!" Patrick called out as they parted company in the hotel lobby.

"I'll throw mine away then," Carradine replied.

He had one more task: to collect the Lilia Hudak passport from Bartok's apartment and to fill a bag with her belongings.

There was a taxi idling on the road at the western perimeter of the Mansour. Young couples on rugs were necking in the long grass,

escaping the summer heat of their homes—and doubtless the prying
eyes of parents. Carradine arranged a price for the journey into Gueliz,
giving the driver the address of a restaurant two blocks south of Bartok's apartment.

The journey took more than half an hour in thick traffic, following
a route almost identical to the one Carradine had taken on foot the previous evening from Jemaa el-Fna. Stepping out of the cab at the northern end of Avenue Mohammed V, he realized that he had been dropped
off within a stone's throw of the café where he had spoken to Oubakir.
Though his circumstances had changed irreversibly since then, Carradine was still fully absorbed in the role of a support agent; he had
simply shifted his loyalty to Bartok so that he could continue to ply his
trade in the secret world.

At no point had it occurred to him to stop and to think and to wonder if he should stay in the game; he wanted to help Bartok and to out-
wit Hulse. The particular characteristics of espionage—the absorption
in a clandestine role; the opiate of secrecy; the adrenalized fear of being caught—were drugs to which Carradine had very quickly become
addicted. At the Mansour, for example, he had deliberately wedged his
mobile phone beneath the cushions of his armchair, to be collected later
from the bar, so that he would hobble any technical surveillance the
Agency might throw at him. Walking in loops around Bartok's street,
he employed the tradecraft he had used in his novels to ascertain if he
was being followed. Using reflective surfaces in shop windows, even the
wing mirrors on cars, Carradine ran anti-surveillance for several blocks,
finding the streets too dark, his natural walking pace too fast and the
mirrors too small to enjoy any degree of success. He remembered a spy
in his second novel stopping on a busy London street and pretending
to answer a mobile phone call so that she could turn three hundred and
sixty degrees and make a full assessment of her surroundings. Carradine did not have his phone, but came to a halt nonetheless and
looked back down the length of Rue Ibn Aïcha, peering this way and

that with a frown and a squint, playing the part of a confused English tourist who had lost his way in the switchback streets of Gueliz. He saw nothing to make him suspicious.

After almost twenty minutes of this, he played the last card in the amateur spy's pack, making a sharp left-hand turn into a quiet residential street and coming to an immediate halt. He counted to ten, then turned around and set off in the direction from which he had come, hoping to bump into anybody who might conceivably have been tailing him. The street was deserted. No pedestrians were coming toward him, no vehicles were loitering on the corner or drifting past at a crawl. Carradine was as sure as he was ever going to be that he had reached Bartok's neighborhood undetected.

Her apartment was on Rue Moulay Ali, a wide residential street with a faux-Spanish restaurant at the northern end. Carradine passed a coffeehouse that was closing down for the night, a damaged strobe light flickering on the street. Bartok had explained that the entrance was about halfway down the road beside a plane tree sprouting from the pavement, its buckled trunk partly blocking access to the door. Carradine spotted the tree and, having checked up and down the road for surveillance, took out Bartok's keys and unlocked the door.

It was pitch-dark inside the lobby. He gave his eyes time to adjust to the gloom, gradually picking out a row of steel letterboxes on the opposite wall. Moving with zombie slowness, a fumbling hand stretched out in front of his face, Carradine eventually located a timer switch and pressed it with his thumb.

Light flooded the lobby. There were pieces of crumpled newspaper and dust all over the floor. A pot plant had toppled over, spilling earth in dried clumps. Bartok had warned him that the lift was temperamental so Carradine took the stairs. Two-thirds of the way up, the lights timed out and he was again forced to fumble in the darkness, his heart pounding with the effort of climbing the stairs and the fear of being caught. He managed to find a plastic switch in the pitch-black and was

able to walk up the remaining flights to Bartok's door, his route illumi-
nated by a series of weak staircase bulbs.

It was a small, stuffy apartment. Carradine was hit by a smell of stale
tobacco and unwashed socks. A Berber rug had been tacked to the wall
next to a poster of Ziggy Stardust. The kitchen was set to one side of
the living room in an open-plan style not dissimilar to the flat in Lisson
Grove. A set of French windows led out onto a narrow terrace. Bartok
had rolled up a yoga mat and placed it underneath a large wooden coffee table in the center of the room.

Carradine closed the door behind him and switched on the air-
conditioning. The room quickly became cooler and the stale smells of
sweat and tobacco partially lifted. Every available surface was scattered
with books, newspapers and magazines. He spotted some cigarette pa-
pers and a small block of hashish on the coffee table. A half-finished
bottle of Grey Goose vodka had been left on a shelf in the kitchen. Carradine took a shot for his nerves then went to the cupboard under the
sink and reached for the bag of dishwasher salt. It was exactly where
Bartok had said it would be, nestled behind a box of soap powder and
a plastic bucket full of cleaning products. He untied the knot on the
bag and felt inside. He plunged his hand into the salt and felt the hard
outline of the passport. He took it out, checked the name—"Lilia
Hudak"—and put it in his back pocket.

Bartok had given him a list of other items to pack. His heart pounding, Carradine went into her bedroom. He was amused by the mess. The
bed was unmade and there were books and items of clothing strewn all
over the floor. It was as if a tribe of monkeys had been set loose in the
room. A small, stained-glass window in the corner fed an eerie technicolor light into the bedroom. Carradine pulled down a soft bag from
an overhead cupboard and set it on the bed. He found a drawer full of
clean T-shirts and stuffed half a dozen of them into the bag along with
two summer dresses from the wardrobe, a pair of denim shorts and
some underwear. He was amazed by the number of clothes she owned.

Bartok had told him about the shampoo bottle beside the bed. He found the bottle, removed the lid and tapped out a tin-plate cigar tube. He unscrewed the cap. The tube was filled with hundred dollar bills. Carradine put it back inside the bottle and threw the shampoo into the bag.

Next he looked under the bed and located the pile of Russian novels Bartok had described, each of them translated into Hungarian. He identified *Anna Karenina* thanks to a picture of Keira Knightley on the front cover looking wan and indecisive. He opened it up. The SIM card was taped to the inside back cover. Carradine placed the book in the bag. There was a laptop and an old mobile phone on a shelf beside the window. Bartok had asked him to leave them behind. Unable to remember what shoes she had been wearing, Carradine picked up a pair of trainers and stuffed them into the bag, mindful of Patrick's instructions for the yacht. Finally, he found the one item Bartok had insisted that he remember: an Art Deco silver bookmark given to her by her late mother. He wrapped it up in a pair of black knickers and placed both carefully inside one of the shoes to protect the bookmark from damage. Then he zipped up the bag and went out into the living room.

The man was standing beside the front door. His arms were folded, his legs slightly apart. Carradine was so shocked that he lurched backwards and had to steady himself on the frame of the door. The man was wearing jeans and a black T-shirt. He was slim and looked about thirty-five.

"You must be the writer." He had a thin voice but with a distinct Russian accent. "Mister Considines."

Carradine did not bother correcting him. Instead he said: "Who the fuck are you?"

Fear boiled inside him. Suddenly he was no longer in an adventure story of his own making, a work of imagination from which he could extricate himself at any time. He was in the center of Marrakech in the dead of night faced with a man who had been waiting for Lara Bartok.

He knew where she lived. He knew that Carradine was associated with her. The game was up.

"Do not concern yourself with who I am. What are you doing here, please?" The man glanced at the bag. "You make a vacation?"

"That's right." Carradine's throat was as dry as coal. He looked in the direction of the second bedroom. He assumed that the Russian had been waiting there, though it was possible that he had picked the lock and walked right in. Had he searched Bartok's room? Did that account for the mess? He wondered if there were other men in the apartment or a team waiting on the stairs. He had been so sure that he had not been followed.

"Who is the bag for, please?"

"My girlfriend," Carradine replied. He knew that he had to play the innocent, to try to find a way of leaving the apartment without exposing Lara or himself to further danger. He could not think of any way of doing that without playing the role of an ordinary man caught up in a conspiracy that he did not understand. "How did you know my name?" he asked.

The Russian ignored him. He was not a physically imposing person, nor particularly sinister to look at. He might have been the landlord popping in to check up that everything was fine with the apartment. He had no gun—at least not one that Carradine had seen—but his manner was very calm and controlled.

"Where is the girl?" he asked. "Where is Lara Bartok?"

Carradine played the innocent. "Lara Bartok?"

"Your girlfriend. This is her place. Where is she, please?"

"My girlfriend's name is Sandy." Carradine plucked the first name that came into his mind. "She's in hospital. She's not well. She asked me to pack her a bag."

"Which hospital?"

The question brought an acid surge into Carradine's throat: he was out of his depth, untrained and untested, making things up out of thin air.

"I don't know the name," he said. "I just know where it is. Near the Medina. The one all the tourists go to." He took a further risk, assuming that every city had one: "The American Hospital."

The Russian nodded. Perhaps Carradine had miraculously stumbled on a version of the truth.

"I am going to call this in," he said. "Please put the bag down. Please remain where you are."

Those words gave Carradine hope. If the Russian had to make a phone call, that meant that he was alone. There was nobody else in the building. His colleagues were looking for Bartok all over town and had spread themselves thin. If he somehow could get past the Russian, if he could find a way out of the building and back to the riad, he could warn Lara and get her out of Marrakech. He had no other choice. If he did as the Russian asked, if he just stood around watching him call his superiors, he was finished. He had to do something. He had to fight back.

"Listen, mate." Carradine stepped toward him. He was suddenly possessed of a wild confidence that he could take him out, that one clean punch would drop his man to the ground. "I don't know who you are or who you're looking for. Sandy is sick. I came to pick up her things. How the fuck did you get in here anyway?"

He was trying to remember everything that his boxing instructor had told him. *Don't swing and hook like they do in the movies. That's just bullshit for the cameras. Drop a low punch into the midriff then drive an uppercut under the jaw. Keep your right elbow close to your body and use the momentum from your pelvis.*

"I can get in anywhere," the Russian replied, taking out his phone. He started to scroll through the contacts, looking for the number that would seal Bartok's fate.

"It's breaking and entering," Carradine told him, moving forward.

He realized that he was at least four inches taller than the Russian, which only added to his reckless courage. He remembered the day in Gymbox when he had missed the pad and accidentally slammed his fist into his instructor's jaw. The instructor had gone flying, as if a rope had been attached to his back and somebody had yanked on it.

"What are you doing, please?" the Russian asked, looking up from his phone.

Carradine wanted it to be the uppercut with which Buster Douglas had floored Tyson in the tenth. He had a vision of George Foreman slumping to the canvas in Kinshasa as Ali loomed over him, his fist primed to strike. He dreamed of recreating the punch with which Sylvester Stallone had floored Drago in *Rocky IV*. Instead Carradine feinted to one side and dropped a hard left hook into his opponent's stomach. The Russian was badly winded, gasping as Carradine brought his right elbow tight to the body and drove upward from his pelvis with all of his strength, landing a sweet right uppercut on the side of the jaw which drove the Russian back against the door. The contact was not as clean as Carradine had hoped, but there was no need for another punch. He was fit and strong and he had put him down. The man slumped semiconscious to the ground, eyes glazed over, legs stretched out in front of him like a cartoon drunk propped up outside a bar. Carradine immediately pulled him to one side so that he could unbolt the door. The Russian was extraordinarily heavy; it was like trying to move a sack of wet sand. His phone had fallen to the ground and he picked it up. Grabbing the bag and checking that the passport was still in his back pocket, Carradine hurried out of the apartment, hitting a light switch with his aching right hand before scampering down eight flights of stairs with the speed of a man trying to outrun a rockslide.

On the ground floor he searched for a back entrance but could not find one. He went down to the basement but there were only two doors, both of them leading to apartments. His knuckles were throbbing; it was as if he had slammed his fist repeatedly against a hot brick stove.

The Russian might already be coming around; Carradine had no choice other than to go outside onto Rue Moulay Ali and take his chances.

The street was utterly still. At the northern end he saw a man walking out of the Spanish restaurant smoking a cigarette. He checked the cars parked along both sides of the street but it was too dark to tell if there was anybody sitting inside them. Using the trunk of the buckled tree as partial cover, he headed in the direction of the restaurant, hugging the shadows, the strap of the bag digging into his shoulder.

An engine started up behind him. Carradine did not dare turn around and show his face. Instead he quickened his pace, running past the restaurant and the shuttered coffeehouse, heading for a busier street up ahead. He dropped the phone into a dustbin. A taxi was coming from the opposite direction with its light switched off. Carradine knew that in Morocco that meant he could share the ride with the other passengers. He waved at the cab. It immediately swerved toward him. There was an old woman in the front. Carradine opened the back door, swung the bag onto the seat and climbed in.

"Where are you going?" he asked the driver in French.

Carradine did not understand the reply but said *"Oui, très bien"* then immediately ducked down, pretending to tie his shoelaces as the taxi passed the northern end of Rue Moulay Ali. For the next several minutes he turned in his seat repeatedly, scouring the vehicles behind him. At one point a young Moroccan on a scooter followed the taxi for four blocks, but eventually turned off, heading in the direction of the Majorelle Gardens. A short time later, the old lady paid her fare and left the cab. Carradine handed the driver a hundred dirhams and asked him to head for the Royal Mansour without stopping to collect any new passengers. The driver did so, leaving him at the western entrance. Carradine walked alone along the private road leading to the hotel. He knew that he looked scruffy and washed out, but he was a white European and the security guard waved him into the building with only a cursory glance.

It was almost one o'clock in the morning. The bar had closed. Carradine found a member of the staff wandering in a corridor, explained that he had lost his mobile phone, then searched the armchair where he had been sitting in the bar with Patrick and Eleanor. To his relief, he found it immediately. He tried switching it on but the battery had died. He tipped the member of the staff and walked back outside, hailing a cab on Mohammed V that took him the short distance to the riad. Battery or no battery, if the Russians or the Agency were tracking his phone, they would still know that he was back at the hotel. If Carradine was going to be picked up, they would come for him in the next few minutes.

He banged on the front door. Twenty-four hours earlier it had taken several minutes for the sleepy night manager in the stained shirt to come to the door. Tonight he opened it almost immediately, recognizing Carradine with a warm smile and inviting him into the hall.

"You are Mister Carradine, yes?" he said.

"That's right."

"There were men here before. Men looking for you."

Carradine's heart popped but he tried to remain calm.

"Which men? Did you get their names?"

The night manager shook his head.

"Americans," he said.

Carradine described Sebastian Hulse: tall, good-looking, slick. He asked if that fitted the description of one of the men.

"Yes, sir. Exactly. It was this man. He says he is your friend."

"He did, did he? What did he want? Where did he go?"

"He says you invite him for a drink. He not find you so they go to your room. Knock on the door."

Carradine had established a system with Bartok: three quick knocks followed by three slower knocks to verify that it was safe to let him in; if he tapped out the rhythm of "Rule Britannia," it was a warning that he had been compromised. He knew that Bartok would not have let

Hulse into the room, but that the Agency was more than capable of picking the simple lock on the door.

"Are they still here?"

Carradine's hand was throbbing. He was physically and mentally exhausted. If Hulse and his accomplice were waiting for him in the riad, he doubted that he possessed the wherewithal to lie convincingly about where he had been or what he had planned with Bartok.

"No, sir. They leave. One, maybe one and half hours ago."

"With a woman?"

"No, sir."

Carradine thanked him. He tipped the night manager, collected his key and went to his room. He knocked on the door using the system they had arranged and prayed that Bartok was OK.

There was no response.

He knocked again—three times in rapid succession, three times with a pause in between each knock—but she did not answer.

He unlocked the door and went inside.

All of the lights had been switched off. The bed was empty. Carradine looked to his left, hoping that Bartok would emerge from the bathroom, just as she had done earlier in the afternoon. She did not. He went into the bathroom and looked behind the shower curtain. He searched under the bed. Her shoulder bag was nowhere to be seen and she had not left a note.

She was gone.

27

Carradine ran back to reception. The night manager was sitting behind the desk looking at photographs on Facebook.

"Hello again, sir!"

"Tell me. Did a woman leave in the last few hours?"

Carradine described Bartok: cropped blond hair, a cream-colored veil, slightly crooked front teeth. He was desperately worried about her. The night manager shrugged and shook his head.

"Not when I am here at the desk," he said. "I do not see this woman."

Carradine returned to the room. He looked for Bartok a second time, pointlessly, even checking inside the wardrobe, as if he expected a woman of her experience and cunning to be crouched inside it under a blanket, like a child playing hide-and-seek. He took out the mobile phone and plugged it in to charge. He was worried for her safety, but his concern was mingled with the prospect of personal betrayal. Had she lied to him? Had it always been her intention to leave once she had rinsed him for information?

He looked down at the phone. The screen showed a thin red sliver of power, not enough to start it up. He was starving. The room service tray had not been removed. Bartok had left a bread roll, a scrape of butter and half a bowl of cold chips. Carradine ate all of it, washed down with two cans of Coke from the minibar. Then he picked up the phone and tapped in his six-digit pin.

There were four missed calls, four unread WhatsApp messages and two texts. He looked at the missed calls. Three were from the same un-identified number, the fourth from his father. There were no voice mails. He tapped on the text message icon. The first was from EE, the second from an old friend in Istanbul. He opened WhatsApp.

Two of the messages were from Mantis.

> You're full of surprises, Kit! Wonderful news about our friend. Well done. Never doubted you for a moment ;)

Carradine muttered "Fuck you" to the screen. He bitterly regret-ted telling Oubakir that he had found Bartok. He read the second message:

> Let me know more about it. Also—will still need the stuff Y gave you in Casablanca. Make sure it comes home safely.

Mantis was referring to the memory stick, which was still in the hotel safe. Carradine assumed that it contained information that would be useful to Moscow and therefore damaging to Western interests. As soon as he got home, he would hand the stick to a contact in the Ser-vice who had helped him, a few years earlier, with a couple of research questions related to his books. Carradine would inform her that a Brit-ish citizen, Stephen Graham, had been betraying his country to Mos-cow for more than a decade. With any luck, Mantis would get twenty years.

The second WhatsApp message was from a UK number he did not recognize. There was no name associated with the account and no photograph. Carradine opened it.

Hi Kit. It's Lilia, your downstairs neighbor. Are you in London? I've tried calling you. A package came for you but I couldn't fit it through your letterbox. I've had to go away on business but you'll find it out the back by the tradesman's entrance. It will be waiting for you there.

Carradine was so tired that, at first, he took the message at face value. Just another package to be collected. Just another note from a neighbor.

Then his brain began to work.

Lilia. Tradesman's entrance.

The message was from Bartok.

28

Carradine packed his bag inside three minutes. He knew that he couldn't take his laptop or phone to Rabat and left both under the mattress, having sent a reply to Mantis and scribbled down half a dozen essential telephone numbers on a piece of writing paper. With luck, he could call the riad at some point in the next two days, explain that he had left in a hurry and ask them to courier the laptop and phone, as well as the memory stick in the hotel safe, to his flat in London.

He opened the door and went out into the courtyard. It was blissfully quiet save for the gentle running of the fountain. He shouldered the two bags and walked in the direction of the swimming pool. He glanced at his watch. It was quarter to three. A light was on in one of the bedrooms on the first floor. Perhaps it was McKenna's suite and he was working late or suffering with a bout of insomnia. Carradine turned past the pool, heading toward the spa. He caught his foot on a loose paving stone and almost tripped but managed to retain his balance. He passed the spa and reached the back gate, checking behind him to ensure that he had not been followed.

He peered over the top. The van had gone from the maintenance area. Carradine could see a car parked on the far side of the street. A cat leapt out in the darkness and scurried away from the wall. As Carradine leaned back, he noticed a slight movement in the front seat of the car, a shadow. He was convinced that it was Bartok's driver.

He looked more closely at the gate. There was no way of opening it; it was padlocked from the street side. A line of barbed wire stretched from one end to the next. If he was going to get over it, he would have to sling both bags through the gap between the barbed wire and the top of the gate, then climb over. The maintenance area was overlooked by several residential buildings, all of which were blacked out, save one. Carradine looked up at the lit window. It appeared to be a stairwell or hall of some kind; certainly there was nobody visible in the building. Looking back at the car, trying to signal to the driver, he wondered if he was making life too difficult for himself. Why not just leave through the front door of the hotel and walk around to the car? There was no need for him formally to check out; the festival was covering his costs. The night manager might think it was strange that Mr. Carradine was leaving at three o'clock in the morning, but he could tell him that he had an early flight to catch. Yet the risk of outside surveillance was too great. By now the Russian would have come around and alerted his colleagues; they would be en route to the riad. Carradine had to go over the gate to minimize the risk of being caught.

He lifted up the first bag. It was heavier than he had expected and banged against the metal gate as he stretched up and pushed it under the barbed wire. He held it at the top with one hand while stepping up onto a narrow metal bar at the base of the gate. The gate wobbled as it took Carradine's weight. He steadied himself against the brick wall. Pushing his arm through the gap as far as it would go, he lowered the bag on the opposite side, letting it drop to the ground. He had packed the bottle of Johnnie Walker and heard a thump against the cement, praying that the bottle hadn't smashed. He then repeated the process with Bartok's bag, letting it drop to the ground.

Having checked his surroundings one last time, Carradine then pulled himself up onto the top of the gate. It was extremely narrow. The barbed wire made it difficult to find a space to plant his feet. The hinge connecting the gate to the wall was also very loose. The gate began to rattle. Carradine crouched down, holding the top with both hands, one leg on either side of the barbed wire but wobbling like a surfer trying to balance on a breaking wave. Feeling exposed, he decided to jump down, almost catching his heel on the wire as he dropped. Pain shot up through his knees as he landed on the concrete. The gate was jangling as though it had been struck by a frying pan. Carradine reached out to smother the din as the cat hissed in the shadows. He half expected the entire neighborhood to wake up and to shout at him to keep the noise down.

He heard the man's voice before he saw his face.

"Monsieur Kit?"

Carradine turned to see a young Moroccan man with a neat beard crouched beneath the wall.

"Yes?" he whispered.

"Come," he said in French, gesturing toward the car. "I am the driver. I have the lady. Come."

Somerville went to the window on the street side and peered through the blinds. Seeing nothing in the stairwell, he turned and walked back toward Bartok.

"You say this was the first time you had heard of Kit Carradine?"

"That is correct," she replied.

Hulse stepped across him.

"Come on. You'd never read his books? You didn't know he was coming to Marrakech? You hadn't been told to make contact with him? He just happened to see you walking out of this Irish guy's book event?"

"That is correct."

"And you expect us to believe that?"

"I have learned not to expect anything from anyone," Bartok replied. "People always let you down, Mr. Hulse. Don't you find that?"

Hulse hesitated. Somerville dug him out of the hole.

"You hadn't seen Carradine's name in the festival program? You didn't look in on his talk?"

"I did not."

"You sure about that?" Hulse asked.

"What reason would I have to lie?"

"To protect him," he said.

"Protect him from what? From who? People like you?"

"Maybe."

Somerville had heard enough. Standing behind Bartok, he shot Hulse a look, telling him to back off.

"Let's not get distracted," he said, filling her glass with water. "Just tell us what happened next."

"When?"

"Pick it up wherever you like," Hulse suggested.

"No." Somerville was rummaging in his jacket pocket and found an almost empty packet of cigarettes crushed beneath a set of house keys. They had been there all along. "We know about Mexico. What interests us is the role the Russians played in all this."

Bartok buried a smile.

"So nothing has changed," she said. "Everybody is still playing catch-up with the Kremlin."

Hulse began to respond but Somerville silenced him again, this time with a raised hand.

"Were you aware of Russian surveillance in Morocco? What did Stephen Graham tell you about their objectives? Did you think Carradine was working for Moscow? Were you immediately suspicious of the Langs?"

"So many questions all at once."

"Then take your time." Somerville tucked the cigarettes into the hip pocket of his trousers and sat down. "You have the stage, Lara. We're all ears."

SECRET INTELLIGENCE SERVICE
EYES ONLY / STRAP 1

STATEMENT BY LARA BARTOK ("LASZLO")
CASE OFFICERS: J.W.S./S.T.H.—CHAPEL STREET
REF: RESURRECTION/SIMAKOV/CARRADINE
FILE: RE2768X

PART 4 OF 5

Why did the Russians want me dead? Why was it so important for them to find me? Was it just because of my activities with Resurrection—or was there something more? To this day, I cannot answer that question. Why did they come for me when they did? Ivan was dead. I had left the movement. I was no longer a threat to them.

I realize that I was extremely fortunate. If I hadn't risked going to the festival, if I hadn't spoken to Michael McKenna, if Kit hadn't spotted me outside the event, I would now be dead. That's certain. Kit Carradine saved my life. Yes, Mantis knew there was every chance I would show myself in Marrakech. He knew I loved McKenna's writing and had always wanted to meet him. He put Kit in my path for just this reason. Mohammed Oubakir also. But I was still very, very lucky.

I trusted Kit immediately. I felt safe with him. It was obvious that he had been manipulated, that he was embarrassed and ashamed to have fallen for Mantis's trick, but I knew he had done it for noble reasons. Many others would have made the same mistake. Every man wants to be a spy, doesn't he? Every child dreams of being a secret agent. How do you turn down an opportunity like that when it comes about, especially given what happened to his father? Kit had a resourcefulness and a courage,

mixed with a kind of romantic naïveté—which I suppose is necessary for any writer—which was very endearing and attractive
to me.

He was brave to go to my apartment. He wanted to help me
and this was the only way he could think of. I don't know how
the Russians knew where I was living. If you can find that out I'll
be fascinated to know. My suspicion is that one of my neighbors
informed on me. He was a creep with a big mouth.

I suppose this would be the best time to talk about Patrick and
Eleanor [JWS: Patrick and Eleanor Lang]. Yes, I was very concerned about them. You can choose to believe me about that or
you can choose not to believe me. Kit had taken them on trust,
just as he had taken Robert Mantis at face value. It was Ivan who
taught me a long time ago that when a stranger strikes up conversation in a bar, in a restaurant, on a plane, that stranger may
be interested in more than some light conversation. Kit knew
that, too. But we had to get out of Morocco. At that very difficult
moment, their boat seemed to be the best way.

29

They ran low through the shadows of the maintenance area. The young driver popped the boot of a Renault Mégane and threw the bags inside. Carradine opened the back door to find Bartok asleep. He was amazed that she was capable of relaxing under such intense pressure.

She sat up abruptly as he moved in beside her.

"You made it," she said.

"We go?" the driver asked in French.

"*Oui*," Bartok replied groggily. "*Allez*."

Carradine felt a vertiginous elation, a belief that he had landed in a life that did not belong to him but to which he was ideally suited. He was certain that the car would not be stopped. He was sure that they would make it to Rabat. He was risking his future to help a wanted criminal but knew that the cause was just. He had not fully thought through what he was doing, nor what he was leaving behind. Looking at Bartok as she stared at the road ahead, he felt like a man walking out of church on his wedding day beside a woman he barely knows.

"What happened to your hand?"

Bartok touched Carradine's knuckles. Her fingers were cool and soft. She caressed his wrist and looked into his eyes with such care that the last of his concerns vanished.

"I got into a fight," he said. He saw that there was a patch of skin on the back of her wrist where the tattoo of the swallows had been removed. "Does your driver speak English?"

Bartok shook her head. "Hardly any. Nothing."

"Somebody was waiting for you in the apartment," he said. "A Russian. He knew who I was."

"How?" She was bewildered. "This is the man you fought? You *punched* him?"

She was still holding his wrist. He played down his feat, as though he got into fights two or three times a week and always emerged victorious.

"You are brave!" she said and cheerfully kissed him on the cheek. "Are you OK?"

"I'm fine." Carradine was watching the pavements on both sides of the road. "He was knocked out. I hope he's all right."

"So do I," she muttered, and just as quickly the thrill of what he had done evaporated. The fact that nobody had come to the riad in the past hour indicated that the Russian was possibly still unconscious. What if Carradine had seriously injured him? He would be no different to Bartok. Another criminal on the run.

"Get down!" Carradine shouted.

The Russian and two other men were walking in the direction of the hotel on the opposite side of the street, no more than thirty meters from the car. He grabbed Bartok, pushing her behind the passenger seat, his head resting on the small of her back as they bent down beneath the windows.

"What's going on?" the driver asked in French.

"That was him. The Russian."

Bartok swore in what he assumed was her native Hungarian. The driver made a sharp left-hand turn. Carradine held onto the door handle, his weight pushing against her.

"You saw him?" She tried to sit up. Carradine made room for her on the seat. "The man from my apartment?"

"Right there," he replied, turning and indicating where he had seen the men. The stretch of road where the Russians had been walking was now obscured by a section of the old city wall.

"So he is fine. And so are you. Did you get everything?"

Carradine looked at the driver. Bartok again reassured him that he would not be able to understand anything they said.

"Yeah. I found the passport. Your place was a mess. Clothes, books, shoes everywhere. I think he'd been looking for it."

She smiled, rubbing her neck. "No. This is just me. I am not a tidy person, Kit."

Carradine laughed. "Ah, OK." He wound down the window, looking out on the deserted streets of Gueliz. "I packed whatever I could. Found the bookmark, the SIM card . . ."

"You were amazing to do this. I do not know how to thank you."

"You don't need to thank me."

For a few minutes they were silent, the car moving steadily along wide, empty boulevards toward the outskirts of the city. Carradine was still hungry and hoped that they could stop on the road once they were clear of Marrakech. It would take about four or five hours to reach Rabat on the dual carriageway. Bartok introduced him formally to the driver, whose name was Rafiq. She explained that Rafiq's uncle had found her the apartment in Gueliz. Carradine asked if it was possible that he was the man who had betrayed her to the Russians. She was adamant that this was not the case and thought it more likely that a neighbor had grown suspicious of her and had spoken to the local police; informers were everywhere in Morocco. If the Russians had their ear to the ground, it would only have been a case of putting two and two together. At the same time, she could not be certain that the men who were looking for her might not now question the uncle and connect the dots to Rafiq. For that reason, she had asked him to leave his cellphone at home so that their journey up to Rabat could not be traced.

"Whose car is this?" Carradine asked. He was worried about number plate recognition.

"Don't worry," she said. "It's his friend's car. It won't flag."

They reached a *péage* at the start of the highway. It was still the middle of the night and there was only one lane open. Two large cameras faced the car on either side of a narrow channel. Rafiq moved forward, stopping at a tollbooth. Bartok had climbed over into the passenger seat. Carradine remained in the back, scanning either side of the highway for police patrols. He saw the headlights of a tailing vehicle reflected in the rearview mirror. There were so few cars on the road that every one of them was a threat. Rafiq opened the window, greeted the guard and paid the toll. The barrier opened and they continued onto the highway. Carradine lit a cigarette to calm his nerves.

"We will be fine," Bartok reassured him, again giving the impression of reading his mind as she turned in her seat to speak to him. "Got one of those for me?"

They all smoked as the light gradually strengthened and the suburbs of Marrakech gave way to a flat, featureless desert stretching out to the horizon. To the east, Carradine could make out the faint outline of the High Atlas Mountains. Bartok spoke in French with Rafiq about his uncle's marriage to a woman who was not permitted to leave the house alone, did not drive a car and had never—to Rafiq's knowledge—drank alcohol nor smoked a cigarette. This, he insisted, was perfectly normal in Moroccan culture. Carradine enjoyed the way she teased him into confessing that he hoped for a similar marital arrangement of his own.

About an hour into the journey Carradine fell asleep, waking to find that Rafiq had stopped at a Shell garage close to the town of Settat on the A7 highway. He sat up and rubbed his face, adjusting to the bright sunlight flooding into the car. Rafiq was filling up with fuel; Bartok was nowhere to be seen.

The interior of the petrol station was no different to a thousand others just like it, from Inverness to Naples: strip-lit aisles displaying crisps and biscuits, fridges stocked with sports drinks and Red Bull. Carradine tried on a pair of sunglasses and looked around for Bartok. There were tables at the back of the shop in front of a cafeteria staffed by two young women wearing aprons and veils. He queued up and bought several pastries and what he assumed was a cheese bun. One of the girls smiled at him and he realized he was still wearing the sunglasses. He took them off and set them on the counter.

Turning from the till, Carradine saw a woman with long dark hair seated at a table overlooking the highway. It was only when she turned around that he realized the woman was Bartok.

"What did you do to your hair?" he said, absorbing the transformation in her appearance.

She invited him to sit beside her.

"Rafiq brought it to me," she replied. "They might work out that we left Marrakech by car. Either we took the road south to Agadir or, more likely, the road to Casablanca. Those were our only options—unless we wanted to get stuck in Essaouira. They might look at CCTV, they might not. But they are searching for a woman with short blond hair traveling with a man who looks a lot like C. K. Carradine." She smiled and sipped her coffee. "You were asleep when I left the car. So I was just another woman in Morocco with long black hair getting out of the passenger seat while her boyfriend filled up with petrol."

"And now?" Carradine asked, gesturing toward the ceiling where he had earlier spotted two CCTV cameras.

"Now you've ruined it!" she said, as if their escape was all just a game and she had not a care in the world. "You shouldn't have bought your food and your drinks. You shouldn't have talked to the woman with the long black wig."

He was stumped for a response, still half-asleep but understanding with each passing moment why Mantis had been so bewitched by Lara Bartok. They hurried back to the car. She took the bag Carradine had packed from the boot and placed it at her feet in the front seat. Carradine shared his food with Rafiq and soon fell asleep again. Seventy miles from Rabat he woke to find that Bartok had removed the SIM card from the copy of *Anna Karenina* and was busy slotting it into what appeared to be a brand-new handset.

"Where'd you get the phone?" he asked.

"Rafiq, too."

"He bought it just now?"

"No. Before. In Marrakech."

He took out the list of numbers he had written down from his phone, explaining that it was important that his father should be able to reach him in an emergency. As he said this, he realized that of course it would be impossible to telephone home. Any intelligence service worth its salt would be covering his father's number.

"Will he worry about you?" she asked.

"It's not that." Carradine did not want to make too much of the situation. He was very close to his father and felt responsible for his happiness and well-being. But William Carradine was a tough old bird with a circle of good friends who kept an eye on him. "It's just for emergencies. I'm his only family in the UK. He doesn't have brothers or sisters. Neither of us do. My mother died a long time ago."

"I am sorry to hear that."

"He won't notice I'm gone for a few days. I'll call him when we get to Gibraltar."

It was then that Carradine saw the cloud of dust ahead of them, about four hundred meters from the car. Rafiq slowed down as other cars in front of him hit the brakes. Bartok asked what was happening and he replied "Crash" in French as the Renault passed the scene. Two vehicles had come off the highway at speed and careered across the desert floor, one landing on its roof, the other folded almost in half at the base of a pylon. Two other cars had come to a halt at the side of the road.

"We should help," said Carradine.

"Kit, we can't," Bartok told him.

He turned and saw two people emerge from the parked cars. She was right. Others would be there to call for an ambulance. If they went back, the police would come and they would run the risk of being identified. Rafiq gradually accelerated away and the crash was soon forgotten. Yet Carradine's nerves had been frayed by the incident—the plumes of dust; the inverted, smashed cars. He tried to wipe what he had seen from his mind. He knew that there had been serious injuries, perhaps even that someone had died, and the knowledge of this acted on him like a portent of things to come.

"Are you OK?" Bartok asked, turning and putting a hand on his leg.

"I'm great," he said and took back the piece of paper on which he had written down the numbers. "How much longer to Rabat?"

"Less than an hour now."

It was past seven o'clock. The other guests at the riad would be awake and eating breakfast by the pool. Had the Russians forced their way in and demanded to see him? Perhaps they had bribed the night manager to let them search Carradine's room. Had they done so, they would now be in possession of his laptop and phone, giving them access to his WhatsApp messages with Mantis.

"You think Stephen Graham was working behind Moscow's back?"

Bartok did not hear the question clearly and asked Carradine to repeat it. He did so.

"I told you already," she replied. "I think he knew they were coming for me. He wanted to save me." Carradine looked out at the dusty road. "Why do you ask this?" she said.

"My phone is in my room. If the Russians see that Mantis was in touch with me, they'll know he's betrayed them."

Rafiq was driving past the suburbs of Casablanca, on the edge of the speed limit. Bartok took off her seat belt and climbed over into the backseat in order to continue the conversation.

"There's nothing we can do about that," she said. Her perfume pushed toward him, a smell he adored. "He made his choice. He probably saved my life by sending you. But I can't protect him."

"No."

"Do you *want* to warn him after what he did to you?"

Carradine found that his bitterness toward Mantis had abated. He was not one to hold a grudge. He understood why "Stephen Graham" had pretended to be a British spy in order to recruit him. Sending him to Morocco to look for "Maria" had been an act of love.

"What will happen to Mantis if they find out?"

Bartok bowed her head.

"He will certainly lose his job," she said. She looked up and met Carradine's eyes. "Worse, perhaps."

He took out the list of telephone numbers. As well as the contact details for his father, he had written down numbers for his editor, his literary agent and two of his oldest friends from school days. The last number on the piece of paper had RM scrawled beside it.

"That's him?" Bartok asked.

"That's him."

Then she did something completely unexpected. Taking the piece of paper, she tore off the bottom section on which Carradine had written Mantis's number, screwed it up into a ball, opened the window and let it fly out of the car.

"There you go," she said. "Now you don't have to feel responsible for him anymore."

30

Less than an hour later they had reached the outskirts of Rabat.

"We're going to need somewhere to stay," said Carradine.

He had blithely assumed that Bartok and Rafiq had already made arrangements. This was not the case.

"Any ideas?" she asked.

"I don't know anybody in Rabat," he replied. "Do you want to pop into the British Embassy?"

"Very funny," she said.

Though he had intended the remark as a joke, the idea took on a certain logic. If Carradine could make contact with the local Service Station chief and tell them about the threat against Bartok, the Embassy might offer them sanctuary.

"Wait," he said. He wondered how to pitch it. He did not want to seem rash. "What if the Service has no idea what the Russians and Americans are up to?"

"Do you think this is likely?"

There was an edge of facetiousness to Bartok's voice which he had not heard before. The patriot in Carradine, that part of him which had believed in his country sufficiently to want to work for Mantis, could not countenance the idea that his own nation's intelligence officers were involved in the murky business of murder. It may have been because of his father's brief career in the Service, but he had always believed that the British adhered to moral values loftier than those in Washington and Moscow.

"Perhaps," he said.

She laughed derisively. "And perhaps they know everything and have chosen to turn a blind eye to targeted killings of innocent civilians. Perhaps they are themselves involved. We cannot know."

Carradine was again struck by the suspicion that Bartok was holding something back.

"What are you not telling me?" he asked.

She looked at him quickly, as if he had intuited a hidden truth.

"What do you mean?"

"It's like you know something. You know the real reason why we can't go to the Embassy."

"The *real* reason?" He saw that she was tired and about to lose her temper. "The real reason is because I was involved in the kidnapping of Otis Euclidis. The real reason is because I assisted in Resurrection operations in the United States and Europe. The real reason is because I was the girlfriend of Ivan Simakov." Carradine was stunned that she had been involved in the Euclidis disappearance. He could see from her face that she had done things she regretted, things of which she was now ashamed. "I have no friends. I have only enemies, Kit. If you are with me you must know this. If we are caught, you will be accused of helping a fugitive to escape justice."

"I'll take that chance." Carradine had come too far to respond in any other way. "I don't think the Service would want you dead," he said. "I don't think they'd be happy to know that their closest political ally has struck a deal with Moscow."

Bartok hesitated. Carradine had again glimpsed the secret which she would not divulge. She turned to face him.

"Then go ahead and think that!" Her temper had snapped. All of the anxiety and suffering of her life on the run was suddenly visible to him: a world in which she was never safe, never certain, could trust nobody. "It does not matter to me what you think. You could be right, you could be wrong. Perhaps the British Secret Service is prepared to sacrifice its good relations with America just to do the decent thing by me. But I doubt it. Let's face it: You write about this world, C. K. Carradine, but you know very little about how it really thinks or how it works." Carradine's ego took a punch as pure and as effective as the uppercut with which he had floored the Russian. "I have to trust my own judgment, my own experience. I have to be able to *survive*. You are helping me to do that and—believe me, please—I am profoundly grateful to you. If you want to leave me now, here in Rabat, I would not blame you. Go back to Marrakech. Go back to your phone with its numbers, to your laptop with its words. Take your suitcase and fly home. If I were you and I were able to do these things, believe me, I would do them. I would not stay here. I would not run that risk. I would make the choice to live my life in London."

"I'm going to get you to Gibraltar," Carradine replied, taking her hand and squeezing it at the wrist. He was not at all certain that it was the correct decision, taken as it was in the face of Bartok's seeming indifference to his plight, but he did not want to walk away or to let her down. "We're going to get on the boat and we're going to get you out of Morocco. Then I'll leave. When you're safely in Gibraltar, I'll go back to my life in London."

31

Then they came to the roadblock.

The first Carradine knew of it was Rafiq swearing under his breath and slowing to a crawl. There was a tailback of about forty cars in two lanes along the main road leading into Rabat. Carradine could see several police cars at the top of the queue, lights flashing, uniformed officials standing at different points on the road.

"Fuck," he said.

"Don't worry," Bartok told him. "Might not be for us. Arabs love a roadblock."

They inched forward. It was hot outside. Carradine began to sweat. He closed the window and asked Rafiq to switch on the air conditioner. It was quickly as cold as a fridge inside the car.

"Tell me about Patrick and Eleanor," she said.

Carradine assumed that Bartok was trying to take his mind off what was happening. Rafiq shunted forward the length of two vehicles and applied the brakes.

"They're a retired couple. Eleanor used to be a lawyer. I'd say Patrick is about fifteen years older than her, looks a bit like Cary Grant.

Very easygoing, very charming. Possible retired ladies' man. Liked the look of your photograph when I showed it to him."

Bartok smiled. "Go on."

Rafiq moved forward another ten feet.

"They live in Kent, eastern part of England . . ."

"I know where Kent is."

"They have a beautiful yacht. *Atalanta*. Custom-made. Showed me some photographs of it at the Mansour. I think you'll be comfortable."

"How did you meet them?"

Carradine remembered his first evening in Marrakech, trawling the souk for LASZLO. It seemed a lifetime ago.

"I was eating dinner in the Kasbah. Place des Ferblantiers. They were sitting at the next table."

Bartok turned to face him. A siren squawked in the distance.

"Sitting there when you arrived?"

Carradine realized why she was looking so apprehensive. She thought that he had been tricked.

"No," he said quickly. "They came in after me."

She looked out at the queue of traffic, visibly annoyed.

"Jesus Christ, Kit."

He leaned toward her. Rafiq briefly turned to look at him.

"I know what you're thinking," he said, trying to make his case. "They're Service re-treads, Moscow illegals, Agency personnel keeping an eye on me. That's not the case, I promise you."

"How can you be sure?"

"Instinct. Common sense."

"Brilliant!" she exclaimed, with heavy sarcasm. "So we are OK then. Your instinct as—what?—a *novelist* tells you that Patrick-who-looks-like-Cary-Grant and Eleanor-who-used-to-be-a-lawyer are normal everyday people. Are those the same instincts that told you to trust Robert Mantis?"

Carradine lost his temper.

"Do you want me to get out? Shall I just leave you here? Is that better? Is that what you want?"

Bartok tried to respond but he talked over her. Rafiq asked them to keep their voices down as he shunted the car forward.

"*Pas maintenant*," Carradine snapped and turned back to Bartok. "I'm trying to help you. I'm trying to do you a favor. What do you think are the chances of Patrick and Eleanor masquerading as a millionaire couple with an Oyster 575 on the *minuscule*, one-in-six-million probability that a British thriller writer might ask if he can sail up the coast of Morocco with them accompanied by his phantom girlfriend?"

"That's what you told them?" Bartok replied. Her anxiety had vanished as quickly as it had surfaced, to the point where she now seemed almost amused.

"Of course that's what I told them!" he said. "That's what we agreed."

"*Phantom* girlfriend?"

Carradine ignored her attempt to lighten the mood. He was still furious.

"Furthermore," he said, "how many intelligence services do you know that have a thousand dollars a night to spend on the Royal Mansour? If Patrick's a spook, if Eleanor is Kent's answer to Mata Hari, why don't they stay at the Radisson and save Her Majesty's government a fortune?"

Rafiq was almost at the top of the traffic queue. Carradine realized that Bartok was no longer listening to him. This infuriated him even more. She spoke to Rafiq rapidly in French, so fast that Carradine struggled to understand what she was saying. He asked her to repeat it.

"OK," she said. "I repeat." It was clear that she had already set aside their quarrel and was focused solely on negotiating their passage through the roadblock. "Here is the situation if they ask any questions." She nodded in the direction of the guards. "We are a couple. Not a phantom couple." To Carradine: a quick, let's-kiss-and-make-up smile. "We were staying in an Airbnb in Marrakech, OK? Rafiq is driving us to

Rabat. We've never met him before. We're flying home to London tomorrow."

Carradine leaned back in his seat, resigned to letting Bartok take
control. He committed her simple lies to memory, rehearsing them in
his mind, as a policeman in a blue uniform walked up to Rafiq's door.
He indicated that Rafiq should wind down the window. Bartok took a
good long look at the policeman and smiled the kind of smile that had
been working on men since she was about fourteen. Rafiq lowered the
window.

"As-Salaam Alaikum."

"Wa-Alaikum Salaam."

The policeman continued to speak to Rafiq in Arabic. He looked into
the car and nodded at Bartok. Bartok smiled back. He stepped to his
right and looked at Carradine. Carradine tried to smile from the backseat but he was still angry.

"Where are you from, please?" the policeman asked through the
window.

"We are from London," Bartok replied confidently. They were speaking in English.

"Where have you come from today?"

"From Marrakech," they both said in unison.

The policeman looked at the bag at Bartok's feet. Carradine dreaded
the moment at which they would be asked to show their passports. Rafiq
posed what sounded like a question, indicating something farther along
the road. The policeman did not react. Instead, he tapped on Carradine's
window and indicated that he should lower it. Carradine did so, his finger shaking as he reached for the switch.

"What is your name, please?"

Oh Christ.

"Christopher," Carradine replied.

"Mr. Christopher?"

Should he lie? If asked to show his passport, there was enough ambiguity in the presentation of Carradine's forenames that the cop could not accuse him of deliberately misleading the police.

"That's right. Christopher Alfred." He did not want to say the surname "Carradine."

"Christopher Alfred?"

"Yes." Bartok was becoming uneasy. Perhaps he shouldn't have evaded the question. Perhaps he should have said "Christopher Carradine" and taken his chances.

"What is your business in Rabat, please, Mr. Christopher Alfred?"

"Tourism," Carradine replied.

"You arrange tourism?"

"No, no." Carradine had been momentarily baffled by the question. "We're tourists. I'm visiting Morocco with my girlfriend."

"Phantom girlfriend," Bartok muttered.

The policeman looked up and stared along the line of cars. Carradine's heart was racing so fast he was concerned that it was affecting his appearance. He could feel his chest surging.

"OK, enjoy," the policeman replied. Without so much as a backward glance, he moved on to the next car in line. An official in front of Rafiq waved the car forward with a red baton.

Nobody uttered a sound as Rafiq engaged first gear and drove away from the roadblock. Carradine felt as if he had survived an examination by master interrogators. Bartok looked as calm and unruffled as a model having her picture taken in a photographer's studio. Only when they were at a safe distance, with the windows closed, did she whisper, "Thank God" and slap Rafiq on the thigh.

"You were brilliant," she said in French, turning to Carradine. "Christopher Alfred! Tourism! A fantastic answer."

"The training kicked in," Carradine replied, slightly bemused that his response had generated such enthusiasm. "I'm very experienced in these life-or-death situations."

"I knew the argument would work," she said.

Carradine was confused. "What?" he said.

"Something I was taught." He realized that she was referring to their squabble in the car. "We were going into a situation in which we were both tense, yes?"

"Yes."

"What does a guilty person look like? He looks calm, he tries to seem like he doesn't have a care in the world. But this calmness betrays him."

"I'm not sure I understand," Carradine replied. They had turned off the road and were heading into central Rabat.

"Who would get into an argument with his girlfriend while waiting in the queue for a police check?"

"An innocent person," Carradine replied.

"Exactly. My window was down. Maybe this policeman heard you shouting at me. Maybe he sees that you look distracted and annoyed with your girlfriend in the front. And your girlfriend in the front seat has a scowl on her face? Throws a flirtatious smile at the handsome young man in the nice police uniform . . . ?"

"Who trained you to think like that?" Carradine asked. He had never heard of such a technique, but marveled at its simplicity.

"I read it in a book," Bartok replied and asked if she could smoke one of his cigarettes.

32

Shortly after eight o'clock, Rafiq dropped them at Gare de Rabat-Ville, the main railway station in the center of the city. Bartok paid and thanked him for all that he and his family had done for her; Carradine saw that there were tears in her eyes as they embraced inside the car. They took their bags from the boot and banged on the roof as Rafiq pulled away.

"Let's get inside," he said.

They walked into the station and had only been inside for a few minutes when a young, bearded man in a white jilaba came up to them holding a homemade brochure displaying photocopied color photographs of a two-bedroom apartment on the seafront.

"Is very clean, very tidy, very cheap," he said. "How long you want stay?"

Carradine told him that they would only need the apartment for one night. Bartok tried to establish if he was the landlord but the young man—whose name was Abdul—was evasive on the subject. In the car they had discussed the importance of finding somewhere to stay that did not use a computerized booking system. They would almost certainly have to show Bartok's Hungarian passport to their host, perhaps

Carradine's as well. They hoped that whoever registered their details would log them, passing them to the authorities only after *Atalanta* had departed.

Abdul led them out of the station. He said that he had a car parked nearby and that they would drive to the apartment together. Carradine was uneasy but knew that they had little choice: doubtless there would be third parties involved in the transaction at every stage. He and Bartok could be shunted from place to place, from person to person, until they eventually arrived at the apartment. Anything was possible in Morocco. The important thing was not to show their faces for too long on the streets. Bartok was paranoid about satellite surveillance, all the more so now that the Agency also had Carradine in their sights. There was always the possibility that they might be spotted by a passerby.

Abdul led them across a busy street toward a large open square surrounded by trees and dotted with park benches. A distant trumpeter was busking the melody from "Michelle." Songbirds tweeted in the trees as they passed beneath them. Everything to Carradine seemed cleaner, sharper, more functional than Marrakech; he had the impression of a European city that was more affluent than anywhere else he had visited in Morocco. Rabat was the nation's capital, the residence of the king, filled with cops and diplomats, ministers and spies. As a consequence, Carradine felt exposed; it was as though a friend from London might appear around the corner at any moment.

"I don't like this city," Bartok whispered as Abdul led them toward a patisserie on the far side of the square. "Sooner we get to the apartment, the better."

"Me neither."

Abdul had other ideas.

"You wait here, please," he told them, indicating that his honored guests should take a seat at one of the tables outside the patisserie. There were customers eating pastries and drinking coffee in the late morning light.

"Why?" Carradine asked.

"I get car."

They looked at each other. It was inconceivable that Abdul was anything other than the man he appeared to be, but neither of them wanted to hang around in such a public place.

"Be quick," Carradine told him. "We'd really like to have some rest."

"Of course, monsieur." The Moroccan gave a low bow before hurrying off around the corner.

"Is it always like this?" Carradine asked.

"Not always."

"We might as well have a coffee," he suggested.

"Yes," Bartok replied. "And text the boat."

She took out the phone. Carradine passed her the sheet of paper. She typed Patrick and Eleanor's number into the contacts.

"Do you want to text or shall I speak to them?" Carradine asked.

"Text. Always," she said.

He knew that intelligence services could identify a person using voice recognition, just as he knew that a spy satellite, orbiting Morocco five hundred miles up, boasted cameras powerful enough to read a headline on the newspaper at the next table. Yet Carradine had never had cause to think that these technologies might be brought to bear on himself or on somebody he knew; they were just gimmicks in his books, details in a hundred Hollywood TV shows and movies. There was an awning over their table, providing both shade from the sun and protection from the all-seeing sky. Bartok was still wearing the long black wig, Carradine a pair of sunglasses and a Panama hat he had bought in the souk.

"I'll be back in a minute," Bartok told him, standing up and going inside.

Carradine assumed that she was off to the bathroom. A waiter stopped at their table. Carradine ordered a café au lait for Bartok and an espresso for himself. He yearned for his phone and laptop and felt an umbilical severing from his old life: what he would have given to check his emails, his WhatsApp messages, just to read that morning's edition of *The Times*. Instead he had only a prehistoric Nokia with which to send Patrick and Eleanor a simple text message painstakingly typed out on an antediluvian keyboard.

Hi. We have made it to Rabat. Having a lovely time and really looking forward to seeing you tomorrow morning. Stupidly lost my phone so using this temporary number. Is 8 a.m. still OK? Lilia very excited to see Atalanta—as am I!

Carradine pressed send and put the phone on the table. The waiter returned with the coffees. The espresso was served, as was the custom in Morocco, with a small bottle of water. Carradine opened it and drank the entire contents without bothering to pour it out. The trumpeter was now playing the theme from *The Godfather* as children ran among the carob trees in front of the patisserie. Carradine's table was positioned on a busy corner section of the square. Pedestrians were passing all the time. One of them, a frail, elderly beggar, was moving from table to table, holding out an arthritic hand as he pleaded for money. He was ignored by each of the customers in turn. Carradine leaned down to fetch his wallet, which was zipped into a side pocket of his case. He had some worn ten and twenty dirham notes—the equivalent of a couple of euros—which he could give to the elderly man. He retrieved the money and sat up as the beggar shuffled toward him. Bartok came back to the table just as he was pressing the money into the man's emaciated hand. She said nothing but smiled at the beggar, who thanked Carradine effusively before shuffling off.

"Got the phone?" she asked.

Carradine looked at the table. He knew instantly that it had been stolen.

"Fuck."

"What is it?" Bartok knew it too. He could tell by her reaction.

"The mobile. The cellphone. Did you pick it up?"

She shook her head, very slowly, coming to terms with what had happened.

"I leaned down for ten seconds to get my wallet. . . ."

Had the beggar taken it? Surely not. An accomplice? More likely an opportunistic thief had swiped it while moving in the flow of pedestrians passing the table.

"Jesus, Kit . . ."

They searched the ground beneath the table. Carradine frisked himself. He asked a young mother at the next table if she had seen anyone taking the phone. She shook her head in the manner of one who did not wish to become involved in somebody else's misfortune.

"What was on the SIM?"

Bartok did not answer him. She withdrew into silence. Carradine could not tell if she was irritated solely by his lapse in concentration or if the SIM contained vital information on which she had relied for months. Every useful number, every precious message: gone in the blink of an eye.

Abdul soon returned to the patisserie. Carradine told him about the theft. The young Moroccan expressed his sympathy but offered nothing in the way of practical solutions; he was keen only that his guests should accompany him to the apartment which had now been prepared for them.

Shouldering his bag, Carradine walked behind Bartok and Abdul as they made their way toward the car. He was furious with himself. The irritation and embarrassment he had felt when Bartok had told him about Mantis returned in full flood. Perhaps he wasn't cut out for the role in which he had cast himself. For the first time since he had arrived in Morocco, Carradine thought nostalgically of home, of the simple writer's life that had so frustrated him. He was not a man prone to self-pity; nor did he wish that he could click his fingers and somehow remove himself from the complications of Rabat and Lara Bartok. Nevertheless, he was tired of living so much on the edge of his wits. He wondered how Bartok had coped for so long and could only assume that she had enjoyed periods of time in which she had been secure and safely anonymous. He presumed that she had lost contact with old friends from Hungary or New York, but perhaps this was not the case. Did she have boyfriends? Carradine could not imagine how she would be able to build or sustain a relationship with another man, living as she did. He assumed that she took her pick of men, whenever desire took hold of her, then moved on before love had a chance to take hold. But what could he possibly know? All that was clear to him was that his own life, as problematic and dangerous as it had become, was nothing in comparison to the complexity of her own.

Watching Bartok as she spoke to Abdul, he felt a great sympathy for her, a surge of feeling for which he was rewarded with a smile as she opened the passenger door of the waiting car and climbed in. His sins had apparently been forgotten. The stolen phone was yesterday's news. Carradine was revived and joined her in the car with a strong desire to prove to Bartok, as well as to himself, that he could get them safely to Gibraltar. He had come this far, suffering only a bruised ego and a swollen right hand along the way. If Abdul came through for them and they could lay low in the apartment, there was every chance of leaving Rabat safely in the morning.

33

The bearded man standing on the crowded rush-hour platform at Oxford Circus was carrying a worn leather briefcase and a furled umbrella. It had been raining hard as he entered the station and his thinning hair was pasted to his scalp. Stephen Graham was a man with a lot on his mind. LASZLO had been found, yes, but nobody had seen hide nor hair of her for twenty-four hours. Ramón Basora had got sloppy, fallen in with the Americans—and paid with his life. Kit Carradine had vanished. Graham's hastily assembled house of cards had come crashing down. He had an ominous feeling that he would be next.

Graham had come from a meeting with Petrenko. Not so much a meeting as an interrogation. Moscow wanted to know what "Robert Mantis" knew about the search for Lara Bartok. Did he realize that she had been sighted in Morocco? Had he had any dealings with one "C. K. Carradine," a British writer attending a literary conference in Marrakech? Graham had denied all knowledge, fending off Petrenko's questions—*Is Kit Carradine working for the Service? Is he romantically involved with Bartok?*—as best he could. If Moscow knew that he had been trying to protect LASZLO, they would have him killed. If Petrenko came away from the meeting believing that Graham had deliberately tried to undermine a Kremlin-sanctioned operation to find Lara Bartok, he was finished.

What could he tell them? That he was in love with the estranged girlfriend of Ivan Simakov? That no woman had ever made him feel the way Lara had made him feel? That their brief relationship had been the most sublime and fulfilling of his life? They would think he was a fool who had lost his mind.

The discussion had taken place at the Langham Hotel. Petrenko, the master interrogator, playing the trusted confidant, the old friend, the world-weary spy. Masking his suspicion of Graham in lighthearted asides, posing questions that were not quite questions, leveling accusations that were never far from threats. Graham had felt that he had survived it all until the moment Petrenko mentioned Ramón. That was when he realized that he was cornered. If he was going to escape with his life, he knew that he would have to give something up.

So, yes, he admitted that he had sent Basora to Casablanca. No, that had nothing to do with LASZLO. Yes, he had heard that Basora had been found dead in his hotel room from a suspected drug overdose. No, he did not have any idea if third parties were involved in the death. Graham explained that he had an agent in Morocco—one Abdullah Aziz—whom he had instructed Ramón to meet at the Sheraton Hotel. Graham himself had not traveled to Casablanca in person because he had been too busy with other projects in London.

It had been hot in the hotel room. Graham had asked if he could open a window. As he did so, Petrenko picked up a black-and-white surveillance photograph from a table beside the bed. He showed it to Graham.

"Do you know this man?"

The man in the photograph was Sebastian Hulse. Graham could not remember how much, or how little, Moscow knew about the American. He tried to maintain a poker face. Should he feign ignorance? Should he say that he recognized Hulse as the Agency's man in Morocco? In the end, he settled on a version of the truth.

"I do. His name is Hulse. He works for the Americans. He was staying at the Sheraton. He befriended Ramón in the bar, took him to dinner, pretended he was a businessman from New York."

Petrenko seemed surprised by the candor of this answer. His wistful smile gave Graham hope.

"You mean Hulse suspected that Ramón was working for us?"

"I can't say. I assumed as much. I told him to break off contact. Next thing I knew, Ramón was being taken to a morgue in Casablanca."

He remembered receiving the text from Carradine, the photographs of Hulse and Ramón in Blaine's. He had wanted to simplify things, to fire Carradine so that he would no longer be in play.

"And you still cannot say who or what may have required him to pay this visit to the mortuary?"

Petrenko's expression betrayed the ghost of a smile. Graham hesitated. It was a toss-up between Hulse and Moscow. He could hardly accuse his own people of murder; better to lay the blame elsewhere.

"My money's on the Agency," he said. "But Ramón was always a maverick. Too much of a taste for fast women, for high-living. Didn't they say there were traces of cocaine in his room?"

"They did," Petrenko replied. "There were."

The distant rumble of an approaching train. Stephen Graham moved forward, pushing through the crowd. He hoped to secure a seat. He was worn out after the long conversation and his thighs were aching after an early morning run.

Two men were standing directly behind him. As the train came crashing through the tunnel, one of them placed a hand on the small of his back. The other put a grip on Graham's right arm.

He knew what they intended to do. He had been through the same training course; he had sanctioned the same hits. To give them credit, they had timed their movements to perfection. Turning around, Graham saw that the closest of the two men was wearing a baseball cap and what appeared to be a false beard. He had been given no time to react, no chance to duck or to move to one side.

He was finished.

34

The apartment was a large, two-bedroom conversion on the first floor of a house overlooking the ocean. With a firm throw from the roof, Carradine could have landed a rock in the Atlantic.

They had the place to themselves. The building was owned by a middle-aged woman who lived across the landing with her mother and two teenage daughters. The family greeted Carradine and Bartok like long-lost relatives, showing them around with the passion and enthusiasm of vendors trying to sell carpets in the souk. They were offered hot food and laundry, sightseeing tips, even a lift to the airport in the morning. Carradine explained that they would be leaving at dawn and had already booked a taxi with a friend. When asked by the landlady if they would be sharing the same room, Bartok took Carradine's hand and smiled beatifically in the direction of her elderly mother.

"Thank you, but we are not married," she said in perfect French. "Until then, we prefer to sleep in separate beds."

"Of course, mademoiselle," the landlady replied, her face a picture of admiration for such old-fashioned sexual mores. The teenage girls looked stunned.

"If we could just have some food this evening, that would be wonderful," Bartok continued. Carradine's cheeks were flushed with embarrassment. "Perhaps couscous? Some salad?"

None of it was too much trouble. The landlady requested only that they enjoy themselves and then closed the door so that the young couple could have some privacy. Minutes later, however, she came back into the apartment, asking if one of them could provide her with a passport.

Carradine fetched his own, as they had agreed, and watched as the landlady painstakingly transcribed his details—in Arabic—onto a registration form. Meanwhile, Bartok settled into what she described as the "more feminine" of the two bedrooms—a large room upholstered in pink and decorated with floral-patterned cushions—closing the door while she unpacked and took a shower. Carradine accepted the landlady's offer of tea and drank it on a small, enclosed balcony in his room while smoking a cigarette out of the window. Traffic was constant in both directions and the room was noisy, but he was glad to be in a place that both of them considered secure and relatively anonymous. By sheer good fortune, they had ended up in an apartment that was not overlooked by neighboring buildings. A man was selling pomegranates from a stall beneath Carradine's window. Across the Corniche, on a stretch of waste ground separating the shoreline from the road, a family was living out of a tent surrounded by oil drums and buffeted by the Atlantic wind. They were otherwise out of sight of strangers. Everything was damp to the touch: the sheets on Carradine's bed; the towels in the bathroom; even the sugar in the tiny packets the landlady placed beside the teapot. He thought again of the riad, of the festival organizers wondering what had become of him, but reckoned it would be at least forty-eight hours before anyone raised the alarm. There was no television nor radio in the apartment and therefore no means of keeping tabs on the developing story in Warsaw. Carradine laid a private bet with himself that the siege would already have been brought to an end. It was just a question of the death toll.

After finishing his tea, he took a shower. The ceiling was so low that he had to sit on a plastic stool while dousing himself with lukewarm water. He shaved and changed into some clean clothes, risked a blast of aftershave, then knocked on Bartok's door.

"Come in!" she said.

She was lying on the double bed wearing a pair of denim shorts and a T-shirt. Her blond hair was damp and tousled from the shower. The room smelled of perfume and the warm sea air.

"You packed my bag well," she said, kicking a leg in the air. He saw that she was reading a book.

"Lots of practice," Carradine replied.

He wished they were together, that they could spend the rest of the day and night in bed, passing the long hours until it was time to leave for the boat. In any other situation, with any other woman, he would have tried his luck.

"What's on your mind?" she asked.

"Nothing much." He walked toward the window, saw the same view he had been looking at while drinking his tea. "We have a lot of time to kill."

"Lots," she said.

"Good book?"

"I've read it before."

She flung it across the room. Carradine caught it like a fly-half as it passed behind his waist. It was a French translation of *The Sheltering Sky*.

"Ah, doomed love," he said, trying to sound sophisticated.

"The wife is called Kit."

He pretended to be furious. "Really?" He flicked through the pages, searching for the name.

"Really," Bartok replied.

"Don't they end up dying in Morocco?" There was a picture on the back of Debra Winger in the arms of John Malkovich. "She gets sick. Or he gets sick. I can't remember."

"Don't spoil it."

"I thought you said you'd read it before?"

"Years ago."

Carradine threw it back. This time the book bounced off the side of the mattress and landed on the floor. Bartok leaned over the bed to fetch it. Her T-shirt rode up on her back. Carradine stole a glance at her waist, tanned and lithe, blond hairs at the base of her spine. She looked up and caught him staring and for an instant the time stopped between them.

The doorbell rang. They continued to stare at each other. Carradine walked to the door. The landlady walked in carrying a tray covered in plates and cutlery. She apologized for interrupting and said that the food was almost ready. One of the teenage daughters followed her in, holding a bowl of salad and some fruit. Carradine noticed how respectful they were toward Bartok, staring at her as though she were a visiting dignitary. Within a few minutes the family had left them in a traditional, tiled reception room at the back of the apartment, plates of chicken couscous, cheese and pasta salad spread out in front of them.

"Do you want to go down to the marina, see if your friends are there?" Bartok asked.

"Together?" Carradine replied.

"No, no."

Her answer was quick and dismissive, as if the notion that she could walk around Rabat in plain sight was nonsensical.

"I don't think I should go," he said. "Even alone. If somebody picks me up, they'll eventually find you."

"Only if you crack under questioning."

Carradine saw her grin as he spooned some couscous into a bowl. "I'd give you up in a heartbeat," he said. "I bet you there's a reward on your head."

Traffic was growling past on the Corniche. He was still thinking about the lost moment in the bedroom. Yet Bartok's mood seemed to have changed.

"I don't want you to be bored," she said. "You can go for a walk. It would be fine."

"I'm perfectly happy."

"You strike me as a trapped person, Kit. Like a caged bird."

"Is that right?" He was by turns flattered by the description and startled that she had intuited his inner restlessness. "I don't feel like that at the moment."

"No, perhaps not. Why would someone do what you have done?"

"I don't understand," he said.

"Become a spy."

"But I'm not a spy." He knew that she was referring to his work for Mantis, but did not want to pretend to be something that he was not.

"I realize that," she replied. "But many people would not have agreed to work for their country as you did. It was an old-fashioned thing to do. Patriotism. A sense of duty. Of course you were not to know that Stephen Graham was a liar, but this does not really matter. You acted in good faith. You wanted to help. You had the adventure inside you, the restlessness. Does your life satisfy you, Kit?"

Several seconds passed before Carradine answered the question.

"In some ways," he replied, taken aback by Bartok's directness. "I'm very lucky. I'm my own boss. I make my own rules. Nobody gets to tell me what time to show up for work, what time I can go home."

"This is important to you? Not to be told what to do?"

It was like being scrutinized by someone who had not yet made up her mind whether or not to like him.

"I prefer it that way," he said. "But it comes at a price. I've started to realize that my life is very solitary. I have no colleagues, no meetings, no team. . . ."

"You have to motivate yourself. . . ."

"Precisely."

He ate some of the couscous.

"Are you married?" Bartok asked.

Carradine almost spat out the food. "No!" he said. "Why so many questions?"

"I am just getting to know you," she said, touching her lips.

"But you know that I'm not married. . . ."

"Do I?"

He realized that the subject had never come up between them.

"Well I'm not," he said.

"Do you have a girlfriend?"

Was she making small talk or clearing the romantic ground? Carradine could not tell. He ate a hunk of bread and said that he wasn't seeing anybody in London.

"What about *outside* London?"

"Nowhere." A sheep, tethered in a nearby yard, let out an anguished cry. "That's probably our dinner," he said. "What about you? Did you have somebody in Marrakech?"

Bartok shook her whole body in a mime of discomfort.

"No. Ivan finished me with men. After him, I was done."

"You mean you're still in love with him?"

Carradine dreaded the answer. The idea of this beautiful, alluring woman holding an eternal candle for the martyred Simakov was debilitating.

"No!" she exclaimed, with disbelief. "I was trying to say . . ." She hesitated. "I was trying to say that I was so disappointed by him that I lost all faith in men."

"In what way?"

"In the sense that he began as somebody I admired. An idealist, a fighter. He was clever and imaginative, full of energy. But he became vain and angry. He betrayed the principles on which he stood."

"Which were?"

Quite apart from the pleasure of sitting and talking to Bartok, Carradine was aware of his own good fortune. To be able to speak to someone who had known Ivan Simakov so intimately was a rare opportunity. It was like listening to a first draft of history.

"Resurrection was intended to be a nonviolent organization targeted against specific people. We always said there would be no leadership structure, no role like that for Ivan. But he quickly became obsessed with the idea that the only way we were ever going to change people was by fighting them. I profoundly disagreed with this. I also saw the way that he cultivated his fame. It became an obsession which has now of course resulted in Ivan being regarded—mistakenly, of course— as some kind of deity. He was nothing of the sort. He was like all of us. He was both good and bad and parts in between. None of us are saints, Kit."

"Speak for yourself."

She made a tutting sound and pushed him playfully with her hand. They finished their food. Carradine offered Bartok a cigarette. He lit it for her, opening a window onto the street.

"What did he feel about you?" he asked. He was aware that he was repeatedly, almost fixatedly, looking at her neck.

"I think he loved me," she said. She was being modest. Simakov had clearly been obsessed with her. "I think he continued to love me. At least that is what I heard from his friends at around the time he was killed. In some ways I still feel responsible for his death."

"Why?"

"Because I think losing me made him angry. He wanted to lash out. He became more vicious, more politicized in his general behavior. He was encouraging Resurrection activists into greater and greater violence with his statements. He was reckless to go to Russia."

This was all true. Carradine remembered the period leading up to Simakov's death, a phase in which he himself had begun to lose faith in whatever it was that had made so many people in the West sympathetic to Resurrection in the first instance. He spoke of his own attitudes toward the movement and told Bartok that he had witnessed the kidnapping of Lisa Redmond. She questioned him forensically on what he had seen, almost as if she was nostalgic for her own days on the front line. For the next two hours they sat in the reception room smoking and talking until Bartok said that she needed to sleep. Carradine knew that she wanted to be alone and went to his room where he tried, unsuccessfully, to doze. When he knocked on her door at eight o'clock, she did not answer. He ate some of the leftover food and read his book for an hour, drinking the Johnnie Walker and wondering if he should have taken up Bartok's suggestion of going to the marina to look for Patrick and Eleanor. What if there had been a change of plan? What if they had decided to leave Rabat without them? They might have sent a text to the stolen mobile but it was now too late.

Just after ten Carradine heard Bartok moving around in her room. He asked through the closed door if she wanted something to eat but she told him that she was not hungry.

"I'll wait until the morning," she said. "I'm just going to rest."

He wondered if he had said something during their long lunchtime conversation that had upset her. Perhaps she had been thinking of him romantically, but had decided against it. The friction between them, the possibility that they might become lovers, appeared to have dissipated. Carradine wished her a good night and returned to his room. Soon afterward the landlady knocked on the door of the apartment and handed him a tray on which she had placed a small pot of tea, two glasses and some baklava. He thanked her and took the tray to his room without bothering to disturb Lara a second time. He had concluded that solitude was her default state; she was not used to spending so much time in close proximity to another person. Perhaps she did not want Carradine to think that they were going to become involved; perhaps she was simply taking her time with him. He was not sure.

He took the tray to the window and looked out over the beach. The wind was howling in from the Atlantic, buffeting the shakily erected tent on the stretch of waste ground in front of his room. Thin clouds of yellowed sand and dust were swirling along the Corniche. The landlady had lined the tray with a fresh sheet of newspaper. Carradine put a lump of sugar into a glass, poured the tea and lifted up the plate of baklava. He was on the point of biting into a small, honey-soaked sponge when his eye was drawn to the newspaper. He set the plate to one side and turned the tray ninety degrees. It was covered in Arabic script. There was a black-and-white photograph of a bearded man hidden within the text. There was no mistaking his face. It was Ramón.

Carradine looked more carefully, wondering if his eyes were again playing tricks on him. He studied the photograph more closely. He could not understand what had been written about Ramón nor why his face was appearing in a Moroccan daily newspaper. Was it a business story—or something more sinister?

Picking up the keys to the flat, Carradine walked outside, crossed the landing and knocked on the landlady's front door. It was some time before she answered. She was adjusting her veil as she opened the door.

"I'm sorry to disturb you so late," said Carradine.

"It is no problem," she replied, in faltering English.

He thrust the newspaper toward her.

"This man." He pointed at the photograph of Ramón. The newspaper was slightly crumpled and sticky. When Carradine tapped Ramón's face with his finger he left a smudge on the bridge of his nose. "Can you tell me what this story is about? Can you translate it?"

He wondered, for a horrible moment, if the landlady was illiterate and would be unable to do what he had asked. Had he just humiliated her? Would she have to wake up one of the teenage girls to ask them to translate? Yet after a moment's hesitation she took the newspaper and began to read the article.

"It says he was a Spanish tourist." She was frowning at the text, as though it contained grammatical errors or content that was causing her offense. "Visiting Casablanca. He has died."

Carradine had somehow known that she would say this.

"Died? *How?*"

"They say with drugs. An overdose of cocaine. He was staying at the Sheraton hotel."

Carradine stood in silence, absorbing what he had been told. He was so shaken that he asked no more questions, merely thanked the landlady and went back to his room. He poured himself a glass of whiskey, wondering if he should wake Bartok. But what would be the point? It would only unsettle her. He could only assume that Ramón had been murdered. Surely there was no possibility that he had accidentally overdosed on cocaine? The coincidence of his death, with Hulse and the Russians at large, was too stark. And yet what proof did he have of foul play? What purpose did it serve to assassinate Ramón? All Carradine knew for certain was that they must get out of Rabat in the morning. If the Russians were going after anybody associated with LASZLO, then he was next on the list.

He drank a glass of water, took a sleeping pill and set his alarm for five. The sun was due to rise at half-past six. He had agreed with Lara to leave the apartment under cover of darkness and to be at the marina at first light. For the next half hour, he lay on his bed fully clothed, listening to the tick of the air conditioner and to the low roar of the passing traffic. Driving images of the dead Ramón from his mind, he waited for sleep to take him.

35

he police lights woke him.

There were no curtains on the windows in Carradine's room. A bright orange beam was strobing against the walls. At first, he thought that he was in the last stages of a dream. Then he saw the lights and felt his heart jolt as though it had been hit by an electric charge. He got out of bed and walked toward the balcony window, trying to remain out of sight.

He crouched down and peered through the window. Two police cars were parked on the opposite side of the Corniche. Three cops, dressed in the same uniforms as the men at the roadblock, were standing on the pavement beneath a date palm. They were facing in the direction of the ocean. One of them was speaking on a walkie-talkie.

The game was up. They had been found. Police investigating the death of Ramón Basora had established a link to Carradine and run him to ground. The landlady had betrayed them. It was only a matter of time before the police stormed the apartment. Carradine wondered if Bartok had seen the lights. He went out into the passage and knocked on her door. There was no answer. He knocked again, this time more loudly.

Still no response. Had she already fled? He turned the handle and walked in.

She was asleep on the bed, naked but for a single white sheet covering her calves and the backs of her thighs. She was breathtakingly beautiful. Carradine felt that he was trespassing on her privacy but he had to wake her. He knelt beside the bed, gently touching her shoulder.

"What is it?" she said sleepily.

She turned over and smiled. It was as though she had been expecting him. She did not seem in any way self-conscious about her nakedness.

"Outside," he said. "Police."

Bartok immediately wrapped the sheet around her and sat up.

"Here?" she replied. She walked toward the window. There was a blanket blocking out the light. She looked out at the Corniche through a narrow gap on one side of the fabric. "How long have they been there?"

Carradine told her that the lights had woken him up only moments earlier.

"What time is it?" she asked, looking to see if he was wearing a watch.

"Almost five."

"Wait."

She had seen something. He stood behind her and looked out through the same narrow gap. His chest was pressed against her back; he could feel the warmth of her body, the shape of her.

"What is it?"

"They're going to the beach."

Bartok pulled the blanket back a little farther. Carradine stepped to one side. One of the cars had driven off so that only one police light remained, sending a clockwise beam, like the beacon from a lighthouse, sweeping across the beach. The headlights of the car were pointing at the ocean. Carradine realized what was happening. The police were clearing the family from the tent. One of them was ushering a woman onto the rocky shoreline while a second policeman, carrying a torch, gathered up their belongings. A child, no older than three or four years old, was being carried in the arms of a man wearing shorts and a dark T-shirt. He put the child down on top of one of the oil drums.

"They're not for us," he said. "I'm sorry I woke you."

"It's fine." Bartok settled her fingertips briefly on his arm. She released the blanket so that the room was in almost total darkness. "We have to be up anyway."

He told her about Ramón. She was surprised, but not shocked. They showered and packed and carried their bags to the door. As Carradine was leaving the keys on a side table in the hall, the landlady's mother peered out from the neighboring apartment and wished them well.

"*Merci pour tout,*" Bartok whispered.

"*Oui, merci,*" said Carradine, and they crept downstairs to the street.

The second police vehicle had gone. The tent had been cleared from the beach leaving only a scattering of oil drums and the black patch of an extinguished fire. The Corniche was deserted save for the occasional passing car. They stood beneath the balcony of Carradine's room waiting for a taxi for more than ten minutes and had almost given up hope when a dented beige Mercedes rounded the corner and pulled in to collect them. The recalcitrant, elderly driver spoke incomprehensible French. They were obliged to give him directions to the marina using a mixture of English, French and hand signals. They drove to the end of the Corniche and joined a road which passed beneath the walls of the old Medina. Carradine could see the lights of the marina to the north, across the Bou Regreg River. He prayed that *Atalanta* was still in dock, that Patrick and Eleanor were fast asleep in their bunks. He was pointing to the bridge which would take them across the narrow river to the marina when it became clear that the driver was refusing to take them.

"*Non.* No go," he said, spluttering at the wheel. "*Pas permit.*"

"*Pourquoi?*" said Carradine.

"No go! *Pas possible! Là!*"

There was a roundabout at the bottom of the bridge. The driver made a full turn and began to drive back in the direction from which they had come.

"*Attends!*" said Carradine, becoming annoyed. "Where are we going?"

It was infuriating to be at the mercy of a moody geriatric who refused to take them where they wanted to go. Carradine produced a fifty-dirham note and waved it at the driver as a bribe, but still he refused to go back. Bartok explained that there was most probably a local law preventing taxi drivers from leaving the city limits; he would lose his license if he crossed the bridge. As if to confirm this, the old man stopped at a set of traffic lights, then made a sudden right turn into a car park at the edge of the river.

"*Bateau,*" he spat. It was as if his mouth were full of chewing tobacco. "*Bateau.*"

Only after he had said the word another three times did Carradine understand that they were being told to take a boat across the channel. Realizing that he had little choice other than to comply, he paid the driver and removed the luggage from the boot. Two men were sleeping on a low wall running along the length of the car park. One of them sat up and waved at Carradine as the taxi drove off. There was a smell of fish guts and salt water.

"Can you take us across?" Bartok asked.

The man shrugged, as if to suggest that it was too early in the morning to make a crossing. The landing point was less than two hundred meters away on the opposite bank; they could have swum across in a couple of minutes.

"How much?" Carradine asked in French.

The man eventually conceded and they settled on an extortionate price for the short crossing. Carradine carried the bags to a wooden jetty covered in fishing nets and coils of rope. Two skiffs were tied up alongside. There was the same overpowering smell of landed fish. The boatman indicated that they should climb into the farthest of the two skiffs.

It was dark and hard to make out the distance between objects: at one point Bartok momentarily lost her balance as her foot landed on a loose wooden plank. Carradine steadied her, helping her down into the skiff, holding her hand as she stepped onto a narrow seat in the stern. He passed the bags, one by one, to the boatman, who was holding one of the oars in his free hand.

"Watch your feet," Bartok warned as Carradine prepared to step into the boat. "It's wet."

He aimed for a point beside her but, inevitably, felt his foot land in a puddle of water. He sat on the seat as the boatman pushed off, resting the foot on a wooden strut. Watching the slow movement of the oars, looking out at the dark channel and the distant lights of the Medina, listening to the sound of the water lapping against the skiff, Carradine knew that this would ordinarily have been a moment for the notebook. But he was so focused on the goal of reaching the marina, and so distracted by his desire for Bartok, that the responsibilities of his profession seemed to belong to a completely different person.

Within three minutes they had crossed the channel. The boatman deposited them at a jetty on the Mellah side of the Bou Regreg. The sun was beginning to rise. They shared a cigarette beside a line of outboard motors attached to a wall at the far end of the jetty. They were hungry and wanted to eat breakfast but there were no cafés or restaurants in sight, only empty modern apartment blocks running east in the direction of the marina.

They crossed a narrow strip of waste ground and walked along a deserted road as the call to prayer rose from the distant Medina. There were no cars parked on the street, no early morning pedestrians heading to mosque or taking a dawn stroll. Carradine was reminded of a deserted movie set on a studio backlot and felt that, at any moment, a posse of cops would burst out of an abandoned building and surge forward to arrest them. He tried to distract himself by thinking practically about Patrick and Eleanor. They would need to be convinced that his relationship with "Lilia" was genuine and that there was no hidden motive behind Carradine's sudden desire to leave Morocco by boat. At the same time, Bartok would have to negotiate customs and immigration using the Hudak passport. If word had got out that she was on the run, or that Carradine had disappeared from the riad, they were finished.

"We're going to have to pretend to be together," he said.

"I know that."

"I said that we'd been dating for about six months. They're going to expect us to share a cabin."

"I know that, too." She shot Carradine a mischievous smile.

"It's just that I don't think they're going to believe that I'm going out with a born-again Christian. . . ."

It was awkward broaching the subject. He wished that he had kept his mouth shut. Bartok put him out of his misery.

"Don't worry," she said. "You don't have to be so English about it. Do I look like the kind of woman who would wait until marriage to sleep with you? We can share a cabin and that is fine."

Carradine spent the next thirty seconds wondering what Bartok had meant by the word "fine." He did not want to get into a longer discussion about how they should behave in front of Patrick and Eleanor. He assumed that Bartok would play her part convincingly and that he would not have to change his own behavior too drastically. It was common in espionage to role-play the part of a couple, though Carradine had never written about an operation of that type in his fiction. As a consequence, he had not had cause to think too deeply about the mechanics of such a deceit. He was sure that body language would play a part, as well as the appearance of a certain easefulness in Bartok's company. But perhaps he was overthinking things and there was no need to be concerned.

Rounding a corner at the end of the street, Carradine sighted the tops of masts and a modern, open-air café on a terrace overlooking the marina. He could hear the ping of halyards, the cry of seagulls on the wind. A man was sitting at one of the tables, deep in conversation on a mobile phone. His back was turned to them and he appeared to be in a state of agitation. It was not clear if he was a customer or a member of staff who had arrived early for work. On closer inspection, he turned out to be Patrick Lang.

"I am telling you . . ." Carradine could hear snatches of his conversation. "They're arriving this morning. At any moment. We had a text message last night . . ."

Bartok took Carradine's hand, pulling him back, sensing the danger. At that moment Patrick turned in his chair and saw that they were walking toward him. Lowering his voice, he quickly ended the call and stood up to greet them.

"There you are! I was just talking about you."

He looked flustered, as if he had been caught in the act of lying. Carradine wondered who the hell he had been speaking to.

"Hello," he said. "Sorry we're early."

Patrick slipped the phone into his back pocket and ran a hand through his hair as he nodded at Bartok. A pair of sunglasses hung from the collar of his canary yellow polo shirt. He seemed distracted and strung out in a way that was completely out of character.

"Yes," he replied. "You didn't answer my text."

"We lost yet another phone." Carradine knew that it was now too late to turn back. If Patrick had alerted Hulse or the Russians to their arrival, they were finished. "This is my girlfriend," he said. "The famous Lilia."

Patrick recovered his equilibrium and made a spectacle of falling for the Bartok charm, kissing the top of her hand as if the ghost of Cary Grant were indeed living inside him.

"Delighted to meet you," he said, offering to take her bag. "Kit said you were very beautiful and he didn't misinform. What happened to the phone?"

Carradine explained that the mobile had been stolen and apologized for not confirming their arrival. Patrick waved away his apologies and ordered three cappuccinos from the waitress. His increasingly relaxed manner made Carradine feel that at any moment they were going to be surrounded by Moroccan police.

"So you're Hungarian?"

"Born and bred," Bartok replied. If she was wary of him, she did not show it. Instead, Carradine was treated to a twenty-minute master class in deception as Bartok spoke of her childhood in Budapest, her work as a private tutor in London, her lifelong fascination with boats and the ocean.

"When Kit told me that you had invited us to come with you on your beautiful yacht, it was the happiest moment," she said, touching Patrick's wrist and speaking with a tenderness that almost convinced Carradine she was telling the truth. "We have changed our flights to go home from Gibraltar. You are so generous. Both of you so kind."

They ate breakfast undisturbed. Carradine concluded that Patrick had been speaking to a member of his family on the telephone and that there was nothing to worry about. Having finished their food, Patrick suggested that they walk down to the boat where Eleanor was waiting for them. Carradine settled the bill, shouldered the bags and followed him out of the café. At no point did Bartok shoot Carradine a look of amused complicity or appear to take any pleasure in their shared deceit. She had dropped into the character of Lilia Hudak solely for the purposes of survival and would play the role only for as long as it was required of her.

"We'll get you settled in, then you'll have to go and see immigration," Patrick announced. They were walking down a gangplank toward a network of pontoons at the entrance to the marina. A young couple with two small children passed them in the opposite direction, nodding at Carradine as he took in the sights of the marina. Patrick pointed ahead at *Atalanta*, sixty feet of teak and fiberglass nestled between two

gigantic Qatari-registered gin palaces with crew in pressed white uniforms scrubbing the decks. She was a thing of beauty, gleaming in the
early morning sun. A red ensign was flying from the stern, rippling in
the slight breeze. Bartok gasped as she stepped on board, walking across
a narrow gangplank connecting the yacht to the pontoon.

"Extraordinary," she said.

Steering wheels were positioned on the port and starboard side of a
cockpit protected by a large canvas roof. A hatch at the far end led into
the interior of the yacht. Eleanor was sitting on one side of the master
cabin at a wooden table spread with the remnants of a classic British
breakfast: triangles of half-eaten toast; pots of Marmite and Oxford
marmalade; miniature packets of Corn Flakes and All-Bran. It was
like a glimpse of home, but for the second time that morning, Carradine
had the sudden, giddy sense that they were walking into a trap.

"Look who I found," Patrick called out with forced cheeriness as he
came down the steps. "They were early."

Eleanor was dressed in dark blue linen trousers and a Breton sweater.
A pair of pajamas and a dressing gown with a White Company label
were draped over the back of the leather seat beside her. She removed a
pair of half-moon spectacles. Just as Patrick had seemed flustered and
evasive when they had first spotted him at the café, there was also a palpable change in Eleanor's demeanor. She looked tired, giving off an air
of impatient agitation. Carradine wondered if there had been an early
morning row.

"Hello," she said, shaking his hand without moving closer to offer a
kiss. "This must be the mysterious Lilia."

Carradine was certain that he caught a flash of wariness in Eleanor's
first glance at Bartok. Did she know the truth about her? Bartok remained in character, smiling beatifically. *What a beautiful boat. So
kind of you to invite us.* Was it Carradine's imagination or was Eleanor
looking for a chink in her armor, for some tiny piece of evidence that
would convince her that their seemingly innocent voluntary crew were

fugitives on the run from the law? Standing in the cabin, watching the two women becoming awkwardly and hesitatingly acquainted, he had to tell himself to remain calm; that whatever circumspection he detected in Eleanor's mood was most likely the aftermath of a row or the natural wariness of a wife who was protective of her husband and all-too-aware that Lilia Hudak was a beautiful young woman.

"Your boat's not at all what I expected," he said, setting his bag on the ground and taking in the state-of-the-art navigation equipment, the shelves of Everyman books, the wood-lined passages leading stern and aft.

"She does us very well," Patrick replied as Eleanor stepped past him.

"My husband and I sleep up here," she said, indicating two separate cabins—one in the bow, another on the portside—both with unmade beds. It was as though she was providing a visual demonstration of the tensions that existed in the marriage.

"It's all so modern," Bartok observed, plainly trying to think of something to fill the silence.

"Oh yes, Patrick likes all the mod cons," Eleanor replied coolly.

She showed them a bathroom on the starboard side before turning back toward the main cabin. "You'll be sleeping here," she said, leading them through a well-stocked galley toward a master cabin in the stern. There was a large double bed beneath the cockpit and a frosted glass door leading to what appeared to be an en-suite bathroom. This would be the room Carradine was to share with Bartok for the next three days. "There's a shower, lots of hot water. Hopefully you'll be comfortable."

"Very," said Carradine, feeling simultaneously as though he had won the jackpot and yet stumbled on one of the most awkward romantic entanglements of his life.

"This is how the TV works," Eleanor continued, banging a button on the bedside table with noticeable force. A flat-screen television rose up from a cupboard on the galley side of the cabin. "State of the art. Apparently."

Perhaps Eleanor was annoyed that she had been obliged to give up the cabin to her guests. The channel was set to Spanish Eurosport. Cyclists wearing Lycra and aerodynamic helmets were bombing around a velodrome.

"So why don't you settle in? We'll see you when we see you."

The two women exchanged wary smiles as Eleanor turned to leave.

"Lovely," said Bartok. "Thank you so much."

Carradine peered through a porthole. He could see Patrick walking back in the direction of the café, again speaking agitatedly on his mobile phone. Who the hell was he talking to? A mistress? His daughter? Hulse?

"Nice place," said Bartok, unaware of Carradine's disquiet.

"Very," he said, closing the door of the cabin. He sat on one side of the double bed. "Nice digs."

The commentary on the cycling was loud enough to disguise their conversation.

"Is she OK?" Bartok asked, nodding in the direction of the main cabin.

"I think they had a row," he whispered.

"Right." She walked to the far side of the room, looking out of the same porthole. Carradine assumed that Patrick was now too far away to be spotted. "You are a very clever man, Kit Carradine."

"Me?" he said. "Why?"

"Finding us such a beautiful way of escape."

Bartok turned to look at him. She touched the ceiling of the cabin and the padded wall beside her, as though trying to acclimatize herself to the latest in a long line of strange, impermanent homes. Quite apart from his concerns about Patrick, Carradine was conscious that they still needed to clear immigration. He took out his passport and placed it on the bed.

"Shall we go together or is it easier for you to do it alone?"

At first it looked as though Bartok had not understood what he was asking. Then she nodded and sat on the bed beside him.

"I want to go with you," she said.

Suddenly she leaned forward, kissing him. The intensity of the kiss, the unexpectedness of it, stripped Carradine of any notion that she might have been acting out of practical necessity. The softness of it was so pleasurable that he grabbed her by the waist and pulled her close against him. No part of him believed that Bartok was engaged in a performance, that she was trying to carry off an illusion of romance. He could sense the desire in her, the excitement, just as he could feel his own.

"What was that for?" he said.

"For everything," she replied, kissing him again, gently and tenderly, on the cheek. "Now let's go and do what we have to do."

36

They walked along a metalled road toward a group of prefabricated buildings overlooking the entrance to the marina. A tram passed overhead, moving toward the bridge connecting Mellah to the old city of Rabat. A television was visible through the window of a deserted restaurant showing a Moroccan news report on the siege in Warsaw. Carradine knocked on the window in the hope of being allowed inside but there was no answer. It was not yet nine o'clock and already very hot. Bartok had put on a hat as protection against the sun.

"It was never supposed to be like this," she said, gesturing toward the television. The picture had frozen on a bird's-eye view of the Sejm, which appeared to be on fire. "Large-scale attacks. Innocent people killed as a consequence. These people are no different to terrorists, to the Chechens or ISIS."

Carradine took her hand.

"If they arrest me or refuse to let me leave Morocco," she said, "I want you to go on without me."

"That's not going to happen."

"I am serious, Kit." She stopped and turned to him, touching his face.

Carradine wondered if she was acting for the benefit of anybody who happened to be watching: a passing immigration officer; Eleanor on the deck of *Atalanta*. "They might say my entry stamp is too old. They might want to know why I have been in Morocco for such a long time."

"When did you arrive?" Carradine asked. He had not thought to look at the dates on the Hudak passport.

"Five months ago."

It didn't seem too long. Surely she could talk her way around the problem?

"Just say you've been recovering from an illness and I flew out from London to fetch you."

"They might not believe me. Five months is a long time."

Carradine was concerned by her sudden lack of confidence. It was the first time that he had seen Bartok display any sign of self-doubt.

"Just tell a version of the truth. Say you rented a flat in Marrakech. I came out to appear at the literary festival. We were offered the chance to leave on a boat owned by a couple who like my books. Simple."

She squeezed his hand as though she were trying to convince her-self that Carradine was right.

"OK," she said. They began walking again. The customs buildings were less than a hundred meters away. "If you say so."

He suddenly remembered their argument in the car the day before.

"Is this one of your tricks?" he asked.

Bartok bristled.

"What do you mean?"

"In the car yesterday, you engineered an argument. Are you genu-inely worried about this or just trying to give that impression to any-one who might be watching?"

She let go of his hand. Carradine realized that he had made a mistake. He had questioned the authenticity of her behavior just at the moment when she had decided to show him a more vulnerable side of her nature.

"I'm worried," she said. "I'm worried all the time."

He had glimpsed the state of permanent apprehension in which she lived. She disguised it with good humor and bonhomie but the months on the run had taken their toll.

"I'm sorry," he said, annoyed to have misjudged the situation. He held her waist. "We're going to get through this. They don't know who you are. They won't recognize you. It's too soon for anyone in London to worry that I've not been in touch. They won't be waiting for us."

"You don't know that. You can't guarantee that."

The passport office was a nondescript wooden shed not much larger than Carradine's room at the riad. Three uniformed officials were seated at desks covered in ashtrays and paperwork. Cigarette smoke hung in the air; there was an absence of natural light. Carradine knocked on the open door and walked in. Bartok removed her hat as the closest, and youngest, of the immigration officers looked up from his desk.

"*Oui?*"

Carradine explained in French that they were staying on board *Atalanta*, the Oyster 575 moored in the marina. The captain, Patrick Lang, and his wife, Eleanor, had already passed through immigration. Carradine was their friend, a British citizen traveling with his girlfriend, Lilia Hudak, a Hungarian. They wanted to clear passport control and to set off for Gibraltar.

The immigration officer looked at them carefully. He stared at Bartok. Carradine was certain that she had been recognized. As if to confirm this, the official called out to his colleague at a desk on the far side of the shed.

"Mahmud."

An older man with a heavy beard, wearing the same light blue uniform, beckoned Carradine and Bartok forward.

"Where are you coming from, please?" he asked in English.

"From Marrakech," Bartok replied.

The man looked at her with an expression of distaste, as if he had expected Carradine to answer the question.

"And what were you doing in Marrakech?"

"My girlfriend hasn't been very well," Carradine replied. He was aware that he was lying to a Moroccan official who had the power to arrest and imprison him. "She picked up a virus in London. She was recuperating in Marrakech."

A chair scraped back behind him, the grind of metal on the hard wooden floor. The younger official who had spoken to them at the door stood up and walked toward them. He settled in a seat beside Mahmud and stared at Carradine, seemingly with the deliberate intention of unsettling him.

"What does it mean, 'picked up virus'?"

Bartok took half a step forward and explained what Carradine had said, this time in French. Mahmud again looked at her as though it was beneath his dignity to have formal dealings with a woman.

"You feel sick now?" he asked.

"I am fine." Bartok produced a relaxed, summery smile. Carradine was boiled by the heat. There was no air-conditioning in the hut, only a fan in the corner of the room which was making no difference to the quality of the thick, smoky air.

"And you?"

Mahmud had directed the question at Carradine. For a reason that he was afterwards not able to explain, Carradine reached into the back pocket of his trousers and took out his passport. Intending to hand it across the desk, he instead managed to lose his grip on it. The passport sailed over the desk and fell to the ground behind the two officials.

"Shit!" he exclaimed. "Sorry."

The third man, seated at his desk in the center of the hut, looked over and grunted. It was not clear whether he was laughing at what had happened or expressing some measure of disapproval. Mahmud slowly turned around and leaned over in his chair, plucking the passport from the ground.

"That is not what I asked," he said. "I asked what you were doing here in Rabat."

As Carradine answered the question, Mahmud handed the passport to the younger official, who began to study it with forensic attention. A seagull clacked in the marina.

"I am a writer. I was invited to a literary festival in Marrakech. We went together—"

The younger official interrupted him.

"But you flew into Casablanca."

Carradine felt that he was being cross-examined by lawyers with decades of experience. The remark had trapped him in a lie from which there was surely no realistic prospect of escape.

"Yes, well, I came to Casablanca because I'm writing a book that's partly set in Morocco. Lilia came up to join me . . ."

Another lie. Mahmud was writing something down as he listened. Was he keeping a record of the conversation, to be used as evidence against them at a later point?

"Lilia?" he said.

"That's me," Bartok replied.

Carradine wondered if it was all a sick joke. The officials already knew that Lara Bartok was standing in front of them. They knew only too well that "Lilia Hudak" was an alias.

"And you are from Hungary?"

"Yes," she said.

There was a sustained silence. The younger official slowly turned the pages of Carradine's passport. Mahmud was writing something down on a pad. He looked up and addressed a question in Arabic to his colleague at the desk in the center of the hut. Carradine was amazed to see Bartok spin on her heels and look out of the window, seemingly without a care in the world.

"This is your first visit to Morocco?"

"It is," Carradine replied.

He wondered what web Mahmud was trying to draw him into. He hated lying. He hated the traps they were setting for him.

"And yet you do not visit this beautiful woman in all that time?"

Of course. It was the simple, gaping hole in their hastily assembled cover story. Carradine did what he could to fill it, improvising as he answered.

"Um, we sort of broke up for a while." He tried to appear as though the official was prying too deeply into his personal life and was pleased to look across and find Bartok lowering her chin toward her chest, as if trying to forget a painful episode in the history of their otherwise happy relationship. "That made it difficult to come here."

"I see," Mahmud replied.

There was another long silence. Carradine could not tell if his story had been believed.

"So now you go to Gibraltar, on—" Mahmud picked up a sheet of paper on his desk and mispronounced the name of the yacht "—*Atlantis?*"

"*Atalanta.* That's right."

"Your passport please, Miss Hudak."

Bartok smiled and reached into her bag, handing the passport to Mahmud. He stared at the cover as if it were the first document of its type that he had ever seen. He turned it over and looked at the back, his head bobbing back and forth as his mouth dropped into a frown.

"Hungarian?"

"Yes."

The Moroccan flicked through the pages, looking for the immigration stamp. Carradine felt that his whole future rested on the next ten seconds. He had no idea if Bartok's stamp was real or forged, if there was a record of Lilia Hudak entering Morocco or if every customs and immigration official in the country had been instructed to search for a woman matching her description.

"You change your hair," Mahmud observed, indicating that the Hudak photograph showed Bartok with a shoulder-length red bob.

"I did," she replied. "Do you prefer that one?"

"I think it looks nice here," Mahmud replied and pressed a stubby finger onto the photograph. Smiling to himself, he handed the passport to the same official who had earlier copied down Carradine's details.

"And why don't you have British passport?"

Carradine assumed that it was a trick question. A car pulled up outside the hut. He was certain that it was a team of Agency personnel coming to haul them in.

"I don't understand," Bartok replied.

Mahmud looked at Carradine. His face was blank as he said: "Why don't you marry this woman?"

Carradine blurted out a laugh.

"I'm thinking about it." For the first time he began to believe that they might be in the clear. "Lilia likes being Hungarian. It's a beautiful country."

"Then maybe *you* should have Hungarian passport."

"Maybe I should."

He felt a surge of relief. They were home and dry. All of his worry and agitation had been for nothing.

Then Mahmud opened a drawer in his desk.

He took out a small black machine and passed it to the younger official. Carradine instantly knew what it was. He had seen similar devices in passport booths the world. The younger official plugged the machine into a computer and switched it on. An eerie blue light glowed from within.

He picked up Carradine's passport. Opening it to the identity page, he scanned it beneath the light, turned to the computer and studied the screen. Various lines of Arabic text appeared inside a small box. Mahmud appeared to be trying to read the text from his position several feet away. The process was taking so long that Carradine began to think that some kind of anomaly had cropped up deep within the Moroccan immigration system. Had a flag been placed on his passport? The younger official said something in Arabic, took Carradine's passport from the machine, hammered an exit stamp onto a clean page, scribbled something on a piece of paper and passed it to him.

"This is fine," he said.

The younger official then opened the Hudak passport and went through the same routine. He placed the identity page under the blue light, turned to the computer, assessed the information in the small box, placed an exit stamp on the same page as the entry visa granted five months earlier, and handed it back to Bartok.

"Enjoy your trip to Gibraltar." Mahmud was beaming, as though he knew that he had released Carradine from a personal torment. "Good weather next three days. Good sailing."

"So I heard," he replied.

Bartok put the passport in her handbag, reached for Carradine's hand and squeezed it tightly to congratulate him on a job well done. Then they walked out of the hut into the bright midmorning sunshine and made their way back to the boat.

37

Patrick was preparing to set sail. When Carradine saw him busying himself in the cockpit, the last of his anxiety about Patrick and Eleanor's true intentions dissipated. If Hulse or the Russians were going to come for them, they would surely have done so by now. The electricity cable had been detached from a panel on the pontoon and the bowline released into the depths of the marina. Carradine had given no thought to the seriousness of going to sea for two nights in the company of an elderly couple who might, at any moment, suffer medical setbacks or become involved in an accident that would require him to take control of a fifty-eight-foot, state-of-the-art yacht conservatively valued at a million pounds. He wanted only three things: to leave Morocco as quickly as possible; to reach Gibraltar so that he could contact his father; and to find some way of protecting Bartok from the threats against her.

He was unpacking in their cabin when he heard a noise of distant tapping, growing progressively louder. At first Carradine thought that it was the sound of rain falling on the roof of the saloon. He looked outside but could see only clear blue sky and the glare of the sun beyond the cockpit. Then he heard a dog bark, the rustle of paws on wooden pontoons, and knew what was coming.

Two uniformed police officers, guard dogs drooling and straining on leads, were making their way toward *Atalanta*. Carradine experienced the cold dread he had known only hours earlier when looking out across the Corniche at the police cars.

"Eleanor!"

Patrick was on deck. Carradine climbed up the steps to the cockpit and saw that the Alsatians were already at the stern. One of them began to bark at the sight of Carradine. The man holding the leash had to tug him back forcefully as he spoke to Patrick in English.

"We come aboard," he said. "Inspection now."

Carradine did not know if the search was related to Bartok or was simply a random customs check on a foreign-registered yacht. The larger of the two dogs continued to bark and was scolded by his master. Patrick indicated that the search party should come on board and explained to Carradine what was happening.

"They're looking for drugs, people smuggling. Best thing is to stay up here. They'll do what they have to."

"I'll tell Lilia."

Carradine went down into the saloon and tapped on the door of their cabin. Bartok was folding clothes into a drawer.

"What's going on?" she asked.

"Dogs. They're going to be coming in here. You're not carrying any weed or anything, are you?"

She looked at him in disbelief. "Are you *kidding*?"

Carradine forced a relieved smile but could not escape a nagging sensation that he had done something wrong or had made a slipup for which they would now pay the price. As he made his way out through the galley, he could hear the dogs scampering on the deck above his head, violent, excited blasts of breath. One of them came down into the saloon in the arms of a customs officer and was released into the boat.

The Alsatian wheeled around Carradine's feet, sniffing his shoes and ankles before hurrying toward the bow. Eleanor emerged into the corridor and jumped back as the dog barked at her.

"Get them under control!" she shouted, at first in English, then in bad, schoolgirl French. Carradine spoke to the officer, asking him to put a leash on the Alsatian. He refused, indicating that the animal could only conduct its search if it was allowed to roam free in every area of the boat.

"You are British?" he asked.

"Yes."

"You are with the girl?"

Carradine thought that he had misheard. Then his mind caught up with the question and he realized that the officer knew about Bartok. Was she under suspicion or had she merely been seen entering the passport hut an hour earlier?

"Which girl?" he said.

"Hungarian."

"Yes. I'm with her."

"Where is she, please?"

The Alsatian now tore past Carradine, through the galley and into the master bedroom. Both Carradine and the officer followed.

Bartok was leaning over in the corner of the room, encouraging the dog with a series of delighted cries and whispers.

"That's it! What do you smell? Good boy, good boy!"

Carradine looked at the officer, who seemed more interested in Bartok than in the search.

"Hello!" she said, straightening up to greet him. "As-Salaam Alaikum."

"Wa-Alaikum Salaam."

The Alsatian had found something. It was pawing at a cupboard on the near side of the double bed. Carradine's stomach turned over. The dog began to bark repeatedly.

"I can open, please?"

Carradine indicated that the officer was free to search wherever he liked. He looked quickly at Bartok, who indicated with her eyes that she did not know what had caught the dog's attention. The officer opened the cupboard and peered inside. Then the barking stopped.

"What is this, please?"

He had pulled out Bartok's black wig. It looked absurd, dangling from his hand like a prop in a school play. A lie sprang instantly into Carradine's mind. He was on the point of saying: "We went to a fancy dress party in Marrakech" when Bartok beat him to the deceit.

"I had cancer," she said in English. *"J'avais un cancer."*

The officer was visibly embarrassed. He was about thirty-five, good-looking and physically fit; to see a man of such apparent authority looking so awkward was almost touching. Reverently he laid the wig on Carradine's side of the bed, murmuring an apology.

"I am very sorry to hear this." Bartok touched her cropped blond hair as though to indicate that it had grown back following radiotherapy. "I hope you will recover soon."

"Oh, she's much better," Carradine interjected, ashamed to be using the illness that had killed his mother for the purposes of deceit.

"We will go now," said the guard and he led the Alsatian out of the cabin.

Patrick was sitting in the cockpit with Eleanor. The second customs officer had made his way back to the pontoon. His colleague soon followed. He waved to Bartok as he left.

"Did they find anything?" Patrick asked.

"Only the dead body in my carry-on bag," Carradine replied.

"And the heroin," Bartok added. "I hope that was OK?"

Patrick smiled. Eleanor did not.

Twenty minutes later *Atalanta* had reached the open sea.

"Sounds like you kids got lucky," said Hulse.

"Kids?" Bartok replied.

"You know what I mean."

"Do I?"

"Let's not play games."

"Lucky?" she said, sounding astonished. "You'd say that what happened to me was fortunate? Losing my freedom. My identity. You call that luck?"

Somerville was tired of the jousting between them. He went outside and finally smoked the one cigarette he allowed himself every day. Walking up Chapel Street, he pretended to make a call on his phone while checking for Russian surveillance. There was movement in one of the windows on the opposite side of the road—a curtain closing two floors up— but no pedestrians, no street cleaners, no vans on a stakeout. He thought about Carradine, grinding out the cigarette underneath his boot, and went back inside.

"Anything?" Hulse asked him.

"Nothing," Somerville replied.

Bartok was coming back from the bathroom. There was a jar of mois-

turizer beside the basin and she brought a smell of citrus into the room, rubbing her hands together as she worked the cream into the skin.

"Is everything to your satisfaction, gentlemen?" she said, seemingly in a brighter mood.

Somerville smiled, watching her as she sat down.

"Almost," Hulse replied.

"Only almost?"

"You were going to tell us about Atalanta," *he said.*

"And you were going to tell me about Kit."

This to Somerville, who shook his head and indicated that Bartok was being taped. He had triggered the voice recorder. The microphone was live.

"Afterward," he said. "The Langs first. Tell us what happened on the boat."

SECRET INTELLIGENCE SERVICE
EYES ONLY / STRAP 1

STATEMENT BY LARA BARTOK ("LASZLO")
CASE OFFICERS: J.W.S./S.T.H.—CHAPEL STREET
REF: RESURRECTION/SIMAKOV/CARRADINE
FILE: RE2768X

PART 5 OF 5

The boat trip was the happiest time I had known since New York. I was with a man I trusted, a man I respected. We had great conversations, we became very close. Kit had been worried at times in Rabat, but he began to enjoy what was happening to him. We were both elated to have got away on *Atalanta*. We felt like we had won, you know? Kit had been a little bored with the sameness of his life in London, writing every day, no proper relationship, also caring for his father [JWS: William Carradine] who had not been well. What had happened to him in Morocco was something out of the ordinary. He loved being part of a story larger than his own life. His father had been forced out of his job because of the treachery of Philby. Did you know about that? Philby befriended him, took him under his wing, taught him what he knew, then betrayed Kit's father to the KGB. There were lots of men and women like him, young spies at the start of their careers who were blown once their identities became known in Moscow.

I think Kit saw what was happening as a chance to show what his family was capable of, what Bill Carradine might have been if only he had not been deceived by one of his own. In this sense Kit was making amends. And he loved the world of spying! My shampoo bottle and the passport in the salt and how careful I was about phones and SIM cards. Second nature to me, but not to him. He was like a kid in a spy shop. It was very endearing.

Of course, just as he talked about his own life and his family, I told him about Ivan, about my role in early Resurrection operations, about the way I had lived since leaving New York. He knew that Stephen Graham had been in love with me, that he had taken me away to a beach house he had rented for us in Mexico, that we had spent a weekend together by the ocean. He asked me about my childhood in Hungary and of course, out of habit, I told the stories I have always told, some of which were true, some of which were not true. A lot of the time I felt as though I should protect him from knowing too much about me, because I was aware that I could hurt him at any moment. I wanted to be with him but I knew, deep in my heart, that this could never be possible.

As you know, I had been suspicious of Patrick and Eleanor. I liked Eleanor particularly and believed that perhaps Patrick was not always true to her. He had a streak of vanity, of arrogance, as if life had always come a little too easily to him. She hinted that he was having an affair, which explained his strange behavior in the marina when we first arrived. He was always talking on the telephone, presumably to his mistress. I wanted to be able to tell Eleanor more about my life. We had many good conversations. She was a terrible cook! Of course, they had no idea who I was. Kit kept up the pretense very well and it was easy to act as though we were boyfriend and girlfriend because we had become lovers.

My worry was that Kit was too concerned for my safety. He had a streak in his personality, a need to be the knight in shining armor. I've noticed that a lot of English men have this. So I had to be ruthless with him. I had to be cruel to be kind. I was trying to find a way to let him know that, sooner or later, it was all going to have to end.

38

Lara and Carradine had gone ashore for brunch at the marina in Puerto de Barbate. They had been at sea for two days and two nights living off cold cuts and salad and both yearned for a decent cup of coffee, some *jamón ibérico* and the chance to stretch their legs. The decision to delay arrival in Gibraltar by forty-eight hours had been Eleanor's; she wanted to take a hire car into the La Breña Natural Park so that she could visit the Barbate Marshes. The last-minute change of itinerary had not seemed suspicious to Carradine, who was in no position to argue with Patrick and Eleanor after they had been so generous and hospitable toward him. Besides, it was not as if Gibraltar held any of the answers to Bartok's predicament. When they had been alone in their cabin, Carradine had tried to persuade her to hand herself over to the British authorities. She had refused. She was reconciled to her fugitive status, insisting that Carradine return to London and forget all about her.

He did not want to. On the first night out of Rabat they had slept together; consequently he was in a state of dazed infatuation and wanted to keep seeing her. He believed that Lara felt the same way and that by trying to persuade him to go home was only demonstrating how much she cared for him. She had explained that she wanted to protect him from the complications of her life on the run.

Their bodies still swaying to the rhythms of the ocean, they walked hand in hand through the marina to a small tapas bar where they ordered fried eggs, *patatas bravas* and *jamón*. Patrick briefly joined them before returning to the boat to fix a broken hatch; Eleanor had gone into town to have her hair done.

"Sooner or later they're going to work out what happened to us," said Carradine, finishing off a second cup of coffee.

"Maybe," Bartok replied. "Maybe not."

It was perhaps the nineteenth version of a conversation they had been having every day since leaving Morocco.

"Where will you go?" he asked. "What will you do?"

"This does not have to concern you."

"I want it to concern me."

She kissed him on the cheek, running her hand along his jaw. They no longer had to pretend to be lovers; a natural intimacy had grown up between them. Carradine toyed with daydreams of smuggling Bartok into the UK so that she could live with him in his flat and make a new life in London. He knew that the crimes of which she was accused in America—armed assault, kidnapping, incitement to violence—would most likely see her extradited to the United States within a matter of weeks. He wanted to believe that he could mount a public defense on her behalf, persuading journalists and broadcasters to campaign for her release, arguing that Bartok had acted under duress from Ivan Simakov and deserved a second chance. He knew that such far-fetched notions were the stuff of fantasy but could not bring himself to face the simple truth: their adventure was over. Looking across the table at the woman who had so bewitched him, Carradine realized that he had only two options: to remain with her, abandoning his life and career in London; or to return home. It was no choice at all. He would have to go back to Lancaster Gate and look back on all that had happened to him in Morocco as a fleeting dream.

"You should telephone your father," she said.

"Yes."

An ancient Téléfonica payphone was bolted to a wall on the far side of the tapas bar. Carradine asked the obvious question.

"Won't they have his number covered? If I call, they can trace it."

"I doubt it," Bartok replied.

Looking back, Carradine realized that was the first sign of what was to come.

Two hours later he was scrubbing the decks and washing down the windows while Patrick caught up on his sleep. The skipper was tired after sailing single-handedly through the night and had retired to his bunk. It was another fiercely hot day, the marina buzzing with activity. Eleanor had not yet returned from the local town. Lara was belowdecks reading a book.

Just after midday she popped her head up into the cockpit and told Carradine that she was going ashore to look for a newspaper. He knew her well enough by now to realize that she wanted to go alone. She was carrying the soft bag that he had found in her apartment, into which she had stuffed various dirty clothes as well as their bedsheets and towels. There was a Laundromat at the marina. They arranged to meet there and to find somewhere in town to have a late lunch. Carradine had not yet rung his father but planned to do so once they were a safe distance from the marina. Lara had agreed that this was a more sensible course of action.

Just before two o'clock, Eleanor returned from the local town smelling of coffee and hairspray. Patrick was still asleep. She seemed surprised to see Carradine.

"Oh. I thought you were in town. I saw Lily in the taxi."

She had taken to calling Bartok "Lily." The two women had grown close in a short space of time. There was an edge to Eleanor's voice, as though she were admonishing Carradine for a sin he had not committed.

"She went on her own," he said, wondering why Bartok had taken a cab when she had said she was only looking for a newspaper. "I'm meeting her in a minute."

"Ah." Eleanor frowned. Carradine sensed that something was wrong. "It did seem odd," she said. "She drove right past me. You were nowhere to be seen. I assumed you two lovebirds had had a row."

"Why did you think that?"

"Because she was crying."

He knew then that Bartok was gone. Carradine felt unbalanced. He asked in which direction the taxi had been heading when it had passed her.

"Out of town, I suppose," Eleanor replied. "Away from here."

"Are you sure?"

"I think so." Her expression softened. "What was the argument about, darling?"

Carradine found himself in the absurd position of confirming Eleanor's belief that there had been a terrible row. What else could he say? That Lily wasn't "Lilia" but instead a fugitive from justice with a bounty on her head? That she had slipped away into Andalucía without so much as a farewell? That Carradine had taken advantage of their hospitality, and potentially putting their safety at risk? It was easier to lie.

"Just boyfriend and girlfriend stuff," he said, numb at the realization of Bartok's betrayal. "Give me a second, will you?"

He went down into the cabin and saw their unmade bed. Only hours earlier they had made love, entwined in each other's bodies, cocooned by the hum of the engine and the hiss of the sea. He opened the cupboard and saw immediately that Lara had taken most of her belongings. Even the absurd wig was gone. Some of her dirty clothes were in a laundry bag leaning against a pile of lifejackets; she had taken one of the *Atalanta* towels to fill out the bag. Carradine opened a drawer on the far side of the cabin. It was no surprise to see that the Lilia Hudak passport had gone. The Art Deco silver bookmark was no longer where Bartok had left it, wedged between the pages of *Anna Karenina*. It was a complete clear-out.

Carradine went out into the galley. Patrick had woken up. He could hear him talking to Eleanor in the cockpit. It was evident that she had told him about the argument because as Carradine came up the ladder he said: "You OK, son?"

"I'm fine," he replied, though in truth he was hollowed out.

"Heard from Lily?" Eleanor asked.

"He doesn't have a phone," Patrick replied.

"No," Carradine confirmed. "I haven't heard from her."

He explained that he was going to go into town to look for her and to apologize for what had happened. Patrick said, "Don't worry, these things go on all the time," and Eleanor agreed, adding: "You two will be fine. You're both lovely people." Carradine felt wretched for deceiving them. He found that he was intensely angry with Bartok. She had humiliated him, used him up.

He walked to the Laundromat. An elderly Spanish woman was removing sheets from a tumble drier and piling them into a plastic basket. She was wearing an apron and a badge. There was nobody else around.

"*Disculpe,*" said Carradine, using what bad schoolboy Spanish he could remember.

"*Hola?*" the woman replied.

Before he had a chance to respond she appeared to recognize him, placing a hand on his elbow.

"*Señor* Kit?"

"*Sí.*"

She hurried into a back office. The Laundromat was very hot. The vast

machines had generated a greenhouse humidity with a smell of soap
powder and artificial pine. Carradine broke out in a sweat and opened
the door, hoping that the hot summer wind might at least make him
feel less claustrophobic.

"Here," said the woman in Spanish, emerging from the back office
holding a large plastic bag and an envelope.

At first Carradine thought it was a bill for the laundry. Then he
looked inside. The shirts and towels had been cleaned and folded. He
searched for Bartok's clothes among his own, but of course found
nothing.

"For you," said the woman, this time in English. "Letter."

Carradine opened the envelope.

My darling Kit

*Forgive me for doing this. We hardly know one another but I
feel as though I have known you all my life. You have saved that
life. I do not know how to repay you except by leaving you in peace.
You must not come with me. You must not __think__ of trying to find
me. This is the only way. Believe me. It is better.*

Carradine's throat was dry. He saw that the letter had been written
hurriedly. Certain words had been crossed out, others underlined. The
first few sentences slanted across the page. He turned away from the elderly lady because he could sense that she was staring at him.

*Go back to London, forget about me. I will go where I have to
go and try to do the same. But please know this. As much as it is
possible for a person to love another person after knowing him for
so short a time, I do love you. I loved what happened between us
on Atalanta. I will never forget it. I will never forget you.*

Lara

39

Carradine waited for the sheets. It was all that he could do. The elderly woman ironed them and folded them and looked at him sympathetically as he walked outside into the blistering afternoon.

He walked back to *Atalanta* and explained that Lilia had gone to the airport in Gibraltar and booked a flight home to London.

"How did you find out?" Patrick asked.

Carradine had been in such a state of shock that he had not even thought that his version of events would be questioned.

"She wrote me an email," he said. Lies now came to him as easily as drinking a cup of coffee. "There's an internet café in town."

It was agreed that Carradine would also leave the boat. Patrick and Eleanor were sad to see him go, but understood that he wanted to get back to London to try to save the relationship.

"It's all such a shock," said Eleanor. "You seemed so happy together."

"We were," said Carradine. "Very happy."

He went down into the cabin and packed his bags. He put the clean sheets and pillowcases on the bed and washed down the bathroom with an old cloth from the galley. It was as though he was erasing what had happened between them: the shower they had taken together on the first morning at sea; the sight of Bartok's moonlit naked body as she slipped out of bed in the dead of night; her eyes looking back at him as she applied makeup in the bathroom mirror. It had all been a fantasy conjured by Carradine's imagination, an affair so fleeting and unreal that he doubted his own ability to believe it in the months and years to come. He went up on deck to find Eleanor mending a broken china mug with a tube of superglue and some cotton buds. Patrick was eating tortilla and drinking a Mahou in the sun. Carradine asked for their address in England so that he could write to thank them and apologized for the muted way in which the trip had ended.

"I know that Lilia loved meeting you and spending time with you," he said, angry with himself for making excuses for her.

"Of course," said Eleanor, hugging him.

"You'll be all right," said Patrick, shaking his hand. "Let us know how it all goes."

Carradine caught a bus to the airport in Seville, checked his emails on a public computer and searched the British and American press for any references to the death of Ramón Basora. He found none. Having expected a tsunami of messages inquiring after his well-being, he discovered only an email from his agent asking how the festival had gone ("Hope you didn't get eaten alive by Katherine Paget"), an invitation to a book launch and a message from the manager of the riad revealing that his phone and laptop had been found under the mattress and were being kept in the hotel safe along with the memory stick. Carradine was relieved that Hulse or the Russians had not taken them and sent a reply saying that he would cover the cost of having the items couriered to his flat in London.

He rang his father from the departure lounge. Though he expressed surprise that Carradine had not responded to a text message he had sent two days earlier, he was otherwise oblivious to the fact that his son had vanished.

"Where are you calling from?" he asked.

"Seville," Carradine replied, relieved at last to be telling the truth about his whereabouts. "Stopped off near Cádiz on the way home."

"Cádiz? Really? I went there with your mother." Carradine was in such a sorry state that he felt tears rising. Father and son, both betrayed and humbled by the secret world. "Took her to a nudist beach. There's a first time for everything. A last time as well."

A flight was leaving for Luton at seven o'clock. Carradine bought copies of *The Times* and *Guardian* and sat in a café eating a *bocadillo*. He had looked at both front pages with trepidation, expecting to find his author's photo blown up alongside that of Lara Bartok under a headline about their mysterious disappearance from the Medina. Instead, turning page after page, he found no reference to what had happened in Marrakech, only detailed accounts of the Resurrection siege in Warsaw, which had been brought to an end by the Polish BOA. Parliament buildings around the world were in lockdown. The Pentagon had been evacuated after a bomb scare. In Budapest, a man and a woman had been shot dead after being mistaken for armed Resurrection activists. The movement had metastasized into an international terrorist phenomenon which could erupt at any time, bringing chaos and fear to governments and citizens alike.

Reading the reports, Carradine began to feel that what had happened to him in Morocco had happened to another man. He had not left Marrakech in the dead of night. He had not stayed in the flat in Rabat. He had not slipped onto an English-registered yacht and spent two nights at sea with a beautiful woman who had vanished from his life as quickly as she had appeared. The whole thing had been as unreal and as fanciful as a film noir, with Bartok as the femme fatale. At no point was he tapped on the shoulder by a plainclothes officer of the *Guardia Civil* nor quietly asked to leave the airport by a representative of Her Majesty's Government in Gibraltar. All that remained was the dismay of losing Lara, the raw disappointment of having glimpsed the promise of love and losing it in the blink of an eye.

The plane was on time. He caught a cab from Luton Airport, sitting in late-night roadworks traffic on the M1, eventually reaching home after midnight. Carradine opened the door of his flat expecting to be greeted by a phalanx of officers from Special Branch, but instead there was only the smell of his neighbor's cooking and a note from the Tenants' Association advising him that the date for the Annual General Meeting had been moved to October. He searched each room for any signs of intrusion, but found nobody hiding in the spare bedroom or waiting for him in his office. He opened several windows to stir the warm, uncirculated air of the London summer and smoked a cigarette in the kitchen, wondering what had become of Lara and wishing that he had stayed in Spain to look for her.

It was only as he was falling asleep that he remembered something vital: he had arranged to meet Stephen Graham the following afternoon. Carradine walked into his study and looked at his diary. Exactly thirteen days had passed since his encounter with Mantis at Lisson Grove. Graham was expecting Carradine to debrief him about the trip to Morocco.

He did not know whether to go ahead with the meeting. Graham would want to talk to him about Bartok. He would want to know what had happened in Marrakech. In all probability, he had sent a WhatsApp message to Carradine's phone confirming that the meeting was due to take place. A single gray tick would have displayed against the message as the phone sat in the safe at the riad. What would Graham have made of that?

Carradine went back to bed. He missed the sounds of the ocean, the swell of the waves in the cabin. Instead, traffic was sweeping along Bayswater Road and his married neighbors were arguing in the next apartment. He tried to imagine how it would benefit him to meet Graham and to continue with the façade of working for the Service. He did not have the energy to lie about what had happened. He would have to tell him everything: about Rabat, about the Russians, about *Atalanta*. As a bargaining chip, should Carradine threaten to expose "Robert Mantis" as a Russian agent? That was surely suicidal: the same men who had come for Bartok in Marrakech would undoubtedly come for him. Perhaps they might do so anyway, grabbing him on the street in the coming days in the hope of finding out what had become of LASZLO. On reflection, this seemed to Carradine the most likely, as well as the most alarming outcome: the Russians knew who he was. They knew that C. K. Carradine had somehow aided and abetted Bartok's escape from Morocco. In this respect, he was going to need Graham's help to get them off his back. If that strategy failed, he would have no choice but to go to the Service and to tell them everything he knew.

40

The courier came at half-past eight, blasting the doorbell and waking Carradine from a deep sleep. He signed for the laptop, the phone and the memory stick, opening the carefully wrapped package from DHL. He wondered if it had been tampered with en route by the Service.

Both batteries were dead. Carradine found chargers and plugged them in. He locked the memory stick in a drawer in his office and walked back to the kitchen. Carradine saw that "Robert Mantis" had written him two WhatsApp messages, four days earlier, both of which had been sent at the same time. The first confirmed the meeting at Lisson Grove later that day. The second was a reminder to bring the memory stick that Oubakir had given him in Casablanca. There was no further mention of Bartok, nor had Mantis attempted to contact Carradine in the ensuing days. Carradine looked at his diary and worked out that the messages had been sent while he was staying in the apartment in Rabat. He replied, apologizing for taking so long to respond and explaining that he had "accidentally" left his phone behind in Marrakech. He said that he looked forward to their meeting later that afternoon and pressed "Send."

The message acquired only a single gray tick.

There were other texts—from his father, from various friends and acquaintances in London. Carradine combed his phone for a covert message or email from Bartok but found nothing. He listened to the voice mails, checked his Twitter feed and scrolled through Facebook looking for clues as to her whereabouts but knew that he was wasting his time. She was gone. He was no different to Stephen Graham and perhaps to countless other men who had fallen under her spell, only to be cast aside when their usefulness had passed.

There were also no messages of any kind from Sebastian Hulse or the Russians. It seemed strange to Carradine that none of them had attempted to make contact, if only to pressure him into giving up information about Bartok's whereabouts. Their absence only added to a burgeoning sense that what had happened to him in Morocco had been part of a dream, a fantasy of escape with no basis in reality.

He spent the rest of the morning replying to emails from his agent and publisher and reading obituaries online of Ivan Simakov, each of them displaying the same photograph of the handsome, martyred revolutionary leader with the implicit visual implication that he was a latter-day Fidel or Che. No fewer than four articles suggested that Simakov had worked for Russian intelligence before setting up Resurrection. Reading the obituaries in his office, Carradine no longer cared who might be looking at his internet history or reading his private correspondence; at one point he even typed the name "Lara Bartok" into Google, finding various articles in which she was referred to as Simakov's "former girlfriend" with little or no further biographical information provided. He was surprised both by how little had been written about her and by the scarcity of photographs of Bartok online: Carradine found only a cropped version of the picture he had seen in *The Guardian* and a yearbook photo of a teenage "Lara Bartok" who may or may not have been the same woman. Either Lara had been extremely careful about her digital footprint from a young age or—more likely—somebody had erased her history from the internet.

Every now and again Carradine would check to see if his message to Mantis had been read. Each time he saw the same thing: a single gray tick beside the text, indicating not only that the message had not been read, but that it had yet to reach Mantis's phone. He began to think that the meeting would not go ahead, but knew that he had no choice other than to appear at Lisson Grove at the allotted time.

As he was leaving the flat, Carradine checked his mailbox on the ground floor. Beneath the piles of junk mail and freebie magazines he found two issues of *The Week,* two copies of *The New Yorker,* a letter from his agent in New York and a handwritten envelope containing what felt like an invitation to a party.

He opened it.

There was a postcard inside. The image on the front showed a four-section collage of photographs from Marrakech: the Koutoubia tower at sunrise; the Berrima Mosque at dusk; the Royal Palace at sunset; a carpet seller in the souk.

There was a handwritten message on the back.

Kit
   Great to meet you in Kech. I'm in London the next few days. Would love to meet up and talk about that girl. You can find me at the St. Ermin's Hotel in St. James. Staying under Hulse.
   I may not be exactly who you think I am.
   Sebastian

Carradine could feel his heart racing as he read the message a second time. Two things immediately occurred to him: Hulse knew where he lived but had elected to contact him via the postal service rather than by dragging him into the back of an Agency van. Secondly, he was being explicit about his interest in Bartok. The postcard seemed to suggest that Carradine had outfoxed the Agency. The tone of the message was conciliatory.

Carradine looked at his watch. It had just gone midday. Even if his meeting with Graham lasted two or three hours, that would still leave him more than enough time to go to the hotel and to ask for Hulse. Better still, he could ring up to his room and—if necessary—leave a message. What did he have to lose? Better to make his peace with the Agency, to get Hulse onside, than to leave himself exposed to the threat from Moscow. It might even be the case that Hulse could help bring Bartok in from the cold.

Carradine walked outside. He lit a cigarette. With the first taste of the tobacco, the sharp hit of nicotine, he felt an absolute confusion. *I may not be exactly who you think I am.* What did it *mean*? Was Hulse a freelancer? Another rogue agent like Mantis? Had he even sent the postcard or was it a trap set by the Russians to lure him to the hotel?

It was impossible to know. Carradine was beyond the point at which he could even pretend to know what might happen to him or who could be lurking around the next corner. He hoped that Stephen Graham might be able to provide him with at least some of the answers.

41

Carradine deliberately followed the same route to Lisson Grove that he had taken a fortnight earlier. There was no reason to do so other than a rather melancholy desire to revisit Sussex Gardens and to try to make sense of what had happened to Lisa Redmond.

He reached the intersection certain that he was not being followed. Vehicles were moving normally in all directions. Pedestrians were walking along the pavements and crossing the road at the lights. The cafés and restaurants were full, the shops were open and busy. To the naked eye there was no suggestion that, just two weeks earlier, a woman had been kidnapped and two men brutally assaulted within fifty meters of where Carradine was standing. He tried to recall what he had seen. He remembered the teenage girl jabbering away to her friend. *I'm like, he needs to get his shit together because I'm, like, just not going through with that bullshit again.* Yet Carradine's memory was otherwise warped and confused: he had conflated his own recollections of the kidnapping with other eyewitness accounts. The photographs and videos of the attack later posted online had become a new version of his personal experience.

He stopped at the pedestrian crossing where the girl had held him back. He checked his phone. The WhatsApp message to Mantis still showed a single gray tick. Carradine was convinced that their meeting would not now go ahead, but nevertheless continued to walk east toward Marylebone Road and the apartment block on Lisson Grove.

He rang the bell. There was no answer so he rang it again. He looked at his phone. Still no response from Graham. Carradine pressed the bell a third time and waited another minute. He was sure that something had happened to him; Russian intelligence had worked out that Graham had betrayed them and he had "disappeared" as a consequence. Carradine was on the point of walking away when the door suddenly buzzed and a cheerful female voice said "Sorry!" on the intercom.

"Hello?" he said, pushing the door ajar.

There was no reply. He climbed the six flights of stairs to the third floor, arriving slightly out of breath and sweating under his shirt.

"There was no need for you to come up."

A diminutive woman in late middle age was standing in the door of Graham's flat. She was holding a yellow duster and a bottle of silver polish and spoke in a cut-glass accent.

"I don't understand," Carradine replied.

The woman looked confused. "Oh," she said. "I thought you were the man from Amazon."

"Me?" He wondered if he had gone to the correct address but remembered the faux Dutch oil painting on the landing. "No. I'm not from Amazon. I was supposed to meet somebody here."

"Here?" Carradine could see various items of brown furniture inside the flat and a rolled-up carpet standing on its end in the hall. The empty room in which he had sat with Graham was in the process of being transformed. He found himself remembering the scene in *Moonraker* when Bond and "M," expecting to find a control room filled with deadly toxins and lab rats, instead walk into a lavish Venetian drawing room wearing gas masks, only to be greeted by Sir Hugo Drax.

"I may have made a mistake," he said.

The woman seemed anxious to relieve Carradine of any notion that his presence was an inconvenience.

"Please don't worry, I've only just moved in," she said. "Were you looking for Mr. Benedictus?"

"Benedictus?"

She picked up an envelope from a stool in the hall. She showed it to Carradine.

"He lived here before me."

Carradine looked at the envelope. It was a charity circular made out to a "Mr. D. Benedictus" at the same address Graham had given to him two weeks earlier.

"No, not him," he said. "Did you know a 'Mr. Mantis' or a 'Stephen Graham'?"

The woman frowned.

"I'm afraid not. You were supposed to meet them here today?"

It occurred to Carradine that she was being unusually helpful. He wondered if she was working for Moscow.

"I was," he said. "Never mind."

He was about to turn around and head back down the stairs when she said: "Somebody else came yesterday."

"Somebody who was looking for Mr. Benedictus?"

"No," she said. "For your Mr. Mantis."

Carradine hesitated. The revelation was not, of itself, particularly alarming. No doubt Graham had used the flat in order to meet all kinds of people.

"Do you remember much about him?" he asked.

The woman wiped a bead of sweat from her forehead. She was wearing three-quarter-length tweed trousers and her hair was cut in a messy, knife-and-fork bob.

"Not particularly," she replied. "As I was saying, I let you in because I thought you were the man from Amazon. I'm waiting for a microwave oven."

There seemed no point in continuing the conversation. They would only go around in circles. Carradine took a last look inside the flat—remembering how the plastic wrap on the cream leather sofa had made him sticky and hot—and apologized for wasting the woman's time. It was only as she was shutting the door that he decided to take a chance. He tapped the four-digit pin into his phone and opened up "Photos."

"If you could just give me two seconds," he said.

The woman lingered in the doorway, throwing the Benedictus envelope onto the ground. Carradine searched for the pictures he had taken in Casablanca and found the photographs of Ramón and Hulse.

"These two guys," he said, showing the woman the shots from Blaine's. As he flicked through them he was conscious that two provocatively dressed Moroccan women were prominent in several frames. "Was it either of them?"

The woman took the phone and looked through the album. She seemed interested in what Carradine was showing her.

"How do you make it bigger?" she asked.

"Which one?" Carradine replied.

"This one," she said, pointing at the photograph of Carradine with his arm around Hulse, their glasses raised in a toast.

He moved his fingers apart on the screen so that Hulse's face was enlarged. He realized that his hand was shaking as he held the phone.

"Him?" he asked.

The woman stared at the screen. Hulse's features were slightly blurred but she seemed to recognize him. She took the phone from Carradine. She held it farther away from her face. His longsighted father did the same thing with menus when he had forgotten to bring his glasses to a restaurant.

"Could he have been American?" Carradine asked.

That was the breakthrough. The woman looked at him as if he had solved a particularly taxing clue in a crossword.

"Yes!" she exclaimed. "I remember now! Rather good-looking. Isn't he well-dressed? Came yesterday, about the same time. Asked for this Mr. Mantis. I only saw him through the camera at the front door, but it was certainly him. Unmistakable accent. American. I could listen to it all day."

Carradine thanked her and walked down the stairs, trying to work out what Hulse had been doing at Lisson Grove. How did he know about Mantis and why had he sent the postcard to Carradine's flat? He wanted to find a blank piece of paper and—in the style of the great conspiracy thrillers of the 1970s—draw a diagram that would make sense of all the names and places and theories he had encountered since his first fateful meeting with Stephen Graham on Bayswater Road. He sat on the stairs and tried to organize his thoughts but found that it was pointless; only a meeting with Hulse at the St. Ermin's Hotel could potentially resolve the myriad puzzles in his mind.

He opened the door onto Lisson Grove. A tall, bespectacled man wearing an ill-fitting lounge suit was staring up at the building. As Carradine came out he smiled at him and raised his hand.

"Mr. Carradine?" he said. "Mr. Kit Carradine?"

Carradine was bewildered. He wondered distractedly if the man was a fan of his books.

"Who's asking?" he said.

"The name's Somerville." It was hard to pick the man's age or to place his accent. "Julian Somerville." His voice had an adenoidal quality and the lenses in his round wired glasses were smudged. "I wondered if we might have a little chat?"

"A little chat about what?"

Somerville had lost much of his hair. Carradine found that he was shaking his hand.

"Oh, about Robert Mantis. About Stephen Graham. About Lara Bartok. About everything, really. Why don't you follow me? I've got a car parked just around the corner."

42

The car was a Jaguar parked near a fish restaurant off Lisson Grove. Somerville opened the back door and invited Carradine to get in.

"Who are you?" he asked. "Where are you from?"

"Just hop inside, Kit. There's a good chap."

Carradine felt that he had no choice. He looked inside the car. There was another man in the backseat. As he climbed in beside him, the man turned. To Carradine's consternation, he saw that it was Sebastian Hulse.

"Kit!" he said, slapping him on the back. "How you doin'?"

As though in a dream where he wanted to speak but was unable to sound the words, Carradine stared at Hulse. All he could summon was the word: "You?"

"Me."

Hulse laughed his seductive laugh, smiled his seductive smile.

"You've given us quite the ride the last few days," he said.

There was a driver in the front seat, staring ahead with both hands on the wheel. Somerville climbed in beside him and they pulled away.

"I don't understand," said Carradine. "Where's Mantis? Where's Stephen Graham?"

Somerville turned. He had taken off his spectacles and removed his suit jacket. The transformation in his appearance was striking. Carradine had thought that he was completely bald, yet he could now see that Somerville's hair was merely shaved close to the scalp. He had guessed that he was most likely in his late forties but realized that he was closer to thirty-five.

"Stephen Graham is dead," he said. Hulse wound down a window. "The man you knew as Robert Mantis has been murdered. Pushed under a train at Oxford Circus."

Carradine felt as though he had thrown a cigarette out of the window and the butt had blown back into the car to burn him. He stared at Hulse. He was somehow hoping that the American would deny what Somerville had told him.

"What? Who killed him? Why?"

"The Moscow men. Who else?"

The car made a sharp turn in the direction of Marylebone Station. Carradine was pushed back in his seat. He assumed that if Hulse was Agency, Somerville was Service, but anything was possible in the looking-glass world into which Stephen Graham had thrust him.

"He was killed by his own side?"

"Now *that* is a revealing question," said Somerville, looking immensely pleased that Carradine had asked it. "How would you know that Mantis wasn't one of us? How did you work that out?"

Carradine's father had always told him that the best policy in life was to tell the truth, even if you thought it was going to get you into trouble. "Be honest," he would say. "That's what I learned from my time in the Service. People can stand anything except being lied to." In recent weeks Carradine had grown used to the business of lying. He remembered deliberately misleading Mantis about the Redmond kidnapping.

He recalled how wretched he had felt drinking Patrick's Rioja and eating Eleanor's food night after night while blatantly deceiving them about "Lilia" and their life together in London. It was time to take his father's advice.

"Lara told me," he said.

"So you *did* find her?"

Hulse looked impressed. Carradine was astonished that the Agency still did not know that he had made contact with LASZLO.

"I did," he said, with an odd surge of pride.

"And?" said Somerville.

"And what?"

"And what happened next?"

So Carradine told them.

More than two hours later they were in the Members' Room at the Royal Academy drinking tea and eating scones. The driver had dropped them off in Piccadilly. Somerville had confirmed that he was an intelligence officer with the Service, showing Carradine a photo ID and handing him a business card almost identical to the one he had been given by "Robert Mantis." Hulse had produced what appeared to be a bona fide security pass for Langley, allowing Carradine to study it closely. It was the first time in his life that he had seen an ID of that kind. A few weeks earlier it would have been a buzz, like handling a moon rock or a first edition of *Casino Royale;* now he didn't trust the evidence of his own eyes. Somerville explained that Stephen Graham had been pushed in front of a train by two assailants who had been conveniently disguised to evade CCTV and sufficiently well-trained to vanish from Oxford Circus station without a trace. The murder had been blamed on a mugging gone wrong, but the Service had learned through a contact in Moscow that Graham had been killed by his own side. His attempts to warn Bartok of the threat against her constituted an act of treason, a breach of omertà for which he had paid with his life. Carradine suspected that

Hulse was hearing much of what Somerville was telling him for the first time.

Their conversation had taken place in full view of the RA members, many of whom had visited the Summer Exhibition and were sheltering from an afternoon storm. Carradine was surprised that Somerville had not insisted that they go to a Service safe house or take a room in a hotel; in his novels he had always staged sensitive conversations of this kind in secure environments. He had told them everything he could remember about his initial contacts with "Robert Mantis," his encounter with Ramón on the plane, the meeting with Oubakir at Blaine's, even his chat with the mysterious "Karel" on the train to Marrakech. At the mention of Karel's name, both men had looked at each other knowingly and decided, by silent agreement, to tell Carradine that "Karel M. Trapp" was in fact a Czech émigré and Agency asset in Casablanca whom Hulse had instructed to follow Carradine onto the train and to provoke him into a discussion about Resurrection.

"I needed to know more about you," he said. "Didn't make sense you were meeting with Oubakir at Blaine's. Basora was shooting his mouth off, we knew he was one of the Mantis agents. When I called London, Julian here had never heard of you, so I figured either you were researching a book, like you said you were, or maybe you were working for Moscow."

"So who killed Ramón?" Carradine was back in the wilderness of mirrors, dizzied by names, stunned by the Karel revelation, and all the time wondering what the hell had happened to Lara.

"Who knows?" said Hulse. "Took a girl up to his hotel room, fucked her, cardiac arrest. Maid found him a day later. Told the cops Basora had offered her money for sex. Kind of a charming guy, wouldn't you say?"

Carradine remembered the girls in Blaine's, the glint of Hulse's wedding ring as his hand caressed Salma's thigh. Had the girls been on the Agency payroll as well?

"So—what?—you looked around town for Lara, you eventually see her at the festival and just follow her back to your riad?" Hulse seemed keen to move the conversation along.

"That's right," said Carradine.

The American smiled, lowering a dollop of clotted cream onto a scone. By Carradine's reckoning, he had already consumed three scones and four chocolate chip cookies. He dropped a scoop of strawberry jam onto the cream and brought it up to his lips.

"And the Irish guy, the writer . . ." He put at least half the scone into his mouth and attempted to say: "What was his name?" without dropping any crumbs.

"Michael McKenna," Somerville replied. "I read his most recent book. Bloody good."

"You think he'd met her before?" Hulse asked.

Carradine shook his head. They spoke at length about what had taken place in the riad. He told them about the fight in Bartok's apartment, the meeting with Oubakir on the street, even his doubts and concerns about Hulse when the American had shown up out of the blue.

"Yeah," he said. "Sorry about that. I knew you were hiding something. Just didn't know what it was."

It was a revealing admission of incompetence. Over a third cup of tea Carradine told the men about the drive to Rabat, the flat on the Corniche, the slice of luck with Patrick and Eleanor. He felt bad giving up their names but hoped that any interest the Service or the Agency had to take in them would be confined to a quick look at their emails and a light vetting. Somerville had been asking most of the questions.

"So you reached Barbate marina," he said, "you went ashore for breakfast, Lara said she was going into town to buy a newspaper, then the lady vanishes?"

"Precisely," Carradine replied.

"She leave a note?" Hulse asked.

"She did."

He could remember every word of it, every full stop and comma, even the slant of Lara's handwriting. He kept the letter in his wallet, folded up next to a photograph of his mother. He wasn't going to tell them any of that.

"What did it say?" Somerville asked.

"Just that she was grateful to me for helping her out. That she was sorry to run away, but didn't want to involve me any further in what she was doing."

"And what *was* she doing, do you think?"

Carradine shrugged. The answer to Hulse's question was surely obvious.

"Running away from guys like you," he said.

Somerville smiled. Hulse did not.

"Did you sleep with her?" Somerville asked.

"Is that relevant?" Carradine replied.

"Man's got a point," said Hulse, licking his lips clean of clotted cream. "Irrelevant."

"I'm not so sure." Somerville moved his head to one side in a rather studied, eccentric manner, as though he was still trying to work out if Carradine was saint or sinner. "What are your feelings toward her? What did you conclude about her work for Resurrection?"

Hulse indicated that he should answer. Carradine wanted to do so without giving the appearance that he was infatuated with Bartok and dismayed to have lost contact with her.

"I thought she was great," he said. "Funny, bright, strong."

"Hot," said Hulse and received a look from Somerville.

"Yes," Carradine continued. "Lara is very beautiful." His interlocutors glanced at each other, as though Carradine had already provided them with cast-iron evidence of the depths of his love. "I found her easy to talk to. She was very straight with me, sensitive around what had happened with Stephen Graham. . . ."

"Sensitive," said Hulse. "You mean finding out you weren't working for the Service, you were actually working for Moscow?"

"Of course that's what I mean." Carradine wondered why Hulse had seen fit to remind him of his humiliation. "She said that she'd known Graham, implied that he'd been in love with her, but that he hadn't known that she knew he was a Russian agent."

"That's about right." Somerville was absentmindedly brushing crumbs from the table.

"How would you know that?" Carradine asked.

"Know what?" Somerville replied.

"That Lara knew Mantis was a false flag."

Somerville reared back in his seat. He looked simultaneously impressed by Carradine's question and extremely cautious about answering it.

"You don't miss much, do you, Kit?"

"Not anymore." Hulse was also staring at him. He smiled automatically when Carradine caught his eye. "Seriously," he said. "Answer the question. How do you know about Lara's dealings with Mantis?"

The two men again looked at each other. It was hard to discern who was in overall command: the Brit or the Yank? Carradine had not yet been able to pin down Somerville's personality or objectives. His mood seemed to depend on what was being discussed and who was discussing it. He could seem distant and formal; he could be jokey and relaxed. These contradictions extended to his appearance: in a certain light Somerville's features were indistinct, even bland; at other times his face came alive with ideas and questions. Even his responses about Bartok had been confusing to Carradine. He knew that Somerville was holding something back.

A mobile phone rang on the far side of the Members' Room. It was a long time before it was answered.

"You've never signed the Official Secrets Act, have you?" Somerville reached into the pocket of his jacket.

"No," Carradine replied. "Not a real one, anyway."

Somerville took out a small piece of paper and placed it on the table. It was identical to the document Carradine had signed in Lisson Grove, down to the texture of the paper. Hulse produced a pen with the flourish of a magician's assistant.

"I suggest that you do so now," said Somerville. "Then we can really start to get to know one another."

43

Fifteen minutes later the driver picked them up on Piccadilly and drove the short distance to a mock French brasserie in Soho. There were reproduction Toulouse-Lautrec prints on the wall, black-and-white photographs of Jeanne Moreau and Yves Montand in the bathroom. The waiters wore black waistcoats and white aprons and spoke with Eastern European accents. Edith Piaf was playing on the sound system. Sitting at a small wooden table close to a zinc-topped bar, Hulse ordered a Diet Coke, Somerville a pint of lager and Carradine a large gin and tonic. He had wanted a vodka martini but thought it would be absurd to ask for one in front of two bona fide spies. No explanation was given for the change of venue. Somerville was very specific about picking the table; Carradine wondered if it was wired. He had now signed the Secrets Act and was effectively under oath. Yet if that was the case, why not take him to a safe house?

"Here's the basic situation." Somerville was picking at a bowl of peanuts and trying to be heard over *"Non, Je Ne Regrette Rien."* "Ramón was a paid agent of Stephen Graham. Let's call him Mantis for the sake of clarity. One of many on his books. Drug problem, alcohol problem, hooker problem."

"So he wasn't murdered?"

"Oh, he was murdered all right," said Hulse. "Moroccan police tried to make out it was accidental. An overdose. But the Russians got to them. Covered it up."

Carradine wasn't particularly convinced by that answer. It could just as easily have been the case that the Agency had killed Ramón and paid the Moroccan authorities to keep it quiet. In fact, Carradine hadn't been particularly convinced by anything Hulse had told him. Throughout the debriefing he had developed a sense that neither man knew as much about him as he had expected them to know. He was being assessed and appraised; it was almost as if they were trying to work out whether or not to keep using him in whatever operation they were cooking up.

"Mantis asked Ramón to keep an eye on you and to help in the search for the girl." Somerville spoke with seeming authority. "Needed to know that you weren't going to blab your mouth off about LASZLO. The irony being that it was Ramón who was indiscreet. Searched for information about her online. Dropped hints that he was engaged in secret work."

"He said that to you in the club in Casablanca?" Carradine asked, turning to Hulse.

Hulse nodded. "Guy was a mess, but I guess Mantis was desperate and using anybody he could find. Bottom line, Moscow wanted to find Bartok and bring her in. Mantis wanted to protect her. Used all kinds of means and methods to achieve that. Moscow found out, pushed him under the train."

"And you?" Carradine asked. "Why do you want to find her so badly?"

"I'm afraid at this stage that's above your pay grade, Kit." Somerville pushed the peanuts away, perhaps remembering that his doctor had warned him not to consume too much salt. "We just want to talk to her. She knows a lot. She could put some pieces of the puzzle together."

Carradine could feel his temper beginning to fray.

"Listen," he said. "If you want me to help you, I need to know what's going on."

"What makes you think we need your help?" said Hulse.

Carradine was stuck for an answer. He found himself saying: "I care about Lara. You're not the only ones who want to keep her alive."

Somerville sipped his pint. Hulse did the same with his Diet Coke. It was as though they were both thinking the same thing.

"You're in love with her," said Somerville.

"Is that a statement or a question?"

"Statement," said Hulse, pulling the peanuts toward him and throwing a handful down his throat.

"I am not in love with her." Carradine was annoyed to be talking about his personal life with two men he wouldn't have trusted to help an old lady across the road. "I'm just fond of her. I like her. I'd like to see her again."

"*Fond* of her?" said Hulse, as if nobody had used the term since the latter half of the nineteenth century. "What does *that* mean?"

"It means he went native." Somerville showed a sudden flash of spite. "It means Lara persuaded him that Ivan Simakov was Gandhi with a side order of Mandela. It means he thinks she's a paragon of revolutionary virtue, a woman of conviction, a misunderstood heroine fighting for a righteous cause."

"You have no idea what I think about her, or Ivan Simakov for that matter." Carradine was shocked by how quickly Somerville's mood had turned. It occurred to him that both men were trying to provoke him, perhaps as a test of his temperament. "I read somewhere that Simakov was a Russian intelligence officer before he founded Resurrection. Is that true?"

Tellingly, Somerville and Hulse both looked down at their drinks.

"I'll take the Fifth on that," said Hulse.

"Me, too," said Somerville then, jokingly: "Come to think of it, we need a Fifth in this country." He succumbed to the temptation to eat a lone peanut and said: "You were going to tell us how you feel about Resurrection."

"Yeah," said Hulse, glad to be switching subjects. "How *do* you feel about them, Kit?"

Carradine looked around the deserted brasserie. The floor was a chessboard of polished black-and-white tiles. It occurred to him that he was most likely a sacrificial pawn in whatever game Hulse and Somerville were playing.

"First of all, I don't think of Resurrection as 'them,'" he said. "It's not a group. Resurrection began as an international movement of individuals, all of whom were seeking the same outcome."

"What, like Manchester United fans?" said Somerville. Hulse smothered a grin.

"If you like." Carradine did not want to be deflected from his answer. "To be honest, when I first became aware of Resurrection a few years ago, the purity of Simakov's intentions, the plain language of the manifesto, I warmed to it. I supported it. The people they were targeting were disgusting. They were liars, narcissists. Many of them were criminals who should have been in jail. I was glad when Otis Euclidis was exposed as a charlatan. I was glad that Piet Boutmy was attacked in Amsterdam. I liked it that the center Left was finally getting off its arse and fighting back instead of wasting time moaning about the animal fat content in the new five-pound note or protesting about the absence of gender-neutral toilets at the LSE." Hulse looked confused. "The world was going to shit and the people who were taking it there were getting a free pass. There had been right-wing coups d'état in my country, in Russia, in Turkey, the United States. Resurrection chimed with me, just as it chimed with many of my friends, my father, with hundreds of thousands of people around the world."

"You didn't think for a moment it was a bit naïve?"

The supercilious tone of Somerville's question suggested that he would tolerate only one kind of answer. Carradine took a long slug of his drink and said: "In what way?"

"Oh, in the way that a bunch of semi-radicalized, ludicrously idealistic liberal intellectuals trying to make the world a better place is *always* a bit naïve. What did they do in those first halcyon months? Throw a pot of paint here. Chuck a shoe there. Kidnap a couple of here-today-gone-tomorrow journalists? 'Give me a break,' as our friend from across the Pond might say. You didn't think human nature might get in the way?" Carradine opened his mouth to reply but Somerville was up and running. "Never underestimate the vanity of self-styled revolutionaries. 'Man the barricades, guys. Let's revive the spirit of '68. We're the new Black Panthers. This is our Prague Spring.' It's all a pose, all nostalgia, like everything nowadays. Revolutionaries? Don't make me laugh. Take away their iPhones for five minutes and they'd have a seizure." It looked as though he was finished, but Somerville added a coda. "What was the phrase Simakov used in the manifesto? 'Those who know that they have done wrong.' Have you ever heard anything so ridiculous? It's a miracle anybody took him seriously."

"What do you mean?" Carradine was wondering why Somerville had become so agitated. It was as though he had a personal stake in some aspect of Resurrection's activities.

"I mean how are we, as human beings, supposed to identify such people? 'Those who know that they have done wrong.' They can't even identify *themselves*. What Simakov and his merry band of followers failed to realize is that most people aren't particularly interested in playing nice. They want to *join* the groups that have their hands on the levers of power. They want to gorge themselves at the same troughs that have enriched the so-called 'elites.' They don't want to smash the state; they want to *assist* it so that they can join in the fun. People are greedy, Kit. Human beings are selfish, competitive. You're a novelist, for Christ's sake. Surely you've realized that by now?"

"The only thing I've realized is that you've been working too long for an organization that sees only the worst in people." Carradine was waiting for Hulse to add his two cents, but the American seemed content to listen. "I have much greater faith in the essential decency of humankind."

Somerville repeated the phrase with scornful condescension—"*the essential decency of humankind*"—and drained the last of his pint. Hulse looked on with an expression of benign amusement. "Isn't that touching? You should have known, just as Lara and Simakov should have known, that ideological movements of the Resurrection sort, particularly those that take on a paramilitary quality, are always hijacked by thugs and bigots, by the intolerant, holier-than-thou 'no platform' crowd, by the self-righteous and the misguided."

"Maybe so," Carradine replied, aware that Somerville had referred to Bartok by her first name twice in the space of five minutes. "Maybe so. But there was nobility at the outset. The possibility of real change. There was hope."

"What a load of cock." Somerville stood up and stretched his back. "Change? Hope? Save me from the romantic delusions of the artistic classes. Save me from the *writers*. Same again, gentlemen?"

"Just a minute," said Carradine. It was important to respond to Somerville's accusations. "I've never been involved in Resurrection actions—"

Somerville interrupted him.

"That's not the point," he said.

"Of course it's the point." To his consternation, Hulse was checking a message on his mobile phone. "I'm here because you wanted to speak to me. I'm here because I'm worried that the people who were hunting Lara in Morocco, the men who killed Ramón and Mantis, may try to do the same to me. I need your help. I want answers. I don't understand why the fuck I'm listening to you ranting on about Resurrection."

"Oh, don't worry about the Moscow men." Somerville placed a hand on Carradine's back. It was as though he considered the potential threat to his life to be no more serious than the matter of settling the bill in the restaurant. "They'll never touch you. They think you're one of us."

"They *what*?!"

Carradine was stunned. Hulse looked up from his phone. "Think about it," he said, taking over the narrative from Somerville. "You turn up in Lara's apartment and beat up on the guy they sent to grab her. You write about espionage with a degree of verisimilitude. . . ."

"Ooh, nice word," said Somerville.

"Thanks, man." Hulse put his wallet on the table. Carradine could see the outline of a condom pressing out through the leather. "Then you vanish from Marrakech without a trace, as far as they're concerned with the connivance of the British Secret Service. . . ."

"That's what they *think*?" Carradine suddenly understood why he had been left unmolested since he returned to London. "How do you *know* all this?"

"Pay grade, Kit. Pay grade." It had become a shorthand for whatever Somerville felt like concealing from him. He ordered more drinks and walked off in the direction of the gents, leaving Carradine alone with Hulse. He had been handed an unexpected opportunity to speak to the American in more detail about what had happened in Morocco.

"What about Oubakir?" he said. "Can you tell me about him, or is he above my pay grade, too?"

"Who?" Hulse was putting the phone back in his pocket. Either he hadn't heard the name clearly or was pretending not to have recognized it.

"Mohammed Oubakir. How did he know you were Agency? Why did he warn me in Blaine's to be careful around you?"

"He said that?" An Ed Sheeran song came on the sound system. Somebody at a table on the far side of the brasserie shouted out: "Oh for fuck's sake, not this shit."

"He said that," Carradine confirmed.

Hulse took a moment to compose himself.

"Look," he said. "I work North Africa. I meet a lot of people. Some of them assume I work for the Agency, some of them don't. Oubakir was on our radar because of his association with Mantis. We knew he was feeding intel back to Moscow thinking it was going to London. We allowed Stephen Graham to continue to operate for precisely this reason. He showed us who the Russians were interested in, where the gaps were in their knowledge, who they were talking to. When I saw you eating dinner with Oubakir, and Ramón told me you were associated with Mantis, I got suspicious. It's what I'm paid to do."

Not for the first time Carradine wished that he could take some time off, write everything down, try to work out exactly who was telling him the truth and who wasn't. He saw Somerville coming back from the gents.

"So, as I was saying." It was as if he had been away for no more than a few seconds. The waiter put a pint on the table and returned to the bar to collect the other drinks. "Here's my theory on the pointlessness of Resurrection." Somerville sat down, took a draw from the pint, and looked as though he expected a rapt audience. "Life is cyclical, gentlemen. It goes in phases. Seven years of famine. Seven years of plenty. The issues that are aggravating us today have been aggravating our forefathers for centuries. There is nothing new under the sun. A noble, articulate, mixed-race liberal icon takes over the Presidency of the United States. Does he make the world a better place? No, he does not. A narcissistic sociopath with a thin skin and a bad dye job disgraces the Presidency of the United States. Does he make the world a *worse* place? No, he does not." The waiter put a gin and tonic in front of Hulse, another Diet Coke in front of Carradine. Carradine switched them around. "We are a planet of individuals. Our happiness is tied to small things: food, water, sex, friendship. Manchester United." A grin from Hulse. "The activities of a tin-pot dictator in Washington, Moscow or Istanbul don't amount to a hill of beans in terms of a man's contentment."

"Try telling that to the people they imprison, the people they humiliate, the people they kill," said Carradine.

"That's my point!" Somerville exclaimed. "In any historical cycle there will be people who suffer, people who die, people who are imprisoned because of the actions of their politicians. But to think that you can make those politicians act differently, to think that you can change the outlook or behavior of a newspaper columnist, a politician, a corrupt banker, a climate change denier—whoever you happen to have a gripe with that week—is the height of fucking stupidity. Nobody ever changes their mind about anything!"

Hulse was about to interrupt when Somerville silenced him.

"Furthermore, it is my personal belief that the more rancid, the more corrupt, the more cynical, the more craven the behavior of our public officials, the more it brings decent people closer and closer together. To condemn them? Yes. But also to remind ourselves that the vast majority of people are well-intentioned, decent citizens and that the targets of Resurrection are therefore a tiny minority of mavericks and outliers who are best ignored, and certainly tolerated."

"I wish I could agree with you, Julian," said Hulse.

"Me, too," said Carradine, trying to square Somerville's optimistic remarks with his earlier tirade against greed and self-interest. Somerville's phone rang. He answered it with a brisk "Hello" then listened as whoever was calling delivered what appeared to be astounding news. Even Hulse seemed surprised. Somerville's facial expression moved from relaxed good humor to profound shock in the space of a few seconds.

"Say that again," he said. "When? *How?*"

There was a lengthy silence. Carradine would have given the world to know what Somerville had been told. Hulse mouthed the words "What's up?" but Somerville ignored him.

"I see," he said. "OK, understood. Yes. We're leaving now. I'll see you as soon as I see you. Bye."

44

Somerville took £30 out of his wallet, handed the money to Carradine and summoned Hulse to his feet.

"We have to go," he said. "Kit, here's a number to reach me at if you're ever worried or get in any trouble."

Scribbling the number on the back of a menu, Somerville apologized for bringing the meeting to such an abrupt conclusion but explained that something urgent had come up at work.

"What kind of thing?" Carradine asked. He noticed that the first five digits written down were the same as his own and that the number ended with a sequence of twos.

"Pay grade," said Hulse, adjusting his jacket.

"That should cover the drinks," said Somerville, nodding at the money. Carradine didn't think that it would.

"So I just go back to my old life?" he said. "Forget about Lara? Forget about Morocco?"

"Forget about all of us." Hulse patted him on the back in a way that Carradine found intensely irritating. "Just keep writing those books, Kit. That's what you're good at."

That last, patronizing remark, delivered as Hulse and Somerville hurried out of the brasserie looking like ushers running late for a wedding, cemented an idea in Carradine's mind. In an instant, his natural curiosity and thirst for risk got the better of him. He pinned the money under his half-finished gin and tonic, tore the number off the menu and followed them out onto the street.

Emerging from the brasserie, he saw Hulse ducking into the backseat of the Jaguar on the opposite side of the road. He assumed that Somerville was already inside. Two black cabs were coming down the one-way street. Carradine raised his hand, missed the first taxi but hailed the second.

"Do you see that Jaguar?" he said, climbing into the back.

"What's that, guv?"

The driver switched on a microphone so that they could hear one another more clearly. He had a central casting Cockney accent, a shaved head and a perfectly horizontal crease of fat at the base of his scalp.

"There's a green Jaguar up ahead on the left."

"So there is."

"How do you feel about following it?"

"How do I *feel*?" There was a pause. Carradine remembered tailing Lara to the riad in Marrakech. "If you're paying, mate, I'll follow whoever you want me to follow. Follow my leader. Follow the money. Follow the yellow brick road. Whatever you want."

By force of habit Carradine fastened his seat belt, a detail he would have excluded had he been writing the scene in a script or novel. He couldn't imagine Humphrey Bogart or Harrison Ford being concerned about backseat safety.

"Great," he said. The Jaguar was about fifty meters ahead and already indicating to the right. Somerville and Hulse could be heading to Service headquarters, to the American Embassy, to a safe house or airport. "Do you take credit cards?" he asked.

"If you've got 'em, I take 'em," said the driver, making eye contact in the rearview mirror. "So who are we following? Jealous husband? Jealous housewife? David Beckham?"

"I really have no idea," Carradine replied, leaning back in his seat. "No idea at all."

45

Hulse and Somerville did not go far. Carradine followed the Jaguar from Soho to Hyde Park Corner then southwest into Mayfair. The driver did such a good job of keeping a discreet distance and concealing himself in traffic that Carradine wondered if he had previous experience.

"Ever been asked to follow someone before?"

"Once or twice, guv. Once or twice."

The Jaguar pulled up outside a large terraced house on Chapel Street. Carradine recognized the road. He had been to a party in an Italian restaurant on the corner less than a year earlier. The cab loitered about a hundred meters away as Somerville emerged from the Jaguar and looked up at the house.

"Suspect number one," said the driver. "Someone should have a word with him about that suit."

Carradine was trying to work out which address Somerville was heading into. Hulse opened the back door and joined him on the pavement. Somerville tapped on the roof and the Jaguar pulled away.

"Now that geezer's gotta be a Yank. You can tell 'em a mile off."

"You're not wrong," Carradine replied, observing the contrast between Hulse's healthy, athletic demeanor and the slightly stooped, anxious-looking Somerville.

"What now?" the driver asked.

"I give you money," Carradine replied, handing over a twenty-pound note. "You've been brilliant. Thanks so much." The change came back but Carradine waved it away. "Do me a favor and forget this ever happened."

"Sure thing. Say no more."

The taxi pulled away leaving Carradine in the middle of the road. He had seen Somerville and Hulse going down a flight of steps toward a basement. They were now out of sight. He jogged toward the house, keeping an eye on a damaged column beyond the gate as a marker for the entrance.

He walked up to the building, staying on the street side of the pavement so that his feet would not be visible to anyone who happened to look up from the basement. He came to a halt and looked down.

Sitting at a table with a piece of paper, a pen and what looked like a voice recorder in front of her, was Lara Bartok. She stood up as Somerville came into the room and shook his hand. There was no question in Carradine's mind that they already knew each other; the body language between them was unmistakable. This was a reunion, not an introduction. As somebody else in the room lowered a set of pale yellow blinds, preventing Carradine from seeing anything else through the window, the beauty and the depth of the operation became clear to him in a moment of overwhelming clarity. He turned away from the house, dumbfounded by what he now understood.

46

Lara Bartok was a spy. Carradine could think of no other plausible explanation for everything that had taken place. Recruited by the Service in her early twenties, she had been played against Ivan Simakov when he had been working for Russian intelligence. She had subsequently fallen in love with him and effectively deserted her post. That was why Somerville had been so agitated by any mention of Resurrection and so dismissive of the movement's ethos. He had recruited Bartok but failed to stop her succumbing to Simakov's charms. He had lost her to a cause greater than his own.

The more Carradine thought about it, the more the theory made sense. When Bartok had decided to leave Simakov, she had not been able to seek the Service's protection. As a common criminal, sought by the American authorities, London had abandoned her to her fate. Carradine thought back to their conversation in the riad. When he had asked her how she knew that Stephen Graham was operating under a false flag, her answer had been vague and evasive. *I just knew.* She knew because there had never been a "Stephen Graham" on the books at British Intelligence.

Carradine lit a cigarette. He was walking along Chapel Street in a heightened state, close to the exhilaration a writer experiences after a creative breakthrough. Yet he was also disturbed by the idea that Lara was so close and yet so out of reach. He wanted to see her, to hear her side of the story. He fought the urge to go to the basement and to ring the doorbell. Quite apart from the humiliation of being followed to the flat, Somerville and Hulse would be horrified to see him. They were hardly likely to welcome him into the fold and make him privy to what they knew about LASZLO. More likely he would be escorted from the building and placed on a watch list. Carradine's presence might also make things difficult for Bartok. It was better to stay away, to use what he now knew to his own advantage. Whatever Somerville might ask of him in the future, whatever lies Hulse may or may not tell, whatever claims were made, Carradine would know the truth. Information was power.

He returned to his flat on foot. It was a beautiful summer evening. As he walked through Hyde Park, Carradine began to unravel more of the mysteries of Morocco. He remembered Bartok's reluctance to go to the British Embassy in Rabat. She had been afraid of arrest, perhaps even of being handed over to the Americans. If that was the case, why was she now in London? Had she been seized in Spain or had she decided to hand herself in?

It was almost dark by the time he reached his flat. He opened the door and switched on the light in the hall. He usually placed his house keys in a small bowl on a table facing the door. The bowl was not there. The cleaner, Mrs. Ritter, had been to the flat while he was away. Perhaps she had moved it.

Carradine went into the living room. As he put his phone down on a side table, he became aware that the rug in the center of the room was facing the wrong way. The black horses in the design usually looked out in the direction of Hyde Park, but the rug had been spun ninety degrees and was now facing toward the kitchen. He wondered if Mrs. Ritter had also been there that afternoon, though she always texted if she was planning to come on a different day.

He walked into his office. Two vintage movie posters hung above his desk. A Japanese advertisement for *Three Days of the Condor* which Carradine had bought online, and a rare French poster for *The Conversation* showing Gene Hackman with a set of headphones clamped to his ear. Redford and Dunaway were always on the right-hand side of his desk, Hackman on the left.

The posters had been switched.

Carradine began to feel unsettled. He looked at his bookshelves. They were usually arranged by author yet somebody had moved the books around. Updike was mixed in with Ambler, Deighton with Philip Roth. He stared at the shelves, trying to think of any conceivable reason why Mrs. Ritter might have put the books back in the wrong order. A complete set of Pauline Kael's collected film reviews were stacked on the ground, as if someone had been dusting the shelves and had forgotten to put them back.

Carradine sat at his desk, aware that his breathing had become more shallow, his body constricted. He looked in the drawer where he had left the memory stick. It was no longer there. He tapped the keyboard to bring the screen to life and entered his password. The desktop opened as normal. He knew that whoever had been in his office would have tried to access the information on the computer. Then he saw that the backup hard drive usually attached to his Dell was missing from the desk. Whoever had taken the memory stick had also taken the drive.

Carradine felt nauseous. The changes to his flat were a Russian signature; diplomats in Moscow regularly had the pictures and furniture in their homes switched around by local goons. He went into his bedroom and saw right away, like a childish schoolboy prank, that the bottom sheet had been removed. A pile of shoes was stacked up by the door. Carradine went out into the sitting room to find his phone. He would call Somerville using the number he had written on the menu. There was no point involving the police.

As he was taking the torn menu from his jacket pocket, he looked into the kitchen. Light was bouncing off the linoleum floor. Water had spilled from the sink, which had been filled to capacity. Carradine rolled up a sleeve and put his hand into the water, looking for the plug. The water was dirty but still warm. He touched something hard at the bottom of the sink and pulled it out. He knew what it was before it had broken the surface. They had put his laptop in the sink.

Carradine stepped back, water dripping from the computer onto the floor. He prayed that he had a copy of his novel backed up in the cloud but knew that whoever had broken into his flat would have the wherewithal to erase it online as easily as they had switched the posters in his office. He put the laptop on the kitchen table, dried his hands and dialed the number.

Somerville did not pick up.

Carradine tried a second time. There was still no answer. He assumed that the phone was on mute or that there was no signal in the basement. For all the times that he had written about mobile phone technology in his books, he still did not know if a phone rang out if there was no signal or if it had failed to connect.

A WhatsApp message came through from the number.

Everything OK? Sorry to leave you in the lurch.

Carradine tapped out a reply. He did not know how to express what had happened.

Slight problem at my flat. Need advice.

Carradine saw that Somerville was "typing." It was like texting Mantis all over again.

Someone will come round within the hour. Stay put.

Carradine didn't bother to give his address. He assumed the Service already knew where he lived. He replied "OK" to Somerville's message, lit a cigarette, and poured himself three inches of vodka.

Less than forty minutes later a new message came through from Somerville telling Carradine to go to a pub on Bayswater Road. Somebody from the Service would meet him there. Carradine knew the pub—it was his local—and described what he was wearing so that the contact would be able to recognize him.

Don't worry about that. They know exactly who you are.

He grabbed his keys, his wallet and his phone and left the flat. He tugged three separate strands of hair from his head and glued them to the frame of the door with saliva so that he might be able to tell if someone had broken in while he was gone. He applied the last of the strands to the bottom of the doorframe and hoped that one of his neighbors wouldn't come out of their flat and ask what on earth he was doing.

He rode the lift to the ground floor. It was dark outside and the street was deserted. The pub was no more than half a mile away. He hadn't eaten for hours and was suddenly famished.

He heard the men coming up behind him before he had time to react. They came quickly, running with light steps. Carradine swung around and saw two of them less than three meters away, closing in. To his consternation, he realized that the man closest to him was the Russian he had knocked out cold in Marrakech.

"Hello, Mr. Considine," he said.

That was the last thing Carradine remembered.

47

Carradine woke up in a comfortable, beautifully furnished bedroom. There was no sound of traffic, only the occasional rush of wind and the regular tweet of birdsong. He felt as though he had slept for twelve hours straight. He was dressed in the same clothes he had been wearing when he had left the flat. His wallet and keys were on a bedside table stacked with antiquarian books. His phone was nowhere to be seen.

Carradine sat up in bed. He was desperately thirsty. There was an en-suite bathroom on the far side of the room. He filled a tooth mug at the basin and drank three glasses of water in quick succession. His muscles were stiff and his head ached but when he looked in the mirror, he saw that his face was unmarked. He needed to shower and shave but was surprised by how calm he felt. He understood that he was probably in a state of shock.

He walked back into the bedroom and pulled back the curtains on the set of windows closest to the door. Carradine was momentarily blinded by bright sunshine but saw that he was standing in a room on the first floor of a dilapidated farmhouse overlooking a muddy yard and, in the distance, a checkerboard of fields. He remembered

Somerville telling him that Moscow would leave him alone on the assumption that he was working for the Service. There was a tiny slice of consolation in that thought. Then he remembered that his flat had been turned upside down and his laptop destroyed. He stepped away from the window and sat back on the bed. He was now afraid.

Carradine tried to shake off a growing dread. He needed to think more clearly. He told himself that he was on a property controlled by Russian intelligence. There was surely no other possibility. It occurred to him that Somerville and Hulse were subjecting him to some kind of training exercise or test, but that theory was too absurd to be taken seriously. Whoever had kidnapped him wanted answers. That was all anybody ever wanted from him. Hulse. Bartok. Somerville. They had all been the same. They had stripped him for information then vanished into the night.

Footfalls on a staircase. Somebody was coming up to the room. Carradine pushed a hand through his hair and stood up, preparing to meet whoever came through the door. He did not know who or what to expect. He assumed that the man from Lara's apartment in Marrakech was the most likely candidate.

It was not him.

The man who came into the room was slim and tan, with shoulder-length black hair tied in a ponytail. He was wearing glasses and sporting a thick, biblical salt-and-pepper beard. His fast, intelligent eyes grinned at Carradine as he flashed him a benevolent smile.

"Kit," he said. "Welcome to our temporary home. Do you like it?"

The voice was deep and rich, the slick international accent hard to place. He was wearing designer jeans and what appeared to be a brand-new pair of Red Wing boots. He oozed the easy confidence and poise of the self-made man.

"Who are you?"

The answer to the question revealed itself even as Carradine was asking it. The man standing in front of him, his appearance subtly altered by the addition of glasses and by the fullness of the beard, was the same man whose face Carradine had stared at in dozens of articles and obituaries over the course of the previous fortnight.

He was talking to Ivan Simakov.

48

You are a hard man to pin down, Kit. Are you just a writer or are you also a British spy? Do you know this world you have fallen into or is all of this a novelty?" Simakov smirked as he gestured outside, loving the sound of his own voice, enjoying the power he was exerting over his stunned and frightened prisoner. "Are you Lara's new boyfriend, the man who has taken her from me? Or did she play you and manipulate you as she has played and manipulated so many others? Who are you, Kit Carradine? A genius or a fool? Tell me, please. I am fascinated."

Carradine felt that he was staring at a ghost, a dream of a dead man. Ivan Simakov had been killed in a Moscow apartment and buried in an unmarked grave. The man standing in front of him had somehow managed to fake his own death and to make a new life in the West. How was this possible?

"You are who I think you are?" he said.

"I am!" Simakov replied, reveling in his own myth.

"How?" said Carradine.

Simakov waved a dismissive hand, as if the whys and wherefores of his miraculous rebirth were of no greater consequence than the sound of the wind outside or the persistent tweet of birdsong. He clutched his hands behind his back.

"Where am I?" Carradine asked.

Simakov tipped back his head and smiled.

"Rest assured you are still in your beloved England, that green and pleasant land. Within two hours, driving along the motorway, you could be back at your desk writing another thriller, another little story about spies."

Carradine was too stunned to be irritated by the slight. He saw that Simakov intended to keep talking. He had the air of a man who was used to supplicants hanging on his every word.

"We are on a farm at the edge of a typical country estate once owned by the English aristocracy, but now lost to those who could afford to keep it in the correct style." Carradine wondered how and why Simakov had been given access to the property; he assumed that it was under Russian ownership. "The British ruling class are inexplicably pleased with themselves, don't you think?" He moved toward the window closest to the bathroom and drew back the curtains. "Your aristocrats can no longer afford to heat their homes. Your banks are owned by Arabs and Chinese. The finest buildings in London belong to Russians. The great English writers and poets have all vanished. Your culture, like so many other cultures today, is an American culture of karaoke, of recycled stories, of political decay and mass stupidity. The great English churches are in the hands of property developers, the schools, so far as I can tell, are controlled not by teachers, but by their pupils. There is no *discipline* in your society. No discipline or intellectual curiosity, only ignorance. Above all, despite this, there seems to be a complete absence of self-doubt in the British character! What is it, exactly, that you are so proud of? You lost an empire and replaced it with—*what*?"

Carradine saw that he was expected to answer.

"With views like that you sound like you'd fit in very well in Moscow," he said. "Everything's a bit binary with you so far, Ivan. Genius or fool? Old Britain good, new Britain bad. I thought you were fighting for freedom of choice, for openness, for decency? I didn't have you down as a reactionary."

Rather than express any discomfort or annoyance with what Carradine had said, Simakov merely touched his beard and looked out at the farmyard, like an admiral surveying his fleet.

"It's true. All through my life I have been confused by your country. I used to tell Lara this." Carradine knew the reference to Bartok was intended to unsettle him. Simakov suddenly turned from the window and looked back across the room. "I thought you would be more upper-class."

"Excuse me?"

"Kit. It sounds like a character in an Evelyn Waugh novel. Nobody is called 'Kit' anymore. What *was* William thinking?"

At the mention of his father's name, Carradine felt sick with worry. Simakov pretended to reassure him.

"Please do not worry," he said, raising a conciliatory hand. "The old man has not been harmed. Yet."

The menace of that last word floored Carradine. He wanted to know what had happened, where his father was being held, to demand that Resurrection release him. But he knew that to show his fear would be to play into Simakov's hands.

"Where is he?" he said, trying to remain as calm as possible. "What is it you want with us?"

Simakov ignored the question.

"Here's the thing." He offered Carradine a cigarette. Carradine wanted one but refused it. Simakov smiled as he placed the packet in his pocket. "Mankind has reached its zenith. *Homo sapiens* has come as far as he can come." He inhaled deeply. "We can eat, we can drink, we can fuck, we can communicate, we can travel, we can do whatever we want. About the only thing we are not permitted to do is smoke!" He smiled at his own joke. Carradine knew that he was listening to a man with no moral compass, no values or kindness, only his own self-love. "There are cures for AIDS and cures for cancer, artificial limbs for the disabled, central heating and hot water and electricity in every home. Every book and film and play and poem and fragment of knowledge ever assembled is available at the click of a mouse or the weight of a finger on the screen of a cellphone. The world has never had it so good. And yet people are still not satisfied! They are so spoiled." Was this a speech Simakov had prepared in advance or was he making it up off the top of his head? Bartok had spoken about being mesmerized by Simakov's words, but this felt more like an actor giving a performance that had been rehearsed time and time again. "It turns out that mankind is so competitive, so adversarial, so frightened of change, so geared to cruelty that he will willfully destroy his own society, his own culture— for what? Independence? *Freedom?* What do Americans mean when they say that they crave 'freedom'? Do they not realize that they are already free!"

Carradine could hardly take in what Simakov was saying. He was thinking about his father, wondering if he was a prisoner in the same house. What would Resurrection try to extract from him in return for his father's safety? Did Simakov know that he had once been a British spy? He wished that he had never set eyes on Stephen Graham, that he had never been so reckless or so vain as to agree to work for the Service.

"I will tell you why they destroyed their own societies." Simakov opened a window. A smell of manure burst into the room. "They blew it all up for the chance to hate. For a sentimental version of an all-white past that didn't exist and can never exist in the future. People by their millions, here and in America, in Poland, in Hungary, in Turkey, voted for going backward when they didn't even need to go *forward*. All they had to do was stand still. Life was never going to get any better. They were never going to be more 'free.' There were never going to be more steaks in the freezer, more ways in which they could be happy and

content. That was the tragedy. Resurrection merely took advantage of
that."

Carradine was confused by that final remark.

"What do you mean?" he said. "What do you mean you took advantage of it?"

Simakov looked as though he had not intended to speak so candidly.
It was the first time Carradine had witnessed a crack in his overween-
ing, theatrical self-confidence. He had the sensation—so familiar from
conversations with Bartok and Somerville—that he was at the edge of
a secret that was being deliberately withheld from him.

"So." Simakov wanted to change the subject. "You must answer me.
Can I expect a visit from the British Secret Service, come to rescue one
of their own? Or are you just another penny thriller writer of no great
importance who spends his life making up stories rather than engaging with the real world and effecting necessary change?"

Carradine knew that Simakov was not interested in the answer. It
was just part of a game designed to unsettle him. All he could do was
wait and bide his time and find out what it was that Simakov wanted.
Carradine's only concern was to work out where he was and how he was
going to save his father.

"Where's my dad?" he said.

Simakov shrugged. "Safe."

"My family is not a threat to you. What do you want?"

Simakov walked into the bathroom, ran a tap at the sink, extinguished his cigarette in the stream of water and threw it into the toilet.

"You are well rested!" he exclaimed. "You feel fit! You feel good! You
want to ask me questions and be direct." He came back into the room
and stood in front of Carradine. "OK, I will be direct with you. You are
here because you have been with Lara."

In that moment Carradine understood that Simakov was still working for Russian intelligence. He had instructed them to find Lara and
to bring her to him. That was why Graham had acted as he did; he had

known of the operation and had wanted to save LASZLO. There was no other explanation for Simakov's miraculous survival. Moscow had detonated the bomb in the apartment knowing that their prize agent had long since left the building. Zack Curtis, the Resurrection volunteer who was killed in the blast, had been merely a sacrificial pawn.

"How do you know I've seen her?"

Simakov looked as though he had been insulted.

"Do I look to you like somebody who is short of information? Do I look like a man who has trouble finding things out?"

"Your friends in Moscow told you?"

Simakov did not bother to deny it.

"Yes," he replied cautiously. "They heard that you were looking for Lara on behalf of Stephen Graham. Is that correct?"

"Stephen Graham is dead," Carradine replied. "But I don't imagine that's news to you. Or to Moscow."

Simakov removed something from his mouth and said, "Stephen caused a lot of problems."

"Really? In the same way Ramón Basora and Zack Curtis caused a lot of problems, or was it something different this time?" Simakov winced. "Tell me, which one of your flunkies threw Graham under the train?"

It was a brave question. Carradine knew that he was pushing his luck. In his sudden understanding of Simakov's real identity, he had intuited a deeper, terrifying truth.

"You deflect very well, Mr. Carradine," Simakov exclaimed. "You avoid the questions you do not wish to answer. You ask me the questions which perhaps your masters have told you to ask. Perhaps you have been trained after all!"

"Only media training, Ivan," he said and regretted it immediately. He knew that Simakov's vanity would be offended by the fact that he did not seem to be afraid. The Russian duly exploded with laughter, the noise carrying outside into the farmyard and beyond to whoever was protecting him, to whoever knew that the supposed icon of nonviolent resistance was in fact a murderous thug still in the employ of Russian intelligence.

"You are funny!" he said, and suddenly swept his right arm across Carradine's face. The back of Simakov's hand connected with his jaw, sending him crashing to the ground. Carradine had been hit before, with greater force and skill, but never with such unexpectedness. The side of his face screamed in pain. He could feel a warm, alkaline pooling of blood in his mouth as he tried to stand up. "You should know when is the correct time to make jokes."

Carradine's mind was spinning in loops, from fear to determination, from despair to hope. He stood up and faced Simakov. He steadied himself. With the awful clarity of a man waking up to a truth long withheld from him, Carradine realized that, all along, Resurrection had been a Kremlin-approved operation to bring chaos to the West. The movement had been funded and organized with the express purpose of bringing chaos to the streets of New York and Washington and Los Angeles, to the neighborhoods of Berlin and Madrid and Paris. Bartok had been duped, Somerville and Hulse as well. There had been so few attacks in Russia not because the friends and relatives of Resurrection activists were being assassinated, but because there were no active Resurrection cells in Russia. There was no other explanation for the ease with which Simakov had been able to fake his own death, to continue to organize Resurrection strikes and to live, like some latter-day bin Laden, on a farm in the middle of the English countryside.

"Who owns this place?" he asked, wanting to swing a punch of his own but knowing that any number of Russian heavies were doubtless on the other side of the door waiting to burst in and defend their boss.

"Why do you ask?" Simakov replied. It pleased Carradine to see that he was rubbing his fist. He hoped that his jaw had smashed a bone in the back of the Russian's hand.

"You're meant to be dead. Anybody sees you, you're finished.

Who's protecting you? Who's paying your bills? A man like you should be cowering in a hut in the backwoods of Montana, living under a pseudonym in Ecuador, shuffling from bedsit to bedsit in the north of England, looking for recruits to your shabby cause. But you're not. You're here, living like a superannuated rock star in a Cotswolds farmhouse. Why is that?"

"I am a lucky man," Simakov replied. "I have friends in high places."

"Yeah. I bet you do." Carradine was gripped by a fatalistic courage, certain that he would never make it out of the house alive, but determined to go out on his own terms. He wanted to express to Simakov the depth of his contempt for what he had done, his conviction that the Russians had picked the wrong strategy, that they would lose in the end, but knew that to do so would be to waste his breath. Instead he continued to puncture Simakov's story.

"I was sorry to hear about your parents."

"Thank you." It was the first time Carradine had seen evidence in his expression of an authentic emotional response.

"It was an accident, wasn't it?"

"Excuse me?"

"The car crash. An accident?"

He wondered if the Great Martyred Leader would bother denying it. He wondered if Simakov would hit him again. Instead, he brought his face so close to Carradine's that he could smell the coffee on his breath as he spoke.

"I hated my parents. I hadn't seen them since I was nineteen years old. Why would I mourn the deaths of two people who had done so little for me?" He paused. "Yes, to answer your question, the crash was an accident."

"And what am I?" said Carradine. "Another Otis Euclidis? You'll keep me here in captivity until everyone assumes I'm dead?"

Simakov looked surprised. "Oh, you heard about that?" he said.

"Heard about what?"

"Dear little Otis has been found in a basement in Indiana. The Brazilian whore who used to rent the house for us tipped off the police that he'd been left there to die. There wasn't much of him left apparently. I imagine the stench was appalling."

Carradine shook his head in disgust.

"Speaking of cars," Simakov continued. "Do you see that vehicle outside?"

Carradine turned and looked out of the window. A large Transit van was parked in front of the house.

"Yes," he replied. His throat was bone dry. He could barely voice the word.

"We found the contents of your cellphone very interesting." Simakov was staring at him, his head tilted to one side. "You and I are going to be getting into that van, Kit. We're going to set out on a journey."

49

Carradine was taken downstairs and served food in a large kitchen by a woman who did not speak to him. Simakov came into the room. He was carrying a small bottle of water and a phone. He sat opposite Carradine at a wooden table and told the woman to leave. She took his plate to the sink and went out into the farmyard.

"I want to know what you think about Lara," he said.

Carradine's jaw was still aching. He had been hungry but had found it difficult to eat.

"Why is that important?" he replied.

"Did you fuck her?"

Carradine had a choice. To lie and to protect himself from further harm, or to make Simakov suffer by telling him the truth. He opted for a sophistry that would achieve both aims.

"What happened between us is private," he said. "My feelings for Lara are my own business, just as her feelings for me are hers."

"Did you fuck her?"

"Grow up, Ivan."

Simakov pulled out a handgun. For a split second Carradine thought that he was going to fire, but he placed the gun on the table—just out of Carradine's reach—and looked him in the eye.

"What did she say about me?"

Carradine looked at him with pity. "That you were the best, Ivan." He laid on the sarcasm, having intuited the extent to which Simakov needed to be praised and reassured. "She said you were unforgettable. One in a million. She's never got over you. What woman would?"

Simakov exploded with rage.

"WHAT DID SHE SAY ABOUT ME?"

Suddenly Carradine understood why the Russians had wanted so desperately to find Lara. Had they discovered that she had been a Service asset and had proof of Simakov's survival? She had left New York because she no longer loved Simakov and had lost faith in the movement; Moscow mistakenly believed that she knew the truth both about Ivan and Resurrection. That would explain why she needed to be silenced.

"Strangely enough, we didn't spend a lot of time talking about you. We were too busy trying not to get killed."

Simakov picked up the gun. His face was flushed with anger.

"Your cellphone," he said. "You've been to Chapel Street. You know that Hulse is there."

"Hulse?"

It was obvious that Simakov knew of their connection. There was no point in lying. Carradine heard the sound of movement in a room close by. He wondered if his father was being brought to see him.

"Sebastian Hulse has become a thorn in my side." Simakov touched the butt of the gun. "He knows too much. He is going to be eliminated."

"Eliminated." The ease with which Simakov spoke of death made Carradine feel nauseous. "Just like that."

"Just like that."

Carradine looked down at the gun. He knew what Simakov was going to ask him to do. He felt that he was caught in a trap from which there would be no escape. He wondered when he would be shown the photographs of his father in captivity. He could not think of any way to get a message to Somerville or Hulse to tell them what had happened. He prayed that whoever had been sent to the pub to meet him would realize that he had been kidnapped. Would the Service bother to come looking for him—or leave him to his fate?

"Why don't you tell me what it is that you want me to do?" he said.

Simakov stood up. There was an apple in a bowl on the table. He polished it on the side of his trousers and took a bite, staring at Carradine as he chewed.

"I had Mr. Hulse followed from his hotel."

"Your Russian friends again?"

"Excuse me?"

"They followed him? The same friends who stole my hard drive? They're the ones who analyzed my phone? That's how you know I read your obituaries, your life story. Moscow does your dirty work."

Carradine saw that Simakov had no intention of answering him.

"What should we find," he continued, "but that Hulse is visiting the same address in Chapel Street that you showed such an interest in." Simakov took another bite of the apple. "So I had the basement watched. And who should we see coming out but a certain Mr. Julian Somerville. Who is this, please?"

"You know who he is," Carradine replied. "He's the man who recruited Lara."

Simakov threw the apple across the table and landed it perfectly in a wastepaper basket on the opposite side of the kitchen.

"Precisely!"

"What's your point, Ivan?"

In a sudden, swift movement, Simakov stepped forward and pressed the gun against Carradine's forehead. The steel was cold, the contact terrifying.

"My point is that you're going to take me to them. You're going to get me into that basement. Lara is inside. I want to see her. I want to ask her about you and I want to finish what I started. She knows too much. You all do. So let's get on with it."

50

Carradine sat in the back of the van beside Simakov. A Russian-speaking driver and a woman were in the front. The woman was slight and wiry and looked Eastern European. She stared outside as they drove south along the M40, occasionally eating a boiled sweet and throwing the wrappers out of the window. Only Simakov had spoken to Carradine since they had left the house. There was an atmosphere of practiced expertise, as though each of them had conducted raids of this kind many times before. They were not afraid. The clock on the dashboard showed it was late afternoon. Carradine had no idea what day it was or how long it had been since they had taken him.

At no point had he been left alone. He had wanted to try to get a message to Somerville using the number he had memorized from the restaurant but had seen neither a mobile phone nor landline in the house. He had thought about scribbling a note on a piece of paper and trying to drop it out of the van at a set of traffic lights, but there had been no pen in his bedroom or the kitchen nor any opportunity to search for one. When he had gone into the bathroom, the Russian-speaking driver had stood outside, the door wide open, giving Carradine no chance to attempt an escape.

"I want to speak to my father," he said. They were a few miles south of High Wycombe. Simakov was sipping from a bottle of water.

"Don't worry about your father," he said. "Why would we hurt an innocent old man?" He checked himself. "Perhaps 'innocent' is the wrong word in this context. Can a man who once worked against Soviet interests as a British spy ever be described as 'innocent'?"

"Where are you keeping him?"

"Somewhere he'll be very comfortable."

"Just let me talk to him." Carradine detested the feeling of powerlessness. "Let me reassure him that he's going to be fine."

"No," Simakov replied.

The plan for their attack was straightforward. Carradine was to walk down to the basement in Chapel Street and to knock on the door of the safe house. Simakov knew that Bartok was being held there because she had been allowed out in the morning and had taken a walk around Belgrave Square. A plainclothes surveillance officer from the Russian Embassy had watched her come out and followed her on foot. A man matching Somerville's description had been with her at all times. There was no security at the flat, not even a CCTV camera showing movement down to the basement. The door had a fish-eye lens. Carradine was to announce himself to whoever answered. Simakov was certain that Hulse and Somerville would let him in. At that point, the Russian driver and the woman would force their way in behind him. They would be armed. Bartok would be escorted outside to the van and driven away. Simakov had told Carradine that he would be allowed to remain at the safe house once Bartok was secured. Carradine knew that it was his intention to kill them all.

"What do you want from her?" he said.

"From Lara?" Simakov screwed the lid back onto the bottle. "Answers."

"Answers about what?"

"Why she left me. Why she disappeared with no explanation. Did she suspect the truth about me, about Resurrection? If not, I want to know why she was so cruel. Why she chose to be with a man like you when she could have stayed with Ivan Simakov."

The sexual jealousy, the bitterness, the self-righteousness: each were as disturbing to Carradine as they were pitiful. He had already seen enough of Simakov to know that he was deranged with power and hate. He remembered everything that Bartok had told him about the breakdown of their relationship and realized that she had been soft-pedaling her reasons for leaving. It wasn't just Simakov's lust for violence that had so appalled her; it was his mania and rage.

"What's going to happen to her?" he asked.

"That is my business."

Carradine thought again of his father. Was it possible that Simakov was lying? William Carradine was a sociable man. He had a girlfriend— or, at least, a companion with whom he spent a great deal of time. He played backgammon twice a week in his local pub with a friend who lived nearby. He regularly helped out at a nearby hospice, reading stories to the patients. In short, his absence would be noted. The girlfriend would call around. The backgammon player would wonder why Bill hadn't turned up at the pub. Before long, the police would be involved, then the Service. They would make the link to Carradine and realize that something was wrong. And where could the Russians hold him? Simakov must have known about his father's ill health. Would he risk kidnapping a recovering stroke victim, an elderly man who might, at any point, require hospital attention? It was a horrifying risk, but if Carradine was going to save Bartok, to avert a bloodbath at the safe house, he was going to have to work on the basis that his father was perfectly safe. Simakov was bluffing.

"Can you at least have a photo taken of my dad, a video, just something to reassure me that he's OK?"

The tiny hesitation in Simakov's response convinced Carradine that his hunch was correct. He knew when a man was being forced to summon a lie; he had done it himself many times in the previous weeks.

"Why are you so worried about him?"

"Because he's my *father*, you fuck. He's sick."

Carradine searched Simakov's face for another tell. There was nothing.

"A photo," he said again. "A video. Can you ask for something to be sent?"

"Afterward," Simakov replied.

With that, Carradine made up his mind: he would work on the assumption that his father was safe. He had come up with a simple plan. He had one chance to warn Bartok, a single opportunity to alert Hulse and Somerville to the danger. The Service surely knew that he had been kidnapped. With luck there would be a weapon inside the flat: an armed officer from Special Branch, a handgun in a drawer. If Bartok understood what Carradine was trying to tell her, she could prepare them for what was coming. If she was nowhere near the window when he knocked, there was very little chance of success.

They reached the outskirts of London. So many times, Carradine had driven along this stretch of road yet now it felt as though he was seeing the city for the first time. His eyes were not his own, his memories were the memories of a different man. He was numb to the point of confusion, as if he had been cast in a role for which he had neither learned his lines nor been directed how to act. He looked at Simakov, who seemed as calm and disinterested as a plumber on his way to a routine job. The Russian driver had his elbow poking out of the window and was smoking a cigarette. The woman was humming along to a song on the radio, sucking on another boiled sweet. The banality of evil.

They turned off the Westway at Paddington, heading south toward Mayfair. A news bulletin reported that a bomb had gone off at the offices of a right-wing newspaper in Paris, killing four people. Simakov appeared to celebrate the news silently, though he said nothing and merely shrugged when Carradine asked if the device had been planted by Resurrection. The van passed a few hundred meters from Sussex Gardens and came within half a mile of Carradine's flat in Lancaster Gate. He felt like a condemned man en route to the gallows being afforded a last glimpse of his hometown. He could not think of any way of changing what was about to happen other than to try to overpower Simakov, to grab his gun and to kill him. He had no experience of firing a weapon, nor did he fancy his chances of overcoming a man of Simakov's training and experience in the cramped rear seats of a Transit van. In the time it took him to do so, the driver or the woman could shoot him dead. He had no choice but to do what he was being ordered to do.

They pulled up in almost exactly the same spot that the taxi driver had parked in a few days earlier. Simakov gave his final instructions in Russian. Carradine guessed that he was making arrangements for his execution and that it was merely a question of which one of them was going to pull the trigger.

"Wouldn't it be a good idea for me to know some names? For us to speak to one another in English?"

Simakov took out two black balaclavas and handed them to the Russians.

"Not necessary," he said. "Just do what I've told you. We park outside the apartment. You get out. You walk down. Lisa and Otis will follow you."

"Lisa? Otis?" said Carradine.

"You wanted names." Simakov was amused by his own joke. "Now you have names."

Simakov took out a third balaclava.

"For me?" Carradine asked.

"Of course not for you. They need to see your face."

Carradine looked at the driver. He was huge and muscular, with dead eyes, almost certainly one of the men who had attacked Redmond. The woman's face was entirely devoid of expression. Carradine cast his mind back to the riad one last time. He could still picture Bartok on the bed, fixing the signals. Three quick knocks followed by three slower knocks to confirm that it was safe to let him in; the rhythm of "Rule, Britannia!" tapped out if Carradine was compromised. He wondered if she would even remember the code.

"Everybody ready?" Simakov asked.

Grunts and nods from the Russians. The driver put the van in gear and pulled up a few feet from the entrance to the basement. As he did so, the woman pulled the balaclava over her head and took two handguns from the glove box. She passed one of the guns to the driver as he switched off the engine. Simakov appeared to be signaling to a vehicle or property on the opposite side of the street. Carradine assumed it was to the same Russian intelligence officer who had tailed Bartok and Somerville around Belgrave Square. Some kind of signal came back—perhaps an all clear, perhaps a confirmation that Bartok was inside—and Simakov gave the go-ahead.

"Now."

He pulled back a side door on the van. Simakov was going to stay behind while the attack took place. If he saw that something was wrong in the basement, he would join the fight. Otherwise he would remain out of sight.

It was a beautiful summer evening. As Carradine stepped out of the van and heard the door slide shut behind him, he saw a young man making his way toward him carrying a picnic basket and a bunch of flowers. Just a passing pedestrian going about his business, perhaps walking toward Hyde Park to meet his girlfriend or heading to a barbecue somewhere in a garden in Mayfair. Carradine waited for him to pass. The young man did not break his stride, nor look back as Carradine stepped toward the gate and walked down the short flight of steps to the flat. The pale yellow blinds were drawn. There were no CCTV cameras in sight. A smell of stale, mossy damp drifted up from the basement. Carradine felt the temperature drop as he reached the bottom of the steps. He looked up to see the driver and the woman at the gate, both now wearing balaclavas and moving with the silence of cats behind him.

This was his opportunity. By staying in the van, Simakov had given Carradine more of a chance. Reaching out toward the window, he knocked on the glass, loudly tapping out the rhythm of "Rule, Britannia!" before coming to a halt at the door. He was aware of the driver and the woman reaching him and crouching down on either side of the door as he waited. He prayed that Bartok had recognized the signal.

He knocked again, loudly, confidently.

Rule, Britannia. Britannia, rule the waves.

At last the driver spoke. "Use the bell," he hissed.

"Who is it?" came a reply from inside.

Carradine recognized Somerville's voice. There was a hesitancy in it, but Carradine could not tell if this was the natural caution of a spy or if Bartok was beside him, warning him that Carradine was trying to send them a message.

"It's Kit," Carradine replied.

"Everything OK?"

"Everything's absolutely great." Carradine looked down and saw the eyes of the woman staring up at him, impatient, primed to strike. He wished that he had had the presence of mind, the imagination to reply in such a way that Somerville would know for certain that there was a problem, but he could not think of a better response. Perhaps he did not need to. When Carradine had failed to show up at the pub, Somerville had surely concluded that he had been kidnapped. His sudden appearance at the safe house would therefore have set off alarm bells.

"OK, Kit. Just a second."

A chain was pulled back on the door. Carradine heard someone reaching for the lock. Instead of stepping to one side and allowing the attack to go ahead, he now did something that he had not intended to do. As the woman leapt up from the ground, Carradine shouted out a warning—"Two guns! Get back!"—as she burst past him into the narrow hall. A shot went off, the woman firing blindly into the living room. Carradine could not tell who she was shooting at or if the gun had gone off accidentally.

Somerville and Bartok were nowhere to be seen. The driver pushed Carradine violently against the frame of the living room door as he surged forward. Carradine was so angered by this that he reached out and grabbed at the neck of his jacket, pulling the driver backward so that he swung around, the gun in his right hand. The balaclava had twisted on his face so that he was blinded. He fired. The shot narrowly missed Carradine, splintering the front door. Sheer rage made him swing a punch at the Russian's face, which knocked him against the wall. High on violence, Carradine kicked him in the stomach and he slumped to the ground. He continued to kick the driver repeatedly in the chest and face, his head jackknifing to one side as Carradine's foot connected with the balaclava. A shot was fired in the sitting room as the gun fell out of the driver's hand. He was unconscious. As Carradine picked up the weapon, he looked ahead and saw the woman lying motionless on the ground. Somerville was standing over her with a pistol. It looked as though he had shot her in the neck.

"Where's Lara?" Carradine shouted.

"Are there others?" Somerville replied.

"In the van, yes. Outside. Simakov is alive."

Somerville looked at him in consternation.

"*What?*"

Bartok walked into the room. She was carrying a kitchen knife. She saw the dead body of the woman on the ground and looked at Carradine.

"Kit," she said. She seemed calm, but had heard what he had told Somerville. "What did you say? Ivan—"

A shadow fell across the room. Somerville looked up toward the steps and shouted: "Get down!"

Carradine grabbed Lara and pushed her to the floor, covering her body with his own as he turned and looked back toward the door. Simakov came in, his head concealed beneath a balaclava, his right hand clutching the handgun which, only hours earlier, he had pressed into Carradine's skull.

Somerville pointed the pistol at his chest and shouted: "Put it down! Put the gun down!"

With his left hand, Simakov pulled off the balaclava and let it drop to the ground. He looked at Bartok. She gasped when she saw his face.

"Jesus," said Somerville.

"Hello, Lara." Simakov sounded as though he did not have a care in the world. "You're coming with me."

"She's not going anywhere," Carradine replied.

Behind Simakov, in the doorway of the flat, the driver groaned.

"How?" said Bartok, climbing to her feet in a state of bewilderment. "How is it possible?"

"Lara, get back," Somerville ordered. He was aiming the pistol at Simakov's chest. Carradine was still holding the weapon he had picked up in the hall. He did not know if he should shoot or if Somerville would want to take Simakov alive. The threat to Lara's life seemed imminent. He had to try to save her.

"There may be others," he told them. "Outside. Russian surveillance. They're watching the flat."

"Telling tales out of school, Kit," said Simakov. "I have a van outside." He was speaking very calmly. "Here's what's going to happen. Lara walks out with me, nice and steady, no big tears or drama. We take off and finish what we started."

"That's not going to happen," Somerville told him.

Carradine could feel sweat on the palm of his hand as he gripped the gun. He was sure that the safety catch was off, that all he needed to do was fire.

"So you were British Intelligence all along?" It was as though Simakov was speaking privately to Bartok and believed that they could not be overheard. "You were so clever. I had no idea."

"Just as I had no idea about you," she replied.

"I wonder why Stephen never told you the truth about me. Was it loyalty? Sentiment? Perhaps he enjoyed the feeling of deceiving you. We all did."

Anger flashed across Bartok's face. "Put the gun down, Ivan," she said. "It's over now. For both of us."

"Not for you," he said, indicating Somerville. "The British will look after you, no?"

Carradine knew then that he had to shoot. Simakov was prepared to die and to take Lara with him. There was a tiny movement behind the blinds on the window of the basement. Was it Russian backup? A faint scuffing noise on the concrete steps outside and an almost imperceptible change in the light. Neither Somerville nor Simakov reacted. Lara was staring at Simakov, as though still trying to come to terms with the fact that he was alive.

"We go now," he said, sweeping the gun toward Somerville, who took a half-step forward but did not fire.

Carradine knew that this was his chance. Shouting "Lara, get down!" he raised the gun, only to see Simakov's chest explode in front of him in an eruption of blood and tissue. Lara was screaming as Sebastian Hulse came into the room. He had shot Simakov in the back at point-blank range.

"Fucking hell," said Somerville.

The driver moved in the hall, reaching out and grabbing Hulse's leg. Hulse looked down and shot him in the head.

"Enough!" Bartok screamed.

Hulse stepped forward, crouched and pulled back Simakov's head.

His face and beard were clear of blood but Hulse did not recognize the man he had killed.

"Simakov," Carradine told him, putting his gun beside the digital recorder on the table. "You just shot Ivan Simakov."

Hulse let the head fall back. He looked at Somerville for confirmation of what he had been told. Somerville nodded. Carradine was holding Bartok as she stared at the Russian's motionless body.

"We need to move fast." Somerville picked up a phone. "All this gets cleared up."

... It is the view of this officer that any information regarding Ivan Simakov's true role in the genesis and development of Resurrection worldwide should remain a matter of the utmost secrecy.

By the same measure, Moscow's hand in encouraging and financing Resurrection attacks in the West must not and should not be disclosed.

Thus:

Ivan Simakov <u>did not</u> survive the bomb attack in Moscow.

Ivan Simakov <u>was not</u> present at the Chapel Street shooting which claimed the lives of two Resurrection activists intent on kidnapping LASZLO. Anatoly Voltsinger and Elena Federova were Belorussian aliens living illegally in the United Kingdom. They were engaged in a burglary of the property at Chapel Street with the intention of stealing jewels valued at over two million pounds sterling. They were overpowered by police and shot dead.

... It is also the view of this officer that agent LASZLO, who willingly gave herself up in Spain, should be played back into the field as part of a broader UK-led effort to foment and cultivate opposition to the regime in Moscow under the operational codename "RETRIBUTION." The chaos and uncertainty visited upon the towns and cities of the West by the Kremlin will be visited, with interest, upon the towns and cities of the Russian Federation, as well as on Russian government representatives overseas. The time for putting up with foreign interference in the affairs of Five Eyes and other sovereign nations is over. An eye for an eye.

. . . Given the well-established links between the current administration in Washington, DC, and Russian organized criminal networks, the Agency should be excluded from knowledge of RETRIBUTION until a changing of the guard takes place at 1600 Pennsylvania Avenue.

J.W.S.

51

Nine days after the shootings at Chapel Street, Carradine was walking through Kensington Gardens smoking a cigarette when he was stopped by a short, jovial woman wearing a bottle-green Barbour and holding an aging black Labrador on a lead.

"Excuse me?" she said. "Are you C. K. Carradine?"

Carradine wondered if it was a practical joke. Surely what happened with Mantis wasn't happening all over again?

"I am," he replied.

"Heard a lot about you," said the woman. She had rosy cheeks and blond highlights in her hair. "Here, take this."

She reached into the pocket of her Barbour and passed Carradine a mobile phone. He recognized it as an old Nokia 3310. He had owned one himself when he had lived in Istanbul more than a decade earlier.

"I'm to keep this?" he asked.

Only a few weeks before he would have wondered why a total stranger was passing him a burner phone in the middle of a London park. Nowadays he knew better.

"Someone will call you."

The Labrador rushed forward and jumped up on Carradine's legs. With his free hand he rubbed the dog's head and stroked his jaw before the woman tugged him away shouting: "Down, Gerald! Down!"

"I'll wait, then," Carradine replied.

"Shouldn't be long," said the woman with an engaging smile. "I'll let them know you've got it."

She nodded at the Nokia before turning away and walking in the direction of Marble Arch. Carradine stubbed out the cigarette on the side of a bin. Less than two minutes later, the phone rang. Carradine took it out of his pocket.

"Hello?"

"Kit! Great to hear your voice."

Somerville. Despite everything that had happened, Carradine felt that old familiar exhilaration at a renewed connection with the secret world.

"Hello, Julian."

"How have you been?"

"Well, thanks. Good to be home."

Two Rollerbladers buzzed past him on opposite sides, sweeping south toward Kensington Palace. In the distance, Carradine could hear a siren.

"How's your father?"

His father was safe and well. On the day Ivan Simakov claimed to have kidnapped him, William Carradine had been playing backgammon in his local pub with a friend.

Took forty quid off me, the bastard, he had told Carradine over dinner at their favorite curry house on Hereford Road. *Doubling dice. Who ever thought those were a good idea?*

"He's fine," said Carradine.

"Glad to hear it. And you? Life going well?"

Lara had left the country. They had spent two days together in a hotel in Brighton before she boarded a ferry for France. Carradine did not know when—if ever—he would see her again. She had told him that she wanted to keep working for the Service, that they had plans for her.

"Life's good," he said. "Going to the gym. Working on the book. Fifty press-ups and a thousand words a day. You know how it is for us artistic types, Julian. Same old, same old."

"Lara is well," Somerville replied. Carradine felt his heart stretch out. "She wanted me to tell you that."

"I appreciate it."

"We've been getting some interesting results from your famous memory stick." It had transpired that Hulse's team had intercepted the stick in Marrakech, filled it with chicken feed and played it back to Moscow. "Our mutual friend, Mr. Yassine, is eager to redress the balance. Now that he knows he's genuinely on the side of the angels. Thought you'd like to know."

"I appreciate that, too."

Carradine wondered why Somerville was disclosing things that he didn't need to disclose. There was a momentary silence.

"Kit."

"Yes?"

"There's a lot of admiration in these parts for the way you handled yourself."

"I'm glad to hear it."

"Some of us think you might be a useful asset in the future."

There it was. The narcotic lure of secrecy, still as seductive to Carradine as it had been on that first afternoon with Mantis, only a few hundred meters from where he was standing.

"Only some of you?" he replied.

"All of us."

Another pause. Then:

"How are you fixed tomorrow? Anything planned?"

They wanted him to continue working for the Service. Maugham. Greene. Forsyth. C. K. Carradine was being presented with a choice. To stay in his office and to stick with his books for the next thirty years, or to work for Queen and country and let the Service decide his fate. It felt like no choice at all.

"I've got nothing planned," he said.

"Good." Somerville cleared his throat. "Why don't you put your pen down for the day and come in for a chat? There's a job we'd like you to think about. Nothing complicated. Nothing dangerous. Right up your street, in fact."

Carradine looked up at the trees. Beside him, two children were giggling on a park bench.

"Right up my street," he said. "Sounds intriguing. Then I suppose I'll see you tomorrow."

Acknowledgments

My thanks to: Julia Wisdom, Finn Cotton, Jaime Frost, Kate Elton, Roger Cazalet, Liz Dawson, Abbie Salter, Claire Ward, Anna Derkacz, Damon Greeney, Anne O'Brien and the fantastic team at Harper Collins. To Charles Spicer, April Osborn, Sally Richardson, Jennifer Enderlin, Paul Hochman, Martin Quinn, David Rotstein and Dori Weintraub at St. Martin's Press. To Kirsty Gordon, Rebecca Carter and Rebecca Folland at Janklow & Nesbit in London and to Claire Dippel, Stefanie Lieberman, Aaron Rich and Dmitri Chitov in New York. To Jeff Silver and Faisal Kanaan at Grandview and to Jon Cassir, Matt Martin, Angela Dallas and Lindsey Bender at CAA.

I am also indebted to: Perdita Martell, Max, Stephen Garrett, Sarah Gabriel, Dr. Harriette Peel, Natasha Fairweather, Chev Wilkinson, Charlotte Asprey, Natascha McElhone, Roddy and Elif Campbell, Amanda Owens, Nick Green, Jessie Grimond, Stephen Lambert and Jenni Russell, Mischa Glenny and Kirsty Lang, Clare Longrigg, Nicholas Shakespeare, Milly Croft-Baker, Roland Philipps, Natalie Cohen, Benedict, Finnian, Barnaby and Molly Macintyre, Charles Elton, Rosie Dalling, Rachel Harley, Owen Matthews, Deirdre Nazareth, Kate Stephenson, Anna Bilton, James Rhodes, Nici and Daphne Dahrendorf,

Noel, Esther Watson, Lisa Hilton, Dinesh Brahmbhatt, Charlotte Cassis, James S, Rory Paget, Boris Starling, Chris de Bellaigue, Mark Pilkington, Guy Walters, Sophie Hackford, Caroline Pilkington, Ian Cumming, Melissa Hanbury, Stanley, and Iris.